Other books

Looking for Jimmy Trilogy

Empty Bottle of Smoke

Some Kind of Ending

Everything That Was

DOWN

AND

OUT

IN

OMAHA

Brave Dog
Dead Dog

Artworks

The Origin Story to the Trilogy

LOOKING FOR JIMMY

CONON PARKS

CHRIS SEMPEK

MIKE MACNEIL

Book & cover design: Vladimir Verano, Vertvolta Design

Front cover collage: Vladimir Verano (images provided by the authors)

Print: 978-0-9975163-6-4
e-book: 978-0-9975163-7-1

Author contact: bravedogdeaddog@icloud.com

Dedicated to our fathers

CONTENTS

PROLOGUE

19,000 fans were watching, it is a play in the final quarter of the important first game of the season as the Rummel High Crusaders go up against arch rival South High Packers. Most of Rummel's first string is on the bench and all-state running back George Kinnick is scoring South's lone touchdown of the game.

After winning this game by a score of 30 to 7, Rummel went on to an undefeated, untied season. The football team was tied with Kearney as the No. 1 team in the State of Nebraska.Coach Don Leahy's boys were also the inter-city and inter-state league champions.

The victory team: being undefeated and untied is the dream of every team at the beginning of the season. Very few teams, however, realize this ambition—the supreme accomplishment for any team. The players and coaches of this year's team have good reason to be proud of their achievements with the leadership of stars like Captain Berigan, J. McGee, C. Ancona, P. Sheehan, V. Finocchiaro, D. Mangan, T. Bolamperti, M. McGuire and J. McGraw.

Andre, very familiar with the names, reads this from the pages of the tattered yearbook and peers at the old black and white photographs while slowly contemplating—and then they went to Korea.

Artist: Bill Vaegemast

CHAPTER ONE

FORTUNATE SON

You make a desert and call it peace.

— Tacitus

Years later and people have died, too many good friends amongst his crew of—the young and the reckless, and all those saints… Andre gets off the train arriving in Omaha just three days before the funeral. Standing on the platform, gazing out upon the bustling enthusiastic crowd, he realizes there is no one there to greet him. People are busy. With their lives, families, businesses, jobs, careers, dreams, scandals and lovers. The air is crisp with an early spring freshness. He looks back at the Amtrak station, it is under a high bridge; kind of a shitty train station. The worst of government meets corporate—dysfunctional fascism laying in a urine soaked wino graveyard. He looks up at the bridge and can see the grand marble castle of the gilded age—Durham Station: the beautiful old train station where the troops loaded up for World War II and how the great jazz bands came to town—you know, how people use to travel, all dressed up with pride and everything. Now it was a museum with a fast food burger diner joint fulfilling its role. Real nice museum, Andre had taken Faye Louise there to listen to the Albanain stone mason's wife, the raven haired classical concert pianist, do a gig there. There was a great photography show in one of the halls of modern day cowboys, ranches and small towns of Nebraska; pretty cool. There was also a great exhibit tribute to Billie Holiday with black and white photographs and her singing the Blues; pretty cool. Was a nice afternoon date. She is so pretty. Andre shudders at the sweet memory. Memories made him shudder. Time...time, time has come today. He is like returning to the scene of the accident. Andre, feeling like a refugee, like he was just pulling into Nazareth—looking for a bed...pulls up the collar on his jacket, knowing the rules have changed today takes out a cigarette and looks at the hard winding steel rail tracks, the scattered old brick warehouses and the muddy brown Missouri River as a gravel barge slowly dissipates with the current into the horizon. Watching the world die. It has come today, time to realize. Andre had wanted it all. He fires up a cig with a Zippo lighter that had been his draftee-to-be second cousin Marine Force Recon's burning down the hooches—like burning down the trailer park... Inhaling deeply—he broods: he's back, he's goddam back, he has re-turned to the scene of the accident, this prodigal son, for he knows... nothing begins where one thinks it should, he misses that woman, he misses the Northwest and the mistress and even the woman that took all his MONEY! and he misses the woman...in Omaha. Andre is just wanting to know which way was home. Dealing with his abandon-ment, he begins to walk where he feels...not necessarily anywhere. Andre recalls when decades earlier, riding in from Cali, his father had picked him up in a silver Mercedes sedan. That's all that was left. Of the business. The family business...and Andre's inheritance. Son of a bitch! Let's call it misfortune that has befallen in our time, all times, many times. Those centuries. The past is dead. The past is alive. Andre ain't Frank Sinatra—he did it his way, but he's got more than a few regrets...with nothing to show for but debt and rebellion. He then hears a screaming come across the sky and then a cello playing hard, rhythmically like a dirty driving rain, like red dice thrown up against a fast-moving freight train. She is possessed. He knows it's a beautiful woman—the musician: a heroine with long brown hair and lips that are full and pouty. Her name is Phaedra, maybe it's all up in his head—this imagination. He was consumed by. This imagination of an insurrection—his own personal. And hers. He knows her. And she will never give him what he wants, what he needs...and Andre has needs. She doesn't understand. But she does. He knows that. He needs to see the tattoos she brandishes upon her body—all of them, he needs to feel. He aspires, he believes that some night, with a candle slowly burning when she is done playing that morning at the Sunday service at the church: Our Lady of Lourdes—they will meet at the Red Lion Lounge for a glass of Burgundy wine and listen to some jazz and eventually that evening he will find that salvation through her, of her. One's got to have goals in life Andre thinks.

Andre crosses the road. Andre wants her. He wants it all... He crosses himself as the cello music fades. It is Pacific Street and thirteenth. Orsi's Italian Bakery and Pizzeria is still closed. He'd gone to high school with some of the Familia Orsi: a good Italian family— well known: like the Salernos, Scarpellos, Caniglias, Procellos, Sortinos, Bolampertis, DiGiacomos and Mancusos. On and on. 'Lot of wops. So many Andre thought, he was just barely scratching the surface. With the names...the names—the ex's and oh's. Gotta throw in the Costellos for fun too with that tribe attending at least seven high schools from South High to Gross, Central, Rummel, Tech, etc. Growing up in Omaha he had thought every third person was either a Jew or an Italian. None of his friends on the Left Coast believe this. To many of them, Chicago is just a bigger black and blue flyover cow town. Funny. Like. What a world. What a fucking planet. It was. It is.

Walking with his working shoes on, Andre seeing what his condition was in, heads up the high hilltop, there's a young woman kind of pretty but rough, in a flossy skirt, army boots and tats with a small girl towed in hand—the child's mom. The woman's blue hair shines in the morning light. A pregnant mean-looking redhead is hooking wearing not much, but ripe as a watermelon. Andre says to her, "How you doing there gal? How soon is the baby due? And is business good?" She tells him: she's doing alright and baby is due in six weeks...and that business is booming. Andre contemplates interviewing her, taking her picture and asking her—how much? Thinking he'd never done a pregnant woman—he could see it. Some Mexican radio plays from somewhere, all around. And Andre thinks—man, this isn't Al Veys' Omaha anymore: old Pollack mayor, hardcore lost a son fighting the Viet Cong in Vietnam, if he could see this scene now he would just roll in his South O St. John's grave. A flock of pigeons soar overhead, fast and erratic, nonsensical. Andre be coming down on a Sunday morning from the drink and the lack of good sleep. The light is getting brighter from the dawn light. Damn! He should have gotten a photo-photograph of the redheaded pregnant hooker: all part of the background like in the Third World where the tin shacks and babies just come with the scenery while the women wash the clothes upon the rocks and wobbly stones along the river bank. The mail trucks are moving. He hears that particular whippoorwill high-pitched whistle going up and down the street—that universal signal: one-time is in the area. He does not know if it's a warning for him or about him: that the heat is nearby. An old rusty Pontiac tools by and from it Janis Joplin wails: "take a little piece of my heart out baby..." For weddings and funerals, weddings and funerals... Andre thinks: how we all get together, all the time, for weddings and funerals... and, about all the women that have just broke his heart eternal. And he was so nice... All the time. Making beautiful poetry out of what he called his unhappiness. Jubilation in the land.

West O Joe gonna tell the world what it is... if you grab them by the balls, their hearts will followas the beautiful jackboot wearing Polish punk prof Anka would often say. Like standing on a beach he blows into his hands and breaks stride like a soul funk brother, deciding to head over to Saint Cabrini to light a candle or two—for the deceased and his own lost soul. With all the shrines: a lot of good statues there, it was a hard to pick one. He reminisces about all the Santa Lucia festivals enjoyed there amongst all those Sicilians mostly from around the sister city of Carlentini—political refugees... real asylum seekers from their bloody war with Mussolini. All those familiar names, so dago, and bred into the fabric hybrid core of Omaha so deep. It's a beautiful old church with no sign of Vatican II. There's a nun wearing a habit walking towards him with a purpose towards salvation. Andre nods at her politely addressing her as "Sister" as he hits the holy water hoping that cuts him a little slack. He talks to her and asks her a few questions but she indicates—she doesn't speak English. He calls her "Hermana" and tells her in Spanish what a fine church it is and for her to have a buen dia. A few Hail Marys later he leaves. Looks across the street; no Sons of Italy today.

Andre, with his rarified air, wanders on like he's been wandering forty years in the desert wilderness and he just keeps running into churches: St. Joseph's (where his associate Sammy Sacco went— giving flowers to the rebels failed), Immaculate Conception (which has a bowling alley in the basement and where Jack McCaslin, the Holy Family renegade priest down in Selma kind of dude, had been the pastor and some of Andre's Polish brethren had gone to school/ church), to St. Ann's on 24th next to Columbus Park—some of Andre's adroit ancestors, bricklayers from County Armagh, Northern Ireland had built it. The neighborhood was mostly Mexican and Honduran now. He staggers along almost drunk with a hangover like a dazed rabbit amongst the dead rabbits, he makes his way—head east. No real reason, never been any reason. With Andre Shit Happens Jones. Comes a time, he comes across Dahlman Park. Andre ponders hard...he knows, he knows. The park is named after "Cowboy Jim" the mayor of Omaha, off and on for decades, who use to take his lasso and rope citizens, and was surrogate for the 'boss' of Omaha—Tom Dennison, who ran Omaha for over thirty years, from 1900 with the turn of the century into the early 1930s. Dennison, the Old West gambler and Faro dealer who had travelled far and wide from New Mexico to Montana working as a miner and cow hand, hailed from Jackson, Nebraska which is in Dakota County, on the northeast part of Nebraska, just off the banks of the tempestuous Missouri River. On Andre's maternal side, his people had settled there in 1850: Irish, coming across on covered wagons being led by a Catholic priest named Father Jeremiah Treci from the Garryowen Parish. The town was originally called St. John's, in honor of St. John the Baptist. They named the church St. Patrick's—imagine that. Some of Andre's relatives became members of the Nebraska Cavalry and later on became embroiled in fighting the battles of the Civil War—most for the North with the Irish Rifles of the Hard Tack Brigade, a few went for the South and Dixie never to be heard from again. Dennison and Andre's people were related...in a sense. On both sides. Back at a wedding, in the day, Andre's maternal great-grandfather inquired to his paternal grandfather whether he knew Dennison and Fast Eddy replied: oh yeah. And Andre recalls vividly the black and white photo of his grandfather at a social gathering carousing with JFK, working the art of the deal, along with a couple of other businessmen with suits on and their cocktails and pretty wives and secretaries...for some reason, Andre deemed it pertinent, that memory. And the meaning. In the late fifties, maybe 1960. Fast Eddy's associate, Dennison, the political intriguer and brute enforcer of the lower ward, never held office and seldom if ever entered city hall, but he ran the machine cunningly, ruthlessly and handily sometimes with a pick-handle and stick of dynamite.

Dahlman, the "perpetual" mayor of Omaha was born in Texas on a small frontier ranch southeast of San Antonio. He left home as a teenager and became a cowboy riding the range with a six-shooter on his hip. Back in Lavaca County, in a small town outside a dance hall he ended up shooting a man dead called Charles Bree who'd done his older sister wrong—abandoning her with child. Jim had considered the man no good and an outlaw—so the story goes. Bree got the first round off missing Dahlman who immediately returned fire with a bullet striking Bree in the forehead—killing him. Dahlman flees Texas for Arkansas where he stayed in hiding for a while. So the story goes. Eventually, Jim and a good friend catch a train to Omaha. This is about 1878 or two years after General Custer and the Seventh Cavalry found their destiny with the Sioux, Cheyenne and Arapahoe up at Little Bighorn. From there they headed west on the Union Pacific Railroad arriving in Sidney out on the panhandle in western Nebraska, then went north by stagecoach arriving at their destination at the N-Bar Ranch, one of the largest in the Great Plains, along the

Niobrara River at the mouth of Antelope Creek, about a dozen miles southeast of Gordon, Nebraska where they were hired on as cowboys.

The cowboy did cattle drives from Texas via Comanche County, Kansas to Standing Rock Agency in the Dakota Territory delivering around 3,000 head of cattle to the Sioux. Dahlman also participated in cow herd drives from Oregon to Montana in his six years working for the N-Bar Ranch. He had explored the barren, trackless wondrous Sand Hills in a roundup after a brutal March blizzard to see if any of the strays might have survived. The 'waste land' had been considered too formidable for cattle to survive—only Indians and buffalo could manage the endless rolling miles. When Dull Knife led the flight of Sioux and Cheyenne into the desolate Sand Hills above Ogallala the cavalry quickly gave up pursuit considering the daunting geography more dangerous getting lost than encountering and fighting the Indians. In April the cowboys went in to see how many they could find and in five weeks the hands had located about 8,000 strays plus another 1,000 without brands, descendants from strays from earlier times. They were fat cows, not the starved creatures all had feared and predicted. From that spring of 1879, the Sand Hills became favored cattle range. The expanse of their continuum reminded Andre of the thirty to forty foot rollers out in the ocean. Andre had done all this recent reading about these characters in his graduate history treatise on Omaha. He thought it was appropriate that a city that's wealth was founded upon the blood and bones and shit of cattle with Omaha's jungle stockyards to rival Chicago's and to some years surpass Chicago—would have a cowboy for mayor. And everybody, from all nations, would be invited to come and see and work.

Andre is getting hungry now and thinking of drugs for some reason—scoring some, any kind of dope really. Looks across the street, sees the Italian contractor's sign up against the stone building: Arcetti. He remembers the associate contractor friend of his father—called Milo...Milo Arcetti. Must be related, probably his office and where he held court. Recalling as a kid meeting those crazy twin nephews of his from back East. Diagonally across he notices the Catracha women are getting ready to open up their little café for some Honduran breakfast. They're pretty. Andre goes sauntering over, thinking about another JFK story—one that Warsocki share with him about his Polack grandfather Joe, who was an ex-boxer, was the union representative for the slaughterhouse workers of South Omaha. Him—with maybe an eight grade education winds up at the Democrat's convention in St. Louis in 1960. Joe is introduced to JFK and they get a talking and eventually Joe goes to JFK: "I think you need me more than I need you." Now that's choppin' wood Andre thinks and Andre wonders how Sergeant Warsocki is doing down in Durango Mexico—with his sweet hermosa South Omaha Mexican wife Concepcion' and family and PTSD and the cartels and the movies and Hollywood and all the weirdness. Sounded like he was doing pretty well in the last couple of correspondences and dispatches, working as an armourer with his Cuban partner on a Netflix series. Guess the Russian/Israeli mercenary associate has a good leads on some security and commodity business in Africa with the Spanish speaking country of Equatorial Guinea—he thought Warsocki's language skills would be helpful. Warsocki also discussed with Andre if he was interested in being a kicker...for his Shin Bet friend Uri, who was learning how to fly airplanes in Winnipeg. Warsocki qualified that he was learning how to land them as well: ja-ha-ha! Yeah, everything was pretty good in Mexico, pretty tranquilo, except for the mass grave they found the other week with twenty seven bodies in it near his little el rancho: 'tranquilo, muy tranquilo...' as they always say. Our neighbor to the south. The border is secure. Fiesta. Just ask Alejandro.

He enjoys the bon vivant vibe of the place with all the colors upon the walls: very tropical, very Caribbean. The place is already packed. He's the only gringo in the joint. The women are sensual and dusky. Some Brazilian-like videos are playing on a TV with beach scenes, music and mucho shaking cula in bikinis going on. He orders in Spanish some chuleta de cerdo—he thought how bad could they screw up a pork chop. They serve it with plantains, rice beans, avocado and diced cabbage with sauce. The meal is delicious. He runs into Angelina, she's very cute, kind of petite and in her early thirties, he knew from a prior construction project before he had left for Portland. He was working as a carpenter framing apartments, she was on the painting crew with all the chapins (Guatemalans) for Arcetti Painting—they're everywhere (like the Caniglias, Salernos and Vacantis). She's ambitious and is working doing side jobs, just grabbing lunch. A couple lite abrazos exchanged with some affirmative squeeze. They talk/chat a bit with his gringo-bad but passable Spanish and her pretty much virtually non-existent English. They share a couple more Indian signals. Then, she goes. To paint interiors. Which she digs doing and is very good at. He finishes up twenty minutes later, departs with his bad imagination, leaving a generous tip and wishing the proprietor Jenny-Jenny well, a handsome woman of African cast—with a buen dia.

Andre, the community organizer, considers the stunning woman with the beautiful restaurant in the Flatiron Building, not far from the Old Market—he still wears the amulet around his neck she gave him. It was her that brought him back, dragged him nearly, to Omaha. She has a heart of gold. They had reconnected so to speak, after decades—she had initiated it in a blackout drunken phone call. He had volunteered as a willing victim who'd been beaten by a stick— figuratively, somewhat…with threats of her immediate arrival via screenshot pics of tickets on jet airplane upon the peaceful pebbled shores of the Great Northwest along the way down below the ocean of the Salish Sea: four days like savage horses they rode each other hard as paintings fell from the walls and lamps tipped over, barely escaping his cheap hotel/motel studio apartment of Whispering Firs in the depressed little methed out logging town of Alger, Washington except to procure supplies of wine and cigarettes then finally hitting the beach once near the end where he was spent on the beach apologizing for his manhood finally failing him as they peered out across the glimmering San Juan Islands off the horizon. Alger where the hippies from the quarry lake commune just a mile north had their big music and naked volleyball party. And the Bandito bikers, crackheads, loggers and long-haul truckers all congregated, communed and survived. Andre still loves her, she with a heart of gold, a heart of gold and kisses like honey...with the amethyst eyes that shine like the prettiest little stars and a tongue as sharp as a torn tin can to rip one to shreds: like being tied to the whipping post. He would go down on his knees like a Mexican penitent and beg for mercy, sweet mercy to worship at her alter and power once again. He was like a bewildered, half-starved stray dog after she kicked him out of her house. He was too proud to ask why. That's when he started hitting it hard—the booze...and whatever other mixes came into the scene at those midnight hours when nothing really good is going on, and the young brothers dealing refer to him as OG. Ah yeah Andre reeling at all the best dives and hole in the wall joints in Omaha—making friends wherever he went. Just couldn't stand the pain, but digging the un-hipness of Omaha the whole way, particularly after the bars are all closed...when he was enjoying a cheeseburger at Bronco's off Leavenworth staring out at the humanity of it all contrasted against the cool neon sign of a cowboy swinging his lariat as the gregarious colored girls who work there ask him: what he wants to drink or what flavored shake he'd like; it was all just part of the scenery. Shaking himself out of his reverie, Andre, the semi-monogamous dude, scrapes his way up the hill to Mandan Park, looks out over the river, raises his hands open towards the heavens to no one, beseeching... and shouts, "I AM A GIGOLO!" Then with his best John Carlos Olympian bronze medalist pose, he drops his right arm and makes a fist with his raised left and lowers his head. A sweet family of many El Salvadorans looks on from a short distance in amazement not understanding but knowing: gringo loco. What the fuck's he going to do to make some scratch? Goddamn carpenters' union around here don't pay shit plus his body was racked from the decades...his books, the science-fiction western romances hadn't sold for nothing, magazine articles paid a couple hundred bucks. Not a good business—'thought he'd be rich by now and reeling out of Betty Ford Clinic for his second or third round. He contemplates seriously—maybe he will become a community organizer. To supplement being a gigolo. It made sense, with him being a social justice warrior kind of dude. Make Agape' proud—don't disappoint him. Up in heaven. Poor old dead Senor Agape'—love gets assassinated: always. Often with sharp steely knives. His was not a figurative death. With evil across the land, out of the shadows—brazen in the open. Maybe he should try and finish the novel him and Walter had been working on prior to Walt's sudden sad and most tragic death: Fifty Shades of Jones. Shit man! He left a loving wife and three young adoring children: fuckin' stroke, wasn't barely fifty. Andre had told him to lighten up on the cigs—damn Pall Malls. Got a lot of dead friends with their lifestyle choices: sex, drugs and motorcycles—and AL-CO-HOL…and just freaky bad luck sometimes mixed with some occasional crime. Andre thinks. Dang son bitch. Too painful, knock-knocking on heaven's door. Andre was a part-time atheist except when he needed a favor from God. And to think that someone bothered to write in the bathroom walls of Rummel High: Andre Jones is a fucking redneck asshole. That was some good hate. Andre took pride in that. Was probably the Walloon. Yeah he bets it was Dean Beauregard who scribbled with sharpie due to the misunderstanding of others. Andre was just roughhousing and drunk—lots of dudes were getting thrown and hit that night, beer bottles were crashing at his feet; must have made out with four or five chicks that night. Doesn't even remember hitting poor old Beauregard in the head. Open palmed—it wasn't that bad. A couple of years later, senior year, Beauregard quite drunk confronts Andre at a party. As only a few empty beer bottles crash at his feet earlier upon his arrival at this party, Andre has no recollection of this faux pas on his part. Pieces of the puzzle are put together…amends are made. Again, it was just some rough housing…the misunderstanding of others, dudes tackling each other, then going about vociferously making out and necking with numerous chicks… With that clarification, they become jolly good fellows. Beauregard understood Andre's affliction. Ah Andre digresses…got to get back to the Re-Search. Speaking of Re-Search, lo and behold, he comes across Kung Fu Sunny Favorite Holiday Spa/Massage. Andre had traipsed upon it a couple of years earlier after he'd been kicked out of the woman with eyes like the prettiest stars, house. His back was sore. A woman named Amber was there to greet him. A lovely woman. Andre only knew a few words of Korean so communication was limited. But, she was so very nice, kind, with a good smile, very thorough and practiced—made him feel like an athlete and soldier, all loosened up. Feeling like a thief— he might have to go back. He contemplates: all those angels of the morning. Sometimes they complained that he fucked them like whores, but he thought that's what they wanted.

He gets a hotel room. Decides he needs to go over all his notes to nowhere with the solitude and loneliness of a refugee. It's downtown and kind of dingy; it's got the required ambience—not far from the old Travel Lodge. Not much has changed. As he brings out the gin bottle and begins rehearsing the process of his disorganization and eternity as these fictional characters wander around praying to God. For Mercy. For Hope (Lord—Andre hated the insipid word hope, the audacity of it). While some are doing pretty fucking dangerous shit in/with crazy faith. Plus he needed to work on: Fifty Shades of Jones. Thought that one could make some mo-nay, maybe throw in a few funny hats and beards for the Amish women genre—there's already too many cowboys and firemen.

Andre earlier in the afternoon had caught an orange Happy Cab over the old construction yard. The taxi driver was a Somali. The bright orange taxi has on its sides the figure of a rickshaw with a conical hat wearing Chinese cat dude pulling it: Happy Cab. They exchanged a few words of Swahili. Andre had asked him if he was Shifta? Hassan put an immediate disclaimer on that one, with his eyes lighting up and a wide smile of his pearly white teeth. It's a clan-based warrior society that comprise raiders, traders and pirates, not good or bad—just the way it is. Back in Seattle, Andre recalls working in a tradeshow shop fabricating large expensive booths to sell products at fancy shows in Vegas or wherever. There was a large contingent of Ethiopians working in the warehouse and who, at times, assisted in some of the construction. Amongst them was one large Somali. Between the shop and the office, nobody knew the difference. Andre turned to the foreman and said—you ain't gonna be able to tell that guy nothing. Andre liked the big Somali, but he knew the Shifta pirate needed to get with his posse and go pillage someplace, or maybe take over an oil tanker and hold the crew up for ransom. Reformers did their best but to no avail. Missionaries: they never learn. They go out to the middle of the Amazon jungle somewhere and try telling the Indians some stuff and the Indians tell them they don't know them and so why should they believe them? Seems like a basic premise... One of good common sense, rationale and sound judgement: a good construct. The Indians know Yanomamo over there in the canoe pretty good and he's part of the tribe and if he says something they'll listen to what he has to say, but these goofy pale strangers start showing up telling outlandish tales—what do they think they're stupid? Don't believe anybody if you don't know them. That's when Andre began to formulate the concept that: good people are stupid. And that—the United States is essentially a backwards country and that progressive notions of modernizing the American people is for the hopelessly naïve and dangerously gullible. The Somali cab driver is the same—he's just not going to believe you and he sure as hell doesn't believe much he heard from the news or what the government has to say. If it wasn't a Somali it could be a dude from El Salvador—they've been around, they don't trust the bad clown show. Now the majority of the American people are like the wild Indians—they just want to love their family, do their job, take care of business, maybe join the military, play sports, get a little golf in, do some hunting and fishing—and be left the fuck alone.

The two share a marvelous discussion upon the merits of Omaha versus the benefits of the Horn of Africa. Andre dispenses with a generous tip to Hassan as they arrive at the old construction yard and tells to return in half an hour or so to pick him up so he may be dropped off again downtown to procure a hotel room.

"Mzuri sana! Asante sana!"

"Mzuri sana"

"Kwaheri."

"Kwaheri mzee."

Like a ghost Andre wanders the old yard for a bit as if seeking a total eclipse of the sun. He sees the steel building he helped build with his cousin Jamie and his wild bunch crew decades ago is still intact. They built it for his old man and his partners, the Trico brothers in some sort of enterprise. There were too many to keep track of with his father. Fast Eddie did not dig Michael getting in business with them Italians.

It was and interesting crew: black and white. Which was normal back then. Andre was mostly running the crane. There was the biggest and most beautiful woman with the V-shaped back of a butterfly swimmer on that crew working as a cement finisher and with the same name as Andre's ex-jarhead cousin and she would get right in Jamie's face and start thumping him in the chest when she got pissed. It was damn entertaining and the brothers be laughing. He wonders whatever happened to Jamie the biggest and strongest beautiful woman he had ever laid eyes upon. In all his travels. And with his body count, in one year sometimes—more than most men have in a lifetime. He adored women. Aw—what a lucky man he was...

Besides the steel building, the train tracks and empty bottles of sweet Burgundy wine, much was gone. It was all remnants of a time, memories: good times, bad times...ghosts, shadows, echoes. Just looking for that home. Like Andre, wanting to believe, just where it was, shake the devil, and wanting to know, just which way to go...he thinks of Tom, Tom Rudloff of the Antiquarium Bookstore down on Harney Street—he could tell the story, he knew Omaha and he knew the wild boys from the early days as they drunkenly and sometimes violently crashed his bohemian scene of artists, beatniks and the dispossessed as he forgave those who trespassed against him... From Holy Name to Holy Family he guides from canto to canto the story, the history, the love, the betrayal, the comedy and the tragedy. Andre knows Tom is good for it. With his espiritu he tells the tale, seeking that truth—the pressure drop, of the matter.

Back at the active hotel, taking a hard swallow of the gin, he grimaces. Andre believes the gin helps keep the malaria and other symptoms of flu and Wu at bay. It's a superstition of his. Richard Burton, the notorious British soldier, scholar, adventurer and sexual explorer of Africa, Asia, Arabia and the Americas strongly believed in the benefits of port as an elixir to anything that ailed you including venereal disease while Andre believed that possible like the other Richard Burton, the famed Welsh actor who also believed in having a drink or two occasionally, as well. He takes another pull and crosses himself thinking the quinine might save him with a little lemon, a little lime. Jones is actually a Welsh name, but according to family mythology and legend—they're Irish. Andre once argued with an English woman that the Welsh were descendants of the Romans that had conquered Britain back in Julius Caesar days. Look he told her—they're kind of swarthy with curly black hair and they're great singers. So—they're actually Italians. Look at Tom Jones, Joe Cocker, Richard Burton the actor... She didn't buy his scientific thesis and seemed almost offended. Fucking pomes (prisoners of Mother England) so sensitive about their standing in the world stage.

　　With the gin starting to really flow and in a state of penitential bliss, and in a fit of passion—self-renunciation/redemption song he pulls out the poem to begin the story, at least part of the story: Andre seeking forgiveness above all other matters.

Down and Out in Omaha

"Oil and Rock"

sad song

happy/sad

the train wreck

mayhem dude—

returning back to the scene of the accident:

the damage done

hoping to repair some

to all my wealthy friends...

to all my wealthy friends...

I give—all my love ALL MY LOVE!

Oh those asphalt blues: to workin' the road gangs　　—

　　with the application of　a back of a shovel　to the backs of the me

when we were Kings!

　　the fights the strikes the Teamsters

the blacks the bikers

the Polacks, the Itais (pizzaland)and

　　those convicts,out on work-release

the stockyards, the slaughterhouses

(with the smell of shit & money & blood)

　　the Falstaff Brewery Milder Oil (Hymie meets Capone)

　　　　politicians!

　　and the steel mill (Paxton Mitchell)

　　　　right next to under the　Martha Street Bridge

with the orange, burning molten iron-ore pouring

fire, heat like a volcano

but loud, constant   unending, deafening

and

winos strewn along the Union Pacific tracks

limping back to

the Salvation Army Center   dejected   sad   broken

the baseball diamond   nearby a little hope   a

little reprieve — college

Creighton U. Jays! Oh take me out to the ballpark

and get me some Cracker Jack

then   Indians!   Wandering

aimlessly—lost,scatteredlike

tumbleweed

a whistle blowsa train a comin'... And!

the hot lunches and the cold beers   at the hole-in-the-wall bars

Sheelytown:Dinker's, Huck's, Deano's)

or to the Sons of Italy!pasta! pasta!

South Omaha   South Omaha   churches Catholic

bells ringing: Immaculate Conception   Saint Joseph's

Saint Cabrini   Our Lady of Lourdes...

with gymnastics and shows and wedding receptions

at Sokol Hall

and butcher shops   Filled with sausage

head cheeseand tacosfiesta!

the smells, the senses   —roll out the barrel

"oompa-oompa" goes the tuba polka!

as the railway cars   slowly clanging their way through the

gravel yard/rock pit like sad steel donkeys

   a cello plays...   hard   insistent   drivingwhile

young boysdarkened by grease and sun GO!

running wrenches for sleeveless tattooed mechanics

      with the honky-tonk on the transistor radio

      blaring   Country!   Skoal   Red Man   —   chaw...

         as acetylene torches cutting metal: sparks flying,

      rocks sailing, bottles busting   —   speed

      on the drug train, baby   call them characters:

      "cuz if we get rid of all the drunks—whose gonna do all the work?!"

this wildness—fueled by al-co-hol, diesel,   heat   sweat   and blood

      withthe corruption and smell of stale cigars

         the nights paving: downtown streets

the hookers walking-stalking the dark vastness

         cigarettes smoking

then,on Interstate 80sun beating down

Sun!

   no shade   eyes stinging   bodies burning   —

   the thirstwater, water

the nonstop whine and scream of the machines:

      Blaw-Knox, Hyster, Mack, Barber-Greene...

   drumming in your brain   roll baby roll   get gas

smooth isn't it? rake that asphalt

   get them contracts—the bidding wars

the asphalt plant's massive smoke stacks
billowing and belching forth with un-ending
   roar and din of the burners,   trucks rumbling,
      sirens wail the drunk wrecking ball,
   the howl of laughter...from outrageous crews
         veterans   of the Magnificent   and Bastard
savage   the victory   savage   the glory
   oh the glory,the vain-glory...
   the heartbreak and   damn tears   agony
      the defeat   the bankrupt!   with
the bid rigging and pay-offs
oil companies and big black Cadillacs
   the unions   the inspectors on the take
      and the lawyers...   FBI   indictments!
in flamesdowndown
      ship goes
   blind with it! bricks falling   dust to dust
      what was, what was
         human folly   —   the tragedy
         the comedy
and the crime(s)
      pick up the pieces   pick up the pieces
like dead bonespiled uphigh
      on prairie   and there!
Once   upon a time
   across these   plains

with the Pawnee, Otoe, Sioux, Cheyenne, Arapaho

    on wounded knee

were   millions of buffalo   baby

millions of buffalo

    run Indians run

    Shoot Andre, the substitute teacher, only part-time, thinks... how am I going to bring back the empire: make it rise from the ashes? Like at the schools he occasionally works at where new students arrive every week with their backs still dripping wet... and the middle school children where the inmates are running the asylum. Fully aware he is an inmate himself—bad mental constructs, kill you every time... Just like the various local, state and federal bureaucracies and some of the larger corporations... Common sense went MIA. French Revolution is here. Got to figure it out—work with it. Andre had declared a long time ago that that mouse was evil—but Andre was still trying to get to Disneyland... Ah damn! Andre considers going missing in action. But Andre seeks revenge. Andre also seeks sex. We lost the company cuz we went soft—kinda like how we're going to lose this country, being soft and we keep going down this silly confused path of slogans with no rule of law and everybody's a victim—with collectivist tomes that divide and conquer propaganda with fucking kumbaya Christian/Marxist sentimental bullshit turn the other cheek WWJD nonsense as Rome burns and Nero plays the fiddle. God—Andre loathes the Republicans. We are a bunch of pussies: Putin knows as does the Mexican cartels along with the Chinese Triads. "No guts, no glory. To be a macho man. Men let me tell you... Put down the books—today, we talk about Life." as Capitan Gerardo Machado the Olympian pentathlete like Patton, would shout at them in Spanish class back at Rummel High as he regaled in the stories of fighting Castro, Che and the communist brigands in the mountain jungles of Cuba. The gin stings his throat. He decides to throw a little tonic and lime with it—the evening is going to take a while, got to get all his vitamin C and minerals. He is giving himself up to the abandonment of the time and the place. For he was born of a tragic father—(this breaks his heart every morning like a prayer). He grabs the leather satchel. It is full of papers. Andre grabs the red file that is tagged DICK. This was the name of the last crook his father got in business with. Andre wants to at least solve some of this mystery: like where'd all the fucking money go?! He starts going through the various assortment of documents. That are from all over the world. Being a science-fiction Western romance writer, Andre can appreciate the creativity. It's some amazing work—make Madoff proud. Andre pours himself another as the beat and bass of the rap music plays loud outside his room in the front parking lot. He refuses to accept the cast of the die. He thought it was Tuesday. It was Wednesday. He might have to change genres. His anger rose.

From:Dick Kelso
Sent:Monday, November 07, 2011 4:13 PM
To:dahirji@yahoo
Subject:Ghana
Hi Cindy,
I'm sorry I haven't got back to you sooner. Here is a progress report on the investment. The money was sent on Oct 13th from Wells Fargo to Charter Bank in Ghana. They originally said it would take 3 to 5 to get top Ghana. I knew from my past experience that it would take at least 5 to 7 days. The money actually got to the bank in Ghana on Monday Oct 24th. The money was taken to the Registers office the next day. I have spoken to my attorney in Ghana and he and a CPA are getting all the necessary paperwork ready to finish up everything.
I have not gone over yet until everything is done by the attorney and CPA. There is no reason to go and sit. When I go it will be to sign the papers and transfer the money to the United States. We are waiting for the final paper which authorizes

my company to do business in Ghana. Twenty Eight Thousand has been paid to the government and am waiting for the certificate to commence business.

Best Regards

Dick K

DEAR DICK KELSO,

OUR DELAY IN PAYING THE CUSTOMSFEES FOR THE CLEARANCE ON TIME YESTERDAY,HAS CAUSED ME SOME QUESTIONING FROM THE CUSTOMS.

AFTER MAKING THE PAYMENT YESTERDAY,I WAS TAKING IN FOR QUESTIONING BY THE CHIEF CUSTROMERS ON DUTY.

IF WE HAD MADE THE PAYMENT ON TIME,I SHOULD HAVE HAD THE CONSIGNMENTRELEASED WITHOUT ANY INTERROGATION.

THE CUSTOMS TOLD ME THAT THE HOMELAND SECURITY HAS ORDERED THAT ALL CARGO COMING INTO THE UNITED STATES MUST BE GIVEN A 100% INSPECTION/SCREENING.

THEY SAID THIS IS DUE TO TERRORIST ACTIVITIES GOING ON AROUND THE WORLD AND THERE HAS BEEN A TERROR ATTACK ALERT SINCE THIS WEEK.

I DID IDENTIFY MYSELF AND SHOWED MY ID AS A DIPLOMAT. THEM WITH A NON INSPECTION CERTICICATE FROM THE BRITISH EMBASSY SINCE AM A BRITISH

SINCE IT'S A DIPLOMATTIC SHIPMENT, ALL OUR CONSIGNMENT HAS IMMUNITY COVER.THEY

ONLY SAID THAT I HAVE TO PROVIDE THE CERTIFICATE,THEN THE CONSIGNMENT WILL BE RELEASED TO ME.

ANYWAY,I HAVE MADE CONTACT WITH THE PERSON INCHARGE AT THE COMMERCIAL AFFAIRS DEPARTMENT OF THE BRITISH EMBASSY HERE IN MOMBASSA

AM ON MY WAY TO MEET HIM TONIGHT AND GET THIS SORTED OUT YOU DON'T NEED TO WOORY ABOUT ANYTHING.I WILL DO MY JOB PERFECTLY

ALL I NEED IS TO GET THE NON INSPECTION CERTIFICATE

AND THE CONSIGNMENT WILL BE RELEASED TO ME
IMMEDIATELY
I JUST WANT TO MAKE SURE I GET THIS CONSIGNMENT
DELIVERED TO YOU ASAP.
ONCE AM THROUGH,I WILL CALL YOU WITH DETAILS OF MY
FLIGHT.IF I CAN'T MAKE IT TODAY,IT HAS TO BE TOMORROW
MORNING.
REGARD'S,
ANTHONY RICHARD

Andre, the part-time substitute teacher trying to make a buck, on the frontlines, working a wide swath around and about the Omaha public school system, speaking/hablo mucho espanol at a variety of them where sometimes his para might not speak English... peruses through this material thinking with all the poor punctuation and spelling that Sir Anthony Richard's public schooling has fallen far short of their heralded stature and reputation. He also believes that the diplomat Anthony Richard is key to solving: where's the fucking money?! But first Andre needed to find out if Sir Anthony Richard, the diplomat even exists. Also, what he's read so far... would make Bernie Madoff blush. He opts to plow through some more of these documents as the pounding bass of the hip-hop rages outside amongst the shouts and laughter of the other hotel patrons and their visitors while Andre assiduously contends with these global affairs and world matters as the patter of feet running to and fro—do not stop. And he concludes that too much money, makes a lot of people stupid—especially if they don't know where it came from with the hard work, sweat, blood, ruthlessness, smarts and luck it took to get it. Oh well. And bad is stronger than good.

A couple shots ring out and a siren wails. From the streets. Outside. Andre checks himself making sure he didn't get hit from a stray bullet in the crossfire—he is too old to die young. He studies further. Just making casual observations. Like on the bus. Looking around. Oh—what a merry bus it is. For all the revelers.

Fwd: URGENT

ROBERT HUANG
IRS CLEARANCE.pdf;

Robert Huang
401 Rockefeller # 1009
Irvine, CA 92612
Phone: 949-374-9404

From: "china bank" —chinacom@asia.com
To: Dick Kelso
Subject: URGENT
DERA MR. DICK KELSO.

KINDLY REFER TO THE ENCLOSE3DE ATTACHMENT AS WAS
RECEIVED FROM OUR NEW YORK OFFICE.
WE ALREADY SENT YOU AN ALERT NOTIFICATION ON YOUR
PHONE.
KIND REGARDS.
MR. HIROYOSHI.

The files, letters and documents were relentless. Why were Japanese names tied in with these Chinese banks? Another point, some email brought up the bay in Madrid...there is no bay in Madrid—it's in the middle of Spain! One would think that the charming sociopath Kelso could do a little better in his facts and global geographical homework. Andre's mind told him—do not confuse the map with the territory. But getting to his more pressing predicament, Andre's bottle of gin was getting low. He wondered how his broken-down Chevrolet was doing besides rusting? Old pickup—out there along the Platte where the Salt Creek conjoins. Maybe it was just the starter—he had changed a few. Would the woman ever talk to him again—this man of constant sorrow? He got a brand-new suit...was thinking about asking her to marry him. Suffering from tactical regret, it was hard on his heart thinking of her. He loved her. He'd work on her café… He'd crawl on his knees a thousand yards to beg at her altar again.

BANCO MEDITTEREAN ESPANA (CAM)
CALLE ANDALUCIA NO 80
28006, Madrid-Spain
TEL/FAX: 0034-911-881-330

Memo: C/A/M-09
Ref: 339 CAM

Date: 14-09-2009

OFFICIAL INFORMATION

Attention: Mr Dick Kelso,

Our bank wish to official inorm you that that on Friday being the 11-09-2009, our bank with bank of spain and Representaive of international monetary fund had an extraordinary meeting for an agreement on a common ground to transfer your fund from Europe to your bank in Wells fargo bank in America unconditionally without further requirements from any financial institution within Europe or in America after the clearnce certificate has been issued by International monetary Fund.

In this communique we wish to notify you that by end of our meeting after going through your file with all this institutions, it was agreed that you have completed up to 70% of the requirements stipulated by European Union, regarding transfer of hugh amount of money out of Europe, 2008/2009 transfer policy. In view of facts, the whole parties involved in this meeting has all authorized the transfer of fund

unconditional after the issuance of the clearance
certificate by the International Monetary fund.

On this note we advice you as a bank to complete all
the necessary requirement From International Monetary
Fund and obtain Clearance Certificate for your fund
to be transferred.

Thanks and Best Regards,

Mr Juande Ramos Esq (Public Relations Officer)
Banco De Medittereano Espana (CAM)

CC: Bank Of Spain
CC: International Monetary Fund
CC: Ministry Of Finance
CC: Dick Kelso

It is all enough to make Andre's chimp head spin. And he is
out of gin. Lonely and tired with only that empty bottle of gin, him
clutching onto it like a farewell nosegay, he, Andre, nonetheless,
bravely decides to forgo the party outside and forge forward with
these X files with all the terrible spelling and grammar. What a bunch
of illiterates like much of our media and too many in Congress—the
teacher in him was offended. It was so bad it reminded Andre of a
Burisma holdings contract—to the Ukraine—how could it be...
with so many Ivy League degrees and law school jurisprudence
certificates? He wonders if the Scientologists were invested in this
hedge fund/rehab nation racket. L. Ron and his brother Lee Bob had
tentacles everywhere. Maybe he could get John Travolta, Will Smith
and Tom Cruise in on this deal. Get the Church of Scientology to
help figure out what this was all about—they being the keeper of the
keys. He had to try to get to the bottom of this so he could get back
to writing and putting the finishing touches on: Fifty Shades of Jones

and figure out what happened to the asphalt plant, the construction company, the lemon groves and all the subsidiaries from so long ago... Try to make Miguel and Fast Eddy proud. Like soaring eagle.

```
From: "Tan Chambers" tanchambers@consultant.com
Date: December 1, 2017 at 11:9:35 AM CST
To: "Dick Kelso"
```

Mr. Dick.
The funds are in China bank here. The bank repatriated the funds from New York bank to Hong Kong that was when we were unable to move it into your bank to cornerstone. It was then the bank decided to open an account for you in their bank and put the money into the account for you in their bank and put the money into the account so you can use online facility and debit card to move your funds around. I don't know how to raise money but I will do my best over the weekend.
Thanks. Mr. Tan

next bit of paper Andre researched had some heading with oriental calligraphy with it:

BANK OF CHINA (Hong Kong)
1021, United Centre, 95 Queens Way,
Hong Kong

ATTENTION: MR. DICK KELSO30[TH] NOV. 2017

FOREX CONVERSION MEMO

DEAR SIR.

WE RECEIVED THE CURRENCY FOREX CALCULATION SHEET
TODAY FROM CHINESE MONETARY AUTHORITY WITH REGARDS
TO YOUR NON RESIDENCE COOPERATE ACCOUNT.
YOU ARE HEREBY REQUIRED TO A 0.035% OF YOUR TOTAL
FUND OF $20 MILLLION USD TOTALLING $7,000 USD.
THIS FEES REPRESENTS THE CURRENCY CONVERSION FORE.X
DIFFERENCE BETWEEN THE HONG KONG DOLLAR AND THE USD.
UPON THE RECEIPT OF THE FEES YOUR ACCOUNT WILL BE
ACTIVATED AND A NEW ACTIVATION CODE SENT TO YOU TO
ENABLE YOU ACCESS YOUR ACCOUNT AND MAKE TRANSFERS ON
THE BANK PLATFORM.
YOU ARE ADVISED TO ACT SWIFTLY AS ADVISED WITHIN THE
SHORTEST POSSIBLE TIME. GET MONEY TO BIG GUY.

YOURS FAITHFULLY,
MR. J.K. LIM.
(FOREX DEPT.)

Getting back to our last episode…and whatever happened to Ghana? Andre kinda feeling like Maxwell Smart knowin' he's gotta go Columbo/Banacek now…to figure it all out. Got to find Agent Ninety-nine. Or let's see—some show that might not antiquate him so: Baywatch? No, that was a while ago as well, back in the day for his girl, Pamela. How about Law & Order: Special Victims Unit? Yes! We've got Ice-T rappin' with the old track "Cop Killer" now selling car insurance working with that Hollywood daughter on TV all the time who plays a cop pitching for the DNC—that's the show! It's all still relevant to today's millennials and gen X-ers. Here's a heavy one—from the U.S. Department of Treasury with the Office of Terrorism and Financial Intelligence…man! He was definitely going to have to go out and get another bottle of gin if this shit keeps up. Fuck maybe NCIS: Los Angeles with LL COOL J tied in with the Bourne Identity—that might be more pertinent. But Andre must not forget about the Illuminati whose headquarters were based in Lincoln, Nebraska at least, according to some old hippy/busker. Andre knew the illuminati liked to keep things understated and looking around Lincoln he could see and sense some of the depth of money of the firm. Andre ended up working on an industrial frame one cold winter since his return. Dudes from all over the states on that project. Saved a dude named Jaime from plunging to his death on that one. Next day: handshake—"Thank you for saving my life sir." A bunch of young blacks from Mississippi arrived on that one, doing some welding, singing in chorus some good chain gang songs... One had said he was from Angola. Andre told him he was from Brazil. All the young dudes laughed. Everybody talkin' some real bullshit. Andre, the part-time substitute teacher, teaching more minority youth about fractions. Had a few cracker hillbillies on that one too with a nuclear white boy in the mix. Some of whom later got drunkenly kicked out of their hotel and had names like Junior and said things casually on tasks like—"I think thaht's about enuf white boys over there to figure that out... and git'r done." It was like 'Deliverance' comes to a giant piñata party with Ray Charles on piano as Tupac raps with some biting verse. The damn weather was Siberian arctic and the pay low. Life kind of sucked as Andre smoked another cigarette peering out at the vast snowy featureless landscape that could have made it in a couple backdrop scenes for Doctor Zhivago. Just before all the commies decide to move into him and his wife's mansion. The monochromatic barrenness would make Boris Pasternak proud. Some of these fucking jobs he found himself in... and a woman of non-color he briefly dated as white as an Irish potato once accused him of being a racist. No–she didn't quite put it that way... she said, Andre wasn't a racist, he just had racist tendencies... Andre always appreciated that one for life; thought she might like to meet a few of the crews he'd worked with. Him being much of the time, the 'minority' construction worker. Pondering his first job back in Omaha on re-arrival, pouring concrete on a hot, hot July with the heat index pushing 107 degrees, and they're in Counciltucky and he's got the pump and they're dumping the mud down these retaining wall and they'd get one truck done and here'd come another one relentlessly. The whole day went like that—with the sweat, he's tripping almost in a hallucinatory haze by end of day and barely looks up on the large expanse of dirt that is the construction site and sees a couple dump trucks hauling aggregate that says Flinn Paving on the sides of their doors. And Andre just says to himself: Fuck me. Later on he would work on the county jail—he could hear the inmates on the other side forty feet up on the lift as he looked out upon I-29 as Hawkins Construction built another bridge (and he would later do finish work on the multi-million dollar lake home of the Hawkins family home—never telling them who he was as his father had regular meetings with Fred Hawkins when the FBI were after them all).. It was times like this, way up high in the air, that Andre considers that he should have gotten to a good psychiatrist about the time he was nineteen/twenty years old. Oh well—the prisoners were really fucked.

U.S. Department of the Treasury
The office of Terrorism and Financial Intelligence
(TFI)

Department of the Treasury
1500 Pennsylvania Avenue, NW
Washington, D.C. 20220

Date: 12/21/2012

To: Managing Director
        Co-operative Bank
        United Kingdom

TRANSFER SUSPENSION ORDER (in red ink)

RE: INTRIM SUSPENSION ORDER ON WIRE TRANSFER OF
US$55,997,881.90
TO A/C#:587014 WITH CONNER STONE BANK, BROKEN BOW
NEBRASKA

IN FAVOR OF DICK KELSO

In accordance with the Council's directives
91/308/U.S. of 10th June 1991 on prevention of use
of Financial systems for purpose of Money Laundering
(Official-L344 of 26:2010) as amended by the Financial
Services Subcommittee and Councial's Directive
2010/9997/U.S of the 21th July 2010, (official Journal
L344 of 28:12:2002).

The U.S Securities And Exchange commissions of 2010
(H. R. 2888), the UN Council Decision 21th July 2010
/646/ US implementing ARTICLE 2(3) OF Regulation
(U.S) No. 2580/2001 on illicit related offences,
the Financial Action Tax Force on Illicit related
offences in conjunction with the Inter Government
Action Group against Embezzlement Act pending due
clearance by this office.

In view of the afore-mentioned, be informed that we
have temporary suspended final transfer of reference
fund to final beneficiary Account until you provide us
with the under-listed documents to enable us clarify
and ensure that the funds is free from any illicit
activities before it can be accepted by Federal
Reserve.

International Criminal Court Funds Declaration
Clearance Certificate

Great Britain Insurance Broker Transaction Insurance
Certificate

Tax Value Added Tax (VAT) 1%

Upon receiving the above listed requirement from the
country of Origin duly prepared in your name and
signed and certify by the International Criminal

Court in Hague Netherlands, your funds will be free
to enter into the nominated bank account with Connor
Stone Bank of Broken Bow, Nebraska within 24hrs.
Kindly assist us to ensure an illicit and CRIME FREE
WORLD as we look forward to receiving your positive
response within the next 72 hours.
Yours faithfully,
Neal Cassady
Deputy Secretary
US Department of the Treasury

Cc: Dick Kelso
This message is highly confidential and solely for
the sighting of the person it is addressed to. If
this message is mistakenly transmitted to you, kindly
return message to the above department.

The Office of Terrorism and Financial Intelligence
(TFI)

Andre What a Wonderful Life Jones reads this in a state of
shock: did Father Miguel ever get a lawyer to go over this hieroglyph-
ic papyrus? It's got to be from a 'Get Smart' script. Control versus
Chaos. Chaos is obviously prevailing. Across the whole nation. Bad
is stronger than good. Screaming emotion versus common sense.
This is less than ten percent of it; a tyranny of the minority seems
to prevail—these days. Andre doesn't need to drink, he wakes up
every morning with a terrible financial hangover. Everything is lost.
Everything is gone. All the pretty paint horses from the Top Hand
Ranch out near Elkhorn, to the lemon groves, the taxi companies,
pizza shop, tortilla factory, sailing yacht, racquetball clubs, trucking outfit, other construction firms, oil wells in western Nebraska,
asphalt plants in Montana...what the fuck, could've been laundering
monies. Also, what's with these fuckin' terrible secretaries? Much
(sic) in these official papers. He starts flitting through more of the
"documents" scanning for the more creative ones... Tricky Dick's

got the whole world, in his hands—from Jakarta to Singapore, South Africa to Accra, Ghana over to Switzerland back to China with a return from the Ukraine and to Russia with love onto Romania and Moldavia and then with the damn Canadians fucking up everything with Castro's son, the French guy... at the United Nations. Amateur hour. It's all an incredible story. Probably a small part of the Biden operation. Probably more LLCs and shell corporations around the globe than the corrupt retard Joe had with his crackhead, hanging out with ultra-fine Ukrainian and slinky Chi-Com hookers son Hunter had going down—one of them was called Fang-Fang, she'd been sweet with California Congressman Swalwell for a couple of years. A glorious operation of incompetence happening it 'twas—call it the Darwin Corporation, a monolithic organization—deep state some call it. More appropriately call it—the Traitor State. Put a guy in Congress who dated a Chinese spy onto the Intelligence Committee. Right along the lines of having a billionaire senator with dementia having a Chinese spy work as her chauffeur for twenty years. She was from California as well. Or just have the Republican minority leader of the Senate just have as his wife the daughter to the largest Chinese shipping magnate. No big deal. Not really a problem. Liz Cheney, her dad, CEO of Haliburton while FOX News sold America that WMDs were all over Iraq rather than WTFs, Andre thought: laughing at the folly and ludicrousness of it all. GOP or DNC—they both sold the American people down the river long ago. Whatever corporate inter- ests, could be BlackRock (traded as BLK), Amazon, WHO, Pfizer, sweater-wearing Bill Gates, Al Gore, Tipper no worries... Or the elected representatives are just paid off by a country or two: Saudi Arabia, Mao Zedong Land, Iran, Panama, etc. Who knows? But pump the brakes! (Andre's was convinced he'd picked up Fang Fang back at the Whiskey after a Soundgarden show—she was so fine: tight, tight, tight Triad; he couldn't blame the compromised congressman) FUNNY. People got to do the math and learn the history—fix the bad constructs like (we are the fucking world) in your head. Speaka my language. Just got too many hopelessly naïve and dangerously gullible people in this goddamn pseudo sophisticate virtue signaling backwards country—cuz we're all going to Disneyland too much and worrying about transgender butterfly week … hey-hey, my my when the sun is sinkin' low so Sergeant Warsocki says. Dang Andre was convinced Tricky Dicky Kelso must be a part of sending kickbacks of ten percent onto the Big Guy—got to keep it layered. And by the way, Andre greatly aspired to party in excess with Hunter someday; and maybe buy some of his art. Looked like a helluva shebang to Andre. All those beautiful women—Hunter had been livin' the dream baby, livin' the dream—with all that cocaine and money. Any man who denies that is either gay and/or saint or simply an unimaginative liar. And—while performing and doing art and selling it for hundreds of thousands of dollars, all at the same time. Truly remarkable Andre thought having been in the art gallery/music party business in Seattle back in the Eighties and early Nineties—a few blocks from China-town. The galleries were either run by trustafarians and/or they were laundering money, except for his dubious crew's sweetheart deal … All so Judy Garland can keep singing, 'Somewhere, oh somewhere over the rainbow' to keep the flying monkeys at bay as John Kerry continues to sailboard across the Atlantic Ocean with his beautiful hair and carbon footprint to make it to the Meister Schwab's illustri-ous meeting at Davos which had been one of the locales for a nasty old brutal prison camp for WW II downed American airmen—run by a Nazi, (there was a Father Meister at St. Joan of Arc parish which was Andre's growing up—he wasn't a bad priest and he wasn't the pederast one) in Switzerland, (we're not going to talk about that …) of course, off to meet the Wizard (possibly Soros—wearing a goat-head amongst blimping, floating Al Gore and all Davos internet elites like silicon sprinkles upon a spanky Starbuck's whipped latte amongst the chosen Illuminati), while peering through the looking-glass and speaking with the mad hatter after eating a special mushroom as an Incan priestess blows magic red dust on the assembled and eager acolytes … Go ask Alice. She'll fucking know as Andre knew; (Andre was just starting to come down off the drugs) David Rockefeller and the Trilateral Commission is involved in this crisis of democracy and passive indoctrination with dubious kinder and gentler bigger better bombs. Definitely a journey to the end of the night: for the republic and the Statue of Liberty. Epstein was the glue that held the whole thing together organizing it all from his private island in the Caribbean. Then they had to kill the intel asset in order to save Prince Andrew, Clinton and Bill Gates (with Melinda clucking: not happy with sweater man dorky-dork husband hanging out with Mossad pimp) from the Lolita Express manifest ledger. It was all right up there with the pandemic/plandemic and Wuhan Red Death hitting us all (the whole world including Italy which sold a lot of their fashion design business to the ever astute Chinese who returned to Italy from their New Year's lunar holiday to the homeland—to lay plague to the Itais while the Chi-Coms locked down travel in their own country: Andre had spoken with the sympatico leftist Dorothy Day Catholic Worker Movement/social worker muther-fuckin flash-grenade hurling ANTIFA/BLM card-carrying Alinskyite Jesuit Holy Family commie bitch Woody for his take from Rome on the early situation and he simply retorted…"it's the gooks, it came from the gooks". Woody was surprised that Andre was so apprised on the Italian garment industry. Woody wasn't really a communist…he was just for the dictatorship of the proletariat). Yes, the Wu got us right in the jimmies to go along with all the soviet lockdowns and the mostly peaceful protests/riots that ravaged many of our once fair cities as the media just keeps pouring a little more gasoline on the fire with their lies, censorship and information blackouts—might as well be Pravda. Woody had been witnessing a procession of old dead dagoe bocce men who smoked too many cigarettes exiting his apartment building with a black drape covering their stiff lifeless bodies as their ancient widows make the sign of the cross and the priests scurry to the next in line for their last rites.

His last correspondence to Woody after the deathly news flash from Italy was:

Slouching towards Omaha baby! U got the Wu or the flu
Woody? And just like Mary Tyler Moore—as we joyously
throw our raspberry berets in the air…we're going to
make it after all!

You, Bono and I

BANCO MEDITTEREAN ESPANA (CAM)
Calle Andaucia NO 80
28006 Madrid-Spain
TEL/FAX: 0034-911-881-330

MEMO: C/A/M 02
REF: 212 CAM

Date: 18-05-2009

Re: BANK GUARANTEE AMENDMENT

ATTENTION: MR DICK KELSO,

IN VIEW OF OUR RECENT DISCUSSION WITH OUR TRANSFER
OFFICER WILSON HUNTER LYMBE DIDIER, WHICH WAS
COMMUNICATED TO YOU THROUGH HIM, WHERE OUR BANK
ACCEPTED TO ISSUE A LETTER OF GUANTEE FOR YOU TO
EUROPEAN UNION MONETARY BUREAU COVERING THE SUM OF
27,500 EURO.
WE WISH TO NOTIFY YOU THAT THE COMMUNIQUE WE RECEIVED
FROM THE EUROPEAN UNION BUREAU TODAY, CONFIRMED THAT
THE LETTER OF GUARENTEE WAS ACCEPTE, BUT WITH THE
RESERVATION THAT THE LETTER OF GUARENTE WILL ONLY
COVER YOU FOR A TUNE OF 15,000 EURO, IN ACCORDANCE
TO THE NEW EUROPEAN UNION POLICY ,SINCE YOU ARE NOT
AN EUROPEAN RESIDENCE AND ALSO IT IS PART OF THE

MEASURES TO TACKLE THE RECESSION IN EUROPEAN UNION
STATES.
IN A NUTSHELL THE EUROPEAN UNION MONETARY BUREA HAS
ACCEPTED A LETTER OF GUARENTEE ON YOUR BEHALF FOR A
TUNE OF 15,000 EURO. WE ADVICE YOU TO COMMUNICATE
WITH WILSON LYMBE DIDIER WITH FURTHER INFORMATIONS.
STILL WAITING ON WORD FROM THE UKRAINE.

THANKS AND BEST REGARDS
MRS ARCELI SANCHEZ
DIRECTOR COMMUNICATIONS
BANCO MEDITERREAN ESPANA.

Here's a special one... from European Central Bank with transfer by Swiss financial Services: the beneficiary is Mr. Dick Kelso of Redondo Beach, California United States of America with the receiving bank being a Wells Fargo. Maybe Dick is smoking crack with Hunter in some posh condo with some nice scantily-clad Russian girls overlooking the sandy beach and Pacific Ocean. It's all probably related. All up in smoke like the lemon groves back in Yuma. Like Watergate was really about a call girl ring: America's Untold Stories... it takes a writer from National Lampoon to bust the case open. Get Nixon was the name of the game according to Rehab Nation investigative journalist Mark Groubert for exposing Alger Hiss of the US State Department as a Soviet spy while working with FDR at Yalta. Maybe Dick Kelso was an infiltrator involved in Russian collusion to bring Hunter down on orders from the Kremlin by getting Hunter hooked on crack. Or so some say. But Tom Rudloff was a teetotaler with empathy. For addicts. Take it all to the Ukraine.

SIR,
PLEASE NOTE THAT THE AMOUNT OF
US$56,000,000.00TRADING TRANSACTION AID HAS OFFICIALY
RELEASED TO YOU,FROM EUROPEAN CENTRAL BANK VIA OUR

AFFILIATE FINANCIAL CORP, Capbchip Finance Company
Ltd.
Capbchip Finance Company Ltd
3 Oroko Street, Accra Ghana
Email: manager@capbchip. Com
Office Land Phone (233 30 2932 349)
Contact person(Victor Kofi-cell phone : 233-54-3678376
ALL CORRESPONDENCE WILL BE SENT TO YOU AS SOON AS
POSSIBLE
TO BE CONFIRMED WITH OUR AFFILIATE FINANCE CORP
(Capbchip Finance Company Ltd)
ALL OTHER CORRESPONDENCE WILL BE FURNISHED TO YOU BY
OUR AFFILIATE
FINANCIAL CORP IN DUE COURSEVIA KIEV.

KINDLY TAKE NOTE OF YOUR CODE NO 7REFERENCE ABOVE
AS IT IS KEY TO OUR AFFILIATE FINACIAL CORP FOR
RECEIVING OF YOUR FUNDS.
REGARDS,
MR.Jean-Claude Trichet
(PRESIDENT EUROPEAN CENTRAL BANK)

This is ten percent of the material, now the question is—how
much money did the old man give this charming sociopath Dick
Kelso? A hundred thousand? A hundred and fifty thousand? A quarter
million? How much madness can one man take/read in a day like the
Spanish Flu killing 700,000 Americans when we had a population of
103 million? It's all too devastating. And how much to the Big Guy
with his crackhead son as bagman in the Ukraine? Andre was trying
to gauge it from what his father had inherited from the largess of his
French and Basque gypsy mother from San Francisco via Montana
origin who had run off with the Benedictine monk—all while chasing
the Big Rock Candy Mountain we all seek. She was quite an artist:
many beautiful paintings—was once married to a banker for a while

as well from the town of Papillion, near the trading post of Bellevue, all part of the Omaha metro area. Andre decides with that Byzantium of documents that he needed to just read some poetic history of the Plains. He grabbed a copy at the airport of Stephen Ambrose's book 'Undaunted Courage' about the Lewis and Clark expedition. Continuing to read Noam Chomsky was depressing him too much with his taut rational claims of the Neo-Liberal globalization and its willful destruction of rural America. And as Noam says the United States cannot tolerate defiance, especially successful defiance. Got to manufacture that consent. No questions allowed: for the lunatic express.

Getting back to the country... like a Canned Heat song, Andre picks it up in the middle of this heroic book of manifest destiny and adventure as is the chaotic way he often reads and comes across a munificent passage:

"Deer to be Seen in every direction and their tracks ar as plenty as Hogs about a farm," Clark wrote on June 30. Now headed north, the expedition was entering a near-paradise. Clark noted, "rasberries perple, ripe and abundant."

On July 4, the men ushered in the day with the firing of the cannon. Private Joseph Field got bitten by a snake. Captain Lewis treated him with poultice, probably of Peruvian bark, (that contains the quinine that is their remedy for the malaria Andre duly figures) that drew the poison. At noon, the party pulled ashore at the mouth of a creek of some fifteen yards wide, "coming out of an extensive Prarie" on the left (west) side. As they ate, the captains questioned the voyagers (French/Indian mixed bloods). No, they knew no name for the creek.

The captains thereupon named it, their second experience in bestowing a name. They called it Independence Creek. * Most of the rivers had French names.

The expedition pulled over for the night at the site of an old Kansas Indian town. "We Camped in the plain." Clark wrote, "one of the most butiful Plains I ever Saw, open & butiful diversified with hills and vallies all presenting themselves to the river covered with grass and a few scattering trees, a handsom Creek meandering thro."

The captains ordered an extra gill distributed. As they sipped their portions, they took in their surroundings and were quite over-whelmed. The country was covered with a sweet and nourishing grass interspersed with copses of trees "Spreding ther lofty branchs over Pool Springs or Brooks of fine water. Groops of Shrubs covered with most delicious froot is to be seen in every direction, and nature appears to have exerted herself to butify the Senery by the variety of flours Delicately and highly flavored raised above the Grass, which Strikes and profumes the Sensation, and amuses the mind."

At sunset, the men again fired the cannon. It was the first-ever Fourth of July celebration west of the Mississippi River.

Perhaps the captains grew philosophical under the influence of the whiskey, as happens to earnest young men carrying heavy responsibilities who find themselves in the Garden of Eden as full dark comes on and the campfire burns down on their nation's birth-day. Clark's last journal entry that day: "So magnificent a Senery in a Contry thus Situated far removed from Sivilized world to be enjoyed by nothing but the Buffalo Elk Deer & Bear in which it abounds & Savage Indians."

Andre falls fast asleep with that line … reminiscing/dreaming of this land of the chokecherries and Elkhorn River of his youth and the racing of the paint horses across the colorful never been plowed rolling hills of wild turnips and the fantastic splotches of pink and purple and yellow prairie flowers imbedded with the green, green sweet greasy grass.

The next morning Andre, the artist and warrior-monk, wakes up and checks himself making sure he doesn't accidentally have any bullet holes in him. Sometimes you don't know what the hurts from. He looks into the mirror in the bathroom, examining his favorite scars—too much of his survival has depended upon drunken luck. But again, Andre is too old to die young. Turns on state media CIA News Network and makes himself a shitty cup of coffee. He realizes they have contempt for us—these let them eat cake elites from the media/bureaucracy complex caught up in their own echo chamber who just repeat themselves like idiotic parrots with the same talking point bullets trying to sound so smart... Enjoying the shitty coffee from the Styrofoam cup, seeking some cake, he looks down at the Gideon's Bible, aware that he is beyond the wire... so to speak. Andre shakes off the cobwebs from the gin and the night's reading of Clark's entries, he recalls the historical marker outside of Jackson, just a little west... that marks the site of one of the encampments of the Lewis and Clark expedition. And Andre thinks—history is everywhere. He has a second coffee and throws in some non-dairy creamer. The cigarette tasted lousy. He looked out his motel window and could see the Union Pacific headquarters and remembers how the main old central train hub had set just a little past that. He had worked part of a summer there busting up the old train tracks and creosoted wooden ties. The fine soot seemed to sink two feet down. The heat was sweltering as they used sledge hammers, jackhammers and large iron bars to break it all apart. They were preparing it for an asphalt overlay; about a dozen of them with his brother, Jimmy Kennedy, Joe Steele and Johnny Walker, who lived up to that name a plenty, Andre was jumping between that project and the airport project that summer. Both very warm places to be in a Nebraska summer, Joe Steele who'd been Andre's partner as defensive tackle puked a couple of times and said working down in that hellhole was worse than two-a-days in football camp. The U.P. insignia was everywhere. With all that, besides what they taught in the public schools back then, he'd become somewhat of an amateur historian on the building of the transcontinental railroad and the Union Pacific. He took out a very unfashionable cigarette—cheap, branded Wild Horse. Lit it and started leafing through his Mari Sandoz books on her love song to the Great Plains—Old Jules, Cheyenne Autumn, The Beaver Men, The Cattlemen and Crazy Horse: The Strange Man of the Oglala. She knew/met a lot of these Indians as a young girl on the ranch. Perusing a bit over some of Willa Cather's books as well about all those old O' Pioneers. It was all about picking the route—to California; through the Nebraska Territory across the Rockies and Sierras. Ex-Secretary of War Jefferson Davis wanted it further south for a more Democratic path. For slave states, of course, wanting to increase their influence, dominion and real estate. The North wanting to check that expansion. A war with Mexico had just been won. War Between the States was looking inevitable.

Lincoln was in the settlement of Council Bluffs in the summer of 1859 giving a speech "setting forth the true principles of the Republican party" as he was running for the nomination to become president and had just finished up the year before the famous Lincoln-Douglas debates. On the other side of the Missouri River was the village of Omaha which translates—against the current. In the audience was a young railroad engineer by the name of Grenville Dodge. He was pointed out to Lincoln after a question/answer session and hopped right to the nitty-gritty with the young Dodge inquiring directly what was the better route for a Pacific railroad to the West? Dodge answered succinctly that the Platte Valley the way to go with the uniform grade all the way to the Rocky Mountains. Lincoln went on with many questions gleaning as much as he could from the young engineer who'd done much surveying west of the Missouri. Going over some of Ian Frazier's work and more of Ambrose's, Andre was realizing how the forty-second parallel was a road running pretty much straight out of Omaha and running right up the Platte Valley till it hit the Rockies. With that little chance pow wow of Lincoln and Dodge, with the help of many others and the sweat and blood of a great deal of Chinese and Irish labor, one of the largest building projects of the nineteenth century was inaugurated.

Dodge dug the Great Plains with the flaming sumac, the ripe wild plum trees and chokecherry bushes amongst the dewy meadow flowers like a Van Gogh painting. In 1853 the enthusiastic young engineer was in his element leading a team of a dozen men to survey the Platte Valley. This is where he saw his first Western Indians, a band of Otoe. He pounced upon and asked every trapper, trader, Mormon, voyager and Indian about any information of the land further west to the Rocky Mountains. On his return he laid a claim on the Elkhorn River, a major tributary to the Platte and about twenty five miles west of Omaha. In 1854 he went back to Illinois to marry Anne Brown. Upon their return he built a cabin and soon took out claims for his brother and father who came out in 1855. Thus they began a farm plowing up the virgin prairie land. Dodge's cabin on the Elkhorn would be the last white man's house an emigrant crossing Nebraska would see till they hit Denver. Andre recalls the beauty of the Elkhorn as a child racing the paint/pinto ponies over the wild rolling hills of colorful pasture that had never been put under the plow. It was beautiful. Less than a couple of miles from Dodge's original homestead. A tear nearly comes to Andre's eye recollecting about the dewy wild flowers and all the pretty horses and everything that was. And to those of us near and those far away. He peers out the grimy window of the Travel Lodge, observing some of the constant street hustle going on; there's a real estate sign in front of an old three story brick building; it reads N.P. Dodge Real Estate. He remembers meeting the kid growing up, great-great grandson or something, nice enough kid. Got shipped off to some fancy east coast boarding school. There's a wee bit of gin left in the bottle, Andre downs it. With self-destruction. He feels like leaving Las Vegas… Leaving Omaha. Contending with the abandonment. Somewhere between lust and despair.

CHAPTER TWO

THERE ARE NO SIDES

We protect our minds by an elaborate system of abstractions,
ambiguities, metaphors and similes from the reality we do not
wish to know too clearly; we lie to ourselves, in order that we
may still have the excuse of ignorance, the alibi of stupidity and
incomprehension.

—Aldous Huxley

Upon further research by Andre the All-American, seeking his historic materialism,
at the downtown Omaha public library amongst the homeless and
disenfranchised (it was a genre thing), by going through the microfiche; it's all about the grassroots: politics, getting out the vote.
As Mayor Daly out of Chicago use to say—vote early, vote often.
Machine spokesmen and workers were selectively picked with care
and consideration of their ethnic background as those they were
responsible for on voting day: an Irishman for Sheelytown, an Italian
for Little Italy, a black for North O, a Bohunk in Little Liberty. Some
of the representative names that represented the organization Andre
was most familiar with through his father and grandfather's connections. Delivering solidly from the Greek quarters was Nick Pappas;
Leo Cantoni, Joe Salerno and Louis Piatti for the Italian block;
making it happen amongst the Syrians and Lebanese were the Dahir
brothers; the contacts for the black community were Victor Walker,
Billy Crutchfield, Jack Broomfield and Harry Buford, who was an
Omaha cop as well as being Dennison's chauffeur/enforcer. Andre
had heard all about the black driver "heavy" from his father who
had been told by his father Fast Eddy. It was business, all to keep the

machine well-oiled and moving. Handling the Irish was a guy named Fitzgerald.

He'd always wondered who was Cantoni? As a kid the familia would always head down to 19ᵗʰ and Leavenworth to Cantoni's Grill because it was run by the Marchello brothers. The Bolampertis' grandfather who Andre had grown up with surrounded by three families of them, had been the chef there. So when you entered you walked into the bar which was always smoke-filled and packed at the bar with dudes. Geno Marchello was constantly in the middle of the crowd usually with a drink in his hand. You'd take a right passing the wooden phone booth before you hit the actual restaurant where Johnny Marchello would greet you. Yellowing pastel wall paper with scenes from Italia were the primary décor. It was a decent sized joint. Many of the old waitresses had known his father since he was a kid hanging out there at the bar with his grandfather. One could take an order and not ever wrote down a thing, and not miss a beat. Andre believed her name was Annie and she could remember every order without ever writing it down. She doted on his father like a caring mother. Sacco's uncles had a car repair and parts store just around the corner. In the recent years he had met some of the Italians for cigars (it was often a mix of crew but often it got pretty Latin) and Sacco says to Andre with such casual outtake—"A lot of shit went down there, y'know—business…" Then he tells a story where he's a young kid with his father and a couple uncles at the bar and a young dude enters and before he's barely in Big Geno has got the guy collared and thrown into the phone booth and is beating the shit out of the guy—just pounding the fuck out of him. He's kind of freaked out as a kid but his father and uncles carry on like…nonplussed cuz it's all normal, guy probably deserved it. Andre reassured Sacco that it was probably good for the digestion of the people in the next room over while they enjoyed their lasagna and spaghetti with meatballs. What a world and just a few blocks away from the Chesterfield Bar which was not too far from the Diamond Bar where the gays and tranvestites hung, back in the day, while howling hounds forsake themselves as sirens wailed against a neon goose and a dark sky.

The Second through Seventh Ward were theirs with some efforts in the Eighth. South Omaha was delegated to attorney John Marcell with a fellow by the name of Rawley as second in command. Frank Kawa and Joe Teshnohlidek were the machine workers delivering the Brown Park area. Kawa owned Johhny's Café where the cattlemen would come to celebrate after arriving by train to sell their livestock at the stockyards. It's also where the slaughterhouse workers might have their breakfast or lunch and could shower off all the blood and muck in the basement area. It's also where Lightnin' Johnson would parade all his girls around, sometimes in protest—stirring quite the scene. Kawa had originally emigrated from Tarnow, Poland as a youth eventually finding himself in South Omaha working on the dock of one of South Omaha's meatpacking plants. He later served in the U.S. Army during World War I. After his discharge, Frank opened up a soft drink parlor in South Omaha at 4636 South 27th Street. With Prohibition kicking in the store served as a convenient outlet for illegal beer and liquor and helped Kawa to become known as "the beer baron of Omaha" though he was moving everything from moonshine to top quality liquor from Canada with Buick sedans equipped with special storage tanks. And kicking so much back to Dennison and his crew. Just all pieces of the puzzle Andre thought as he went through different articles, microfiche and books on the pertinent subject of the river city empire.

Going through the vast array of information he comes across a friend of his grandfather's and his grandfather's brothers so to speak—(there were nine brothers and three sisters with one sister becoming a nun, Sister of Mercy, probably to pray for all the rest ...). The name is Milder. As a boy working in the construction yard with his brother, just under the bridge across from the Paxton/Mitchell Steel Mill was Milder Oil where his brother and him out there in the hot sun would cut lots of weeds and with acetylene torch cut lots of steel up. Didn't see much of the Milder brothers but could never forget all the red oil trucks and that long black sleek Cadillac tooling about occasionally.

One brother, Morris, was a long-running associate in the organization. He had a sharp pencil and was an expert bookkeeper. Morris started as a collector and eventually made it to controller, keeping track of all the collections for the protection payments. With all that, Morris went into the oil business where with his relationship with Dennison he was awarded the fueling and lubricating contracts with the city and county vehicles which of course included all the fire, police and public works equipment. Morris continued his work with Dennison as well as assisting during election time. Andre wonders where was Jimmy Carter back then? Gotta be pushing a hundred years old, he must've been around then? He was probably off in distant lands to meet strange and unusuale people. To monitor their elections. Off in Zimbabwe. Or Bolivia, Waziristan or Stroessner's Paraguay. Like now. We are going Third World—banana republic is here. After supporting every Latin American bastard across the decades and wondering why the peasants thought they'd try out communism. We gots to quit lecturing the world all sanctimoniously about free and fair elections. Revelations, revelations every week of the fraud, corruption and lies. History is right before us. It's a choice to know.

Morris crossed Dennison and paid a high price. His business ruined from the city and county contracts to any garage owners and taxi companies. Then his house was blown up. That's when Morris decided it was time to move to Kansas City and seek the protection of Boss Pendergast with protocol as such—Dennison couldn't hit him. So it wasn't good to cross the boss. He might kill you or have you killed or at least kick the hell out of you as a black lieutenant of the name Walker who ran the third ward found out. He'd been a policeman then bought the Midway Saloon at 12th and Capitol with Dennison's backing/blessing, but then was deposed for some unknown reason at least according to a book by Orville Menard and found himself grabbed out of the bar one night and wrestled to the ground by a policeman to find Dennison kicking him. That was the end of Walker's career in Omaha politics and his reign at the Midway. He eventually left down to become a waiter on the Union Pacific Railroad. This was a man who'd been a sub-boss and lawyer of the third ward, his power alleged to have been second only to Dennison's. Andre continues his research in this academic setting, reading more and comprehending that if you were loyal to him, he was loyal to you.

Thus, comes a man named Jack Broomfield into the organization and to run the Midway. He was a native of Savannah, Missouri. Until he lost a leg in a train wreck, he'd been a Pullman porter. He came to Omaha in 1887, doing different jobs till a man named Crutchfield with him took over the Midway. Besides drinks, the Midway had dice, roulette, faro and cards. It was known far and wide being Union Pacific was headquartered in Omaha and the center of the country thus the name. It catered to mostly blacks and people came in from coast to coast. The Midway was a booming success and made Broomfield a wealthy man. It remained open until state prohibition closed it in 1917. Broomfield dies ten years later and Dennison is one of the pallbearers at his funeral. Dennison extolled him, "He was true blue and always loyal…one of the old school of political workers and could always be depended upon to take care of the colored vote and he never failed." Well—that was the world then Andre concludes. For this vast byzantine puzzle he was trying to solve. There you go. And boys will keep chasing girls…just to get a kiss. And soldiers march off to war. That '60s song is stuck in his head. Fuckin' hippies. He reads on. The book is 'Cigars and Wires' by an Omaha cop named Blecha. Jon L. Blecha. Another Bohunk Andre surmises—very appropriate. A number of dudes he went to Rummel with became cops, especially amongst the brothers. He's hip to the names as he peruses the non-fiction, scanning the sentences…Gorat, Gorat… Louie "Little Napoleon" Gorat being described as a prolific bootlegger who, aided by his brother-in-law Joe Mandolfo, made his payments through Western Union. Gorat's is a famous restaurant steakhouse in Omaha. His grandfather Eddie's moll Charlotte loved being taken to Gorat's. She'd been voted prettiest girl of Benson High of the colors green and white esteemed Benson High Bunnies where a lot of good svelte athletes came out of—they almost beat Rummel in football that senior year; there was big DT Billy Vechio trying to chase down the hundred yard state champion sprinter who had broke into the open for a long rush touchdown. From there Charlotte with girlfriend took a bus and headed to Hollywood where she got work at the Beverly Hills Tennis Club where she got all the stars' autographs: Burt Lancaster, Barbara Stanwyck, Gary Cooper, Liz Taylor, etc. They all played tennis there. Eventually Charlotte came back to Omaha with child. She worked as a waitress at the Holiday Lounge where she met Eddie who was there carousing and making deals and he took a shine to the pretty waitress with a young boy. Thus they got married. Sometime in the fifties. Eddie adopted the boy and bought her the biggest bronze/gold Cadillac. Jumping around in that thing with his siblings as a kid—it was a boat, with a black plush interior as they pulled out of Happy Hollow Country Club as Simon, the old black waiter would bring out a little cake for them on their birthday and sing 'Happy Birthday' for them. It was the sixties—things were different back then. Andre's father would occasionally bring up, or bark, that Charlotte had been a waitress when she met Ed—Andre wasn't sure what that meant about his grandmother as a child. She had served cocktails at the Holiday Lounge—back in the day. So it goes. Since he got back he loved going with Faye Louise to Gorat's Steak House and the Green Onion, occasionally drifting into the Holiday Lounge—them both being/feeling like existential refugees from decades between the two of them from being away—back in Omaha. Making the rounds, getting back to their Omaha roots, attempting to make the connections to who they were and where they came from, after their long exile from. He had met her in Portland through her cousin who was now back in Rome working for the Jesuit envoy as the scandals assistant. Cousin Woody had lived there and introduced Andre who was just back from Dutch Harbor and was on his way to do some scuba diving for a Greenpeace action in the Salish Sea, along with Jimmy just up from Chico and working at the fruit juice factory, and had gotten to know Faye with her exquisite French Montreal accent and was now living in the Northwest where/when she had become more of a hippy back in Eugene, Oregon while living in a teepee with some pot grower where sometimes it takes a great notion. Just like Andre's kin the Freres brothers had abandoned Nebraska to go out and become loggers in Oregon. Pretty old school, hard-core rednecks, Andre got along with them fine. They were familia. And Freres Brothers semi-trucks would pull up in these semi-trucks to unload bunker after bunker of plywood at these huge construction jobs Andre would be working at and he would tell his union brothers from the Carpenters that they were his kin and they would just start scoffing at him—laughing. So Andre would just shrug like Atlas: fuck it. His grandfather from Ponca, not too far from Jackson, had occasionally driven out there to see his cousins. But Faye Louise would eventually have to return to Montreal to reunite with her children—back in Canada: Oh Canada...where the French guy was ruling like a Cuomo and dreaming of his idol Fidel. As he would have to make sorties to Seattle for a change of vibe. That is, of course, before what The Clash foretold of—the clampdown and others call the Great Reset with Klaus Schwab and Bonnie Prince Charlie, before the Wu hit the shores and careened across this fruited plain of the United States of America and Italy and the world...that is—just before the nanny-state/fun-haters and all the "well-meaning" authoritarians took off their sheep's clothing to exert their insatiable thirst/lust for power—for the "good" of the rest of us. To save us. But not the whales. Destroy the village in order to save it, or something like that—duh. Was probably never even ever said; some political hack fluffer apparatchik propagandist reporter just made it up. Elected representatives are not leaders—they're elected representatives: think of the dweebs one voted for back in student council days... Some states remained free, some went Soviet. Constitution or no constitution. A declaration of independence. The liberty of the individual. Everybody thinking Australia, Canada and New Zealand were cool countries—they locked down as stupid as New York and California. Rudloff tries to imagine that: truth as a distraction, follow the science. We only have the rights we can defend. Warsocki had enunciated something along those lines a few soused evenings down in Durango quoting Solzhenitsyn—"Human beings are born with different capacities. If they are free, they are not equal. And if they are equal, they are not free." Andre concurred—Warsocki always coming up with a good Russian quote be it Dostoevsky, Gogol or Solzhenitsyn. Andre was at the epicenter in Seattle when the shit first hit and he knew the nancy boys in Seattle would go full retard lockdown. And he was right. And he thinks, good people are stupid—believing all the time. A bunch of fuckin' hopers...and what was up with so many of his liberal brethren thinking that French kissing these un-Democrat politicians was gonna make things all better. Ye-ah... But Andre the Sandinista digresses often...as does Tom "the Narrator" Rudloff occasionally, who often had admonished Andre—for his lack of manners. Too many good texts from Warsocki. Ja-ha! Incendiary. And Sergeant Warsocki—fresh from fighting America's battles overseas against terrorists—just before the whole military went woke and was thoroughly emasculated for tranny inclusion because everybody's a racist—in order to save the postmodern butterflies. And the lovely nice people in America would hear what Warsocki would have to say about the wars in Iraq and Afghanistan fighting with the Kurds, Shinwari Pashtuns and Tajiks but would grimace and shirk at the bluntness of the truth and horror, preferring to hear what Anderson Cooper, Don Lemon or Chris Cuomo on CNN would have to say on what was going on in these American Wars on Terror, as well as what was happening down in Mexico and the border—yes...much better to not talk to somebody who has been there. And then the Wu and the riots cometh. It was a lot of bullshit, wear a mask, don't wear a mask...six feet, not six feet, the doctor Alfred Fauci E. Neuman couldn't make up his mind...drink Bud Light beer or don't drink Bud Light beer? Tran or not to tran? Take a shot or not take a shot? It's all abou choice. But you were a hero nurse—oh, now you're not... Because you didn't get the shot— you're fired. You're gone—to fireman as is the Army sergeant who endured four deployments in Afghanistan and Iraq. Oh—all the people love our heroes in America like we love our Indians. Might even send the IRS out on one's ass if you step out of line or be the investigative reporter Matt Taibbi for the Rolling Stone. Maybe free Julian Assange—how about it Barack Obama? But show me your "papers" or you can't go into this restaurant or bar. WTF. Fucking Nazis. Oh well, as Andre wearing a rich crimson damask waistcoat buys his plane tickets, shows his ID over and over, gets scanned and still gets padded down three times, three flights. It's like a banana republic now fraught with kangaroo courts who punish the businessmen, but free the violent thieving criminal without bail. The Beat poet Allen Ginsberg declared or howled in one of his more famous and ironic lines—beer just make you fat and gay (nothing wrong with being gay, but just come out of the closet—it's not the 1900s anymore). The country's been drinking too much Bud Light. Coming from that great poet—this should mean something. Andre contemplates the nation's been drinking too much Kool-Aid as well. Ah— one's gots to keep a sense of humor, for it was all just too much money getting handed around: LLCs, Ukrainian shell corporations, Chi-com Confucious institutes, kumbaya make you feel good rock guitar mass mega churches, climate crisis centers and big pharma compnaies. Andre hates equally. Fucking gay Republicans and cross-dressing J. Edgar FBI lying Indian-killing conspiring with Russian collusion while getting played by Boston mobster Whitey Bulger playing sycophants as the DOJ eunuchs run interference for them (something like Crow Dog and Russell Means would say Andre imagines in their political diatribes). So to speak. But Andre thinking, the song remains the same—shoot, move and communicate, we only have the rights we can defend, part of: a bright shining lie, and much of the history of this world as we send Jimmy Carter out to monitor other countries elections as FDR blue blood WASP minions got the nod from Luciano, Costello and Lansky while golfing because Costello didn't think a President of the United States should have a Bronx accent like their Irish gangster pal Al Smith, the governor of New York who bawled like a baby on the boardwalk when they gave him the news saying, " I would have given you guys everything," and then he got deathly calm and still, collecting himself and said with cold flint eyes, "He's going to break your balls." And Luciano realized they totally fucked up. Oh well, the narrator Rudloff, who never made it to the annual Al Smith Dinner gala extravaganza in NYC, shakes his head at how random the world is as he continues telling the saga of such infinite jest that it just breaks his heart about this thing called Life—no matter how beautiful it is sometimes: makes you want to just hang down your head and cry. He quotes in Latin: Dolorem ipsum, quia dolor sit amet, consectetur adipisicing elit, sed do eius modi tempora incididunt ut labore et dolore magnam aliquam quaerat voluptatem—Cicero. Through suffering... All that good seminary training. No pain, no gain. Lessons in Latin from real men/good teachers like Father Kane and Father Kalamaja at Rummel High of Julius Caesar's book: The Gallic Wars.

CHAPTER THREE

TRIGGERING VISHNU

Those friends thou hast, and their adoption tried

Grapple them to thy soul with hoops of steel

—*Hamlet*, William Shakespeare

Their relationship was at times a debauch. Both forlorn and homesick. They remedied the situation with heavy drink. And passionate reckless sex. Just fucking like savage horses. Him seeking her holy grail. She was a wild cat. He got so torn up by her the first couple of rounds he thought he might have to make his way to the emergency room. The last time he'd been ripped up like that was back in the early Eighties with a Puerto Rican girl named Eva that he'd guessed had just been dying to meet him. At an apartment in downtown Benson. She scarred him good. Lord have mercy, he'd be seeking grace and succor, Andre's back looked like a tiger's striped markings—but in shreds. It must have been the French in Faye Louise or maybe the Irish banshee. My, my: Lord have mercy... He liked pulling hard on Faye Louise's pretty pony tail. She taught him advanced French. He learned like an honor student. Hippy, hippy shake! She was so ENLIGHTENED. And gratuitous. They were so vain. And it made him wonder—why are women always trying to reform themselves and lying about their virtue?

They did a lot of cool groovy hikes around the many rural parts of Nebraska amongst the bobcats, deer and red fox when they weren't drinking heavily at the Green Onion or dancing wildly to the cool jazz and steamy soul being played at the best parties of the Omaha Lounge downtown where the old girls would dress to the nines and you could imagine Charlie Parker, Duke Ellington or Billie Holliday could come sauntering up on the casual stage to slay it—like they would at the old Red Lion Lounge back in the day, across from the Blackstone Hotel, Andre's old man as a kid would hang out on the stoop of the stairs listening...like the little orphan/street urchin he was before getting shipped off to a monastery. Often the two would head to Fontanelle Forest over towards Bellevue along the banks of the Missouri. Bellevue had been the fur trading post for the lucrative business of beaver pelts that made wonderful hats in Europe. The French trappers had named the area Belle Vue because of the beauty of the view from the bluffs overlooking the Missouri River. It was run for a while by a fellow named Lucien Fontanelle who represented the American Fur Company and traded amongst the Omaha, Pawnee, Otoe and Missouri tribes. The next town over was called Papillion which means butterfly in French. Andre's French grandmother had been married for a little while to a banker from Papillion. The book Papillion by Henri Charriere was Andre's favorite book and movie. Steve McQueen was awesome in that movie as he hypnotically stared out at the open sea. To freedom.

The trails were pretty-pretty, the talks good. She was recovering from a rough acrimonious and financially disastrous divorce that she'd been making most of the money while believing her husband. Earlier on she'd gotten her degree from NU in Lincoln in accounting and had gone to work for the prestigious Omaha accounting firm De-Loitte, Bush and Associates, but the CFO Marc Martin had a habit of grabbing the young female accountants underneath their dresses during meetings. Like the allegations on the last two presidents Orange Man Bad and Colonel Corn-Pop—grabbing them by their pussy. Young Faye Louise with her sweet French accent brought the issue up to the HR lady, which was useless, for Marc Martin was the CFO...the nice lady from HR shrugged and said it had been brought to her attention from other young women accountants: oh my, he's a little frisky—just going to have to buck up girl, Title 9, girls sports—we're making progress... That's when Faye Louise decided to get out of corporate business with such good assistance from HR, and go into education, eventually getting her master's degree out in Oregon. Andre the Benevolent, of course, assisted her in taking off the strait jacket she'd found herself in, along with her bra. They'd look out over from the cliffs and try to imagine what it was like back in the 1700s and 1800s with the Spanish, French, English and Americans all vying for control and power of the vast area amongst the many tribes. Battles ensued. One of the more noteworthy was the Villasur expedition of 1720. It was a Spanish military venture to put in check the French from Louisiana and their growing influence, expansion and interest upon the Great Plains with their explorers and fur traders. The Spanish had proclaimed ownership of the Great Plains since the conquistador Francisco Vasquez de Coronado explored this region seeking the gold from the fabled Seven Cities of Cibola and looking for his wealthy nation of Quivira, of the 16th century, but with no such luck they had exerted little to assert this claim for Coronado found none of the mythical cities of gold and had eventually referred to it as simply—the Great American Desert. So up until then the Spanish had mostly stayed around Santa Fe and had not ventured much northeast of what is today New Mexico.

But with the advent of the French entering the Platte River west of the Missouri River the Spanish got nervous and ordered Capitan Villasur to capture French trappers on the Plains and gather intelligence as to what the French ambitions were in the region. He left Santa Fe in early June of 1720 with a priest, a Spanish trader, a troop of forty cavalry called Cuera, sixty to seventy Pueblo Indians and about a dozen Apaches to lead them as scouts. The Apaches were tribal enemies with the Pawnee. The leader of the scouts was a man named Jose Naranjo who was of African-Hopi parentage and believed to have been to the Platte River area previously.

The outfit makes their way northeast through Colorado, Kansas and Nebraska establishing contact with the Pawnee and Otoe along the Platte and Loup Rivers. Villasur makes attempts to have negotiations with the Indians through a translator—some captive/slave who spoke Pawnee. The translator disappears from camp. This is about the middle of August just south of the confluence where the Loup and Platte meet near Columbus, Nebraska about fifty miles west of Omaha. Villasur is concerned about the growing number of Pawnee and Otoe Indians and their increasing belligerence.

At dawn, they attacked. Shooting with muskets procured from the French and unleashing a cascade of arrows, they charged into combat against the sleeping Spanish encampment. According to survivors, Frenchmen were fighting along with the Pawnee and Otoe warriors. The battle was brief and soon thirty six Spanish lay dead, including Villasur and Naranjo with ten of their Pueblo Indian allies.

The surviving Spanish and Indians arrived back in Santa Fe on September 6. The defeat marked the first and last attempt of the Spanish that far north and east to exert any influence upon the central plains. Ironically at a place eventually named Columbus. History was funny that way, Andre thought. He'd always been amazed by the conquistadors. The sheer brass of these men upon their horses wandering out into the featureless steppe of the Llano Estacado with millions of buffalo surrounding them, lost with the seamlessness of the sky and the smooth plain of the land as to feel as if they had been swallowed up by the sea. According to Coronado. The imagination is vast like the Plains Andre thinks...just trying to give peace a chance. With vast cities of gold and wealth. Like Quivira.

And what about scalps? Where'd that shit come from? Blame it on the white man, Andre figures. Imagine surviving one! He'd had that feeling with a couple old timey barbers—Bud for one at Loveland Barbershop next to Hinky Dinky grocery store across the street from the VIP Lounge. Brother and neighbor boys they'd ride their bikes down Center Street, read the WW II comic books or the Old West cowboy/Indian ones, watch Skelly Jim, the mechanic from across the street, reading the newspaper as the other barbers, George, Bud and Tom, yacked with him and whatever other dudes came in: talking about the times…Watergate, Vietnam and sports. They'd pretty much ignore the boys especially Skelly Jim who'd pay no heed to them even though that was his gas station and garage their parents used every week along with a multitude of repairs. He had enough kids with five or six of his sons working at his shop. The boys were there to listen and learn. Subby Florida's barbershop school was another place for a good scalping. Andre touches his hair and rubs his head recalling the tale of William Thompson, the most celebrated scalpee possibly of all time.

Mister William Thompson rode into this notoriety on a railroad handcar in central Nebraska. He and five other men set out from Plum Creek depot to fix a broken telegraph line on August 6, 1867. They were ambushed by a party of Cheyenne. Thompson started to run. A bullet hit him in the arm, but he kept running with desperate hope as a mounted Cheyenne warrior overtook him, clubbing him to the ground and stabbed him in the neck. Whence he jumped down off his horse and began to twirl his fingers around William Thompson's hair to commence sawing and hacking away at his scalp. Poor William remained awake throughout the whole ordeal with all the popping noise peculiar to the process of the hair follicles separating from the skull. Andre shudders at the prospect period but particularly at the notion of consciousness while enduring this sort of operation.

With the job finished and well done, the Indian hopped back on his pony and trots off back to the merry band tossing his treasured prize into the bushes. It was really bad luck for Bill and his crew. An hour earlier or an hour later, they would have missed the gang of Cheyenne who were just freshly returning from a raid into Pawnee country. They had observed the hand car making its way down the tracks and had decided to wreck it by piling up logs upon the tracks. The Cheyenne then hid themselves until the car passed by them. Thus they sprung upon the hapless six yelling and shooting. According to Cheyenne lore, they decided that taking the hand car worked so well they ought to do the same to a train. Thus a train arrived that night and derailed. The Cheyenne pounced upon the wrecked train killing the engineer and the fireman. The brakeman and the conductor jumped out of the caboose and sped away into the night. The train was packed with whiskey, tobacco, flour, saddles, and an abundance of plumage for frontier ladies. The victorious Indians celebrated their success and got drunk, dressing up in the finery of silk, velvet and calico as they staggered around the bonfire. Around dawn the Cheyenne set the boxcars on fire and throw the dead bodies of the engineer and fireman into the flames. That's when Thompson who had been lying motionless since the hand car was wrecked decided it was time for him to make his break. He recovers his scalp, and crawls and lurches his way back along the tracks till he arrives at the Willow Island depot. How long William hung out at Willow Island with his scalp along his side is unclear. Eventually a train arrives to take him back to Omaha. He is accompanied by the immolated bodies of the engineer and fireman.

Rumors had abounded throughout Omaha so there was quite a gathering of the curious at the Union Pacific station, waiting for the arrival of the burnt offerings. A couple boxes contained what was left and for the benefit of the public, one was cracked open. Part of a leg fell out with a charred trunk resembling a large log. The gaping crowd stood in awe, that's about when the horrified spectators heard about another spectacle. There about 3/4s alive was Mr. Thompson with his scalp riding in a bucket of water. Quite weak of course, with a bullet wound through one arm, a knife wound to the neck and part of the top of his head gone—the aghast spectators flocked everywhere in horror. Andre can only imagine having worked down there at the sweltering train hub as a portrait of the artist as a youth, busting up tracks, jackhammering pavement and breaking rocks in the hot sun in the summers with his brother and deplorables the likes of hard partying Johnny Walker and hard drinking Joe Steele who was a helluva defensive tackle. Joe eventually joined the Glaziers Union Local 109. Andre last heard Joe was just about getting ready to retire. He use to hitchhike to get to the school to make the games. Joe, Walker and Beauregard had a road trip infamy out to Vegas via Phoenix back in the early Eighties. Like Costello. Joe won a football scholarship with the Mavericks at University of Nebraska Omaha, but they didn't give him a parking space so he quit.

The operation proved unsuccessful. A local surgeon had attempted to stitch the scalp back upon his head. There is a photograph of the patient taken after the surgery. He is a full-bearded man seated in a chair wearing a stunned, shocked look like a dazed rabbit in an overly large frock coat. His skull does look peculiar. It was said that thereafter William Thompson wore a black skull cap and converted to Judaism. A reporter who peeked in the bucket when the Union Pacific train arrived in Omaha claims the approximate nine inches by four rectangle resembled a drowned rat as it floated and curled up in the water. Thompson later on donates the specimen to science where it eventually finds a home in a jar of alcohol and is prominently displayed at the downtown Omaha Public Library up until 1967.

Andre considers that one hard and thinks what a goddamn backwards country he is in. Andre he came, he saw—ain't nothing progressive here: 'cept for a few pockets of the wealthy dropping some baubles to cultural elites—it was a wasteland. But Andre liked the palooka factor—they were real, like the Indians. Later on he reads that each tribe had a particular way of scalping and that the Indian scouts could tell the troopers what tribe had done the deed anytime they happenstance came upon the scalped. What a world. Where it all came from—nobody knows for sure. Was it the Parthians that Herodotus refers to in his fifth century B.C. historical record? Was it the Byzantines? Genghis Khan and his Mongols who got the ball rolling? The Spaniards? The Caribbean natives were a pretty rough lot. The Yaquis of Chihuahua and Sonora? The French explorer Jacque Cartier recorded it in the sixteenth century along the St. Lawrence River. It is said that American bounty hunters were getting $250 an Apache scalp and that they'd head a little further south to supplement their income by taking Mexican hair. The practice never

gained traction west of the Rockies. Thus Andre would return or as
that little red-headed Raggedy Jen-Anne Psaki press secretary liked
to constantly say—he would "circle back" to—the lying liar's line:
what a world... now at least they've got the cute little Raggedy Anne
Karine Jean-Pierre... making up all the inane nonsense. What up
Chomsky? And, what would Orwell think? Re-read *Homage to Catalonia* is Andre's constant default:

> Philosophically, Communism and Anarchism are poles
> apart. Practically—i.e. in the form of society aimed at—the
> difference is mainly on emphasis, but is quite irreconcilable.
> The Communist's emphasis is always on centralism and effi-
> ciency, the Anarchist's on liberty and equality.

So much political capital has been made out of the Barcelo-
na fighting that it is important to try and get a balanced view of it.
An immense amount, enough to fill many books, has already been
written on the subject, and I do not suppose I should exaggerate if
I said that nine-tenths of it is untruthful. Nearly all the newspaper
accounts published at the time were manufactured by journalists at
a distance, and were not only inaccurate in their facts but were inten-
tionally misleading.

Andre the ramblin' man walks the concrete sidewalks alone
with his shadow, hitting the Happy Bar on North 16th Street, the
mythic enigma reminisces those beautiful days recalling the return
trip to with that sexy rapturous woman Twohig with violet eyes like
the prettiest stars who hurt him so good—contemplating how he
would be destroyed by one woman, saved by another, over and over:
a vicious cycle—story of his life feeling like his heart being tossed
amongst a beating pile after an Aztec sacrifice. He recalls the beauty
and the glory with her of what life use to be: tent camping in Montana
and Yellowstone, visiting the Little Bighorn Battle monument, to
being on the Crow Indian Reservation and to picking up some fuel
and supplies at the gas station and talking to the store attendant, a
woman from Finland who'd been married to a Crow and her giving a

quick history of the tribe and informing them of all the cartel planes hauling drugs onto the Rez as an outlet—the Rez being a sovereign nation; she got quiet as some Indian women entered, he reminisces going to the Paha Sapa/Black Hills with a couple nights at Spearfish hiking the trails, visiting Deadwood, pilgrimage to Wounded Knee and talking/interviewing with chief who'd been in the church there at fifteen years old with the 'Nam vets, the American Indian Movement and Crow Dog as thousands of rounds flew from the FBI and Brave Bull and his wife speak of all of Custer's descendants that are up on the cemetery hill with the name Yellow Hair who came from the Cheyenne woman Custer took and they spoke how those descendants were still all around the Pine Ridge and Rose Bud Reservations. Aware that a Cheyenne woman warrior was reputed to have been the one that took Custer down in the battle and the Twohig women took their sewing awls to pierce his ears so that he might hear them in the afterlife... Andre found that a curious detail—Custer's offspring were alive and well here on the Rez. Him and the woman went up the hill and investigated and saw the headstones. One of the woman's certifiably crazy-crazy sisters (she had to escape a polygamous cult in the Northwest by jumping on/signing up with a NOAA ship heading to Polynesia—same boat his pal Connelly was on) had actually lived decades earlier on the Rez in a teepee with her sincerely delusional hippy wannabe an Indian boyfriend and was going to become a member of the Lakota tribe no doubt. The woman came from a creative artistic family. It was all a kind of a flim-flam reservation scam. The Indians at the bare desolate stand said the Sioux don't own much of the actual land—that it was all big on paper, but that the whites and Yellow Hairs owned most of it. Andre interjected to the aging couple that they were still being punished for killing Custer. Eventually, hours later made it to the Sand Hills of Nebraska, down a long barren gravel road to the great writer Mari Sandoz's gravesite and Fort Robinson which had been the Spotted Tail and Red Cloud Indian Agencies in northwestern Nebraska where the Oglala and Brule' Sioux, Arapaho and Northern Cheyenne had their initial Rez to get their paltry inmate rations, etc and the place Crazy Horse and his warriors who had defeated Custer and other U.S. Army forces eventually surrendered and where he came to his tragic and timely death. Andre drinks a whiskey neat in the joint. Then another. It makes his mind wander, remembering as the firewater cascades down his throat. He closes his eyes. The desolate Great Plains. The despair of Crazy Horse. With the loss of the buffalo and the loss of the people's freedom. Andre imagines all the peoples: the English and Cromwell's crushing of the Irish, the Mongols decimation of the Russians, Poles and the other five percent of the world population, the Turks genocide of a million Armenians, the Herero and Nama of Namibia, the Holocaust, Yugoslavia, the Hutus slaughter of the Tutsis, on and on. Where to start, where to stop—many trails of tears... Follow the chimps in the jungle, but try not to get the monkey-pox. So much for Rousseau, Christ and Marx. Andre orders a third round of Jameson. It's just enough to hear the Hotchkiss guns as they opened up in the winter of 1890 upon the ghost dancers. He's got to prepare himself before he hits the downtown public library. He recollects a little before he makes his way, buoyed by the elixir and the ambiance of the swell joint catering to dissipation.

Crazy Horse arrives. There is great mistrust. It is the end of the good life. Like the Comanche who hunted and raided from Nebraska to Durango, Mexico, the Sioux are a nomadic people. They're about freedom and liberty. They didn't dig all them progressive notions about how they were getting instructed how to live and be and how it was all for their own god-damn good, etc. and not being allowed to be a backwards people with their own beliefs, culture and traditions and told (forced to) that they had to pretty much become organic farmers growing blueberries and endives to be hip. It just offended the warrior in them. And all that toxic masculinity them Sioux, Comanche, Kiowa, Cheyenne, etc. had—it was no good. Next the white man was going to tell them they could only have one wife, hunting was bad and that they couldn't eat fat young dog anymore. The crass savages needed to get civilized from their deplorable condition according to the moderns.

So it's all a setup. Crazy Horse has been beating the US Army bad on several recent battles going back to the Fetterman Massacre or the Battle of a Hundred Slain during Red Cloud's War to the Battle of Rosebud just prior to the Little Bighorn, killing Custer was just the most notorious and symbolic and for that he was going to be punished. Sitting Bull and Crazy Horse are hampered with the burden of the women and children as the cavalry relentlessly pursues them. Sitting Bull just about makes it to Canada, but Crazy Horse eventually arrives near Fort Robinson at the Red Cloud Indian Agency. A contingent of soldiers with ten wagons full of presents and a hundred head of cattle go out to entreat Crazy Horse and his disparate band. General Crook who'd lost to Crazy Horse at the Battle of Rosebud had promised Crazy Horse that they'd be allowed to hunt buffalo in the fall. Thus, Crazy Horse was given the impression that as long as he quit fighting that it was temporary at the reservation. More soldiers came out from the fort. The Indian warriors came down the White River in five bands of forty each chanting songs as they filed across the stream. Observers remarked that the cadre paraded down more like a victorious army than one about to surrender and lay down their arms. Crazy Horse handed over three good Winchester rifles. The ponies were given to Red Cloud's Indians as rewards for their cooperation in subduing the hostiles: divide and conquer, always the name of the game. Red Cloud and Spotted Tail were two Sioux chiefs that had given up the game years earlier even though Red Cloud, the Oglala chief had driven the Army out of the northern plains back in the 1850s through 1860s until the signing of the 1868 Laramie Treaty that gave the Sioux the Paha Sapa or Black Hills with a whole lot more territory. The treaty was broken as soon as gold was found in the Black Hills. Red Cloud got dragged back East and saw it was going to be a lost cause. Crazy Horse avoided all contact with the whites never even allowing a photograph of himself taken. He wasn't giving up the ghost and not going on parade or speaking tour or getting an acting part in Buffalo Bill's Wild West Show out of North Platte, Nebraska like Sitting Bull, Geronimo and Quanah Parker did to varying degrees. Sitting Bull was with Buffalo Bill's traveling show for a while till they assassinated him. Geronimo made pretty good dime but went through hell and sometimes drank too much getting chastised by Quanah Parker who lived in a mansion with a couple of teepees out front for him and his five wives. Quanah Parker and the Comanche collected money on each head of cattle that the cowboys drove across their Rez so they kind of managed to stay in business. Unlike the Sioux and Cheyenne. But all these complexities made for bitterness, jealousy and murderous rivalries. Crazy Horse was getting all the attention. It's just human nature—chimps in the jungle: civil war, plots, tribe against tribe, internecine battle. Back to Hobbes. Forget about Rousseau. He's utopic with his flowery language of the noble savage—seeking this is his paradise. Like a workers' paradise Marx and Lenin promised, like a Benedictine monastery or a Jewish kibbutz over in Israel with everybody singing camp songs around the camp fire like Camp Fire Girls.

There was no official written agreement or formal treaty, Crazy Horse signed nothing. Then they killed him. They lied to him with the complicity of the Loafer Indians as the wild ones called them, General Crook gave orders to have him arrested, jail him and send him east under guard via railroad. Crazy Horse's fate was to be the Dry Tortugas in Florida which was a small atoll in the Gulf of Mexico where the Army had a fort and prison with holes dug in the coral with iron bars across the top. Brutal. Crazy Horse went riding in to discuss matters, but it was too late when he figured out the setup. He got bayoneted a couple times with the help of some Indians and died a very rough agonizing death. A doctor gave him shots of morphine to ease the pain. His final struggle ended near midnight. His father cried at the loss of his son.

News of his death spread a pall across the Indian camps. The eighteen hundred man garrison stayed on alert all night long. The death wail rose all at once across the darkness for miles around. The people of Chadron, Crawford, Gordon and the Bourdoux fur trading post all slept with grave concern that evening. The next day Crazy Horse's parents took his body by travois from the fort to Spotted Tail Agency. They placed him on an outlying hill upon a platform in the traditional manner remaining with him for three days straight. Later his body was moved to a secret burial site. No one knows where the bones of Crazy Horse lay.

Recalling Wounded Knee in 1983, the ten year anniversary from the FBI/Indian War of 1973 which was at the same site of the My Lai-like massacre at Wounded Knee in 1890 where nearly three hundred Lakota perished that bitter cold day in December to be buried in the bloody mud and the ensuing blizzard. As Black Elk declared… for the nation's hoop is broken and scattered—there is no center any longer, and the sacred tree is dead. Through the famous motorcycle riding/bronco busting Jesuit artist Don Doll who'd worked for years up at the mission in Pine Ridge, Andre ends up side-kicking around and working as a photographer covering the story for the Minneapolis Tribune. Things were warm. Choppers in the air. Hostility and sorrow hung in the air. Anger rose with one young warrior who got in his face accusing Andre of being CIA/FBI. The cat wanted to go right to the mat with him. Andre confronted him but wasn't about to start fighting him. That would have definitely ended badly—for Andre and a few other Wasi'chu. It was exciting. Almost like being back at a military coup with full on war breaking out with machine gunfire, mortars and screaming jets in East Africa. With all the feds, guns—M-16s, high-powered deer rifles with scopes and all. It was very spiritual as well with the marches from four directions all converging. Except for having a young Indian wanting to go to the mat with him to kill him. Andre caught the fucker messing with the car. It was the first time Andre had been accused of being CIA—it wouldn't be the last.

And then there was Chief Standing Bear of the Ponca tribe… trying to just get the hell out of Oklahoma hell. Standing Bear and six others didn't like what they saw so they decided to walk the whole way back from the red dusty land of the Flower Moon people, the Osage, to the verdant rolling hills along the beautiful Ponca valley of the Niobrara River of northern Nebraska. Forced back this trail of tears his daughter Prairie Flower died in the town of Milford, Nebraska. He became famous as he argued successfully in U.S. District Court in 1879 in Omaha that Indians are "persons within the meaning of the law and is entitled to its rights and protection" and have the writ of habeas corpus—a fundamental right in the Constitution that protects against unlawful and indefinite imprisonment. With the victory of this landmark case, Standing Bear became the first Indian judicially granted civil rights under American law. On the trek back of this Trail of Tears, others perished besides Prairie Flower. White Buffalo Girl, the daughter of Black Elk and Moon Hawk, also died and was buried in Neligh, Nebraska. The folks of Neligh provided a Christian burial for the poor girl with an oak cross over the gravesite. Black Elk requested that the grave of his daughter be honored. In 1913 the town of Neligh erected a marble monument. It is still there.

Standing Bear went on to travel the eastern United States to advocate for Indian rights. After returning from the East, in 1883 he settled on the Niobrara, their traditional land, with other Ponca Indians. Now there are two tribes recognized by the federal government: the Ponca Tribe of Oklahoma and the Ponca Tribe of Nebraska.

In his address to the court at his trial, Standing Bear raising his right hand said the words: "That hand is not the color of yours, but if I prick it, the blood will flow, and I shall feel pain. The blood is the same color as yours. God made me, and I am a Man."

Andre reads more…having gone to the public downtown library to procure books by some of the people on the wagons. He also wants information about Mari Sandoz, the Nebraskan writer with books like The Beaver Men, The Buffalo Hunters and The Cattlemen. He had done pilgrimage, seeking Old Jules, driving down the desolate gravel road, to her ranch gravesite between White Clay and Gordon in the Nebraska Sand Hills on his fateful return back to Omaha with the beautiful Twohig woman with the fine dining restaurant. He grabs some books on Willa Cather as well, author of books like My Antonia about the Bohemian Immigrants settling upon the Plains. She was from Red Cloud, Nebraska and recounts how there were thirteen newspapers in vicinity in thirteen different languages—Czech, Swedish, German, Danish, etc. for it was the end of the line for homesteading in this harsh, choking, dusty empty-quarter: enough to make Febold Feboldson proud as he tries to capture the wind to sail across the Great Plains. Andre peruses through a diary of a woman written in 1863 who is heading to Montana before going through letters written by Sandoz—not sure what he's looking for. He reads from Biscuits to Badmen—Omaha to Bannack: Summer by a Harriet Sanders who wrote in a journal about the travel on a wagon train.

> June 16, 1863. We all left the Herdon [Hotel} in Omaha about 6 p.m. in a large carriage...overtook our teams and went two and half miles and camped, our first night on the prairie.

> Wednesday, June 17. In the morning, one yoke of cows were gone...

> Thursday, June 18. Last night we had a terrible thunder storm. It rained very hard... Met this a.m. wagons, Mormons going to bring friends back to Salt Lake... Camped for the night west of the Elk Horn. Had considerable trouble crossing the bridge. It swayed from one side to the other under weight of our teams. And the oxen were determined they would not cross, but after some urging, we all reached the other side in safety.

Saturday, June 29. —- ... This p.m. I rode the pony and carried Jimmie for an hour, and then walked three miles.

Sunday, June 21. This has been a lovely day. We camped last night in a beautiful part of the Platte Valley a few rods from the river... We are now sixty two miles west of Omaha. Have had a regular Sunday supper, if we are living on the Plains, coffee, ham, beans, warm biscuits, canned peaches, and it was all good. I am now sitting in my chair in the wagon writing and watching the glorious sunset, I never saw a sight so grand you can see it fall, it seems as though it drops, it moves so fast.

Monday, June 22. —- ...Camped tonight on the Loupe fork at Columbus... There are about seventy teams of Mormons camped about a half mile from us.

Tuesday, June 23. We are now ready to be ferried across Loupe fork...I am now sitting on the opposite shore. Our team was the first to be ferried over. We had a great deal of trouble: the river is filled with quicksands, and it is very necessary to keep the oxen moving... We have just heard of a battle fought yesterday between our troops and the Indians only twenty miles from here [sixteen miles up Loupe Fork of the Platte.} The Sioux beat the Pawnees and our troops, and they telegraphed for more of our men to come. I hope we shall have no trouble with Indians. Tonight we have camped fifteen miles from the battle-ground, and the hills on the right are guarded by Indian scouts. A Government company of nineteen men taking provisions to Fort Laramie have camped near us, and we are going to keep guard all night so that we feel pretty secure. The men have their guns all loaded and ready for a brush.

Wednesday, June 24. —- …Here we are camped in a most beautiful flower garden on the banks of the Platte. It is a most singular river, it has been in many places today one mile in width, dotted with beautiful islands, very deep in place, and in others so shallow that a good sized fish would get aground. It is completely filled with sand bars and quicksand.

Thursday, June 25. We are now 115 miles from Omaha and about 65 to 75 from Fort Kearney.

Saturday, June 27. —- … It is raining, the wind is blowing very hard, and I have never saw such grand lightning. Sheet after sheet, it darts through the heavens, but I must go to bed; the children do not seem inclined to go to sleep till I come.

Monday, June 29. —- …Our attention was attracted to a very strange and unusual appearance between us and the woods, at a great distance on the plains. It had the appearance of a prairie on fire or a lake with the waves rolling. When we returned to the wagon, Mr. Booth told us that it was a mirage and even on the plains, an unusual thing. This afternoon we passed two villages of prairie dogs… But Oh! What a shower we have had. I have heard of thunder storms on the plains, but I never before imagined anything like it. A perfect blaze of lightning and the most terrific thunder. It was really awful.

Wednesday, July 1. —- … Saw as many as three buffalo grazing, also ten beautiful antelope bounding over the plains but not near enough for a shot.

Thursday, July 2. This is our first day on the plains without good water. We left the ranch at Fort Kearney, have found good water ever since until today our canteens are empty, except as fill them from the pools at the side of the road… Today we have seen eight or nine antelope. The men tried to a number of times to get a shot at them but failed, as they are very shy and run like the wind. Last night about 1 o'clock, the cattle commenced running; they took a regular stampede.

Sunday, July 5. —- … I went to the top of a hill near our wagons about 200 feet high. There we had a fine view of the Platt Valley, the high bluffs on the opposite side of the river and the North and South Forks. I never saw a finer view in my life… We learned that there are fifteen hundred Sioux camped for the night on an island five miles down the river from us.

Saturday, July 11. —- … Passed a grave this A.M. We have passed, since we left Omaha, as near as I can remember about fifteen graves by the roadside. Oh! How sad to bury a friend on these plains.

Thursday, July 16. —- … This A.M., while our team was about a half a mile in advance of the others, we saw two animals crossing the road about ten rods ahead of us. We stopped our team, and Mr. Sanders took his gun, but it was no use, they were soon out of sight. They ran as fast as a deer. They were panthers, almost as large as Nero [a large dog]. We came in sight of Chimney Rock a little before noon at the distance of about fifteen miles.

Fascinating journey—now they were in Old Jules country, Andre went to read what Mari had in her notes.

To George Lorimer, Editor

Saturday Evening Post

July 23, 1932

...My father had many friends among the Sioux and these spent part of every summer on the Niobrara, camped before our house. Those young Indians were our best playmates... I've spent much of the last three summers on the Pine Ridge and Rosebud agencies where many of the Oglala and the Brules are.

To Mr. C. C. Calhoun

Washington, D. C.

November 17, 1932

...The interviews are with such people as: American Horse, chief under Red Cloud in 1876; Herbert Bissonette, son of Joseph, full blood French, long with the Sioux and official interpreter at Camp Robinson; Louie ...The interviews are with such people as: American Horse, chief under Bourdoux, breed interpreter at Red Cloud, member of the 100 who went to the northern camps with Young Man Afraid in 1875 with the council tobacco; Mrs. Ellis Brown, daughter of Big Bat Pourier and raised with the Sioux; Slim Jim Burdick, chief of dog scouts for Custer and Stanley, back and forth from the Black Hills to Red Cloud and Laramie; Mrs. Charles Clifford, relative of Little Bat, daughter-in-law of Hank Clifford; son of Chardon after whom Chadron, creek and town, were named, always lived with Sioux; James H. Cook, of Agate, Nebraska, strong Red Cloud man; George Colhoff, breed working at Yates store in 1874-8; Cornelius A. Craven, with beef herd

at Red Cloud 1875, etc.; Mrs. John Farnham, daughter
OF Big Mouth, wife of saloon keeper between Red Cloud
[Agency] and Camp Robinson; William Garnett, raised by
Sioux, scout and interpreter, son-in-law of Nick Janis; Mrs.
Nettie Goings, half-sister of Frank Grouard, famous scout of
"Sandwich Island" fame; Mrs. Nick Janis, wife of trader for
American Fur Co., whose first daughter was born at Horse
Creek during trading of 1851; Mrs. Maggie Palmer, daughter
of Antoine Janis, son of Nick; R. O. Pugh, married to breed,
agency hand 1876, etc.; Red Cloud, the chief; Rev. Amos Ross,
Episcopal minister with early Sioux; Jack Russel, Buckskin
Jack, bullwhacker at Richards bridge over Platte in 50's, later
assistant farmer for Pine Ridge; later assistant farmer for Pine
Ridge; Richard Stirk, charge of beef herd, with Ben Tibbits,
1875-6; Mrs. Emma Stirk, sister of Little Bat Garnier; Ben
Tibbits, wagon master with Custer, with Indians to Pine Ridge
from Sod agency and from Red Cloud; Wm. Young, mule
skinner about Red Cloud; Sword, Indian capt. Of police, on
dog council, etc. These interviews go on endlessly...

(C. C. Calhoun was a lawyer representing the Sioux in their suit
against the U. S. government asking for indemnity for the Black Hills
area they claimed was taken illegally)

Andre becomes further engrossed in these letters of history...

To H. L. Mencken

American Mercury

February 13, 1933

... anyway, I think it is high time that someone wrote an opera
on the American Indian—what concerns me is that something
more than a few moth-eaten war bonnets and scalps should be
preserved of this magnificent people.

Every time I go to the Sioux reservations I see fewer of the
old aristocrats, fewer of the lean old meat-eaters who made
fortitude their wakan tree of their existence through the
tribulations of vanishing hunting grounds, whiskey traders
and fork-tongued treaty makers, even to starvation. Soon
(Ah, this is about the only topic on this earth that can bring
a mist to my eyes) soon they will be gone. Their seamed
faces, the faded eyes, the toothless gums emphasize the need
for haste. It is not comforting to know that their kind will
never walk the earth again... He Dog was born in the same
village as Crazy Horse, the famous Oglala war chief; they
grew up together, became Shirt-Wearers together, and chiefs.
It is this Crazy Horse I suggest as the central character of
an Indian opera, Siouan because over a long period of years
they were the white man's fast friends; they were the most
feared fighters if not as foolhardy as the Cheyennes and their
resistance was the most prolonged, the most spectacular and
the most successful. Recency too is an element, for there are
still pre-agency Indians at Rosebud and Pine Ridge, men and
women mature when the whiteman first drove the Sioux to
war... the life of Crazy Horse offers a great deal of material,
humorous, romantic, dramatic, tragic. He was an outstanding
youth called Curly because his hair was fuzzy and the color
of young prairie chickens, which suggests white blood to me,
coming greatness to the Indians. Then came his coups; the
event that gave him his father's name Crazy Horse; the vision
saying he would never be harmed by bullets... the wooing of
his wife Black Shawl... the shortage of the buffaloes, pressure
of the whiteman; soldiers; the death of his only child and his
fast for four days at her grave...and through these difficulties a
legend arose among the Sioux that if the white soldiers were
surprised, their horses stolen, and the dead on the field mostly
rifle-armed soldiers, Crazy Horse had been there. Often it
happened so swiftly the wagon guns were of no use at all...
but after these victories he made no talks. Even in council he

let others speak and look to him in the final decision. He never painted, wore only one feather, as ordered in his vision. Even after the days of mourning on the Little Big Horn were over and the wild victory dance proceeded, Crazy Horse sat apart. He had never heard of manifest destiny but he understood its essence…one after another his brother chiefs were hunted down and defeated and yet they must separate to hunt for winter was near. It came so cold that soldiers froze. There was no joy in the tipis, for a summer spent in defeating the Army of the Plains yields no meat and robes, only scalps and badly fitting blue uniforms, full of holes. To test him still further, the Cheyennes, driven from their beds in a forty-below blizzard, came for help in their nakedness…promised that he was to go to Washington and be given a reservation for his people he left Black Shawl with his uncle, Spotted Tail and went to Fort Robinson with the officers, only to discover that he was not a guest but a prisoner in the guardhouse…bayoneted, died that night. And about all the knolls and buttes rose a keening of women and a mourning from self-mutilated braves. They knew this was the end. Crazy Horse was dead. The keening lay heavy on the wind…the next morning his father and mother moved slowly northeastward toward the breaks of Pine Ridge, out of the valley of White Earth [River], on two ponies, a buckskin drawing the travois with their dead son. They left behind them, in the purple mourning dress of the Indian woman, the faithful Black Shawl…He Dog saw the killing, and as he speaks of it to me, a white woman, dangerous fires glow in his fading eyes. He throws the cigarette I brought and lighted from him. But in his generosity he soon forgets and as I leave I am once more his grand-daughter, his white grand-daughter, Little Boy…the Sioux offers a great variety of "ballet" material, ranging from the dance of the virgins to the wild Sundance on the Little Big Horn and the wilder victory dance a week later…the ruthless dignity of the tragedy…it seems vastly important to me that the Plains Indians be given a place in the opera, if not the

Sioux then the Cheyenne, in all the violence, ferocity, humor, courtesy, generosity, poise and tragedy of his nature.

Whoah! Andre thinks—Mari is casually corresponding with H.L. Mencken, the famed satiric acerbic essayist and journalist, who covered the "Monkey Trial" and was credited with dubbing it that... With trial lawyer Clarence Darrow pitted against Nebraska Democrat three-time presidential candidate William Jennings Bryan in the Scopes trial, formally The State of Tennessee v. John Thomas Scopes—the high school teacher accused of teaching human evolution in 1925. High profile attorney Darrow served as the defense for Scopes while William Jennings Bryan argued for the prosecution. It was basically a fundamentalist-modernist controversy: First Amendment censorship kind of stuff. Mencken was an attack dog is his combative style for a free press. H. L. was a wild man. Wow, Mari was proposing a great project to him... how badass would that be—an Indian opera?

To M. I. McCreight

January 27, 1937

Dear Tchanta Tanka:

Thank you so much for the fine little book, Chief Flying Hawk's Tales. It is a beautiful thing, and very valuable historically but more than that—you have caught the essence of the laconic Indian tale... I assume that when Flying Hawk speaks of the Custer battle on the Big Horn he means not the river but the Little Big Horn, or the Greasy Grass as the Lakotah called it. Could the soldier Crazy Horse pursued half a mile p.29, have been Harrington, who was never accounted for until about ten years ago, when the skeleton of a soldier was found down the river, in a thicket?...I didn't get up to

Rosebud for the Sundance but I saw the one at Pine Ridge in 1930. We camped out on White Clay creek about nine miles from the agency, in White Calf's pasture for several weeks. They were very friendly to us. We spent all the time we could with Old He Dog up beyond Oglala. You mention his camp up near Rosebud in 1928. Must be another He Dog. The one I mean died last winter—a brother chieftain and shirt-wearer of Crazy Horse, one of the hostile leaders who came in the spring of 1877. He was blind in 1930, and his legs were bad, but he always recognizes my step and told us long stories of his youth. We brought him the two things he loved, cigarettes and fresh beef. And once he had stood with Crazy Horse and Sitting Bull and Gall against the entire nation. It makes my vocabulary inadequate to think of these things. And now he is dead, and with these old plains Indians dies a culture and a courtesy that will never be seen again.

It is enough.

Reading the footnotes, Andre gathers that McCreight is a rancher from Chadron, Nebraska who had been adopted by the Sioux tribe and given the Indian name Tchanka Tanka—Great Heart or Big Heart. He published Chief Flying Hawk's Tales: The True Story of Custer's Last Fight.

All interesting stuff. To Andre. And people act like we don't really know what happened at the battle…with only about a thousand or so living witnesses. Some things never change. Our press is like Pravda. The song remains the same. Time. He continues in his Re-Search, in this academic tangent style approach.

To Bernard De Voto

July 27, 1938

... Among these, page 239, is a letter signed by O. P. Wiggins, giving a terse resume of his life from the time he went to Fort Laramie, 1839, to his wounding in the Battle of Monterey, Sept 23, 1847, also a list of the party of Mormons he says he and [Jim] Beckwourth (who was born into slavery back in Frederick County, Virginia) guided to Salt Lake in 1846. He says Jack McGaa was first hired to go with Beckwourth but his wife was sick down in Taos, New Mexico, compelling McGaa's return there, and so Wiggins was hired to go instead ... and Wiggins checked up on the government list of troops and civilian employees in the battle's casualties. While I've never traced Wiggins, I'm familiar with his name in the Fort Laramie region, also McGaa's. The first white child born in Denver was supposed to be Denver McGaa and in my childhood I knew a slew of the handsome Irish-Sioux breeds. The McGaas were the aristocracy of the Pine Ridge, South Dakota, reservations; wealthy cattlemen and the boys all good dancers. Jack McGaa was a great uncle to some of the lot, I always understood.

To Louis Lightner

Judge, Sixth Judicial District

Columbus, Nebraska

March 3, 1938

... I'm sorry I can't do anything just now about another novel. I'm deep in Flight to the North, the story of the Cheyennes' last revolt against starvation and malaria in Indian Territory and their desperate trek across Kansas and Nebraska with winter upon them, hoping to at least die in the land they loved ...

So Dull Knife and his Cheyennes (the old and the small were

with the old chief) were shot to pieces by 12 pound guns in the gullies above Fort Robinson, Nebraska. But Little Wolf and his able-bodied men and women got away and finally obtained a home, an agency in the north, as they had been promised years before. But it cost them half their numbers, and the United States army a million dollars. The material is magnificent in both heroism and tragedy, and damning to the white man. Something of these things I hope to capture upon paper in a book length narrative...

Now that was a writer, Mari Sandoz, living firsthand amongst the Sioux and Cheyenne doing what she could to help them, Andre thinks... as he falls steadfastly asleep in his new digs. Gets a little loud when the MMA fights are happening next door or the hockey tournaments are in full swing—lest we forget Floor Nine when the swingers come to town or the COVID payment comes that week and the big girls from North O stay-cationers with multiple children in tow rock it out for steaks as forty three kids running around empty the swimming pool by midnight. Then there was the time the cops blew out the windows on the fourth floor on a meth lab bust. That was exciting. It never stopped. And his pal running the bar and at the hotel about every day, Hochek, never quit laughing as he would pore over the security videos with the inquiring cops in pursuit of the bad boys.

Andre has changed venue and is now back living in the Howard Johnson's Hotel off 72nd and Grover Street—kind of back revisiting the past in his old neighborhood and parish—Westgate and Saint Joan of Arc while continuing further in his Re-Search. So unlike his down and out in Seattle, it was like the song remains the same here in Omaha—Westgate Plaza still having the same marquee with commercial brick buildings like the American Shorthorn Association and all the little cracker box houses from fifty years ago when they'd all assemble in front of Mangelsen's Dime Store next to the Paradise Lounge, La Casa West and the same desultory apartments

Andre grew up in as a toddler, to do the Little League parade in their colorful tee shirts down to the baseball diamonds they marched—his first team was Kennedy's Mets named in honor of the '69 NYC World Series champion New York Mets team with pitcher Tom Seaver. The sponsor and dude who picked the name was an artist by the name of Kennedy with a wild redhead for a wife and a whole mess of kids (Andre had gotten his ass in the sling with her at CCD classes up at St. Joan). Got a deal worked out for his new digs with Little League/ peewee football onto Rummel High teammate and offensive tackle, Charley Hochek who is manager of the bar/restaurant The Bacchanal with Hochek's cohort Sal Amalfi the manager of the motel who had happened to spend a little cooling time in Leavenworth for the mis-understanding of others and some technical discretionary creative accounting mishaps, alleged embezzlement issues and errors. Got the best suite in the house—seven stories up: a suite. He definitely wanted to stay off the ninth floor: funny juju there, where the swing-ers would rent out the whole floor; Hochek delivered the food up there, he didn't allow any of his young waitresses to bring the steak and pizzas to Floor Nine when that party was happening while the most Catholic Pope Paul Society is reserving the large banquet rooms down on lower level. They give him a break, for the room, the cocaine, the working girls and the nights out at the American Dream strip club. It's all about connections and Hochek was very connected knowing the owners of all the various clubs and pawn shops. The Bacchanal is the place where he first met Terri Baby with a crew of Rummel dudes up for sodden drinking and playing poker, like Costello, Vescio, Billy, Donnie, Mancuso, Beauregard and Harrison (Suds would have been there but Suds was dead). But it was at Vino Paradiso, Mavis's place, where Hochek, the maestro of circumstance, did the formal intro... He was sitting in between them. Told him, looking and sounding like Rocky Raccoon, "Here, sit here...she really likes you..."as he moved on to his next prey. And Andre, delusions of—what life use to be before it all went black... about half-believed Hochek. She didn't have any idea who he was or that they had ever met. Andre finds out later. After she picked him up and took him back to her place where he had to fend off the whole night to snarling pit bulls sprawled out on the king-size bed. Could've been a waterbed, the next morning it is very foggy out and not just in Andre's mind. He looks about remembering how they ended the evening at the Green Onion—closing it down, the beginning of a tradition; they didn't call her West End Terri for nothing, for the bad girl often preyed upon her hapless Bumble victims at the West End Lounge—looking for Mr. Goodbar: a woman who'd been on the rodeo circuit a while like a good cowgirl barrel racer picked up her prey at times as Andre would slam her up on her kitchen island as he begged for mercy and tried not to pull her hair too hard. Warsocki, in town to assist his father, happens to send him a text that morning inquiring as to Andre's whereabouts. Andre truthfully responds that he can only vaguely claim to be in some hazy taupe beige suburban ghetto somewhere on the periphery of Omaha in some barely middle class borough aspiring to be bour-geois called Papillion—he believes... After they getting their fill... satiating themselves—she'd kind of drop kick him off every Sunday morning. After that routine for a while. Andre kind of feeling like a good whore—with a blessed Magdalena feeling. With the drop and go program, after several months of Andre getting kicked in the head like that every Sunday morning, they kind of finally went on a date of sorts one Sunday... to the Santa Lucia Festival. It's in East Omaha, Omaha being the sister city to Carlentini, Sicily. Omaha, New York City same-same to the residents of Carlentini—it is known. The fes-tival is set next to Saint Frances Cabrini Church right across from the Sons of Italy building. They get some mostaccioli as Andre saunters over to the old church to light some candles and pray, but first he asks Terri Baby if she had ever been in a church before. He thought it was a valid question given what kind of heathen of a pagan demon she was. In bed. Poor little drunk kindergarten teacher claims she had been once in a church on a trip to Italy along the Amalfi coast. That reassured Andre some—he didn't want to get kicked out. Or hit by lightning. Or some kind of Omen thing happening... You just never know Andre thinks—embracing his religious superstition. Besides that was enough coupledom for Andre anyway…couples get on Andre's nerves. And there was consensus by everybody, including his old friends, that Andre, who had never gotten in no trouble, and was always a pretty good kid—till he started running with Terri Baby.

*It's important to note that sometimes Terri Baby picked up her prey at the Ozone Lounge at Anthony's Steakhouse. This was a common sexual tantric ritual practice amongst the free women of Omaha… Andre, the anthropologist was to learn this cultural system the hard rough way. He was beginning to believe that his arrested development was starting to get the best of him…definitely the best of his love and physicality.

He listens to Buffalo Soldier by Bob Marley to get in the groove and to distract him from all the noise of the patrons and police that occasionally arrived to deal with lawbreakers.

Buffalo Soldier, dreadlock Rasta

There was a Buffalo Soldier

In the heart of America

Stolen from Africa, brought to America

Fighting on arrival, fighting for survival

Woe yoy yoy yo yoy yoy yoy, yo

Said he was a Buffalo Soldier

Win the war for America

Troddin' through San Juan

In the arms of America

Buffalo Soldier, dreadlock Rasta

Woe yoy yoy woe yoy yoy yoy

Woe yoy yoy yo yoy yoy yoy yo

The Buffalo Soldiers, the all-black regiment of the 9th and 10th Cavalries and the 24th and 25th Infantries fought in significant military actions in the Red River War (1874-1875) and in Cuba at the Battle of San Juan Hill during the Spanish-American War (1898). Formed in 1866, up and down the Great Plains they rode—fighting the Comanche, Sioux, Apache, Yaquis and Utes as well as taking on the bandits that roamed free across the Badlands. They came up from Nebraska to keep the peace at Pine Ridge after the Wounded Knee Massacre. And they were expedited west to Wyoming to quell the violence in the Johnson County War in 1892 between small farmers and wealthy ranchers. Andre is reading some more Mari Sandoz of Old Jules fame with Vigilantes gunning down people in saloons in Verdigre, Nebraska and lynching horse rustlers…all to further his education. Man—he thinks, these Buffalo Soldiers, dreadlock Rasta got everywhere. They took part in the Philippine-American War from 1899 to 1903 to heading down to participating in the Mexico Expedition with Patton and Pershing, chasing Pancho Villa and fighting with the Mexican federales and militia forces (1916-1918). They carried the buffalo insignia with them to France in World War I. Dreadlock Rasta…lest we forget all the black, Mexican and Indian cowboys working with all them colorful whiskey-fueled white cowboys with their Colt six-shooters, riding and roving upon their painted ponies—on the cattle drives across a western ocean: to feed all the thousands sailing to this land of opportunity.

He had picked up some good books at the vast bibliotheque publico where the security were kept pretty busy. From her book, Love Song to the Plains, Andre reads…and Andre reads, trying not to pay too much attention to the buzz from the TV as the propaganda and advertising blares from the news and the commercials selling soap and dope. They're not on our side. He picks up from some old magazine articles that the oldest human remains found on the Great Plains date from twelve thousand years ago from the end of the last Ice Age. The archaeologists split the early inhabitants into the mammoth hunters and the buffalo hunters. The killers of the elephants came first with a distinctive type of stone point, called the Clovis point. After the mammoths died off from some climate disaster, the hunters used a smaller point called the Folsom point to kill the prehistoric buffalo. This is believed to be around eight to nine thousand years old. Before the asteroid hit. Maybe.

The big game vanished from the Great Plains six thousand years ago and archaeologists have found little evidence of game for about two thousand after that. The experts in paleo-climate believe that from 4,000 B.C. to 2,000 B.C. the region went through a period of scorching heat and extreme arid conditions. Damn buffalo and their flatulence Andre thinks after a road trip to Cody, Nebraska to drink at the White Elephant Saloon which provided fine liquors for family use and choice cigars he decided to head up towards the Verdigre Creek Valley and onto Royal, Nebraska—Antelope County to check out the Ashfall Fossil Beds—with petrified rhinos and camels; had better get in contact with floating and bloating free-blimping Al Gore and the continuing to windsurf across the Atlantic pond John Kerry. Eventually the rains returned and the temperature cooled. With the moisture, humans again moved in with the animals following the river valleys. And four thousand years later with fifty million bison covering the Great Plains with the elk and the antelope and wolf and grizzly bear like the Serengeti, we start plowing up the buffalo grass, bluestem, sage, threadleaf sedge, Indian ricegrass, soapweed blossoms, prairie onion, sumac, blue grama grass and wild rye to plant hardy varieties of wheat from Russia and a couple dry years occur and we got the Dust Bowl, Woody Guthrie and hard work while Lawrence Welk lives in Omaha awhile trying to ride out the storm. But Charlie Parker and the band keep playing in Boss Pendergast's Kansas City—it don't shut down, not for Prohibition, Great Depression or no Dust Bowl.

Andre is contemplating some Ezra Pound prose and connects how his constructs/deconstructs apply to these non-binary mad, mad times we are living of—burning down the house, the neighborhood, the country, what the fuck. And the police station. And the federal courthouse. And the churches. And the town. Or city in general. During the riots in Omaha—coming out of the Old Market and hitting Dodge Street, they really hit the wine, beer and Cheetos section, according to the clerk out on 72nd that Andre interviewed. He had talked with some of his pals who lived in that central part of Omaha and had been in the army all had their ARs out because nobody knew how out of control it was going to get—a little necessary backup insurance...just in case. As he made his rounds, Andre could definitely see some of these cats had flown in and were not from Omaha. If you were at the airports you could see some of these herds jumping on flights to the next hotspot city to stir it up. What a world. Next thing you know, there will be a ten day week...after the names of the months are changed and all the statues of Abe Lincoln and Frederick Douglas are torn down as ex-presidents and ex-presidential candidates say nothing like deaf mutes. But of course, is what Andre thinks. In doing some of his more academic Re-Search. On the French Revolution. While. Waiting for Thermidor. Or, reading Mao Tse Tung's Dialogues on: the white man's burden.

Gold and Work

1944

THE WAY OF UTOPIA

On the 10th of September last, I walked down the Via Salaria and into the Republic of Utopia, a quiet country lying eighty years east of Fara Sabina. Noticing the cheerful disposition

of the inhabitants, I enquired the cause of their content-
ment, and I was told that it was due both to their laws and
to the teaching they received from their earliest school days.

They maintain (and in this they are in agreement with
Aristotle and other ancient sages of East and West) that
our knowledge of universals derive from our knowledge
of particulars, and that thought hinges on the definition of
words...

Andre jumps around in the reading with his attention deficit
disorder:

A VISITING CARD

...language of Dante, and set about speaking a language of
shopkeeper and hairdressers—and not even the language of
real hairdressers: a language no hairdresser would use.

If Dante has used a word that word belongs to your language.
The same goes for 'l'amico suo', Cavalcanti.

'VOI'

The banning of the 'Lei' marks the beginning of the great
task of salvaging the Latin strength that underlies the deca-
dence of the Italian language. May this revolution continue,
until we have regained the full force of the Latin language
and the Ghibelline poets!

Damnit all! One might at least consider Dante's own terminol-
ogy in his classification of words: "pexa", "hirsute." Sleek words and
shaggy words he calls them.

When Caesar conquered Britain he didn't have to say 'la sua' every time for 'sua', or 'il vostro' for 'vostro'. The article 'il' is sometimes superfluous.

Who denies his great-grandfather would deny his race.

It seems to me that many departures from Latin usage and syntax not to mention the insertion of useless words, might well be dispensed with. They are born of ignorance, medieval or other. I don't mean that we should create a latinising snobbery, but that when a writer, faced with a problem of style, falls into Latin syntax he should not correct it simply because some louse of a pedagogue has decreed a 'rule'. The Latinist, on the other hand, should not interfere by correcting whomever writes in his mother tongue as he has learnt it from a speech, whose forms have perhaps arisen from Latin as it was spoken.

It is ridiculous that when I write English I can use Latin words and forms that you don't dare to adopt (mal franxese); and that you are afraid to adopt the verbal force and syntactical freedom of the Ghibelline poets. The damnable Della Crusca: chaff but no grain!

Ah—it all made perfect sense to Andre and he agrees whole heartedly with the poet Pound that monetary theory is worthy of study because it leads us to the contemplation of justice... Andre was doing this study—all for: just in case. Those that missed the twentieth century. But now it was time for further Re-Search upon the streets, dives and alleyways of sweet home Omaha. Even though he wasn't a biologist, Andre bets Ezra could define a woman.

Andre, the card-carrying liberal who questions authority and hates equally while being fully conscious that drunk chicks dig him, and NAFTA if you HAFTA, takes a break from the media/press hysteria circus about Orange Man Bad because he's American like a lot of fukkin' Americans, brash, obnoxious, and full of themselves. Orange Man Bad reminds Andre of his father Miguel; the visionary entrepreneur, the consumate salesman, the Monte Hall of let's make a deal… They—the Media/Industrial complex loathe businessmen in general but they seem to really like the corrupt retard Manchurian candidate…with his grasping wife: the doctor. Nobody ever wants to hear from a liberal like Andre who thinks George W. was our dumbest president but was telling people back twenty years ago—we got a choice between a doofus and a dweeb; Al Gore being the doofus and W being the dweeb. Just one man's opinion. Nothing personal. Now we got a dozen octogenarians running the country: great. Andre figured Orange Man Bad was just promoting his stupid celebrity show when he announced his candidacy. He thought it was a joke. His popularity rose from not speaking politicalese…y'know saying a lot of verbiage while saying absolutely nothing. Orange Man Bad is just a symptom of the failure of both corrupt political establishment parties to deliver to the unheard and forgotten. Andre's going with RFK Jr., because Andre's eaten bear before and thought it was pretty good…out bear hunting with the Whitcombs of Fall City: methedout logging town. Besides, RFK Jr. is an ex-junky and junkies know a lot, and, he wants to make America healthy again y'know…eat healthy foods and exercise. Also, he who wrote the definitive book on the Wu lab and big pharma racket with the complicity of Dr. Alfred E. Anthony Fauci Neuman, Billy-Bob Gates and the WHO—World Health Organization gonna save us all…got to fight the power. He also broke down in plain English a lot about what was going on with Russia and the Ukraine like they don't want NATO in their front yard, as the Ukrainian men kissed their wives and babies along the Polish border and headed to the front—many of them to die. Andre had been for the Iraqi war veteran Tulsi Gabbard, but then the Hilary called her a Russian asset. Well there you go…guess the DNC didn't like Hawaii Five-O Tulsi—he couldn't believe the Dems didn't run with her, didn't back her, the beautiful Samoan was too independent, too tough, had too much character for their likes. He recalls being in a bar in downtown Hippieville, Washington—the Horse Shoe Café since 1886 watching the Dem debates…Tulsi was great, Lunch-Bucket Sleepy Joe was bumbling and stumbling around and behind the podium. It blew Andre's mind that Alzheimer's victim got the nomination; Clyburn got South Carolina to deliver, the corrupt retard had been in the dust up until then. So with all that political contemplation, Andre decides to do further humble practical scholarly endeavor with the poet/critic extraordinaire from Boise, Idaho, Ezra Pound—

PROVINCIALISM THE ENEMY

Civilization means the enrichment of life and the abolition of violence; the man with this before him can indubitably make steel rails, and, in doing so, be alive. The man who makes steel rails in order that steel rails shall be made is little better than the mechanism he works with. He is no safeguard against Kaiserism; he is as dangerous and as impotent as a chemical. He is as much a sink of prejudice as of energy, a breeding ground of provincialism.

The history of the world is the history of temperaments in opposite. A sane historian will recognize this, a sane sociologist will the value of 'temperament'. I am not afraid to use a word made ridiculous by its association with freaks and Bohemians. France and England are civilization, and because they are, more than other nations, do recognize such diversity. Modern civilization comes out of Italy, out of renaissance Italy, the first nation which broke away from Aquinian dogmatism, and proclaimed the individual; respected the personality. That enlightenment still gleams in the common Italian's 'Cosi son io!' when asked for the cause of his acts.

Humanity is a collection of individuals, not a whole divided into segments or units. The only things that matter are the things which make individual life more interesting.

Andre Jones would have liked to share some of these luminary ideas of Pound on Twitter. But Andre got cancelled. By the FBI. Could be… Or the nose ring guy running it? Zuckerberg? Who knows? It's all about the psychiatry… back after the Italian partisans picked him up and the proper U.S. authorities hauled poor old Ezra away to Galinger Hospital, three court-appointed psychiatrists including Winfred Overhosler, superintendent of St. Elizabeth's Hospital, decided that he was mentally unfit to stand trial. They found him "abnormally grandiose… expansive and exuberant in manner, exhibiting pressure of speech, discursiveness and distractibility". A fourth psychiatrist appointed by Pound's lawyer initially thought he was a psychopath, which would have made him fit to stand trial. Kind of an interesting point Andre thought—psychopaths are fit for trial… Well—no doubt, Ezra Pound did go full Mussolini. Never go full Mussolini.

Thinking of drunk chicks that dig him, as he reads the OWH an article about a young beautiful Czech psychiatrist that was offing her patients via poison, a little push or stabbing them—all for their own good, he reminisces upon that one stony Sunday morning from a year ago he shared with Emka from Alderman's Bar just across from Bud Olson's Bar—she was a pretty serious looking girl and he had asked her if she had any superpower credentials. She replied that she could drink three bottles of wine and still be normal. Andre thought that wasn't too bad for a Sunday at 10 in the morning—like going to church, seeking some audacity in hope. Emka was cool. She'd probably be like a La Llorona which Andre was convinced he'd run into a few nights across the vast continents over the decades. As Gertrude Stein said so succinctly, so correctly, "Rose is a rose is a rose." And Andre says, "Woman is a woman is a woman."

'Ye-ah… crimson and clover. Over and over…'

The electricity that flowed through her when his strong hands caresses the back of her neck made her flower bloom. His tongue was like brush strokes as if he painted a canvas on the way down. She inhales as her hips arches upward to meet his face. She was high out of this world. All she had to do was enjoy it. He gripped her hips with both hands. She rejoices. He lowered her hips back and moved up to kiss the nape of her neck as he cupped her breasts. One hand stayed on her nipples while the other slid down the flat of her stomach where he made little circles working his way down between her legs. She exhales fully. Inhales catching her breath. He parted her sea and entered her. It had been so long. It was so good… He sees—as her dusky velvet torso swells and heaves like the ocean billows. Naked and sexed she rolls. All of her. Ablaze with furious ardor, with generous breasts and gleaming thighs, he kisses her mouth full. Love and hate, despair, lust: amongst pity, rage, disgust, cruelty, war, and sweet tenderness… a beating heart. To fornicate. Waiting for the wild dogs to bark. Into the end of the night—hear'em howl. Loudly. Go Kama-Kama-Sutra—she screams, in joy, pain and exultation, "Fuck yeah!"

He is back at his hotel suite. Andre reads it… and says aloud, "Not bad Walter, not bad." It was some of Walter's work on Fifty Shades of Jones. Andre didn't write any of it. But it makes him wonder how his old stripper friend Mindy was doing? She was a finely built Filipino/Japanese woman who worked back at Pandora's in Portland—they tripped some together well, going out to some dinners and shows: memories, memories. Walter and Andre would just go get drunk at the Interlude Lounge and Andre would tell him these tales of western romance. It was going to be a side project for them. To try and make some money—might try and get an Amish theme going; women loved this stuff. But then, Walter suddenly died leaving his loving wife, Judy, and a couple of sweet young kids that adored him. Life is not fair. A degenerate like Andre lives to satisfy his carnal lusts and appetites like a brute beast that understands nothing while a good loving husband and father like Walter dies at an early age. No rhyme, no reason. And for that reason, Andre does not believe in artificial intelligence. He was an atheist—that way. It's a stupid machine. No heart, no soul. Inherent vice like winter ice as the starlight bends upon the surface of a lake. Mystery finally claims us. In mystical union, reverently, discreetly, advisedly—in the sight of God…Judy-Judy Judy-Jane and Walter did marry betwixt Christ and his Church. Rudloff thinks it might have been a half-Lutheran kind of ceremony because it was a kind of done soberly and in the fear of God unlike a very drunken Catholic affair maybe involving some polka and beer. He was there—Rudloff, still alive, with Jack McCaslin and Senor Agape'. Andre didn't make it—big surprise. So, according to the letter Senor Agape' wrote, Andre who was in Bali, it was instituted by God in the time of man's innocency and it is not by any to be enterprised.

The love was so deep that when Walter died, friends would get together with Judy and their three children over Big Fred's pizza and share Walter stories of adventure as Judy continued working as a teacher. She told Andre one night—she knew she would never marry again. Andre knew she wouldn't. Seven years later, she goes to bed one night and dies. Andre told the children simply—that she died of a broken heart. Somewhere in the medieval divine, with the tyranny of faith, Rudloff and Senor Agape' sigh and shake their heads at the bitterness and beauty of it all. Nothing fair about it. Life. The immortal soul of it…makes Rudloff contemplate from the classic Greek saying: Count no man happy till he be dead. Senor Agape' often cited that.

CHAPTER FOUR

HOMECOMING QUEEN

They tell me I murdered Custer. It is a lie...
He was a fool and rode to his death.

—Sitting Bull

Warsocki remembers. Or does he recall? How did he get here? As he patiently nurses a glass of mezcal with a chaser from a cold can of Tecate looking out across the dry scorched low mountains of the Sierra Madres of Durango, Mexico sitting in the plaza playing dominoes in the middle of Cartelandia. He takes it all in—thirty years of smoke veneered the ceiling with a patina of good times along with the walls and old wooden tables of the tavern. Catering to the rebellious in music and life, it even motivated the timid to—go there... Walking out of the head he sees Andre sitting at a table near the entrance. He looked like he had rode a hundred miles in the back of a pickup truck. His face was wind and sunburned, a shock of black hair everywhere. Like from across the Plains, buffalo, Crazy Horse...

"Hey bro! Co sluchasz? Que pasa?"

Andre looks at Warsocki, his eyes distant, but coming into focus..."Chop! Lookin' strong!"

Warsocki replies, "Well, running screed on the Blaw-Knox, sweating-paving asphalt for your old man, working swing shift at the

Stockyards Hide Company and hitting the gym should do something. You get back from France? Rob enough banks?"

Andre dryly replies, "No Africa, and it was my buddy, Shibumi Schwartz, that did the robbing, I just helped with the logistics and spending. I think he might work for Mossad."

"Well that explains your face and the funky rucksack," laughs Warsocki. "What's it made out of?"

"Monkey fur," said Andre.

"No shit!" exclaims Warsocki. "Big ass ape!"

"Yeah, also makes for a good toupee. I hit Kenya and the Congo," mumbles Andre still getting his bearings back in Omaha like with a thousand yard stare.

"Well, only you would be gone two years and come back with a monkey rucksack," Warsocki grins conspiratorially, "But it beats a priest with a monkey puppet groomin' your ass! Ja-ha!"

"As my brother always said—keep an eye on that goddamn monkey. So it's deep-ass symbolism Chop: kill the monkey, kill the messenger, kill the priest."

This is what set the ball in motion, according to Warsocki—why not ramble on around the world? Andre says—you just go there. He kind of got it with his stint in the Marine Corps and the brothels in Tijuana. You just go there… But this was different. Warsocki went to university got his degree in Russian and next thing you know he's got a Czech wife and is running around partying in Prague, to hanging in Berlin witnessing and participating in bringing the Wall down so people could escape communism, then catching a train to Petrograd, winds up out on the Russian Steppes riding ponies with Tatars and then eventually a few years later in the middle of the civil war in Yugoslavia. Just to fill in a few of the blanks…besides teaching English to the Mexican kids at the South Omaha public schools, or working down in Carter Lake at Future Foam Incorporated or taking care of the rhinos at the Henry Doorly Zoo while designing the desert features of the zoo's massive solarium because of his deep experience at two years of war in the deserts of Iraq in places with biblical and exotic names like Nineveh, Mosul and Mesopotamia. It's been a dance: a rhapsody of life amongst us banished children of Eden. He can at least say that. Lest not we forget a year in Afghanistan with the Shinwari tribe working as an advisor for the U.S. Army. Always be wary of the word "advisor" when it comes to foreign policy. So they say, so they say. Another word to keep track of is "aid" or more specifically, "USAID" especially when it comes in large burlap bags of rice and unmarked wooden crates. Just details Warsocki had picked up on and felt like sharing with idiot America. And we use to just call it shell shock Warsocki thinks—right to the point. Two words, two syllables, a swift command of the English language. Right to the point. Not going to get lost in translation like post-traumatic stress disorder.

He recalls the chance reunion with the Shinwari here in Omaha—nothing is chance. He's back up in Nebraska to help and assist his slowly deteriorating dying South O Polack father. He's got a vicious disease for a man who kept in top physical condition his whole life. Andre is in town doing somewhat the same with his ailing father. Andre is building a deck in Dundee neighborhood for a hillbilly artist guy. It's one of those extreme humid muggy summer days. It's a Sunday. He calls him and proposes a late lunch. Andre retorts that he smells like a goat. Warsocki says, "Well then let's get goat."

Warsocki text a pic of a joint. It's not Mexican, it's Afghani. A time is set. Andre a few hours later arrives at the address. It is right behind Big Fred's Pizza. There is a small grocery store beside it. The café is closed due to Ramadan. He sends a text to Warsocki and informs the place is closed due to Ramada he then goes inside to the grocery store where there are about six Afghani looking young dudes. He talks to them a bit and goes to the cooler and gets a cool drink, pays for it and heads outside. He sees Warsocki driving around looking for the place heading slightly in the wrong direction. Polish Warsocki eventually arrives. They go into the grocery store. Warsocki lumbers in with his prominent nose proboscis; stocky built and long arms, wearing a black ball cap that has golden embroidery written on it that says in Arabic—advisor. He exchanges some words of Pashto and Dari with them. Andre observes. One guy had been a 'terp a few years after he'd left Afghanistan back in 2005. He heads back out to retrieve his phone. Andre saunters back to the counter as a hetman shows up Andre hadn't seen before. All of the sudden the hetman bursts out, "Is that Sergeant Warsocki?! Is that Sergeant Warsocki?!"

Andre replies with aplomb, "Relax dude, he'll be back. He's just going out to get his phone."

He returns. They exuberantly greet each other. They fought against the Taliban together. They hadn't seen each other since 2005. An Afghani jirga ensues like an Indian powwow. They talk of the war: Shaheen and Sarge. Andre listens like he knows what the fuck they're talking about. They talk of many things; ambushes, battles, the Russians and finding themselves in the middle of old Soviet mine fields … and of course, the Taliban, with the communists, Tajiks, mercenaries, Blackwater, the CIA, the DEA, Saraf and different players and all the sergeants—Afghani and American, and how close they were to victory; the history, the history, the tumbling time. Hours later, after discussion of Warsocki's career in the movie business is discussed; Shaheen says he likes the show Narcos. Warsocki tells him that's one of the shows he's worked on. Shaheen rolls with it and then says, "Mexico is like Afghanistan."

There were many other jirgas, goat butchering banquets with occasional bouts of buzkashi (when they could round up enough horses and a poor little goat) after that initial one—with many Shinwari joining along with Iraq/Afghanistan war veterans, operators and associates with nebulous and vague credentials of Warsocki. Andre got to meet other soldiers Warsocki fought the Taliban with: Afghani and American. Andre thought some of these Afghanis were the nicest stone cold killers he had ever hung out with. Reflections of … Warsocki has them. Of how life use to be.

And then he gets to thinking about his jolly buddy Johnny DeCamp who he ran his bar, Johnny D's, for a while. Johnny had been a state senator for the Nebraska unicameral. He'd also been a LRPP in Vietnam. Chop's job as manager of the bar, The Company, was to drink scotch with Johnny and get him home safely to his tough, willful Vietnamese wife. And then Warsocki thinks of a night when Chuck happened to join them at the bar for a scotch or two while going into more cogent details about what he and his brother Tom had been up to in their year of war in Vietnam, walking point or being the "slack" man about three yards behind, chopping their way through the jungle with machete, breaking brush, hacking it out in the bush, perspiring, looking for trip wires, booby traps, buried mines, unwelcome movement, broken branches, footprints, with only a few hours of sleep, measuring distance every hundred yards, keeping pace, compass, leading the platoon. Johnny had another. Chuck went on how it was good to have his brother with him as they went hours at a time with no words as shards of hard bamboo flayed arms raw to go along with the oppressive heat and humidity of the primeval canopy where one might never see the sun. Johnny had another. Chop poured Chuck one. And poured a double for himself, cuz Chuck was talking about the year 1968, for as an Airborne Ranger who Andre and Warsocki had worked asphalt with, one of the five Harris brothers who worked for the company, this was the white one Timmy, who'd been there in 1970 said: Ah yeah 1968 ... that's when the real shootin' was goin on ... And Warsocki recalls how the burly mechanic, one of the Cihachek brothers from Missouri Valley, would drop heavy metal objects from behind Timmy Harris just to watch him hit the roof from the shell shock—now that was FUNNY. Some good old boys. Hard work. That farming. Hogs, cattle, cold beer, the heat. Get the drift...

Stay off the trails like stay off the wall, it be the Ides of March, maybe later. We come upon, wading into the water along the Mekong Delta, the remnants of an old French Michelin Company's rubber plantation ... the greenery was so pretty. Trying to make old General

Julian Ewell proud, but he loved his damn 101st, I mean, the one hundred worse—ja-ha, Airborne so much, especially them Pathfinders… Hackworth was there in the Delta as well—he'd threatened to court martial some Pathfinders who had the gall to refuse to bring birds down cuz they didn't have the perimeter secured. I knew one of the dudes—his call name was Hazard…ja-ha! Well, we'd been guarding a bridge when the radio call came out and we got the M113s moving started moving out. We had four tracks of which Ewell hated the mechs. for they were always breaking down in the quagmire and keeping one platoon out of the bush from killing VC. So we check out a village, go through all the bunkers or holes in the ground, find nothing in this VC-held hamlet, Tom is in the open-topped turret manning the .50-calber machine gun and then BLAM! A fireball explodes. I'm crawling out. Can't hear anything—waiting for the ammo to go off, looking for Tom. Find him. Drag him from the fire. A few weeks earlier he was staunching the wound, stopping the bleeding, just a sucking chest wound, keeping me from bleeding out when the Claymore booby trap went off killing Summers instantly, a good steady dude from Baltimore, eighteen years old, no open casket for John—and Charlie's AK fire hit us from everywhere. Twigs and branches and bamboo showering us. Infantry School manual not applying in this dense foliage. Dang—oh yeah and then a couple weeks later; we get blown up… Thought it was the least I could do. After saving me earlier. Aw hell, face is on fire—still can't grow a beard on that part of my face. Checking out everybody. My brother's all fucked up. Medic birds are on the way. This is no shit—we're all half-dazed. Getting loaded up and taking off, can never forget…Linda Ronstadt is on the radio—You and me travel to the beat of a different drum…

Seemed like the right song at the time. Two brothers, three weeks, four Purple Hearts.

That's fuckin' crazy! Name a fuckin' bridge after them. Or an old fuckin' Indian chief. What the fuck—bad ass. Chopper quips, sipping his scotch solemnly in sorrowful mystery.

Johnny has another double. He appreciates somebody else around the table to fill in on the true narrative of this history. Soldiers march off to war—Johnny bellows.

A salute to Linda Ronstadt!

Salud to Linda Ronstadt!

A tinking of glasses ensues.

How about our Omaha girl Jane?

I think she was in Hanoi at the time. With flowers in her hair.

To Hanoi Jane!

She's still a beauty. God bless her.

The bitch.

God bless her!

Love her. Anyway.

To beautiful women!

Love them.

The bitch.

To beautiful women and war!

To Helen of Troy!

To Helen and Troy...

Samson and Delilah!

War is hell.

Drums of war.

The bitch.

And then another round of Tet hit. We got goddam good at killing.

Love.

Hue.

Bitch.

Johnny slams the shot, throwing the empty bottle of whiskey against the wall of his bar as the glass shatters into many pieces and snarls: "and the beat goes on... Helen of Troy! Boys just wanting to get a kiss while wondering—where have all the flowers gone? Long time passing. Men still go to war. From Carthage onward."

And Warsocki follows, humming, thinking of Linda Ronstadt: and the beat goes on, to a different drum. He'd hear it all again—later, over in Afghanistan: the Stone Poneys and the beautiful temptress Linda Ronstadt. In Afghanistan. In some other fucked-up shit. In a daze. A blurred world, after the Katyusha rocket hit. Pretty seriously wounded, but intact—not believing, deafening. Hit like a wave. Shit literally flying everywhere. They were covered in blue like Picts attacking Hadrian's Wall fending off the Roman Legions. Just before Captain Billy was about to constitutionally hit the latrine. They looked around at each other embrace the Suck, Laughing hysterically, shaking their heads—grinning, then pulling it together... and start barking orders. All kind of like a weird déjà vu. As Warsocki's cousin just fresh out of Fallujah had said to him as he first arrived in Iraq FNG: "it's all just LUCK..." as his cousin's tour of duty was over and he was heading home. Oh yeah, that song plays. Over and over... Choppers come down from the sky. Dust to dust. Load up the wounded and the dead. And the beat goes on.

Andre later on hears some of that tale... of woe and war from Warsocki. Speaking of Helen of Troy, Linda Ronstadt, Jane and homecoming queens, Andre is doing further Re-Search: it has become by now another addiction and compulsion thinking, believing it may hold the key to how things have come to be. This time it is in a more academic setting. He is reading Josie Washburn's The Underworld Sewer. It is her account of life in the trade as a prostitute in Omaha from 1871 to 1909, back in the crib days with little twinkling Christmas lights traversing across the narrow alleyways. He flits through the pages taking notes. She's got a bar named after her now—a pretty cool one in the Old Market with great architecture. He writes down these words... her words.

THE EVIL

THE MODERN SYSTEM IS A PRETENSE lawful control of the evil.

The modern system is founded upon the basis that this evil is necessary for the safety of the community.

But the system pretends at times to ERADICATE THAT WHICH IT SAYS IS A NECESSITY.

The system stands for inconsistency, lack of principles and insincerity.

The system calls itself regulation of evil. The system stands for avarice, tyranny, viciousness, crime, degradation, and death.

The system of regulation stands for fraud and corruption.

The system stands for oppression and graft.

The system of REGULATION REQUIRES THAT THE REGULATORS BE THOSE ONLY WHO WANT THE EVIL TO CONTINUE.

OUR SOCIETY

Most of the girls learn to smoke cigarettes as they enter the underworld.

Among her customers is the rich society gentleman who is noted in his "set" for his eccentricities. The truth is he is addicted to the habit of smoking opium and in the underworld is known as a hop-fiend.

He takes the girl to apartments furnished for the occasion, which is being presided over by a Chinaman dressed in white linen...

...has a small streak of light over which the opium is cooked... Over this blaze the opium is held on a long bladed knife until it is hot.

This hop joint becomes the rendezvous for society dude and the belle of the underworld. She becomes stupefied with opium and cares less for her surroundings. Two years elapsed and she was no longer the belle of the underworld—other girls had taken her place. Another year passes and—behold a wreck. She has parted her belongings and even her clothing for opium, and would now beg, borrow or steal the money to obtain the drug. This is the end of the beautiful and wretched human being, at the mercy of conditions of today.

The dope and cigarette habits are simply appalling among us—more than half of the underworld girls use morphine, cocaine, or hop in some form or other. On account of the lax drug laws there is no restrictions upon them. They are able to buy as much as they want and the amount consumed can scarcely be equaled by the smart set.

I am not writing a myth, but of facts which I have come under my observation.

Andre looks at the front pages of the book and sees it is first published in Omaha in 1909. His grandfather was up in Dakota County riding horseback out running cars. About twenty five years after Cody puts on the performance of his first Buffalo Bill's Wild West Show with Annie Oakley, Calamity Jane, Pawnee Bill with Lakota, Arapaho, Comanche, Cheyenne, Pawnee and Crow Indians in Omaha. Harsh lucid observations by Josie that resonate equally today. World chase me down, Andre thinks... was a lot going on back then. The Nebraska state penitentiary break where two black inmates attempt an escape and the deputy warden is stabbed to death in the ensuing riot and chaos and three white convicts carry out their own prison break with guns of unknown provenance. John Dowd, Charley Morley, and Charles Taylor shoot their way out killing the warden and wounding his brother. They are hunted by the last posse of three hundred deputized men riding horseback across the Nebraska Plains through a blinding blizzard. People get kidnapped, robbed, shot and hung, all a couple of years after this book is published.

Andre can relate to that part about the coming out of the opium dens... out of Morocco or San Francisco—he'd been that guy... just like a picture of Dorian Gray. Yo! This is all a happening—a few years before Josie wrote this treatise; the biggest kidnapping in the country went down with a butcher kidnaps the teenage son of Omaha's wealthiest meatpacking tycoon Mister Cudahy for a $25,000 ransom in gold. Pat Crowe becomes the most wants man in America. Everything went down—stealing horses, river rafts, Dennison and his crew, more posse shooting and chasing within the city bounds and trains. The chase covers a great deal of the southern Plains eventually ending in north New Mexico. Nothing new under the sun Andre thinks of the Beastie Boys and 'Sabotage': the Black Tom munitions explosion in NYC by German agents with the Zimmerman telegram sent to Revolutionary Mexico and then Pancho Villa invades New Mexico, World War I, the Great Depression, Bonnie and Clyde, Pretty Boy Floyd, Ma Barker and eventually, eleven dead later, Nebraska gets to Starkweather with a sawed-off .410 and a meanness in this world with his pretty baby Caril Ann Fugate on his lap. What a world like Walter always said…what a world, Andre thinks. Where the fuck is Dubois when you need him? Probably back praying to Mecca. Andre knows he's going to have nightmares tonight back at the Howard Johnson, if he gets any sleep tonight at all—there's an MMA fight at the Ramada next door and a big narco-corrida FIESTA happening at the Liberty Arena less than a quarter mile away. Later on that evening, American Indians have a fight down the hallway from his suite. It was loud, he didn't dare go out. Not sure what tribes were involved. He knew the head of hotel security—and he knew Jackson was high as a Chinese weather balloon floating over North America with his loyal pit bull dog Hazard always carrying his stash. What would Howard Johnson think? With that one shooting right in the parking lot as Andre just drives by with Terri Baby moments after the cops arrive and there's one dead Mexican… Well there was no shortage of carjacking and shootings right at the gas station next to the hotel. No shortage of mayhem and wild crime here… In Omaha, there old neighborhood. Like a bad Bruce Springsteen song. And America, with a dislocation from reality—in this post-civilization world and theatre of the Absurd. Andre thinks maybe he should get his M1 carbine out of hock at Sol's Pawn off Cuming Street. He heads to 88 Tactical to stock up on some bullets—he's getting low on 9mms. But probably get his 7.62s for his M14 at Guns Unlimited—lot better pricing for the heavier stuff. And get some shotgun shells: double-aught buck. Recollecting how his .380 packing brother described returning to Atlanta after the fishing/camping trip visit in Nebraska with his two teenage sons during the recent riots…smoke curling and fires ablaze in the disparate parts of the city: Downtown, Midtown, and Buckhead…wasn't no police to be found nowhere and their neighborhood shopping mall with a dozen some businesses all in shambles less than a half mile from their home: looted and destroyed… as the sound of irregular gunfire broke out at all hours. His beautiful calm hardworking brunette wife looks at him in the comfortable air conditioned living room. Welcome to Costco. Welcome to Walmart. Welcome-welcome-welcome. MARTA, the Atlanta transit system is a fast moving mobile homeless shelter now. Welcome to Dystopia. A Hobbesian State of Nature. Apocalypse Now. This is the End...a Dadaist End. And it was just beginning. Revelations, everything piling up in mounds—every month, every week, but a lot of people refused to hear or see...because in this society of convenience, we're goin' to Disneyland, as the empire melts like ice cream. No border, no country. Habla espanol ANYBODY?

CHAPTER FIVE

POLICE BLOTTER

It is not necessary to censor the news.
It's sufficient to delay it until it no longer matters.

—Napoleon Bonaparte

More from—back in the day, of cigars and wires, of the underworld, the belly of the beast: Andre peruses through the bounty of material, back at West Gate at the Genealogy and Local History Room of the Omaha Public Library on 84th and Grover near where the old Woolco Department Store just across from the Paradise Lounge stood, had been and the seedy carnival would set up shop in the parking lot with their rickety dangerous rides and freak show wagon of three breasted women and babies in pickle jars and the boys in the neighborhood would ride their bikes down and read excerpts from the Happy Hooker. His neighbor Pots knew just where to go as they tried to figure out what was really going on in that shower scene and jelly. Then maybe they'd ride their bikes to Westridge Swimming Pool making sure they were packing their Speedos. He cross references with the cop Jon Blecha's book Cigars and Wires with the public records. Two bootleggers, Louise Vinciquerra and Joe Mandolfo, testified for the government. Louise was known as the queen of Omaha bootleggers. She testified that one of the defendants, Joe Vaccaro, explained to her that she had to buy her liquor from the syndicate with specific fees and fixed prices per gallon of whiskey. In discussions with her Vaccaro would often refer to the syndicate as the "company" and that if she didn't pay she'd be raided by law enforcement authorities and that the company would break her. The prosecution presented six checks as evidence Louise wrote as payments for liquor. She claimed she would give the checks to either Vaccaro or Carl Mangiamelli, another defendant. The checks would be endorsed by either one of those two or Frank Calamia. She states that when she was paying the company she had only one raid and that was by federal agents, but as soon as she quit doing business with them in October of 1931 she was raided six times in forty days.

Joe Mandolfo was running a still that got raided by the local authorities and was informed by an Alfio Laferla, another defendant who ran a pool hall down on South 13th Street that if he didn't want his still to get hit he'd have to pay the liquor syndicate $200 a month for protection. According to Mandolfo, Laferla said he'd get tipped off if a raid was going down. He also told Mandolfo that he'd have to buy his yeast and sugar from the outfit. Mandolfo testified that he refused to pay and his still was raided two weeks later.

This was all part of the Liquor Syndicate Trail as it was called. This was in October of 1932. On a cold windswept evening Dennison called a meeting with several of the prime defendants in the case two weeks prior to the trial. At 18th and Douglas Street, Dennison walks out of the Fontanelle Cigar Store around 8:00 p.m. and meets with the former Chief of Detectives Paul Sutton on the sidewalk. They are joined by Harry Buford. Buford realizes they are being watched by Prohibition agents from across the street. According to the files, Dennison walks back into the cigar store but later comes out where he is met by Joe Patach who is armed with a shotgun placing it in a nearby car. They remain outside discussing matters till about 9:00 p.m. when Roscoe Rawley who had been inside the cigar store joins them. Dennison eventually gets into Buford's vehicle with Buford as driver. Patach and Rawley follow in their separate vehicles. Where they headed remains a mystery.

The big shake-up occurred in 1931 due to the hit on prominent Omaha businessman Harry Lapidus who was murdered as he was driving home from the downtown Jewish Community Center. He was shot near Hanscom Park three times in the head as he slowed his LaSalle sedan in front of 1915 Park Avenue. Witnesses saw two men talking with Lapidus then heard the gunshots and saw the car sped away down Ed Creighton Boulevard heading east. A couple of the witnesses ran up to the LaSalle to find lifeless body of Lapidus slumped over the steering wheel. Lapidus also happened to be the father-in-law to the Assistant State Attorney General. This was the beginning of the end for Dennison's thirty plus year reign in Omaha. An investigation ensued and theories roiled in the hurly burly of Omaha's political landscape. It was revealed that Frank Calamia met with Lapidus several times at Lapidus's Omaha Fixture and Supply Company, but there is no record of them having any kind of business relationship.

Andre is going through all this material recalling tales he'd heard from his grandfather, some of the old black dudes, his old superintendent Morgan who was a tanker back at the Battle of the Bulge and the mouthy retired inspector named Brick who were all by the mechanic shop every day. His father would casually bring up some pertinent details also. No wonder Andre like the TV western *The Big Valley* with the tough Barbara Stanwyck and beautiful Audra so much as a kid. They just took what they wanted and needed. They had the muscle and the power from the barrel of a gun with the tough man in black—Nick, the law, statutes and sheriff with the attorney Jarrett and got the work done with the six million dollar man Heath the Lee Majors, gonna marry Farah Fawcett, and was some extra brawn for battle. It was awesome. Just hang the horse thieves, kick out any woeful homesteaders crossing their land in their rickety shitty wagons, and burn down the teepees and tell the Indians the way it was going to be. They were gangsters. With smoking hot sister riding her horse. That's how Andre interpreted the show as a kid. Like how you gotta be. Something obviously went wrong with the constructs…

with the company, and the country: too much kumbaya—it's not natural, it's not following the science and biology... Got to watch the fucked up constructs. That's what the Mutual of Omaha show Wild Kingdom was all about. Marlon Perkins hid in safety while he had Jim go out there and wrestle the crocodiles and pin down gorilla chimps after witnessing wildebeests and baby gazelles being taken down by a couple of lion or cheetahs as a pack of hyenas and jackals converge to try and steal and devour the recently dead prey from the lions and/or cheetahs. Nothing fair about it.

So there was some outrage, just a few blocks from the Jones Construction Company on Martha Street Bridge where the Paxton Mitchell Steel Mill resided just on the other side not far from the Falstaff Brewery and the Milder brothers ran their oil company and the train tracks ran and the smell of the stockyards still faintly permeated the aura of the area along with the Kitty Clover Potato Chip factory. You can shoot your rival criminals but you can't assassinate the civilians especially a prosperous one who is a reformer.

After all this research at the Genealogy and Local History Center of the Omaha Public Library, perusing through the microfilm and the obituaries as he sat next to a disheveled gentleman with Tourette's syndrome. Just par for the course as he continues his quest to write another great American novel. Andre thinks he might take cue from the Wect Center Skelly dudes and go get a haircut from Bud who was just up at the nearby barber shop across from West Gate Plaza according to the fighting Tritt team, who when they weren't brawling were drag racing as kids all night in North Omaha. Fast women and fast cars, they were mechanics and brothers still doing business, producing, working hard, contributing. Andre had known them now for fifty years, maybe meet them guys later at the VIP Lounge the old neighborhood place where in the Sixties and Seventies the gangster Lavelle had held court and the private detective Sonny Whelan kept his office, all working out their various business arrangements and deals. All part of the belly of the beast. That joint hadn't changed nothing in fifty years. Andre loved that about Omaha. He starts going through the ancient phone books from the 1920s, 1930s, 1940, into the 1950s. He reads the newspaper clippings; takes notes. Reads about the Polack side via marriage—he remembers the stories told to him from his father's half-brother. Eddie must have had it out with one of Rose's many sisters before knocking up Andre's seventeen year old grandmother. The guy looked just like Andre's grandfather—Eddy. Andre couldn't talk when he first met him. Brother Miguel, Andre's father, had set up a golf game and had kept it real vague about Charley; said he was kind of an orphan and had lived with Johnny and Rose for a bit who Andre remembers visiting as a kid back at Holy Cross parish. Andre was in visiting from Portland. The guy knew the Jones clan and had lived with a crew of twenty seven Polacks on 29th & Q Street as the old babooshka speaking only Polish would collect money from them every day as they entered the house. Charley had told the tale about when the nuns came for Irene—his young cousin, in an almost haunting recounting as if he was was witnessing it in the present. He spoke of how James J., Andre's great grandfather, was handy with taking the back of a shovel to the backs of his men—to maintain order amongst those rebellious crews. Ruthless, all interesting stuff: to Andre—kind of rough…them days. The house was not too far from his buddy Alfie's Lithuanian Bakery—his brother Joe was a tough Omaha cop, the oldest got drafted and had gone to Vietnam working as a bodyguard/bullet magnet for the generals. The Mackevicus brothers were big Butkus boys—Alfie had been an offensive tackle at Rummel. Andre scours over birth certificates and police reports. He scans over Blecha's book and Menard's files and it goes something like this…

Billy Maher met up with Johnny Finelli, one of Al Capone's emissaries from Chicago. Finelli checks himself into a hotel in downtown Omaha where Maher meets him around 6:00 p.m. Only a few know what the discussion entailed. In the later part of 1931, Maher and Calamia make several phone calls to Finelli's residence in Chicago.

The next day, George Kubik and his son attended a boxing match between Jack Dempsey and Ed "Bearcat" Wright at the Aksarben

Colesium. They eventually make their way to Staskiewicz's soft drink parlor at 42nd and L Street. George has a couple of beers. His son and he then make their way to Kubik's speakeasy at South 27th Street. The son attends to the trade filling pints for the next day and leaves in family truck. Around one o'clock that night George drives to his home at 4004 South 26th Street. He is jumped by three guys with guns. One of them called him by his first name. They said it was a stick-up. The gunmen took his wallet with about five hundred dollars in it and a diamond ring he was wearing. After that they forced him into a car parked in a nearby alley driving to 60th and F Street. That's where they shoved Kubik out while two of the assailants shot him. That didn't kill him so one of them jumped out and shot him two more times, one to the shoulder and one to the face. The killers then drove off, but Kubik was not yet dead.

He managed to crawl two blocks to a house where the home-owner called the police. Kubik was hauled to the hospital in critical condition. Kubik described his assailants as of Italian descent (Andre thought that could be considered racial profiling). He claims he does not know them, but one seemed familiar to him. Kubik ends up dying that morning about 6:30 a.m. The coroner finds that Kubik was struck by six bullets. He recovers two .38-caliber rounds from Kubik's body. A couple of hours later Kubik's brother, John and friend John Staskiewicz go to the crime scene and recover a .32-caliber revolver. Five bullets had been fired. They turn the pistol over to the police and find that it was purchased recently from a sporting goods store in Springfield, Illinois. The name of the person purported to have bought the revolver was a "Joseph Lacoski" for what it was worth.

On November 13 the police put out a dragnet and rounded up about a couple dozen bootleggers. One of the more popular boot-leggers was Yano Salerno was picked up in East Omaha at 6th and Pierce Street with a couple of associates. The cops also arrested his brother Tony at his residence on 8th Street where they seized thirty five gallons of hooch. The arrests of the bootleggers was made under a charge of an open investigation. Upon Inspector Sutton's orders the Salernos were later that day released from custody.

On Saturday, November 14 Kubik's funeral was held. There was a mile long procession starting from his house that ended at St. Francis of Assisi Church at 32nd and K Street. Roughly a thousand people packed the church to attend the mass while others huddled outside in the pouring rain. Bootlegger Charlie Hutter made the service. Others with names like Butch send flower arrangements. Kubik was later buried in a crypt at St. John's Polish Cemetery.

A few days later, the police commissioner of Omaha ordered Police Chief Pzanowski to shake up the Morals Squad and remove Detective Brosnihan and Sergeant Patach from their assignments. On November 23 Prohibition agents led by Newton Splawn raided an old warehouse at 2116 California Street. They found hundreds of gallons of whiskey and other alcohol. They also arrested Lawrence Scavio who was at the plant that was Billy Maher's main still. Maher was the liquor syndicate's north side's key representative.

Andre moves on sifting through the archives, rap sheets, books and newspaper clippings; taking notes and often recognizing the names... with his ancestors' name occasionally prominent in the reports amongst charges and protests. The names remain the same. Like pieces in a large puzzle. They called them cigar stores... where one placed their bets and gambled. At 15th and Harney Street in downtown Omaha was a place called Baseball Headquarters. It was opened in 1919 by a minor league pitcher by the name of Billy Fox (Fox was another family name in Andre's quartet—great grandmother Ada Fox out of Billings, Montana: real crazy, take the old man as a kid down to skid row just to scare the hell out of him)) Hanging on the walls of the establishment were proudly hung the photographs of boxers such as Jack Johnson, Joe Gans, Jack Dempsey, and Mickey Walker. Blackboards were written up on many of the walls with the country's racetracks along with the names and numbers of each horse and their current odds. A Western Union telegraph was also prominent and essential with information ticking in on last minute scratches, track conditions, jockey weights and latest odds. Over the cigar store's loudspeaker system "the call" would go out as some special talent would read the ticker and describe the race to the anxious bettors. How it was done...back in the day, Andre tried to visualize the scene and the smell of the stale cigars with the rat-tat-tat of the telegraph as the baseball scores after each inning were disseminated.

In 1923 ownership of Baseball Headquarters changed hands from Fox to Omaha gamblers Packey Gaughan and Sam Ziegman. The cigar store was in the same building as the Carlton Hotel. These guys were serious and knew their business. They had their bookmaking as well as running blackjack and poker games in the basement. The popularity of the joint grew. It became a favorite hangout for professional athletes, gangsters and gamblers. The two of them take on a third partner by the name of Barrick who was one of Omaha's top gamblers. This guy was a heavy and became known throughout the country as the "millionaire bookie" due to the amount of doe he handled in the business. Bookies laid off some of their heavier bets with Barrick for insurance against heavy losses. Throughout all this they paid tribute to Boss Dennison and his political machine. After Prohibition kicked in the bootlegging intertwined with the illegal gambling business.

In October 1925, the troupe decide to open a cabaret at 1517 Howard Street called the Gay Paree. The American Legion convention was being held in Omaha and they thought it be a good idea to sell alcohol that they were now bootlegging along with running gambling joints. Federal Prohibition agents raid the Gay Paree. A federal grand jury in Omaha set indictments for violations of the National Prohibition Act including conspiracy. Some of those charged were Ziegman, Packey and Casey Gaughan, Patrick Boyle, Harry "Babe" Markel, and several others. The indictment accused them of conspiracy to transport a large quantity of "gin, whiskey, alcohol, and beer" to the location of 1517 Howard Street with the intent to sell.

There were other bookmaking establishments with their wire services that flourished in Omaha in the 1920s. One had the curious name of the Friars Club. It was located on the third floor of the Bankers Savings Building at 315 South 15ᵗʰ Street. It had formerly been known as the Elks Building. The listed organizers of the corporation were Paul Weyerman, Frank Polito and Dave Lindstrom. Articles of incorporation had been filed at the Douglas County Clerk's Office on October 11, 1924. Dennison and his trusted colleague Billy Nesselhous were silent partners in the enterprise. Dennison's official office was located on the floor below the operation and Nesslhous' real estate office was also conveniently in the same building. The chief operators of the enterprise were Dennison workers Frank Housky and Tony Hoffman with loyal ally Pat Boyle, a fight promotor and newspaper reporter, helping run the club as well: a well-oiled machine making these principals a million dollars each in its few years of operation. As far as Andre is concerned, the best part is the purpose of the Friars Club according to the articles of incorporation, was for "athletic and social advancement of its members" and he reads on it was key, "that such applicant is endorsed by a member in good standing." How could anyone disagree with that Andre thinks? His grandfather Fast Eddie was a member of quite a few athletic clubs Andre recalls though he only heard stories of him playing golf. Maybe having season tickets to the Husker football games count as well? Doesn't sound like him or any of his brothers played a lot of ball at South High either—guess he was an active bettor.

And there was another renowned cigar store called the Office Cigar Store. It was also situated in the Bankers Savings Building with its address 317 South 15ᵗʰ Street. Eddie Barrick and Whitey Petty were the operators of this gambling establishment. They also owned the P & B Cigar Store at 203 South 19ᵗʰ Street. Both joints handled bets on horse races. Barrick was the bookie beast while Whitey Petty had the underworld connections with Al Capone of Chicago and Arnold Rothstein and Owney 'the Killer" Madden. Andre is reading all this material trying to digest the gist and drift of it all, and thinking this is getting pretty complicated: all these connections. It's a mixed up world. Andre is just trying to get laid and finish his romance novel—Fifty Shades of Jones. He continues in his academic research and ethnic studies. It's important work and somebody needs to do it.

He's reading about the Aksarben Racetrack where Terri Baby had been an under aged cocktail waitress back in the late Eighties, and a number of buddies from Harrison and others had walked the ponies as a high school summer job, a job Walkin' Willy had who brutally murdered the beautiful young woman McManus, whose brother Tom was a friend of Andre's growing up; was a flock of kids living in that unit raised by their mother at the Village Apartments, was kind of a pink ghetto with a few blacks—cops were there a lot with baby daddies just getting back from Vietnam. Be friends one minute with them, then they'd be throwing dirt in your face taking some swings at you and you'd be fighting: the haves and the have-nots. Andre happened to be visiting Omaha and was in the Irish bar Barret's when they put the juice to Walking Willy. There was a countdown to midnight as Willy sat in the electric chair—waiting to meet his maker. The lights were getting flicked on and off as people cheered. Andre thinks he had just gotten back from France about that time. Andre digresses, shaken out of his reverie… he thinks—how even back in the twenties different do-gooders like State Attorney General Christian Sorenson allied with the Douglas County's Woman's Christian Temperance Union were trying to shut it down as well as shut down the cigar stores and pool halls. Barrick and Whitey Petty get arrested on gambling charges. The race wire office is raided. D.W. Young and Harry Calloway, employees of Barrick and Petty are also arrested at another location which was part of the General News Bureau. Which is what Eddie Barrick claimed they were "news bureaus" to give the public what they wanted, what they needed… supply them with racetrack information. The results from the raids produced records that showed the local investigators that Barrick and Petty were part of a bookmaking network that operated coast to coast from New York to San Francisco on down to New Orleans. Sorenson pushed for these crackdowns with much publicity claiming the gambling, bootlegging, vice and crime was organized and controlled by the political boss, Tom Dennison and his top lieutenant, Billy Nesselhous. Andre was surmising there was some political battle going on between waspy Lincoln, the state capital desiring to exercise and lord their authority over the local but much bigger and way more cosmopolitan and multi-ethnic city of Omaha, which in Indian means "against the current" which seemed quite an apropos name to his childhood city now that he had cultural reference to push off from with cities in the likes of Paris, Nairobi, Istanbul, Miami, Portland, Albuquerque, Belgrade, Cairo, Yakima and El Paso. He'd be betting on the ponies and often his horse would win.

In December of 1929, Baseball Headquarters suffered a major blow that had nothing to do with the political pressure and police actions—Packey Gaughan died. According to the Omaha World-Herald report his death was due to a bowel obstruction. They neglected or were most likely uniformed that that the obstruction to his gut happened to be a piece of lead. At least according to underworld sources, Gaughan had been running a load of booze into Nebraska from another state when he got shot. Casey Gaughan, his brother subsequently took over Baseball Headquarters.

More heat is applied. More raids continued. Andre reads fast over the names, dates, locations and charges.

At Baseball Headquarters Sam Ziegman is arrested and charged as a keeper of a disorderly house. Eight other people are arrested as "inmates" but Sam protests claiming they were just playing rummy for merchandise.

Cops hit an apartment in the Lafayette Apartments at 17th Avenue and Jackson Street. Izzy Ziegman, Sam's younger brother, and Jimmy Abdo are arrested at the apartment. Two telephones are used to manage the bets. They are both charged with operating a betting establishment. Izzy is also the manager of the card room at Baseball Headquarters. They are later released on $500 bonds.

Officer George Lynch led a raid on the Loyal Smoke House. The cops found Sam House running the business. Whitey Petty was also present at the cigar store.

On January 7, Sergeant Sutton and officers hit the Orpheum Cigar Store at 418 South 15th Street. A major bookmaker by the name of Frank Lenahan ran the cigar store. He was arrested for keeper of a disorderly house. Twenty two other people were issued arrests as inmates. Not only did the joint take bets on horse races in the United States but also from the Havana, Cuba and Agua Caliente Racetrack in Tijuana, Mexico.

Inmates! The language was the best Andre thought…keepers of disorderly houses, etc. It was brilliant. This all made him laugh. Thinking of Orwell. And Damon Runyon: Guys and Dolls. What a world. Fast Eddie and Charlotte survived and thrived in. And pretty international: Bahamas, Tahoe, Vegas.

The Office Cigar Store changes its name to the Cornhusker Cigar Store as does the names of the owners. The new owners listed were a Joe Connell and Pat Boyle, both known associates of the Dennison machine.

On Sunday, January 12, 1930 police raid 831 North 42nd Street, which was the residence of Casey Gaughan. Gaughan refused to answer the door so the officers bust into find Gaughan in the basement burning bet records. Seven telephones were discovered in the basement. Casey was running a clearinghouse for horse race gamblers. The bets were made through the telephones connected with a direct wire to the General News Bureau. The raiding party also found six quarts of whiskey which Gaughan was issued an arrest for unlawful possession and a charge of investigation.

July 25, 1931 driving down Commercial Avenue near 17th Street in northeastern Omaha, Sam Ziegman and a friend were suddenly overtaken by another car by several armed men who tried to force them off the road. When questioned later on by the police, Ziegman claims he jumped out of the car hitting his head and blacking out, not remembering a thing. He refuses to identify his friend and claims to have no comprehension why anybody would want him dead. Dennison didn't like Ziegman. Say no more.

Andre recalls from a few years earlier. He and Warsocki are tooling around the metro. Warsocki's back from Cartelandia, Mexico, this is before all the Haitians invaded his town before heading to the border…to help with his father who's got a raw deal with his health. The man had been a powerhouse lifting weights way up in the air down at South High in the fifties, coaching football—he'd been a handsome Neanderthal of a Polak man: formidable and intimidating with a casual stoic stare in a calm casual way. Warsocki still was edgy with the PTSD. He said sometimes there was more gunfire in Durango sometimes than there had been in Afghanistan, or Absurdistan as he liked to call it sometimes. Warsocki liked the Kurds a lot and he liked the Afghanis, whatever tribe they descended from Pashtuns, Tajiks, etc. They'd hit Boyer Chute for some back to nature therapy. Andre really wasn't doing much better than Warsocki at the time. The alcoholism was starting to rock him good and whatever drugs that popped up around the midnight hour…nothing good is really happening after midnight—unless you're in the bed of a beautiful woman.

They amble around the trails along the Missouri River, four thousand desolate acres of it—just trees, creeks, prairie and wild animals. It always seemed empty of people whenever Andre brought hippy chicks and nature gals down here, only ten minutes from North Omaha and historic Florence. Just a little north of the Mormon Bridge where the Mormons gathered and camped a deadly cold malignant winter prior to the Later-day Saints taking their handcarts as directed by Brigham who received revelations to cross the Plains to get to their Beulah and promised land of Zion: Utah. Must have been one helluva trip for those LDS pilgrims. They must have died like flies. About five hundred perished along the banks of the Missouri during Winter Quarters… Andre considered it amazing, nobody was around—just a very few were ever here. If it was Seattle or Portland there'd be five hundred people bumping into each other. Guess everybody was bowling, drinking ice cold beer and shooting pool. At Chop's or Western Bowl.

Warsocki had just completed working on a movie in DR. He was the armorer and military advisor for a Hollywood movie. With his work on the series Narcos he was in pretty high demand. Prior to heading to the Caribbean he had texted Andre—Hotel Cocaine: 1978 Miami, Cubans, Haitians, cocaine, orgies, Hunter S. Thompson, Rick James, CIA, DEA...what could go wrong? Guess the production went pretty well. Or at least the party did: till the Hollywood strike... Andre almost made it—his passport was clean and he still had his IATSE film mechanic's card to work on the show, one of the Pashtuns was to go with him.

So they talked about the movie, the Dominican Republic, Mexico, the working conditions of their fathers, women, politics and Hollywood. As they tooled through North Omaha and the election was so near—they couldn't help but notice there were no Biden/ Harris signs about. Virtually none. This was the 'hood as they drive right by Skeet's Smokehouse where the dancers would come around from the back to fraternize with the cops as everybody enjoyed the tasty ribs... On they toured by the Viking Ship off Redick Avenue where keggers for seventeen bucks a keg from the Falstaff brewery happened, on past where the Quebec Club use to sit off Ames. Occasionally one beleaguered sign would sprout up, but there was no buzz or excitement, enthusiasm or agitation amongst all the brethren here. You had to go out to the affluent white neighborhoods like in Loveland and Dundee to catch all the Biden/Harris support. "Guess they aren't black"—Warsocki quips. "Ja-ha! That old racist Dixiecrat hanging out with Grand Wizard KKK Robert Byrd, trying to keep Hunter from attending a "jungle" in public school, then legislating crime laws that threw more blacks in prison in the early 90s—damn people got no memory... Make Bull Connor proud. Democrat, Democrat, Democrat. Better call that radio host Charlemagne. Taking that shit from old white man. Post him up. Ja-ha! Better head to the barbershop, see Jermaine and tell the Senator what the fuck's going on. Let Ernie know. And what's up with fifty intelligence officers all signing on to the Russian interference? Christ! Brennan the CIA director voted for Gus Hall and Angela Davis under the American Communist ticket for prez and vice prez. Now I have known beaucoup wacky characters, but I don't know if any of them were that nuts to vote for those two clown payasos—aw wait a minute, maybe quite a few back at Ho Chi Magee, Rudloff and your Holy Family Catholic Communist Church did… Angela did speak there. So we're obliged to believe these spooks—they think. I've run with a bunch of them overseas. You never know. But it's called fake news now cuz it's fake. And that really offends them because it's very important to them to be taken seriously—even though they have to know they're frauds." Andre smiles with amusement because truth is often funny.

"A-ha! The cultural elites. Yeah, yeah—what can be unburdened by what has been… Ha! Just keep saying that Kamala. You're the Veep! Willy Brown's little party girl/school girl—my SF artiste' pals saw her regularly with him; at the finest establishments—she's a good looking woman. Running California and partying were his specialties. Just listen to Judge Joe Brown go off—he takes no prisoners. He's rough. Ah yeah—over and over man—everything is racist… coming from the racists. Got a wild one on that. You remember Teddy Nickels—he joined the army, was in the 10th Mountain Division—funky white dude with an afro his hair was co curly? His family owned a butcher shop in North O off 30th Street not that far from Canfield's military surplus store off Cuming. Anyway, he tells the story when the heat was up and shit was burning in the late 60s that some Black Panthers were going to hit their store. All of the sudden Ernie pulls up in his chopper and pulls out a .357 and puts it to one of their heads and says—these people help our people…you rob them and fuck with them I'll blow you all the fuck away."

"A man of peace ... Ernie Chambers. Dude has got stones. Use to love shopping at Canfield's; all that old military gear, get our camping gear before camping was cool."

"The son of a preacher man—Ernie could press some weight: literally, those pics of him at the barber shop. Yeah Beauregard's uncle wasn't so lucky at the construction yard near there—pulls out his piece, misses and gets wasted. Korea didn't get him, but North O did. Yeah Canfield's—what a place, that old Hebrew Jack got the best shit from militaries all over the world. Before REI, before Cabela's ... there was Canfield's down on Cuming Street. We wore the coolest shit! And camped like Call of the Wild Jack London. That warehouse was like walking into a war museum."

"Yeah, like Ceuta for la Legion'—the Spanish Legion: Morocco. Damn had forgotten about that one, Deano's unc... Didn't know about the butcher shop. Always liked his style: the Senator with the cutoff sweatshirts. He was saying all the way back in the 70s that them college athletes needed to get paid ... Met him through that cute chick I was dating back in early 80s. Her brother and I hung there at his barber shop. She was a Playboy bunny when about one of the last Playboy Clubs in the states opened up. In Omaha. I think they were all closed within five years. You know it was over when your aunt and uncle from Broken Bow are heading over to it. Ja-ha. Old Hef wandering around in his bathrobe."

"Yeah, pretty fucking dopey. You know the scene is toast once it arrives in Omaha. Shit! I remember her. She was a real doll. Kismet or something—what was her name? Dang! Smoking ... a non-blonde."

"Kaya—that was her name. She was cool. Where the fuck are we going?"

Andre is not sure ... But Warsocki's PTSD seems a little better—maybe they could get him in that vets program where they ship 'em down to the Florida Everglades to capture and kill pythons. Fuck! Andre laughs—Warsocki had PTSD coming straight out the chute when he left his mama's womb: shit everybody who knows him from the wild boys' days knows that…it's just more accentuated now. He heads back to Mexico later this week: back to Cartelandia. Andre will give him a lift to airport. And then out of nowhere they come upon a small Jewish cemetery that neither one knew existed. Warsocki comments on how Andre seems to have a funny proclivity for taking him to unique places. It's not a very big cemetery. They slowly tool around in the F-150 on this low westerly sloping hill. They recognize many of the names as they drive up the narrow one lane concrete paths… Then they come upon the largest stone almost mausoleum-like monument that had simply inscribed the name: Gaughan. And Warsocki and Andres stare at it for a bit till finally Warsocki gruffly retorts—"Wow, that's where those fuckers are buried."

"Jackie Gaughan was a buddy of my grandfather's. Him and his moll Charlotte would go visit him and hang when he was operating the El Cortez back in Vegas. They had great shrimp according to my mother who would occasionally accompany my father and them on these conventions extravagant. Believe he owned the El Dorado in Reno as well."

"Well that don't surprise me one bit—remembering Eddie pulling up in his lime green Mark IV Continental back there at the construction yard slapping five with the brothers, bullshitting with that retired irascible city inspector Brick and going over matters with Morgan that old superintendent of his who was a tank commander back at the Bulge… No surprise at all. No sirree—no surprise at all. The Doyles worked as his heavies—they called Patti Doyle "the Chef" for some reason."

"I'd heard that too. Guess he liked to cook. The old West O madam Peppermint Patti was his paramour. That was a long time ago. All of it."

"Yes it was…lectio, meditatio, oratio, contemplation."

"Ha! The old Polack priest, the steely–eyed cat assasinating shootist Father Kalamaja teaching the Latin. Ran into you at Huck's back when you were working at Allied Oil. Was with the mechanics Cihacek, Roy and Stirling for lunch: drinking beer. It was high school. Before you joined us at the company, and before you joined the Marine Corps."

"That's right. Got with Huck's daughter. She was fine. And got higher than a kite with her—high-high-high…like velvet underground shit."

"Good dog ja-ha! She was Sweet Jane. Yeah Richie Cihacek would just go AWOL sometimes—six to nine months. Trouble with the law or trouble with women. A wild bunch. Ungovernable brutes. All the asphalt guys had guns as that drug-addled Italian paving inspector Mike something R from Brooklyn was always rambling on about—coming from the rotten Big Apple… Get ya good deal on TVs and steaks. Funny shit."

"Those were the days. And that other inspector, spent some time in Chu Lai, good friend with that foreman Julian—his Mexican wife was as pregnant as a watermelon—he took off with that hooker one night we were paving. Made Julian the temporary city inspector. A-ha!"

"Yeah, yeah he was a pretty funny dude…we were paving across from the Kitty Clover Potato Chip plant."

"The smell of victory—potatoes, asphalt, molten steel, beer, brewery and the stockyards. Indelible."

"Yes it 'twas."

"What do you thinks up with all the Jew-hating going on these days? Shit it ain't just in Israel and the Arab world—hell its right here!"

"Got members of Congress that straight up hate Jews—it's appalling. But they hate Americans also. Probably they hate themselves too—what the fuck. We're deplorable. Ja-ha! This is Hee-Haw here man. I don't care what they say—this is Hillbilly Nation. Doesn't matter if ur white, black, brown or red. The Rez is hillbilly. The 'hood is hillbilly. They just don't get it. And they never will."

"We're backwards alright. These blue dot hee-haws here in Omaha; they're just virtue signaling with all their bullshit inclusive signs about caring and shit. They just need to relax. Anyway, I love my Sabra woman."

"Amen to that, ain't nothing ever really changing in Nebraska—there's the New York Dolls but we got the Nebraska Dolls and they got big medicine jujuj vooddo power...at the governor's mansion—I'm telling you man. Shit's for real. Like Gypsy stuff. We all got some white trash/po' buckra to us. They shouldn't be so insecure... Ah yeah—the Sabra: they're simply stunning. I've talked about this matter with my 1/2 Russian Shin Bet motherfucker. Israel is kind of like us—got a lot of Spartans: Raid on Entebbe-type bad asses, but it's got a lot of airy-fairy, tie-dye wearin' kibbutz'n hippy-dippy 'nice kid' utopics who can't get their light brown dreadlocked nappy heads around the cold reality that...the world is Fort Apache, especially if you're a Jew."

"Hey man I was on a kibbutz for a couple of weeks. It was a date farm—literally and figuratively, a date farm. Real nice time, peace concerts and all. Ended up picking pistachios as well. Yeah-yeah so well—they call it antisemitism. That's very euphemistic sounding like Orwell—control the language, control the thought. They need to just call it what it is: Jew hatred. Never thought I'd see it this crude and rampant as it is here now across our fruited plain of America. But what the fuck...these days nobody is suppose to be able to defend themselves. That's what they want—a helpless populace. Be like lambs. Turn the other cheek—nonsensical Christian sentimentality."

"Was that before picking coffee beans for the Sandinistas or afterwards? A-ha! To quote Gorgeous George 'He who controls the past controls the present/ He who controls the present controls the past' kinda apt. While they defund the police and our cackling nonsensical posting bail for Minneapolis rioters Veep Kamala and Hollywood court jesters post bail for criminal antifa rioters and BLM looters. Everybody's a victim. It's a bad clown show. But, hate the Jew. They're fuckin' Brownshirts—ain't nuthin' liberal about them at all. But a lot of liberals are always pretty liberal till you disagree with them. Ja-ha! Peace Nazis. And by the way, the first veep of "color" was Charles Curtis born in the Kansas Territory. His mother was of the Kaw/Kansa and Osage tribe. The dude rode horses out on the prairie amongst the buffalo and lived in teepees with his Indian maternal grandparents on the Rez in Indian Territory aka Oklahoma. This was President Hoover's VP back in the Twenties. Ulysses S. Grant had Indians in his cabinet as well. The totality of the lying is overwhelming."

"Those aren't fucking liberals, that's the fuckin' Left—liberals think outside the box. We don't follow doctrine. We believe in the First Amendment. You know—free speech, not censorship. Antifa hates liberals. The naïve dipshit mayor of Portland goes out to "talk" to them, to "reason" with them and he barely escapes with his life. Ja-ha! Look at what the bad clown show did to that boat people dude: Ngo. His family flees the communists in Vietnam after the fall of Saigon. They get thrown in the killing fields re-education camps till they can barely make their escape from the Marxists upon dilapidated boats across treacherous shark-infested waters to hopefully bob over and make it to the Philippines to eventually randomly accidentally wind up in the Rose City of utopic, keep it weird, Portlandia...dude's just being an investigative journalist and is getting attacked and beaten nearly to death a couple of times by ignorant chicken shit dopes wearing black masks. They don't want the truth."

"Yeah—it's the Left. They're cowards. A bunch of pussies attacking the helpless old ladies eating at a restaurant—they're always in a pack. Like the Brownshirts—stupid ruthless thugs with their PLO Jew-hating keffiyeh scarves. They'd get their asses kicked if they tried that shit here. Why do you think they were called the National Socialist Workers' Party—the fuckin' Nazis. Believe me, they're just getting started. Give me one good platoon of Marines with a couple Afghanis and Kurds—problem solved in a few short hours. All this Orange Man Bad hysteria is a bunch of feminist chicks with daddy issues...and the sneaky-fucker sissies "boyfriends" running around with them wearing their pink pussy hats pretending they're sensitive and sympathetic to the Cause…and the women believe them cuz they can control them; ah they due tend to live longer. Anyway. Incredulous!"

"Ja-ha—mock the hysterics! It's about the control. Power—absolute power. They'll say anything for it. Give the masses what they want to hear. Am pretty sure a niece of mine would say to my brother and I just as she put us up against the wall to be shot—that it was good for us! Ja-ha! Said that to him over seven years ago. Got to love her…and her zeal, fanaticism and commitment. Well, not sure if the UN would sanction that or our anemic senate. Ja-ha! Praise be to this little religious plot of sacred land—that all their hard work and blood, sweat and tears—was not in vain. All these Jews buried here. Love that Sabra woman. Back in Tel Aviv. Got to get back there and see her. Again. She's so mean. Hitting me with a flower…packing an Uzi by her side. Jew noses are the best. Almost convinced me to join the IDF. What a recruiter."

"Right… Another hell of your own making, like you haven't had enough chaos in your life. But God bless them beautiful Sabra women, packing them Uzis."

Then they solicitously, almost like surreptitiously, make their exit out the unknown little Jewish cemetery in North Omaha. Crossing themselves a couple of times…like altar boys. Tom Rudloff smiles shaking his head—knowing they're right to seek some slack… cuz he's knowing they're devils. Andre then pulls out onto Military Avenue and cranks up The Clash's Clampdown:

The kingdom is ransacked, the jewels all take back

And the chopper descends…

What are we going to do now?

Taking off his turban, they said, is this man a Jew?

We will teach our twisted speech

To the young believers

We will train our blue-eyed men

To be young believers

Hah, get along, get along

Yeah, I'm working hard in Harrisburg

Working hard in Petersburg

Get along, get along

Work

Work

Work

And I give away no secrets

"That's a badass song," says Warsocki, "more relevant today than ever…"

They tool through downtown Benson. "Remember the Lift Ticket Lounge… And the Rebates! Your brother Ben on bass tearing it up. And Charlie Burton lining up to six shots of whiskey, with everything else, getting ready to sing: Breathe for me Pressley!"

"Costellos getting kicked out. With Jimmy like riders of the storm tearing it up on dance floor. With any chick he wanted. He was Johnny Depp before Johnny Depp was Johnny Depp I repeat myself.

Dat was FUN. Charlie is still alive! And the Costellos are famous. Meet all hundred of them at Starksky's Bar—a couple of them will take your bets: y'know—old school."

"Old school indeed. Kickin' the jams. No fucking way—that's incredible. Breathe for me Pressley: great sing of theirs. I think some of the Costellos might have done some substance abuse issues... besides just taking your bets. Am just speculating. Great hockey players. And football linemen. Before I met him as a kid I remember Schmitty's old man who coached them said they'd rather fight than play hockey—he's talking about them as kids. Ya-ha!"

"That's funny cuz that's the truth. Lived it with them. What the fuck's with your brother running all over Arabia and the world and now living in Poland?"

"Ah, y'know I think it all started for him after partying with Clarence "Gatemouth" Brown after a gig at the Howard Street—they were doing lines all night... It seems to have set him on the trajectory of slouching towards Mecca and he ended up teaching English and got himself one Polish princess for a wife and then another. Just did a gig with Kobza who was playing in London and decided to bop over and see him."

"Got a thing for Slavic women... I get it. I dig borscht. The LA man, playing in a rock 'n' roll band Timmy Kobza—part of the Peony Park Jazz Quartet back in 1978 with "the" Ray Williams, Rudy Can't Fail Barrajas and Gene Genie Giroux. That's awesome. I know you don't drink anymore but I'm gonna hit the Musette and have a couple shots of whiskey. We can play some eight-ball pool. Or snooker."

"Peony Park the amusement park and adventure land: the roller coaster and rides, the beach, Sprite Nite, the ballroom, the pinball, and lest we forget—them long-haired, cigarette-smoking hoods."

"Like crimson and clover."

Tom Rudloff continues narrating the story—let's call this chapter The Book of Omaha. He reads…working on putting a greyhound dog track together for the Omaha metro area, Meyer Lansky decided that across the river in Council Bluffs would be a better site—not to conflict with the thoroughbred horse racing at Aksarben (Nebraska cleverly spelled backwards). It's the 1940s and Luciano, Siegel, Costello and Lansky are looking for other avenues and opportunities to increase their business expansion. According to FBI records, Frank Costello and Joe Adonis were partners with Lansky in the dog track operation in Council Bluffs. It was called the Dodge Park Kennel Club. The dog track operated on an "option" system. This was so bettors could get around state gambling restrictions. They would purchase an "interest" on a dog. So if a dog won, placed or showed the dog's value increased thus the bettor would turn in the "interest" to collect one's winnings. The "interest" in a losing dog was immediately deemed useless until a bet was placed on the dog in the next race. A bettor or investor had to collect their profit or "option" from the "interest" within thirty minutes after a race. Pretty ingenious. That's what Luciano liked—anything to make money and make the enterprise grow.

He was born in Sicily. Forming a national syndicate after the death of Rothstein, he called for a summit in Atlantic City, New Jersey under the safe haven provided by the political boardwalk boss Nucky Johnson. It was an all-star cast of gangsters in attendance: Meyer Lansky was one of the key organizers along with Costello and Johnny Torrio, the predecessor of Capone. Reported at the gathering with Luciano and Adonis was Dutch Schultz, Lepke, Albert Anastasia, Al Capone and Jake Guzik from Chicago, Moretti and Longy Zwillman from New Jersey. Gang leaders from the cities of Detroit, Kansas City, Philadelphia, Boston and Cleveland were all represented as well. It was the first of many meetings to organize a nationwide criminal enterprise—also trying to keep the killing under control. It was bad for business Luciano, Lansky and Costello thought. Not so much Siegel who was purported to be a part of Murder Incorporated tied in with Lepke Buchalter and his notorious gang of cut-throat hitmen psychopaths.

Lansky and Luciano forged criminal alliances across the country to create more successful business ventures. Thus Lansky seeking more opportunities ends up in Omaha trying to make it happen— with the dogs. Lansky's rationale for building the track was to create an opportunity for his bookies on the East Coast to make bets when his Florida racetracks were closed for the season. According to an associate of Lansky's he initially wanted it on the Nebraska side but the influence of Aksarben hindered that prospect.

While visiting Omaha, Lansky would often stay at the Fonta-nelle Hotel and frequent the Paxton Hotel where he was friendly with a waitress at its coffee shop. He'd hit the Chez Paree club run by Eddie Barrick and Sam Ziegman. It is not known whether Lansky held any ownership in the Chez Paree. In 1972, Ziegman and Lansky would be charged for conspiracy by a federal grand jury in a skim-ming operation involving millions of dollars at the Flamingo Hotel in Las Vegas.

Andre recalls his grandfather mentioning how the ancient one-armed bandit slot machine had come from the Chez Paree. It was a nickel slot machine—all gray cast steel with some colorful lines to accent the beast with its cherries. Funny how it ended up back at his old man's bar in the basement—a fixture of history. He tried remembering other stories Eddie would share. They tended to come out more forward when he'd been drinking and we were all enjoying a family spaghetti dinner at Cantoni's. Eddie would get on about tales of the Stork Club located on the South Omaha Bridge Road. It had dinner, floor shows, dance bands with booze and slot machines, roulette, craps, black jack tables and a race book for the ponies and dogs. The Outfit from Kansas City had some ownership in the establishment which changed the names of the proprietors often in this murky web of liability.

In the 1950s a federal grand jury was investigating the Kansas City Syndicate. The findings in the report states that a Mahoney and Hill initially owned the club and in 1945 they sold it to Chickie Berman, Cy Silver and Al Abrams. Al Abrams was the brother-in-law of Jackie Gaughan.

Later that year, according to the federal grand jury's report, Abrams and Berman sold their interest in the establishment to a new group of gamblers that consisted of Silver, Tiny Barnes, Fred Wyerman, Einar and Maxie Abramson two weeks after a mysterious late night explosion occurred that some suspected was from a bombing. Tiny Barnes claimed it was from "defective wiring" which lends to the notion of how one has to keep an open mind sometimes.

In the later part of 1946 Cy Silver with the financial support of his pal, Chickie Berman, bought off his partners. The Omaha World-Herald published an article that the sale went down for $110,000. According to the report Berman and Silver would manage the bar. Two weeks later one night, an explosion occurred in the bar. Andre guesses there were no hard feeling, Chickie Berman was the younger brother to Dave Berman who was a partner with Meyer Lansky and Bugsy Siegel in the Flamingo Hotel which opened in December 1946. Six months later Virginia Hill takes off to Paris, Bugsy is hanging out at her place in California one late evening and is clipped off by a shooter with an M1 carbine as he merrily swills on his sherry talking business with an associate. Dave Berman, a WWII vet with the Canadian Army who tried to sign up in Omaha but because he was a felon the U.S. Army wouldn't take him, with a couple others takes over operations of the Flamingo for the Lansky crew.

It was reported, according to rumors, newspaper clippings and microfiche acquired at the genealogy branch of the Omaha Public Library and grandfather Eddy's recollected versions that on April 6, 1947, after closing the club for the evening the owners and associates piled into a vehicle and headed back to Omaha at approximately 4:00 a.m. when machine gunfire burst across the hood of their car. That stopped them in their track as five hoods jumped out brandishing Tommy guns and barking at those in the ambushed vehicle to do as they are told. The five were representatives from Kansas City. In the ambushed vehicle was Silver, Busty Stanger who was part of the club's management and Einar Abramson who was the driver were escorted back to the club. With due diligence Busty shows the highwaymen where the safe was located and the robbers leave with just under a $100,000.

Ironically, according to more reports and rumors, a couple days before the robbery two mobsters from Kansas City, Gus and Charles Gargotta were arrested in Kansas City on warrants charging them for the February 23rd robbery of a dice game at Vernon's Chicken Hut located on the outskirts of Harlan, Iowa. The brothers had reputedly blown their roll so they decided to just go ahead and rob everybody in the basement of this gambling oasis. The gangsters were hauled off to Iowa with $15,000 bond. They contact their associates back in Kansas City and tell them their problems. Several hours after the Stork Club heist a couple of characters arrive in Iowa with $30,000 in crumpled bills to make bail to free the Gargotta brothers. It could be coincidence. Nobody wants to rush to judgement. Or use racial profiling...but, Gus and Charles Gargotta were later never brought to trial due to the memory loss of all witnesses at Vernon's Chicken Hut. Speculation and suspicion arose like the mist along the Missouri River—all, against the current, the Indian meaning for the word OMAHA.

In time, under the leadership of Charles Binaggio, the Kansas City crew would take over the stewardship of the Stork Club with methods akin to Mao—from the barrel of a gun... For negotiations broke down at the first meeting between the Kansas City Mob associates and Silver when he informed them that he was not interested in selling. The second meeting went different after a couple of the KC goons dragged Cy Silver out to a Nebraska cornfield and put a pistol to his head. That was just enough encouragement for Cy Silver to sell his interest at the recommended price. Abrams and Berman, the other partners were held at gunpoint back at the Stork Club by other thugs as they relented in their interest in the club. Later on, Mister Silver would deny that this incident had ever occurred.

According to some sources, like Susan Berman daughter of Dave Berman, Chickie originally refused to give up his interest in the club as guns were pointed right at him. Syndicate representatives from Kansas City contacted Dave Berman in Las Vegas and made it clear to him they would kill his brother if he didn't cooperate with their request. Dave called up Chickie and eventually persuaded him to let go of his interest in the festive establishment. Force and intimidation gets things done—how the mob works as the means justifies the end. In crime and revolution…

Later on from an interview with the FBI, Berman says he could have handled Binaggio, but the younger Italians were rough and just wanted to kill everyone including Cy Silver and Berman could not allow that. Dave who had first come to Omaha as a kid and sold newspapers would save his brother Chickie innumerable times over the years as Chickie was a compulsive gambler and would incur substantial gambling debts to underworld elements.

The cast of characters grows larger after KC takes over the Stork Club. Earl Kennedy and George Beskas of Kansas City become involved: both gangsters. The Omaha perennial heavy Charley Hutter springs upon the scene. Another hood by the name of Duke Sarno also of KC goes to work at the club after the hostile takeover. Hutter fulfilled the role as enforcer at the drinking establishment with his nasty reputation as a very tough dude respected and feared by many. He was introduced to the KC crew via Lew Farrell of the Chicago Syndicate. Lew Farrell's original name was Luigi Fratto—didn't like his slave name Andre guessed….

About a month later Buster Stanger is shot four times with a shotgun by unknown assailants as he walked to his car parked on

15th and Jackson Street. Incredibly he survives the attack. He informs the police that he will handle the matter and is visited in the hospital by Charley Hutter as he recovers from his injuries. And almost three years later a bomb goes off at the Bell Cigar Store damaging several other buildings in the vicinity. The owner of the cigar store was Weyerman. Omaha police go to 114 North 35th Avenue to question George Beskas about his involvement in the bombing. Beskas claimed he had nothing to do with it. Disputes amongst rival factions was the motive. All part of the bombing investigation. Underworld stuff. Grandpa's world with his eight brothers and one sister in the nunnery and another one who flew the coop.

A guy named Scavio was later on picked up by Omaha police along with a couple brothers named Meehan. All three were released on bail. Beskas would later on go down to Hot Springs, Arkansas to meet with Kansas City crime boss Tony Gizzo along with capo Tony Accardo out of Chicago. Not long after that pow wow Gizzo would die of a massive heart attack and Nick Civella would emerge as chief of the Kansas City Outfit. Underworld stuff. Grandpa's world. Straight out of Damon Runyon musical.

Meanwhile back in Omaha, some dudes are just trying to sell Hamm's beer in a civil orderly fashion as others killed for distribution rights. It's all about the money. You just got to follow it and it will usually take you right to the politics. And that's how Frank "the Enforcer" Nitti came out to Dodge, Nebraska to do some pheasant hunting—distribution. And then there's religion. And possible suicides all due to distribution. Take the case of Frank Polito who was found inside his tavern at 1006 Howard Street sitting in his swivel chair with a fatal gunshot wound to the head by a .45 handgun fired once at his side and a half-smoked cigar clenched in his left hand. The coroner ruled it a suicide. Polito's wife and two brothers said the thirty four year old said he had no interest in capping himself. Everybody said he was in good spirits and had visited his pal Mondo Marcuzzo, whose nightclub had just been bombed a week earlier. His business partner Whitey Tobias had testified that the business was in good order. A coroner's inquest was convened with a number of witnesses. The night watchman at around 3:00 a.m. had exchanged small talk with Polito as he saw him cross the street and meet someone in the shadows. Polito had suggested to a friend that he ought to get a life insurance policy after the murder of the beer distributor by the name of Butch Hanfelt who had purportedly bought the interest held by Paul Weyerman in the Log Cabin nightclub in Carter Lake the same club that had sustained damage from a bombing just ten days prior to Butch Hanfelt's murder. But according to the operator of the Log Cabin nightclub, Tommy Abdo, a serious gambler and cohort of Sam Ziegman, Hanfelt did not buy interest in the club, but was just there to loan him money to loan him money to pay off one of the original owners. Fucking complicated Andre thought—just trying to sell some goddamn beer. The coroner determined later on that Polito died from a gunshot wound at the hands of a person or persons unknown. Polito? Abdo? Salerno? Et cetera. So many of these names were familiar to Andre who played ball with their grandsons down at the Westgate baseball diamonds, peewee football at Prairie Lane or wrestled with them at the District 66 Club or just went to school with them. It's like we're all related: going to Sortino's for pizza or King Kong for cheeseburgers with monkey statuary everywhere or a having a wrapped cabbage and beef pie from a Runza Hut. All matters of distinction facing extinction…like where you at? As motorcyclists careen up and down streets in Omaha sans helmet. Kids still ride their bikes without helmets and definitely they fly on their horses that way—in Nebraska. Like the Indians. And the law abiding citizens are well armed. Like the Indians. A dog goes bad you might have to shoot it. There's a lack of supervision. It's a backwards fucking state. The narrator Tom sighs, but look at and examine the history further…

This was all just a couple weeks after Hanfelt was murdered at around three in the morning after leaving the warehouse of his United Beverage Company at 12th and Leavenworth. He was a approaching his brick house at 4416 Hickory Street when he took two blasts to the face from a 12-gauge shotgun. The assailant had hid in the bushes

near the porch. A number of theories on arose on the string of bombings and slew of hits. One source had it that Hanfelt was in financial
arrears with the Manhattan Brewing Company in Chicago for $5,000.
This was run by the Chicago Syndicate that Johnny Torrio ran prior
to Capone's reign. Louis Greenberg handled the books and had been
tight with Capone. After Frank Nitti took over Greenberg continued
to handle the finances of the brewery and other issues of accounting
that Nitti had. A week before the killing representatives from Chicago
had been in Omaha to collect from Hanfelt.

There had been a dozen other bombings of businesses that year
after the repeal of National Prohibition on December 5, 1933—kind
of like Cleveland in 1976, which had more bombings than Beirut that
year. It was tough to kill an Irishman sometimes Andre thought. One
of the bombings had been at 1512 Howard Street at the plush nightclub owned by Billy Fox, the ex-baseball player who was the original
proprietor of the cigar store Baseball Headquarters. Another couple
earlier in the year in June were at the Metropolitan Billiard Parlor at
1516 Capitol Avenue. The explosion was devastating enough to blow
out many of the windows of the building and blast debris across to the
other side of the street. A few weeks later, at 3:50 a.m. another powerful bomb goes off at 2039 Harney Street where the Culver Cigar Store
was located on the first floor along with the Culver Hotel that had the
second and third floor. All windows on the first and second floor were
shattered as were many on the third floor. Shrapnel from metal and
concrete were almost a hundred feet from blast. Andre is reading all
this and thinking the community organizer Dennison had only been
out of forced judicial retirement for a little over a year and had barely
made it through his honeymoon and divorce with his nineteen year
old wife Navajo Truman and it was already going to hell in Omaha.
That's what reform does—tommy guns and bank robbers... as Boss
Tweed of New York's Tammany Hall and Boss Pendergast of Kansas
City are hauled off to prison that same year Dennison goes to trial
with his partner Billy Nesselhous, Billy Maher, Jimmy Mardi, Harry
Buford and fifty four other associates. The bosses were going down in

1932. They couldn't beat them at the ballot box…so their reforming opponents discovered the courts would deliver their political aim and aspiration. Many witnesses were assembled to refute the state from former newspaperman Patrick Boyle who was the proprietor of the Cornhusker Cigar Store denying the assertion that Dennison had a private office there. Some government witnesses came from the state penitentiary who was serving a four year sentence for man-slaughter. He claimed to have participated in close to two hundred hijackings and that all the stolen goods were delivered to Billy Maher. On and on various claims went. Much of the rancor was over the as-sassination of Lapidus—it was one thing when gangsters killed one another… But could they prove it was carried out upon Dennison's orders. City attorney Bernie Boyle castigated the government's case against Dennison. With his cold gray eyes Dennison takes the stand on November 15. Led by questions from his attorney Dennison had a litany of denials: no, he had never met Capone, no, he had never tried to influence police commissioners, no—he, Dennison, had never told the state witness that Buford was in charge of the black district. He was acquitted eventually along with Nesselhous, Maher, Calamia, Buford, Marcell, Roscoe Rawley, Sutton (detective) and the rest. Dennison had evaded jail time but his reign was over by 1934. He died and his funeral was February 20, 1934 at St. Peter's Catholic Church with an attendance of more than a thousand with members from the legitimate business community as well as the illegitimate business community. So to speak. Billy Nesselhous who was also in the horse business gave Father Flanagan a thousand dollars for Boys Town—how it works… If you want a perfect church—don't go to church…

The legacy—it was all about the connections. Arrangements were made. Requests for assistance or information summoned. Un-derworld figures traveled between cities with essentially visas. They could hang out in Omaha without getting hassled by the cops till it chilled out in Chicago or Kansas City as long as they didn't commit any crimes. A telephone call would come in for Dennison from his old friend Vaso Chucovich, the boss out of Denver that a criminal was heading to Omaha after a misunderstanding between factions had occurred. The criminals would be monitored to make sure they weren't making any trouble. This network functioned from San Francisco to Butte, Montana back to Omaha. The intercity relationships weren't just based out of Chicago, Kansas City and Omaha. Trade for ghost voters happened between Pendergast and Dennison with loans being repaid. It was the stock in trade. Under the banner of the Democrats they operated. Mayor Cowboy Jim Dahlman, who'd take his lasso and rope citizens on the sidewalk, lost his election to reformers in 1918 who were making a stab at it of cleaning up the city from all the perdition, vice and corruption. And to Dennison and his lieutenants with their adroit and vicious thinking, the best way to get rid of the reformers who were ruining business was to create mayhem, and mayhem is what the civic reform-minded people got. For one of the ugliest chapters in Omaha history was about to occur—by the incitement of the Race Riot of 1919 against the candidates who won.

It started with the newspaper The Bee. Under Dennison's watch crime was syndicated and highly structured, vice was abundant but territorial. Business was managed under a sub rosa network of committee with Dennison as chairman of the board. Basically like the Mexican plaza. With Cowboy Jim out and the new reform mayor in—anarchy ensued. Outside forces of organized crime were allowed in to create mayhem. The new mayor by the name of Smith with his well-meaning new administration filled with a sense of goodness, duty and reform the fresh crusader of a police commissioner by the name of Ringer—were doomed. The Boss got the newspaper The Bee to write a slew of articles about how all the fine citizens of Omaha were prey to criminals due to the effeteness of the new Smith administration as Dennison recruited and brought in criminals from outside organizations to ply their trade to embarrass Smith. At the Karbach Building which is where Dennison's lair/office lay—the nickname for new police commissioner was "Lily White Ringer" as daytime bank robberies were carried out to display his incompetence. This was a concerted plan executed by Dennison and his cronies with the exact effect they'd strived for plus with WW I ending the national scene was also a little warm with racial strife and black soldiers returning wondering what had they been fighting for.

It began with an inflammatory bullshit piece by The Bee (Andre reflects how: they write lots of lies now, they wrote lots of lies back then—gotta sell the dope and soap) they'd been drumming up stories of white women being assaulted by black men. Omaha after LA in 1920 had the largest black population west of the Missouri. That's where poor Will Brown, a cripple, who couldn't have done it, comes into play. He's taken by police as a suspected robber and assailant. A mob gathers. A noose is thrown around his neck, he is beaten as a few officers manage to get him to the police station, the on to the fortress-like county jail for more security. That Sunday morning in front of the Bancroft School a gathering of three hundred set off to the jail as a lynching mob. It grew to about a thousand as they lurched their way downtown. About two dozen police met the mob at the county courthouse. The two parties banter back and forth. A message is delivered to headquarters that the situation is not too critical. Meanwhile an idiot on a white horse is circling the crowd waving a rope inciting the melee. By late afternoon there are close to 4,000 people gathered. More police are summoned. It's a hundred against 4,000. By 5:00 the aroused angry mob starts fighting with the cops, throwing stones at the courthouse and smashing windows, breaking down doors and setting buildings on fire.

The mob then looted the pawnshops and hardware stores taking arms and ammunition, scaring the nation. Gunfire broke out. People dropped wounded or dead. A rush was made where Will Brown and other prisoners were being held. Firemen arrived to the burning building only to have the hoses slashed. People attempting to assist the police or firemen were chased down streets and alleys and beaten. Mayor Smith who'd been present for several hours came out of the courthouse to reason with the mob (somewhat like the Portland mayor Wheeler who in 2020 came out to talk and sing camp songs with antifa and the BLM mob as they ransacked and torched a federal building, to barely escape with his liberal life) and within a short time he was knocked unconscious and dragged down Harney Street to the intersection of 16th Street. Three times a noose was tossed around his neck. This is the mayor mind you—of Omaha, Nebraska. Andre wonders if The Bee would describe this as a mostly peaceful protest. Anyway, Mayor Smith is in big trouble. The rope has been thrown over a traffic light post. The mayor is getting pulled up and down, clear off the ground. He is unconscious. There's a couple variants about the mayor's rescue but it is understood that a couple detectives and a state agent by the name of Danbaum who drove through the mob with one of the detectives cutting the noose and getting the mayor into the vehicle as Danbaum punched the gas hitting and knocking down several men in the process. They rush him to the hospital where he remained for several days in serious condition. Danbaum had been a Dennison man who'd been relieved as a detective by Smith and Ringer in February 1919 and had taken a job with the state sheriff's office. After the rescue of Mayor Smith, Danbaum got put back on the police force.

Poor Will Brown was not so lucky. They stormed the courthouse as the officers scramble him and the other inmates up to the roof of the burning building only to be shot from rioters in higher neighboring buildings. It's a terrible scene with the smoke and confusion and to the end Will Brown proclaimed his innocence to the sheriff who lost him to the savage mob. Will Brown gets taken by the herd and beaten into unconsciousness with his clothes torn off and hung from a lamp post at 18th and Harney Street on the south side of the County Courthouse, it is just before 11:00. His hoisted body high in the air is shot to hell with bullets. His limp body is cut down to be dragged through the streets of Omaha. To ultimately be burned to charred remains at 17th and Dodge. By three in the morning the army troops were called in with machine gun nests set up to greet the awakening city with a goddamn bad hangover. Plain Jane Fonda's father, Henry witnessed the brutal lynching as the black man dangled from the end of a rope with tears in his eyes at the horrendous sight. Two cops die in the fray trying to do their job and protect poor Will Brown.

The Bee and its propagandist editors ranted later on about inefficient government and weak policing, not that they had nothing to do with it. The Smith administration lost in the next election. The machine was back in the driver's seat for the next ten years. But the question remains—how responsible was the Dennison machine involved in the fomenting of the disastrous ugly riot. Billy Maher and others said Dennison had nothing to do with it. General Leonard Wood who led the army troops to restore order in Omaha put the responsibility on the newspaper The Bee for stirring up the racial strife and the 'old criminal gang' while other cops and firemen claimed it was just a bunch of punks and hoods who just got out of control. Church leaders and blacks blamed The Bee in its reporting and even questioned if some of the attacks were being carried out by Dennison's men. The truth is out there. Just nobody knows for sure the depths of what it was. But after that fiasco and stab at progress and reform—it was business back to usual with Cowboy Jim lending a helping hand and roping people on the streets of Omaha as mayor again. The machine rolled with vigor and panache after that little recess and reset. Smooth isn't it? Andre finds it daunting. He leaves the library, gets a taxi downtown and decides to take a hike over to these streets he has walked—where Mayor Smith was strung up and Will Brown murdered. Wondering if his grandfather and brothers were there? They were definitely a gang right off Missouri Ave there and nineteenth. The horror, the horror. What a world. Propaganda worked then, propaganda works now.

Andre, the predator and sometimes designated drunk—with a normal amount of girlfriends, kicks a can and says: fuck it and heads back to his hotel room at the Howard Johnson. He might have to read some more Ezra Pound or work on Fifty Shades of Jones via writing or Re-Search with a comely waitress. He decides on the Re-Search end of it. He goes downstairs and meets friends—new and old at the Bachannal. The band is good. A lot of good acts straight out of

Austin were coming to Omaha because so many states were under lockdown. The dancing is raucous, people are cutting loose—everybody's there like Washington Square. Could be the end of the world. It's closing time. She works at the Bachannal as a waitress... She's a pretty Botticelli. He invites her up to his room for some fine wine. Mavis is the bar manager, Hochek's Tonto, and is expressing much blonde concern for the welfare of her waitresses with Andre. He tells her: it's all good...relax, we're just gonna drink a little red, red wine...

It's quickly a very physical affair, and real sport with certain jiu-jitsu grappling techniques in play. The next morning it looked like a baby seal had been slaughtered in the upheaved room with bloody sheets and empty wine bottles everywhere. In the morning, her phone was blowing up. Children were calling, ex-husband; the melodrama—deal breaker. He walks her down to her car in the parking lot and they kiss sweetly, but that was going to be the end of that action, baby daddy. But, she was an angel of the morning....got to dig that.

After the death of Dennison others filled the ranks but none achieved the status of boss. It was all factions after that with Kansas City and the Teamsters pressing hard at times. Bennie Barone became a key figure for one. With his brother-in-law Tony "Crow" Variano he gets involved in a stolen car ring. Bennie's brother Nosey is also involved in the rackets and gets busted in 1936 for selling morphine. He does six months in the Douglas County jail. After release, he gets involved with his brother Bennie in the Omaha race wire feud. He is a prime suspect for two bombings that happen in 1938.

From fencing to smuggling liquor and drugs the Barone brothers were deep in it with associates like the Biase brothers: Sam, Louis, Benny and Tony. It wasn't just bookmaking and moving narcotics, they were also aligned with the Scavio brothers, Tony and Lawrence who were known primarily for pulling off burglaries. Billy Maher and Scavio were picked up in 1942 for attempting to commit arson on a restaurant at 3011 St. Mary's Avenue. They were caught pouring a lot of gasoline. The place was owned by Scavio's sister—doing a little insurance work for sis to put a couple more potatoes in the pot. Besides bad news in the arson business for the crew, that same year Nosey Barone along with Millio Militti, an ex-prize fighter were busted stripping a stolen car in the southeast part of Omaha. Militti was muscle Barone often used in his criminal enterprises. It had been stolen in Chicago four days earlier.

Unfortunately for Nosey Barone, at the end of 1943 in the Cornhusker Cigar Store Nosey got shot. He'd been beating up and regularly threatening the owner of the establishment, Henry Sorkin, as well as attempting to strong arm him for a thousand dollar loan. The business owner's partner was Sam House. According to Sorkin, he walked into the Cornhusker and saw Barone coming at him and figured he was going to get delivered another beating so he pulled out .32-caliber pistol he had stored beneath the store's counter. And thus began shooting at Nosey hitting him several times. Sam House claims he had heard some loud noises, but thought they were from light bulbs exploding because often the streetcars passed the cigar store and would shake the building so much that the light bulbs would break. Andre reads all this and thinks that sounds like—a likely story.

A couple of weeks later, Barone dies from his wounds. Peritonitis was the cause. One of the bullets punctured his intestines. The doctor working on him said that Barone was uncooperative and belligerent, refusing treatment, declining an operation and disconnecting medical equipment. Maybe the bullets had a toxic effect on his mind. Anyway, Sorkin gets charged with first-degree murder.

At his preliminary hearing, Sorkin was represented by attorneys Hugh and Bernie Boyle. Hugh at the trial described Barone as "turbulent, bloodthirsty, dangerous," and a member of a "gang of killers" who inspired "deadly fear' in Sorkin who shot him in self-defense. Sorkin claims he'd already been beat up and robbed several times by Barone and two of his associates, Tony Scavio and Milio Militti. Sam House testified that he did not see who shot Barone. Sorkin was found not guilty of murder and soon moved out of Omaha.

Just before the death of his brother Nosey, Bennie Barone was involved in another case that was a shooting. Charlie Hutter, Barone and a Benny Biase were eating at the Green Gables restaurant at 72nd and Dodge when a farmer from Elkhorn ended up on the wrong side of Charlie Hutter's gun. It started with an argument in the parking lot. The prosecution was going for murder. Bennie Barone testified for the defense led by lawyer Eugene O'Sullivan; that Hutter was attacked and was protecting himself. The District Court Judge Henry Beal reduced the murder charge to manslaughter. It was a hung jury after nearly twenty four hours of deliberation. Beal declares it a mistrial. It goes back to trial again for manslaughter and the second round Hutter is declared a free man—not guilty.

Out of Barone's circle was a fellow named Kenneth Kitts who made his living robbing. He preferred to do his burglaries outside of Omaha, many of them banks. He kept his headquarters in Omaha as he and his gang of marauders picked their targets. Kitts had expensive tastes in clothes and cars buying many Cadillacs and Chryslers.

In the late forties, Kitts and Tony Biase with Charles Robinson broke into the bank early one morning in Hurley, South Dakota clearing nearly $50,000 out of safety deposit boxes. They bound and gagged a husband and wife that happened to come upon them—restaurant owners who lived in an apartment in building adjoining bank. The wife looking for her husband, got shot in the shoulder after screaming and then took a hit to the head by the butt of a gun. The gunshot to her shoulder was fortunately not serious. Just a flesh wound. The bandit trio would a few years later find themselves in court in front of a federal grand jury in Deadwood, South Dakota.

The Biase brothers ran the Turf Cigar Store on 610 South 16th Street. That was there HQ for operating their criminal activities which ran the gauntlet including moving heroin. It was a place to be for underworld figures, local and out-of-town guests to hang amongst fellow hoods. This was possibly where the plan was hatched to hit this New York jeweler by the name of Goldberg. Kitts and two other hoods got him on the outskirts of Oklahoma City with $100,000 of uncut diamonds and ring settings. The unfortunate jeweler was left on the side of the highway bound and gagged. Obviously this was some kind of inside job. The robbers return to Omaha metro area and head to Barone's place The Last Chance Café. A call is made to Al Rotella whose sister happens to be Stella Rotella. Al is also an associate of Max Abramson. Andre starts thinking everybody is an associate…and this is getting complicated considering Andre was pitching writing an article for Mother Jones on the link between Jeffrey Epstein and the sex trafficking of children in the Franklin Cover-up. But he's doing his Re-Search. He wants to get to the roots of it all.

So Al Rotella takes the diamonds and puts them in the safe of the Venetian Music Company owned by Maxie's brother Harry. Al Rotella had some interest also in this music vending company. Now allegedly, according to Kitts who was trying to cut a deal with the Feds, Rotella delivered some of the diamonds to a fence in Chicago. Now Al's day job was running the Harney Drug Store at 17th and Harney Street. This drug store was owned by Maxie. An Omaha jeweler had given Kitts the description of Goldberg's vehicle and where he was headed. A couple of years later the whole crew gets charged with conspiracy and crossing state lines with stolen jewelry, but he case gets dropped by the U.S. attorney because criminals like politicians occasionally lie and they decided that Kenneth Kitts was just too prone to exaggeration and thus not considered a strong witness given he was scrambling to save his own hide. Imagine that.

Back at the nondescript Last Chance Café on West Broadway with two windows with neon signs, crimes were being planned. (Terri Baby's grandma would have her run in there as a little girl to go drag grandpa out of this very club under a different alias. He was a heavy equipment contractor—her uncles lived hard lives and didn't live to get too old—and she got mad at Andre for giving her a hard time for being from Counciltucky: he saw it from a hundred miles away as she playing like some kind of sorority girl before he knew even much about her background, with her grandparents orphans on a potato farm and married at fifteen years old…her sliver of the family somehow made it out of the pitfalls of the web and became prosperous on the other side of the river). Barone had an after-hours club in the basement of this dingy joint. Lots of discussions held amongst the local banditti—Kitts included. The next big bank heist for Kitts and cronies was to be in Laurens, Iowa. Kitts had gotten word that some of the safe deposit boxes had a lot money. He discusses the matter with another associate by the name of Pasquale Belcastro. He runs over in his 1950 Nash to Iowa and cases the bank out. They are joined by Yancy Hardy who flies in from Texas on a commercial flight to Omaha's Eppley Airfield.

The burglars break into the Laurens State Bank and do pretty good collecting about $8,000 in dead presidents, $5,000 in silver coins and about $25,000 in traveler's checks. They then proceed to Sioux City, Iowa to meet up with associate Tony Prochelo at his nightclub, the Turin Inn. They give him a cut for the score. Andre grew up with the Prochelos. They lived right across the street from them. A neighbor had casually said when they moved in that he really hoped they'd get the right house if there hit someday. It was certainly fun having the Prochelo brothers in the neighborhood with their little Mexican sister. They bought the house that the Goldsteins use to live in. The old man Charley never really had a job, but they lived pretty well. Andre's father did business at times with them. And they were family friends going way back prior to them moving in—all part of the same parish down there at Holy Family to do street ministry and salvage the peripheral lost cause Catholics (Faye Louise and Woody's fam was down there—along with the wild hard-partying Twohig clan would also gather—this is where he saw the Twohig sisters and others dancing to the musical Godspell and Andre fell in love with the beautiful willowy Kat Twohig who would become the owner of the fine restaurant…circle unbroken: say no more, say no more) so Andre had met the five brothers since he was around five. And later on would go on a few business trips with his father up to Sioux City to meet Leo who was Charley's father. Andre and his brother on those field trips never really knew what was going on as they ran with two of the sons, Smokin' Joe Prochelo and Crazy Tommy Prochelo. It was a riot. But something was...going on. A continuum of the mystery of business with Mike. Sometimes it involved much magic thinking. Charley could get some pretty good deals on things. He was definitely a hustler with a nervous cigarette always at his side. Andre's father, Charley with fedora and pals would all go coyote hunting out at the horse ranch near Elkhorn. They'd put buckets of Kentucky Fried chicken out there on the hill as bait. Then they'd get roaring drunk. About ten of them. Sometimes Andre and his brother would retrieve the dead coyotes dragging them across the pasture to bring them to the barn. There'd be firewood cutting parties too. Andre's mother was up from around those parts and recalled frequenting the after-hours club of the Turin Inn as young Charley poured drinks as bartender for his father Leo—back in the fifties. It's a small world after all.

So Kitts calls the Last Chance Café to talk with Bennie to discuss the proper steps to take for untraceable conversion of the dough. Bennie give his best advice and they make tracks to Omaha. They arrive at Barone's house at 1314 South 24th Street and count the silver. The criminals then load up the silver again and head to a close friend of Barone's named Lou Varda. Varda owned the Wishbone Nightclub at 76th and Dodge. He also had a bar on North 16th Street. A partial exchange is made and three days later Barone meets Belcastro at the Harney Drug Store and gives him the balance retaining a decent commission for his part. Eventually the walls close in, arrests are made, federal complaints filed, Belcastro gets picked up in Chicago. Kitts escapes from jail in Cedar Rapids, Iowa with the assistance of John F. Quinn who is Barone's business partner at the Last Chance Café and also Maxie Abramson's son-in-law. Criminal defense attorney Hugh Boyle comes to the aid of both Kitts and Quinn as the authorities are still looking for Kitts. He is found in an Omaha motel room. Boyle manages to get charges dropped against Quinn.

The state of Nebraska convicts Kitts of being a habitual criminal, but that's just the beginning of Kitts' problems. Different states are coming after him along with the U.S. District Court. Then Kitts' wife divorces him while he's in the prison as everybody's throwing twenty years at him. She proceeds to move in with Maxie Abramson. The walls close in on Barone as well and he gets three years as an accessory at the federal penitentiary in Leavenworth.

Tom closes the book for a pause of reflection…says a quiet prayer, hearing the dialogue and contemplations of his associates and acolytes. Over the decades—down at the Antiquarium Bookstore in the Old Market.

CHAPTER SIX

CLIFF NOTES FOR CRIMINALS

Well, it is too bad, Chief Warren...

—Jack Ruby to the Chief Justice of the United States

Andre starts compiling an outline from the era of the forties, fifties and early sixties of a few of the names of the after-hours nightclubs and roadhouses that offered drinking, gambling and other entertainment of Carter Lake, Council Bluffs and unincorporated East Omaha: the Moonlight Club, the Chez Paree, the Gay Club, the Midnight Sun, the Royal Café, the Ha Ha Club, the Stork Club, the Lakeside Steak House to name a few. Quite a few happened to be located on an East Locust Street. Incidents occurred such as: large fight breaks out in club that left three customers stabbed, arrested was owner Carl Mangiamelli and one of his employees George Mrzlak.

At the Midnight Sun on 2501 East Locust Street just a block from the Gay Club a fight breaks out around 2:00 a.m. Four customers get into a fight with the owners, father and son, Sam and James Lombardo. The slugged and beaten customers told police that the Lombardos pulled out guns on them and that James took out a club and commenced to beat them over the head. The Lombardos got felony assault and the place was padlocked for a year by order of the judge.

Pete Bonacci, a good friend of Bennie Barone, was the operator of the Gay Club which stayed open until 6:00 am providing food and dance bands

In 1956, Gaughan moved much of his interest from Vegas to Tahoe. He also might have had controlling stock in The Eldorado in Reno, at least according to Andre's pal Joe, the union glazier who played next to Andre back at Rummel as defensive tackle and would hitchhike to games to catch the team bus since Rummel didn't have a stadium.

Weyerman and Eddie Barrick took points in the Fremont Hotel which was under construction in Vegas. Weyerman with three percent interest moved to Las Vegas where he became the manager at the hotel's casino. Connie Hurley had four percent in the Fremont. There were approximately a dozen investors from Sam Ziegman to Torres who was a trusted associate of Lansky.

In the mid-fifties a new group of investors took over The Flamingo. It included Ziegman, Gaughan, Eddie Barrick. Most of them relocated to Vegas, but some like Ziegman kept their official residence in Omaha. One of the first Omaha gamblers to permanently migrate to Nevada was Joe Rosenberg. Dave Berman and Greenbaum still maintained control and management of the Flamingo.

Mayor Rosenblatt put Sergeant Mahoney in charge of the Vice Squad. In several inspections of various cigar stores in downtown Omaha, Mahoney and his squad reported finding nothing illegal going on. But another raid was soon followed up by a different police detail without informing Sergeant Mahoney and his Vice Squad that it was going down and they busted several bookie joints located in the various cigar stores with all kinds of evidence. The detectives arrested Tony Higgins, Soddy DiMauro, Peggy Nocita and Charles LaFerla in the raid. Mayor Rosenblatt publicly stated that the bust in no way reflected poorly upon Sergeant Mahoney and his Vice Squad's work. The mayor had been the sponsor of Mahoney to head that department. Other public servants agreed wholeheartedly with the mayor and his recommendation. Higgins had been arrested several times prior to such offenses. His partners included a Clarence Matya, Dutch Volker, Sam Scarpello, Fred Scarpello and a Frank Kessler who owned a television and appliance store at twelfth and Farnam Street. In the early sixties, Higgins was considered the head of the Omaha bookies. At his what were called lay-off centers the likes of Anthony Ligouri, an ex-boxer and associate of Babe Bisignano, a known underworld figure. Ligouri claims he was just a casual bettor even though phone records in a nine month period were nearly a thousand to the likes of Tony Higgins and Joe Marfisi to name a few. Many calls to Kansas City as well. The bookies moved around, buildings would get condemned and demolished and the bookmakers would find new homes such as Joe Digilio who weathered federal grand jury indictments as well as losing his space in downtown Omaha. He remained undaunted and repositioned himself at Turk Abboud's billiards parlor at Twenty Fourth and Leavenworth. Not far from Four Aces Package where Andre got ripped off picking up a pack of cigarettes in no time flat parking his truck right in front of the joint in broad daylight—lost a dozen CDs and and a Milwaukee impact driver. You got to pay attention and you got to pay your taxes: so they say. Even thinking about that hash deal in Marseilles, Andre in all his travels, had never been ripped off so quickly.

With the racing season opening Lansky stayed at the Fontanelle Hotel and frequented the Paxton Hotel often at its coffee shop where he was pals with a waitress there. Meyer made friends everywhere he went.

In the spring of 1950, the Kansas City mob bosses, Gargotta and Binaggio were knocked off. If they can prove you're crazy—it's good for assassinations. From the past: Democrat Louisiana governor and senator Huey Long, the Kingfish, got too big for his britches and wasn't kicking back enough to the mob. Weiss, the doctor, was a patsy. He never fired his .32 at Long—he didn't even bring it into the capital in Baton Rouge—it was planted there later on. Decades later after investigation by the state police it was determined the pistol had never been fired. Long's bodyguards Joe Messina and Murphy Roden supposedly opened fire on Weiss after he punched Huey Long with bullets flying. By ricochet Huey goes down, but the official version was in 1935 a young doctor Weiss defending his father-in-law's reputation, a judge and rival to Long shoots him in southern chivalry. Later in the 1950s, an affidavit by Louisiana state trooper investigation has witnesses go to a bar owned by Joe Messina where he is introduced as the man who killed Huey Long. Messina does not deny the claim. Andre knows of this from reading a take by Chicago Boss Sam Giancana's half-brother, Chuck, who didn't even want to be in the Mafia. He picked the book up for a buck at the St. Vincent DePaul Society store off 23rd and Leavenworth Street while he was getting a nice suit so he could go to an old friend, who'd been poor as a kid with a single mother and a flock of kids, fancy country club party at Happy Hollow—the dude had become fantastically wealthy. Andre needed to make a good show of it and wear a tie since nobody had seen him in decades. He applied some pomade to his hair…might meet some rich broad. They'd been in scrapes together, guy had a wicked right…they'd nearly been kicked out of Rummel together for putting a Volkswagon the linebacker McCoy had rolled that had sat in the front yard of their house for a year or two. Like Seal Team 6, the crew of them had put it in the front entry of the library on the second floor. In reality, Stevie Doyle got underneath the thing and dead lifted it the whole two flight of stairs. There were a couple of mannequins in the front seat they'd picked up at Crossroads Mall on Dodge Street, dressed up as a priest and a woman of the night or maybe she was a nun or somebody's mom…kind of wholesome looking back. It wasn't like the crew threw an altar boy with his pants down in the backseat (that's all they were missing). There was some choice graffiti. There had been some deliberations amongst the brethren that night due to the political ramifications… Andre had said leave it. Damn the torpedoes. Turned out it wasn't a crowd pleaser with the clergy. What a motley crew of Dead Rabbits, these bastard sons of Erin: Kirby, Kieny, Mangan, Hogan, Kennedy, McCoy, Suds (bulldozer operator and worked briefly as a taxi driver up in Dutch Harbor when Andre ran into up there commercial fishing in Eighties) and Doyle—can never forget Doyle. Anyway, Andre the barauder, repeats himself and digresses, sometimes in French, sometimes in Swahili, as he looks for the right tie. Erin go Bragh.

The same goes for the attempted assassination of FDR according to that book—if it's true… FDR is down in Miami. The Great Depression has kicked in. He has just beaten Hoover. He is the president-elect and has gone on a 12-day cruise in South Florida on a yacht owned by multimillionaire Vincent Astor. It sails into Biscayne Bay. FDR is heading to the train station for a New York bound trip. Prior to that he attends a rally in an open car with Miami mayor Redmond Gautier. He gives a short speech to a large crowd. Tony Cermak, the mayor of Chicago is standing nearby. FDR says hello and waves Tony over. At that moment, Joe Zangara begins firing a revolver at the car. Cermak is doubled up. Four other people are hit. The Secret Service agents are shouting. A woman next to Zangara grabs his arm— mayhem. He is nabbed. Cermak dies. Roosevelt becomes president. The book Chuck wrote claims that Cermak was always the target. The mayor wasn't kicking back enough and believed he was immune. FDR was never the target. Zangara was hired. It was an inside deal though he was portrayed as an unemployed Italian immigrant brick-layer who was an anarchist that hated capitalism. Maybe Chuck Giancana is making the whole thing up. Andre is open to that. But he's the dude who said all the way back in the Sixties that China was about: SLAVERY. And then again, maybe these politicians' heads get too big sometimes and they forget who they need to pay—who they owe. On it goes. And by the way, FDR, the patrician grandfatherly figure the American school children have been groomed to cherish and worship, wouldn't shake hands with Jesse Owens after he won Olympic gold in Munich. He shook every other medalists' hands. Jesse didn't think much of that and didn't vote for him. Also, he could have saved thousands of Jews from the Holocaust. His administration obstructed many rescue opportunities for European Jews as they rounded up the American Japanese to put them in prison camps—

the narrator is just saying. But none of this should be that much of a surprise given the overt racism of the high- academic president of Princeton, the most racist president of all time—Woodrow Wilson, who after watching The Birth of a Nation in the White House and promised to keep the US out of World War I, but JP Morgan and the banks were going to lose their ass if Germany won, so a massive anti-Hun propaganda campaign was unleashed onto the American public as the progressive Woodrow Wilson threw the US into it where in 110 days of battle and 110,000 American deaths later—victory was achieved. But the question is—for who? Tom Rudloff, the light keeper and antiquarian digresses… He ponders could it be to save the British Empire? He takes note Andre, the part-time substitute teacher educating across the OPS was up at downtown Central High School working as a social studies instructor and went over the names of the dead inscribed on the bronze plaques paying tribute to those killed in the wars: twenty seven killed in WWI, fifty in WWII, six in Korea and fifteen in Vietnam. Those numbers had Andre and Tom scratching their heads—one gets WWII with fifty dead; Vietnam was a fifteen year old war… how'd so many get slaughtered in WWI in less than a year?

Berman had spent time in Sing Sing Prison for the kidnapping of a New York bootlegger at the behest of Frank Costello and Lansky. His partner in the crime got shot dead by the police for attempting to shoot the police. Berman had pulled his pistol out but a detective grabbed him before he could start firing. This was all near Central Park. Later on, he's in Omaha, World War II was braking out, but because he was a convicted felon he couldn't join the U.S. Army to fight. He went to a friend's nightclub, the Chez Paree in Carter Lake to get the name of a contact that could get him into the Canadian Army. Dave Berman got discharged from the Canadian Army in August of 1944.

Berman got involved with Bugsy Seigel to purchase the El Cortez Hotel. He needed to get permission from Lansky so he flew back to Omaha to pay him $160,000. Lansky was in Omaha working on the dog racing business. Also, according to Susie Berman, Berman's daughter, her uncle Chickie was given a suitcase full of money to pay for the casino. Chickie liked to gamble and found himself in a craps game in a downtown Vegas casino and lost all the money. That put a delay in the purchase forcing Berman to get back to the Midwest to acquire more money to finance the purchase of the casino.

Another professional gambler with Omaha connections who became a well-known player In Las Vegas was Bowser Rosenberg. Bowser left Omaha in 1941 to relocate in Vegas where he worked as a dealer. After 1945 he began investing in casinos with his pal Dave Berman. Prior to moving to Las Vegas, Rosenberg had worked at a number of gambling houses in the Omaha metro area. He had also helped running race books for the likes of Sam House and the Silver brothers. Omaha was where he learned the ropes as he would later become a partner in the El Cortez as well as the El Dorado Club. Frank Housky who'd been one of Tom Dennison's major lieutenants had owned a piece of the casino located on the first floor of the Apache Hotel at Second and Fremont Street. Funny how the world turns Andre thinks—he'd been down to Vegas a half dozen times or so. He'd also worked construction on a casino before. A grandfathered thing in the hood of Seattle. In a little self-incorporated entity called Skyway. The tiny rough borough was surrounded by Seattle and most of Seattle didn't even know Skyway even existed. It wasn't tied in with the Indians and there were two of these little casinos—one was called Romans the other called SkyBowl because along with the casino was a large bowling alley. Everybody was there. The place didn't shut down. Retired ladies from Boeing and the like showed up in the morning for bowling league. In the afternoon the Asians would constantly be coming up to Andre to ask when the casino would reopen. At night, Crip ganger-bangers and Hispanic girls dressed to the nines like the finest houris—all smoking cigarettes like it was the '70s would be hanging out. It was a wild scene. With family center birthday parties—joint was a scene, can't make this shit up. The new owners of the casino were an Armenian faction. Andre worked hard on it for three months or so had some interaction with the Armenians and just checked out and absorbed the scene as Vietnamese dudes in their conical hats ambled around the streets with a wooden yoke over their shoulders hauling wooden buckets of rice and water or whatever; Andre didn't know. He got these kind of jobs through his associates. His career was one constant gig from bartending, driving cab to construction jobs and working along the Seattle waterfront in the maritime industry as a commercial-fisherman, merchant sailor and itinerant longshoreman. That's all Andre could say—about the Viet Cong dude missing his water buffalo. Later on he would work on the Romans Casino. In the slums of Skyway (Seattle). It wasn't Las Vegas. And Andre wasn't in Kansas no more… Talk about America coming together. It was all too much Re-Search.

Bowser Rosenberg would eventually become an investor in the Las Vegas Club along with Berman, Siegel and Icepick Willie Alderman. And a little later Bowser bought some interest in the Flamingo as did his old friend Ben Goffstein who back in the 1920s they had sold newspapers on the street corners of Omaha. Andre thinks of that Neil Diamond song: They're Coming to America. He flashes back to a scene at a Menard's Home Center and Lumberyard just a few years ago in the early Wu days that happened they said because the Chinese eat bats (but that's not racist) and the controlled demolition of society was just getting rolling… and Andre's building a deck for some old friends and he's in the parking lot and it's goddamn hot and in some dilapidated car like an AMC hornet or gremlin or something is some red-faced, semi-bearded, wild-haired un-kept irrefutable and irredeemable dude tooling around the parking lot with that Neil Diamond song blaring: They're Coming to America. It was a sight and scene to behold as Andre hung in a tenuous existential balance between hilarity, pride and horror. It was awesome. What a world and Andre recalls they were still trying to encourage people to wear useless masks upon entrance to the store back then. Those were the days my friend… Andre thinks—we thought they'd never end.

Later on in 1951, the Omaha bookies Sam Ziegman, Jackie Gaughan and Eddie Barrick were given the opportunity to buy points in the Flaming. Bowser Rosenberg and Goffstein were in management positions there. The casino was controlled by Gus Greenbaum, Dave Berman and Willie Alderman.

In 1955, the Riviera Hotel had recently opened up. It was losing money. Chicago bosses Jake Guzik and Tony Acardo persuade Gus Greenbaum to take over management of the operation. He owed them a million dollars from an earlier loan. Rosenberg, Berman, Alderman and Goffstein all become partners in the Riviera.

In 1956, Barrick buys interest in the Fremont Hotel getting built. Connie Hurley and Ed Torres are investors as well. Ed Torres is a close associate of Meyer Lansky. Barrick gets his former partner from the Chez Paree to buy three percent stock in the enterprise.

Different deals were made, transactions happened, hotels and casinos changed hands. Eventually Jackie Gaughan establishes his headquarters at the El Cortez at Sixth and Fremont. With that Gaughan brought in some of his old dealers who had worked for him at the Chez Paree and Stork Club back in Omaha. Tiger Novak bought some percentage, moving to Las Vegas in 1962 where he went to work at the El Cortes. Weyerman, Ziegman and Barrick also took ownership the Horseshoe Club. Andre was surprised in his research as to what presence the Omaha bookies had in the inception of Las Vegas. Kind of made him proud like soaring eagle. Andre believes that Jackie Gaughan was married to the sister of dominant Omaha architect, Leo Daly. And Leo Daly was good friend with Andre's grandfather Fast Eddie. He was going to have to ask his mother about that one. Got to get the facts right.

From 1967 to 1978, they all got indicted for skimming and tax evasion. Some paid fines, some of them had charges dropped and a few spent some time. But not all the bookies and gamblers out of Omaha moved to Las Vegas. Some continued to pursue their fortune locally. The likes of Tony Higgins, Sam Nocita, Dutch Volker, Leo

Imolati and John Salinitro prospered in this complicated web and underworld network of wires services. And alliances. Some of them were old going back to the bootlegging days and others were young doing their apprenticeship in the lucrative business. There was no shortage of appetite for gambling. Andre concurs thinking he hasn't been in a good craps game in a while and was missing the pai gow while getting hectored by the Asian women about what a lousy gambler he was: "YOU NO GOOD GAMBLER!" Andre, like Dostoevsky, was more of a roulette guy—red/black; math was hard. For him. Like Barbie.

He reads on perusing through some old Omaha World-Herald clips… Maxie Abramson and Joe Tool set up a lay-off center for bets with the business front Rotella Engineering. The owner is Al Rotella. Police bust the operation. He denies any knowledge of bookmaking happening. With that heat they set up shop at the Baldridge Building at 20th and Farnam Street. The business is called the A&A Brokerage Company. That business gets busted as well with telephone records billed to Rotella Engineering amongst calls to a vast array of distant cities like Chicago, Kansas City, Denver and Minneapolis.

Tony Higgins goes to Chicago to meet with representatives from the Chicago Syndicate and procure the syndicate's wire service. He partnered with the Sam and Fred Scarpello relatives to the famous All-American wrestler Joe Scarpello who later on would be tag team partner with Verne Gagne. Andre recalled watching the All-Star pro wrestling with Baron von Raschke and the Mad Dog Vachon crew on Sunday morning right after the rough roller derby bouts and the commercials by the hyper hawker used car salesman Joe Zweiback selling Gera-Speed. As kids they'd go down to the Civic Auditorium and watch the pro wrestling live—adults would be freaking out, sometimes there'd be midget wrestlers. He remembers a black gentleman screaming at the top of his lungs at the referee that one of the wrestlers had a knife. Andre kept looking for the knife but they were pretty high up with around thirty thousand people. Andre digresses. The brothers owned Scarpello's Club 22 at 22nd and Pierce. This bar was also a horse racing operation. It was different in they received the information from Chicago via telephone and not from traditional telegraph lines—cutting edge at the time.

In the late Fifties into the Sixties, Tony Higgins was the main player for bookies in Omaha along with his associates: Sam Scarpello, Joe Marfisi, Dutch Volker, Soddy DiMauro, Clarence Matya, John Abboud, Tony Manzo and C.J. Van Ness. They managed to pull this all together with the help of Frank Kessler who owned Kessler's Television and Appliance Company at 1210 Farnam Street. Frank's son Tommy was Tony Higgin's son-in-law. Frank and Tommy put the phone system together with a transformer board to make a central wire room for a switchboard that could handle eighteen connections for seven phones set in a row. A very high-tech operation for 1961. Busts are made locally and by the Feds and IRS, committees are assembled by Congress because they weren't getting their piece as they saw it—it wasn't about morals except amongst the chumps and inexperienced and hopelessly naïve. Andre laughs because he went to school with some Kesslers—guess the apple didn't fall too far from the tree they sez. (The Kessler they went to school with got blown up in some kind of deal—he was always funny; looked like a goddamn pirate now. Not quite as bad as the alumni a few years older who became president of the Omaha chapter of the Hells Angels, Rummel High really covered the gauntlet). The lawyers made money defending them as they would drag the likes of Jackie Gaughan from Las Vegas back to Omaha to testify in 1970 in regards to corruption charges with the Sarpy County Sheriff by the name of Whitted being one of the defendants. Gaughan claimed he may have picked up a tab or two for the good sheriff on the occasional visits to his casino in Vegas. Then towards the end of his testimony Gaughan said, "I can see more than a half a dozen people in this courtroom that I have picked up tabs." The Chief Judge Robinson didn't groove on that posit and interjected with alacrity that Jackie had never picked up the bill for his court. Gaughan let it go…he'd already made his point. Didn't want to further ruffle the feathers of the judge of the Admiralty Court. In September of that year, Sheriff Whitted was found guilty by a federal jury on three counts of perjury. In November, while on appeal, Sheriff Whitted got re-elected for his third term by the good people of Sarpy County.

The good sheriff continued in his job arresting John Salinitro at 6817 Chandler Acres Drive in Sarpy County where they came upon a bounty of betting slips. Salinitro was using the telephone in the bedroom at the place to handle business. Andre recalls answering the door sometimes and a stocky grinny dude would hand him a brown paper sack and tell him to give this to his dad. Andre never was sure if it was from the unions or the bookies. Later on John Salanitro comes under investigation by the Nebraska Liquor Control Commission for his ownership in the Cabay Lounge at Tara Plaza in Papillion. He is not listed as a corporate officer in the company that owns the Cabay Lounge. The Papillion City Council approve the license renewal application to the Cabay. The Cabay Lounge is owned by Vernie Belfiore, Paul Belfiore and Mary Barrios of La Vista who happens to be Salanitro's sister. The Papillion City Council still recommended the approval even though Salanitro was facing a multitude of federal and local indictments.

As the world turns, Tom Rudloff flips over a few more pages and quotes to himself some Shakespeare—some rise by sin, and some by virtue fall. He pets his cat. Somewhere near Heaven, he is like Virgil. Somebody's got to tell the story. He consults with his old cohort Senor Agape' occasionally for some clarification of the details…for it's all—in the details. The cop who wrote the tale knows. To get the nuance right. Senor Agape' is not completely comfortable being this near Heaven. He heads back to Purgatorio—just making the odd visits to see his old pal Tom and to interject on some of the finer points of the narrative. It's all in the details. It's all in the timing…

It's a new era in the underbelly of the United States—the Sixties

and Seventies were a new era in a lot of arenas back then Gloria
Steinem and Helen Reddy—I Am Woman hear me roar… girls need
to play sports: Title Nine—with girls; to sex, drugs and rock 'n' roll
and feminism…another austerity program for men and women as
they burned the bras and wore halter tops, which were cool, with
bellbottom blue jeans seeking a brand-new key. The times they are a
changin'…as the poet laureate Dylan strums his guitar and sings with
his unusual and distinct nasal voice while occasionally petting his
Siamese cat as he probably thinks of Joan Baez as she plays her guitar
crying a protest folk song of political import like "One Tin Soldier"
all of this much before gender dysphoria had kicked in and gone
rampant across this home of the brave. This was all way before girl
swimmers had to put on their bathing suits: NOT A DUDE. Before
Nebraska state senator Machela Cavanaugh had her epic meltdown
gone viral on floor chanting hysterically about loving trans-people
like an out of control preschooler. That should have been the end
of the Cavanaugh political dynasty, but like the Kennedys—they'll
keep going. All much before this…back when it was sane in the
Seventies. So in 1968, Congress authorizes court ordered wiretaps
be made available to the FBI and other law enforcement agencies for
criminal investigations: another game changer. In Omaha they start
going after bookmakers Clarence Matya and John Salanitro. Matya
had around two hundred bars in Omaha working essentially as his
agents—getting the bets the customers wanted to make on this football game or that horse race. His headquarters was Paltani's Lounge
on 45th and Center Street not far from the Fan Tan Club, Jimmy's
Place (sometimes Tommy's) and Petrow's Restaurant, all favorites
of Fast Eddie's. Andre remembers the joint as a kid—it wasn't that
far from the old asphalt plant and construction yard. Paltani's was
owned by Don Paltani, Matya rented the place as his office. By the
mid-70s they were turning up the heat on these guys. They started
bugging all these joints in Omaha from the Green Onion to Cohen
and Kelly's Lounge. The local cops with the FBI also did surveillance
on these bars and many others observing different associates from
Kansas City coming and meeting Salanitro for a drink at the Green

Onion. In 1978 Paltani's Lounge was raided as well as a couple of houses on Poppleton that happened to be owned by Sam Scarpello. This was around the same time of the Abboud murder where he'd been reported missing until his body was found along a creek bed in a rural area just west of Omaha. It was gangland style with a back shot to the head by a .22 caliber pistol just like Sam Giancana and many others. The cops had their suspicions, but no proof. Abboud had a commercial realty company. His family hired a private investigator by the name of Whelan. They believed it was a couple of associates of Abboud that he was in business with or were employees of his. So it was mob-like in style but was unrelated to the Mafia. A couple characters are arrested for the slaying with Whelan's tenacious pursuit of them. They get convicted but pull off a daring escape from the sixth floor of the jail and make it 3/4s of a mile to the Canadian border near the Red River in North Dakota. The motivation for the killing was business. Abboud pissed off a couple of associates and they hired a young man named Hochstein to carry out the hit for $1,500. It was all as murky as the Papio Creek. Another murder that occurred a few years earlier was that of Frank "the Barber" Mason. He ran his bookmaking operation with Tony Manzo out of a couple apartments off Dewey Avenue and Leavenworth Street. One night at his home at 3116 State Street "the Barber" Mason was shot and killed by two intruders as he returned fire but was unable to hit either one. They were after his dough. Reportedly Manzo continued with the business after the slaying of his partner. The perpetrators of the Mason murder were never apprehended.

Nate "Lightnin" Johnson operated the Seventh Ward Improvement Center which was an after-hours club that sold liquor in an unlicensed premise—sometimes he'd put on parades of protest with his stable of girls. Andre recalls some of the older dudes from the crew howling about all the good times with the booze and girls had at the Seventh Ward Improvement Center. Charges were brought up against Johnson for illegally selling alcohol, running prostitutes and other vice charges. Andre living off 33rd and Lake would traipse on by some of the "private clubs" of North Omaha wondering how he could attain a license and membership. They were paving the streets next to Skeet's Pit-barbeque on 24th Street across from St. Benedict the Moor church, and the all-stars Quincy Jones, Bobby Jones, Macarthur Keyes, foreman Tech football star, '68 the Nam Army Airborne/Black Panther mutherfucker Julian Harris and others told him it wasn't just barbeque getting sold there—they had go-go girls dancing in the back of the well mentholated barbeque pit. You just got to be out there walking and talking—what Andre thinks… Rudloff concurs returning to the story of John Salinitro with everybody knowing the government was only busting all these dudes' balls just because they weren't getting their cut.

So Salinitro serves his time at the Federal Correction Institute in Sandstone, Minnesota. This is 1971. It's for perjury. He gets released and goes right back in business because people got to bet on the Cornhuskers and the ponies. Then in 1975 there's another large raid on Salinitro and his crew which included Abramson, DiMauro, Paul Cappellano Jr. and Sr., Wayne Womochill, Jerry Krajenski, James Bonofede, Michael Scavio, Ronald Dean Nelson, Clarence Smaldone, Paul Villano, Ed Wisniewski, a couple of Murphy brothers with a few Quinns thrown in and others with the most interesting being former city prosecutor Anthony Troia. Salinitro's betting operation extended to other cities including Denver, Kansas City, Minneapolis and Chicago. The judge from the Eighth Circuit Court gives Salinitro two years for conducting an illegal gambling operation. It's July 1976, Salinitro's lawyer appeals the conviction. Salinitro has dinner with Kansas City Mob top bookie John Costanza and other key representatives of the Kansas City Syndicate. They have a late night dinner in midtown Omaha. Salinitro goes to the Ramada Inn West at 107th Avenue and Pacific Street where the KC crew was staying. About three o'clock in the morning Salinitro leaves the motel in his car. He runs out of gas at about 100th and Pacific. He walks the thirteen blocks to his house at 88th and Pacific streets. He is greeted by his wife and then suffers a massive heart attack. She calls the rescue squad, but he dies on his way to the hospital. Omaha detectives thought it was highly unusual for Salinitro to run out of gas given how much he relied on it for his business that handled millions of dollars in bets. Maybe just a convenient death—for KC Syndicate as they continued frequently visiting Aksarben to make inroads into Omaha with the vacuum of power like Dennison wielded.

So Costanza out of KC and Salanitro were both facing prison due to FBI wiretaps. Salanitro dies, Costanza gets a reduced sentence to three years—this is all happening while KC's River Quay areas blowing up: literally blowing. With bombs. It was all part of the fireworks for the bicentennial—gangland murders included. The River Quay was a downtown Kansas City development along the riverfront started in the early seventies by businessman Marion Trozzolo. It became a wildly successful shopping and entertainment center. But a conflict arose between a Willie Cammisano and David Bonadonna. Cammisano was a ruthless force in the Kansas City Mob. David Bonadonna and his sons had major business capital in the River Quay. Bonadonna was acquainted with Cammisano and had an established relationship with the syndicate going back to the days of Charles Binaggio. They both had brothers and sons that wanted different interests in the development. Eventually, in 1976, David Bonadonna is found dead in the trunk of his car with a bullet hole to the head: eternity. What were his last thoughts? As narrator, Rudloff wants to know things like that.

The bombing in Kansas City in the mid to late Seventies is about as bad as Cleveland where there were thirty four in 1976, many of them trying to kill the Irishman Danny Greene who allied himself with arms trafficker John Nardi who fought for control of Cleveland against gangster James Licavoli. Cleveland and Kansas City had more bombings than Beirut in those years. Beirut was a great cosmopolitan place till the PLO invaded.

Where this ties together is on a Sunday in 1977 a powerful bomb levels a building in the Quay where a Patrick O'Brien ran a bar names Pat O'Brien's. His real job was a bookmaker for the syndicate.

The building is owned by two sons of Bonadonna, Tony and Fred. More messaging one could infer...

Patrick O'Brien ends up in Omaha hanging out at the Trentino's Restaurant on 10th and Pacific that Bonofede has recently bought and now calls Angie's after his sister. A lot of underworld figures hang out there from the narcotic dealing Biase brothers to Coonie Dinovitz who is an associate of the Kansas City Mob. He has recently been released from jail after serving two years for loan-sharking in KC. Dinovitz is made restaurant bar manager. Pat O'Brien is frequently hanging out at Angie's because he has been sent by the Kansas City Syndicate to establish a bookmaking operation upon their behest and benefit. Sometimes when O'Brien was in town he would stay at the Old Mill Holiday Inn at 655 North 108th Avenue, not far from the Green Onion. Especially during the horse racing season at Aksarben would it get busy with visitors from Kansas City. Costanza would arrive and meet Omaha gambler John Giangrosso driving around in his Lincoln Continental. Room reservations at the Old Mill Holiday Inn were made by a Quinn who would place the name under "Green Onion" with the contact number being that of the Cohen and Kelly's Lounge at 130th and West Center Road. Quinn was a known felon and held hidden ownership in both establishments. As the world turns, deals are made, bets placed and the ponies run... Tony Civella, the nephew to Nick Civella who was the Kansas City mob boss by this time drops in at the Old Mill on occasion. The police are doing surveillance and acquire authorizations for wiretaps on Angie's, Cohen & Kelly's, and Westside Billiard's on 72nd Street owned and operated by Tommy "the Greek" who was an associate of the late Maxie Abramson.

The narrator Rudloff thinks it's hard to keep track of all these names (and he grew up with them) as so much of the song remains the same...coming together like a naked woman in a painting. Kind of a wild town Omaha.

By 1981 and 1982 the FBI is doing a massive investigation on the KC Outfit and Vegas on skimming hundreds of thousands of dollars from the Tropicana Hotel Casino in Las Vegas. A federal grand jury issues indictments for eleven members out of Kansas City and Omaha including Nick Civella, Carl Civella, Charles Moeretina and Carl Caruso who was one of the main couriers delivering $40,000 bundles back to Kansas City. The heat is on. It's so bad—Bonofede, Costanza, Coonie Dinovitz can't even go to the Aksarben Tracks without getting harassed and kicked out. Omaha attorney Anthony Troia gets a temporary restraining order from Douglas County. Bartenders at Field Club Countru Club were busted for laying off bets for O'Brien who was a member along with John Giangrosso. These guys were all paying their bills. Sometimes going to the racetrack sitting at a season table at the Aksarben clubhouse (where Terri Baby had worked as an under aged cocktail waitress one summer) payed for by Danny Lawson who was a friend of Nick Civella's and had also been convicted along with Coonie for loan-sharking. He maintained it under the alias Jack Daniels. A place for the Kansas City Outfit to come and socialize with the Omaha gamblers to discuss their mutual interests. By 1983, the whole crew gets thrown in prison for a year or two. In Leavenworth. No more, no less. Probably didn't get invited to the Aksarben debutante ball where little rich kids had to dress up like medieval court jesters wearing silken leotards while carrying soft pillows around and get their picture posted in the Omaha World-Herald—pure child abuse that one Andre thought. Kind of all along the lines of the voodoo Barbie-like larger dolls of the wives of the Nebraska governors' in a display case in the front entry of the governor's mansion down in Lincoln which was the HQ for the Illuminati according to that very high hippy busker Andre happened to work with one miserable winter. The dolls are extraordinary with one Ken doll for Governor Orr's husband. People called delegates, from all over the world get to walk into the front entry for official luncheons and the first thing they get to see are these voodoo dolls straight out of 'Chuckie' make you cringe at what happened when they'd come to life at midnight during a full moon: Nebraska/Alaska. Outposts, unsupervised hee-haw backwards countries—where a man can breathe wide open. The type of places that give you Sarah

Palin as governor. What a world. It was. She might even shoot her dog—if she felt she had to. How it is on those farms and ranches across the fruited plain where the deer and the antelope play. The dogs can't be killing the livestock and/or they got to be able to herd and hunt—earn their keep, ain't no free lunch. Out on the ranch. Out on the farm. Or the Reservation, at least not for dogs. Andre recalling one early morning waking up at the farmhouse to the report of a .30-06 as his uncle William sent a wild dog to his eternity as it came upon the front field where his hogs and some cattle be. And it was just beginning. Or ending. For the mob. Run Bambi run. Andre heads to Scheels Sporting Goods Store to buy some ammo. And get a little fishing gear, got to catch him some good catfish along Salt Creek before it conjoins with the Platte and his father Michael's ashes lay.

And then one evening the basketball coach for Rummel that play like the Harlem Globetrotters, Coach Chuck who was Mavis's fancy man and king of getting the technical foul with five daughters (his Indian name), proposes to the crew that they all leave the jazz of the Red Lion Bar and head to the VIP Lounge and that's where Andre gets to meet Gonzales and his wife. He's running to be the Douglas County Sheriff, his wife is an Omaha cop. Mancuso and Sacco grew up with him and though he was a Democrat—they vouched for him and said he was cool and attended his fund raising parties at their Coach Chuck's and his Georgia cracker blondie girlfriend, Mavis's, dago red wine place: Vino Paradiso. Teachers Gone Wild Terri Baby was waitressing there and later told Andre she had run into a couple of his friends there—Mancuso and Sacco. Well it was a pleasant and entertaining evening as Coach Chuck had regaled in the story of how city councilman Vinnie Palermo had been at the fundraising gala and had slapped Coach on the back saying gregariously, Chuck—"anything you need, anything you need…you give me a call, anytime."

He tells the troupe as Andre scans his surroundings looking to see if he recognizes anyone in these ancient haunts of his. Andre informs Gonzales that he'd spent the other evening smoking cigars at the Havana Garage with Sacco and Mancuso—some of his boys from the hood…get things relaxed. It was a good night and a lot of live conversation and laughs. Later on, Terri Baby, the enchantress, took him back to her place to drink shots of tequila and get the pit bulls braying at the full moon. She abused him.

The race was tight. Politics, politics, politics and the powers that be… A few weeks later Gonzales loses by a few points…and a couple of weeks later it hits the fan as Vinnie Palermo is indicted along with another dude named Palermo who happens to be a cop and is not Sicilian but is Mexican, along with Ritchie, a brother of Gonzales who happens to be an Omaha cop and not just a beat cop but a captain. Andre reads the headlines of the Omaha World-Herald which is owned by Warren Buffett who happens to get his haircut by the same barber Andre's Lebanese bookkeeper went to. Andre digresses to give the general drift of how things work and happen all the fucking time. In Omaha. Andre also watches the local TV news as Quanecia Fraser laid it this tale of woe about some accounting discrepancies and inconsistencies in the Latino Peace Officers Association. One of the main charges that came up was titled; conspiracy to commit wire fraud. Andre shakes his head—does anything change in South Omaha? Almost a hundred and fifty years and the song remains the same. It would make Andre's ancestors proud. He reads and watches more of this as he peruses the mug shots of the alleged culprits in their orange jail suits. A cop from Counciltucky named Jack Olson— he was one of the primary fundraisers. He was residing in jail as well. It sounds like quite a bit of the fundraising involved trips to Las Vegas. Kind of a simple story. Andre reads. He also watches local TV news lady Julie Cornell break it down—oh heavens, ring a ding-ding and for a more complete coverage on the subject matter he dialed into Erin Hartley's reportage as Nebraska National Guard with Nebraska State Troopers head down to the border because of dough-head's executive order. The local TV babes giving us the news better than the national news... if one was paying attention. There's all kinds of grifters.

Later on at Big Red Keno, to choose some numbers and smoke a couple of cigarettes, Andre talks with Mancuso. Mancuso says, "Vinnie's a good guy—he just can't stay out of trouble. And later on later on, near the Platte River where dead cows float on by during floods... Andre is fishing along oxbow lake near his trailer with his Nicaraguan Sandinista cohort Tuco who brings an amigo from El Salvador with him named Flores who has a lot of ink on him. Andre asks him if he's a member of MS13—who had recently taken over an apartment building in South O—he says, "Nah," but he went to visit his abuela, little grandmother... and had to escape El Salvador after just a couple days because of his ink—that wasn't gang affiliated. They do some fishing. The guy's a tree cutter. Andre asks him who he works for... Flores replies that he is employed by Vinnie's Tree Cutting. They all fish for a few more hours. It's hotter than hell. They get talking a little more—and it dawns on Andre that Flores works for Palermo. He didn't know what the dude's business had been; so he begins asking questions... Flores says the son is trying to keep it together, but the latest wife is trying to take the business while divorcing Vinnie's as he hangs in Federal prison. And again, Andre knew Vinnie had a son because Terri Baby is friends with the nurse at Indian Hills Elementary off 31st and U Street (where Andre has also substitute taught sometimes as a gym teacher) and Terri Baby's been instructing kindergarten for twenty-five years (lot of hijabs there—got to get out the prayer mat) and it's a few blocks from some of the oldest public housing projects in Omaha, with a sister who was married to Palermo. Andre is not up to speed with how many wives Vinnie has had. But Flores like Mancuso, says Vinnie is a good guy— he just can't stay out of trouble. The way the world turns—in Omaha, one to two degrees of separation. What would Marlon Brando say? Or Malcolm X? It'd all make protesting, fighting Nick Nolte proud— drunk as he is, having worked at the Falstaff Brewery in his youth while selling counterfeit draft card documents. So goes the beat, the hustle and the house edge.

CHAPTER SEVEN

TEAMSTERS

"This is the truth," we say. "You can discuss it as much as you want; we aren't interested. But in a few years there'll be the police who will show you we are right."

— *The Fall*, Albert Camus

Like a French movie, Andre remembers the strike with Teamsters as a young man. He was kicked off operating heavy equipment sometimes by the business agents of the union. He would call up Donnie Dickau the big, tough black haired, dark complexion truck-driving superintendent cowboy who'd been in KO-REA... and ask him what he wanted him to do—refuse? Donnie who was quick with a hook at dropping mouthy foremen, would start laughing, "Oh I don't think you should do that. A lot of these guys are ex-boxers and besides I don't want to get Rudy and Roy all worked up. Just get off the machine."

Other times they'd get hit on site with a crew and get to hear a little speech by the organizers and Andre would inquire if they had any "literature" available. That kind of seemed to throw them.

Andre liked the truck drivers and he liked filling in when needed, hauling the rock and asphalt. If the day was rained out maybe it's six in the morning—them Teamsters are hitting the bar: Deano's or Huck's, maybe the Hickory and some eventually to Sparano's go-go club called Mickey's at 15th and Harney for cocktails and dancing. 'Lot of cops hung out there. Funny thing, Jimmy Hoffa didn't drink.

A couple years ago he found himself back truck driving and running front-end loader. The project was building a new golf course on hills five hundred feet high—half a million cubic yards of material moved. Most of the hundred working on it were Mexican nationals with their bracero temp cards; they'd do their seven months, go back for a visit and vacation for a while and then rotate back. Some of them had been doing it with this construction company or others for over twenty years. It didn't seem that difficult or complicated to Andre—they weren't storming the border. The rest of the crew were blacks or hill-billies. Everybody mostly got along just fine, having a lot of laughs doing some hard-ass work, six days a week, ten hours a day, making money. The company was out of Lincoln and went all over the world building golf courses. Andre talked to the owner once for about ten minutes—he was pretty cool. Andre flew across them hills, driving them trucks hard wanting to make them old Teamsters he worked with from the past proud—especially ex-Marine big toothless brawling son of a bitch Duane Honze, a hard man.

Tom continues in the narrative: by the early Fifties the Teamsters were over a million members strong and one of the most powerful unions in the country. There's a fellow named Barney Baker who roved these parts of Omaha as an organizer for the Central Conference of Teamsters out of St. Louis back in the fifties and sixties. It was an eleven state region with the nice fat Central States Pension Fund—to make loans. For casinos. The mob had inculcated itself into the unions over the last couple of decades. Initially for muscle to fight against the employers hired thugs. The mob was good at playing both sides. Hoffa gets the rap a lot, but it was just doing business: what it took. He didn't buy all the revolutionary workers bullshit—he was just trying to get his members the most money and best deal he could. He also didn't know why the Italians were kissing each other all the time. Baker stayed at the Blackstone Hotel, a swank joint, at 36th and Farnam when he came to Omaha. That's where Andre's grandmother lived for some time after she got divorced from Fast Eddie. She ran with the Austrian pianist who played there. Andre's aunt was a young girl at the time lived with her mother at the hotel. His aunt, who looked like Joan Baez, after attending the upscale Duchesne Academy in North O, would later on as a teenager become homeless in Omaha, then ends up joining a nunnery for a short stint, then becomes a hippy with flowers in her hair, then winds up stationed in Hawaii at a military base married to a guy over in Vietnam. Andre thought it was hard to keep track of history sometimes. Andre would much later on visit his paternal grandmother and hippy aunt in California—San Francisco and Tahoe respectively. His hippy aunt there Tahoe, with the Vietnam vet husband whose brother Jack showed up at their place in Hawaii still in his boonie gear straight out of the bush AWOL after the Ia Drang campaign, brought up to Andre how she had some Italian friends from San Fran-North Beach and that they all seemed to know Ed and his mol from socializing back there in Vegas, from back in the day… as they say. She seemed surprised. For some reason.

Barney Baker was originally out of New York working the waterfront as a collector for a gang of thugs headed by a Dunn and Sheridan. Before that career he had been an ex-prizefighter. He worked for them till they opened fire on a hiring boss in the Greenwich Village who wasn't being cooperative. He didn't die immediately and identified his assailants accordingly adding a Danny Gentile to the roster. On the waterfront with the heat being applied, Baker headed to Hollywood, Florida. He works as a doorman at a nightclub owned by Meyer Lansky and Lansky's brother Jake. Sheridan locates to Hollywood and gets arrested and while waiting in the jail cell for extradition to New York, Baker visits him. They ask him where Gentile is—he makes up a story. He decides the cops are going to be pissed when they find out his ploy. So Baker runs off to Las Vegas and hides out in the Flamingo Hotel. Bugsy Siegel is still supervising the last finishing touches to the casino royale. Gentile, Sheridan and Dunn are all caught and convicted of murder with Sheridan and Dunn being eventually executed by the State of New York.

Strong-arming, intimidation and violence are all part of Baker's retinue for doing the job. Slashing truck tires, pulling trailer pins, ripping the wiring out of rigs went on to employers who did not comply along with threats, boycotts and strikes. When he was in Omaha, Baker worked with business agent Pete Capellupo. They would present contracts to the recalcitrant contractors. Fast Eddie and his lieutenant brothers paid the money. Eddie always said that—just give them a little money... Andre's father was less negotiable and to avoid the vandalism and having trucks set on fire down at the construction yard in South Omaha just off Martha Street—he always packed heat, usually in the style of a 9mm German Luger. It all seemed pretty normal growing up. Except for the occasional strikes and bouts of maudlin drinking and brown paper sacks full of money that occasionally got delivered to the house by scrappy men in crew cuts.

When in Omaha, Barney Baker would be supplied with a Cadillac and driver by his good friend Julius Novak who was the owner of a major car dealership. From the Blackstone Hotel Baker would often go to eat at the Del Reo Café at 211 South 15th Street. That's where lots of union organizers would congregate and make their plans. Lew Farrell representing the Chicago Syndicate and also working as an organizer for the Teamsters would often join Barney for dinner at the Del Reo. It's all about the relationships. Andre ponders...

In 1958, Baker is subpoenaed to testify before Congress at the McClellan Committee which was investigating illegal activity by the Teamsters and other unions. Baker was asked by Bobby Kennedy about his work with the Teamsters and his stake in the Epicure Restaurant back in Omaha. Baker replied that it was a social club and a non-profit deal. What a great response Andre thinks—everybody knows non-profit usually means lots of profit. Barney was fuckin' brilliant. Asked by Kennedy if he had any interest in the corporation, Baker replies—no. Then asked how and why was he listed as the vice president of the corporation? Baker claimed—it was to use his name for the labor end of it and it was just a title they gave him... and that he derived no money from the restaurant. Bobby Kennedy asked

Barney Baker who "they" were and he replied he could probably remember the names of the officers if the corporation if the names were
told to him. Kennedy then asked him if he knew Stella Rotella and a
few others and Barney answered that no he did not.

In 1959, Baker gets indicted in Pittsburgh by a federal grand
jury on three counts of violating the Taft-Hartley Act. He was getting
payoffs from the president of a trucking company for which he was
the union representative for the employees of that company. Kind of
sounded familiar to Andre… between the politicians and the union
representatives—Eddie paid them all, which political party or which
union, it didn't matter… when you got 53,000 tons of asphalt business
on the line to be split with Dambrowski's Land Paving Company. In
1957 or was it 1965? So Barney gets busted and they sentence him to
two years in prison. He appeals and gets off with a $5,000 bond and
travel restrictions outside of Pennsylvania and Illinois.

In 1961, Baker gets a call from his old friend Julius Novak, the
Omaha car dealer, for some help with the Longshoremen. Novak had
around a thousand Jaguars on the docks in Newark, New Jersey in
open storage and wanted Baker to use his influence with the Longshoremen's Union to ensure that his cars weren't stolen or stripped.
Novak and Baker fly out of Chicago to Newark to meet some
Longshoremen representatives to work things out. It is a violation
of Baker's travel restrictions by the federal judge. A bench warrant
is issued for his arrest. Baker is picked up by U.S. Marshals in Miami
and he is delivered to Pittsburgh where he is sentenced to federal
prison. Baker spends two years in Sandstone, Minnesota. Andre
wonders what happened to Julius Novak's Jaguars? Andre's father
had an old Jaguar E-Type convertible from that era. The color was a
beautiful dark British racing green. Andre drove it around on dates
occasionally. His father probably did as well.

Andre recalls company parties and how drunk everybody got.
Big Frank Raabe was the truck boss and he ran the crew with his fist.
He was brown as dark leather with these gray crystalline eyes staring
out always smoking a cigar. His wife was raven haired and rough

looking, but sexy for an older woman. He'd brag everyone how she could beat the shit out of them all. The he'd piss his pants. Those J.J. Jones Asphalt and Construction company parties (picnics and circuses) got pretty out of order sometimes. Those were tough dudes, veterans many of them, from WW II, Korea to Vietnam—magnificent bastards. Looking back Andre wondered about how Abbie Hoffman and his yippee ki yay crew were planning on dosing the public water supply with LSD, but instead Andre thinks maybe elements of Soros financed government gender preference confused elements have been dumping estrogen into the public water sources. What happened to all the dudes? Andre recalls living with a devout feminista Democrat and how he would get these hysteric lectures every morning over his bowl of Grape-Nuts before heading to work. She eventually decided he was an incorrigible sexist narcissist Neanderthal (which he was/ is) and got herself a more pliable emotionally nose-ring wearing with his man bun deftly intact, sensitive gumby beta morph-male. But the fighting and sex had been great though the general relationship was a train wreck (she would strike out at him for what he often said sometimes lashing out that it was "mansplaining" swearing she had never hit anybody ever before—so it was Andre's fault because he was possessed of toxic masculinity). Yet it was ultimately another cautionary tale racked up for the files which some mistakenly call wisdom. He'd been down so long… Andre hadn't known which way was up. Thus he would repeat the cycle (he thought it was normal to be in a constant state of anger and turmoil with physical violence in relationship)…with more beautiful high-strung women who zealously regarded estrogen charged matriarchy as the only answer to all the world's ills. Throw in some mythological Aztec/Santeria/ Gypsy voodoo with some Appalachian snake handling and you're in business: Poor Mother Earth.

Hoffa loathed the Kennedys and had warned the Mob not to get behind the Kennedys in the election—that Joe didn't have any control over those boys: Sinatra was wrong he told them. Hoffa was a realist and a violent man having fought the employers' goons a lot back in the thirties. He unabashedly threatened violence publicly and in private against them. Bobby pursued him with the possessed vengeance of a fanatic. Ironically, the Democrat, RFK might have done more to destroy the organized labor movement more than any other politician with his hatred for Hoffa. The assassination of JFK would get a lot of heat off Hoffa. He stood to benefit greatly with JFK's death. But so did LBJ, the mob, the CIA, etc. Hoffa had some liabilities, he had close links to the likes of Santo Trafficante of Tampa Bay and Carlos Marcello of New Orleans. These two Mafia dons names come up most often in regards to the assassination along with Sam Giancana who shared a girlfriend with John Kennedy—Judith Exner and Russell Bufalino whose cousin was longtime counsel and attorney for Jimmy Hoffa who was also tight with Chicago mobster Red Dorfman who was childhood pal of underworld figure Jack Ruby who of course as everybody knows...silenced Oswald, the patsy, Marine and supposed defector who had four months prior to the killing of Kennedy had given a lecture at the Jesuit college of Spring Hill in Alabama. Why are Jesuits and the Marine Corps so often involved in nefarious and clandestine operations? The seminarian- narrator Tom digresses.

It is known that two months prior to the assassination that Ruby was making telephone calls to Teamster associate Barney Baker. Ruby may have just been calling for professional in getting some muscle to deal with some labor problems at his juke joints. The Warren Commission and other committees considered Hoffa but concluded it was improbable he had anything to do with it. The Teamster not discussed much was the president of the local out of Delaware—Frank Sheeran who was involved with the Bufalino crime family out of Pennsylvania. He was a truck driver who had fought in World War II in Patton's killer division—they took no prisoners, from North Africa to the Italian campaign (Sicily, Salerno and Anzio), through southern France all the way to Germany. Sheeran gets into some trouble and his union attorney, Bill Bufalino, gets the case thrown out and decides he should meet his cousin Russel because maybe he thought Sheeran was a handy guy who could make a good house painter. Sheeran ends up working for Bufalino as well as becoming a president of a Teamster local out of Delaware besides running with Jimmy Hoffa a lot. He often worked as a driver for both Russelll Bufalino and Hoffa. He claims to have helped load up a bag of guns that were put in an airplane heading to Dallas in 1963. He also called a strike on a newspaper so that an expose' article on Lunch Bucket Joe wouldn't come out before an election in Delaware—he bragged afterwards he could get whatever he wanted from Biden with that favor. The military records show that Sheeran was in 411 days of combat. He spoke of massacres of prisoners, revenge killings and reprisals to Nazi concentration camp guards at Dachau. Also he made it clear that if one went AWOL with their unit going back into combat—one had better keep going cuz if caught the officer would just shoot you without even bothering to blame it on the Germans. Orders were given, come across a German pack train of mule drivers in the Harz Mountains—have them dig their graves, then kill them. Sheeran states that this inured him to killing. It was a job. A job that he would later take up with the mob as a hit man—or, one who painted houses. While working as a Teamster organizer and president of a local. And possibly being the assassin of Hoffa, his friend, with two bullets to the head, who was just trying to wrest control of his Teamsters from the mob after just getting out of prison with a pardon from Nixon. Fuckin' rough sport, Andre thinks...this union organizing. There were definitely some baddies out of his union experiences back in the Northwest, back in Seattle, between the Carpenters, the Iron Workers and the Longshoreman lest we forget the Merchant Seamen that frequented the New Museum of Hysteria and Indecision—the artists Walker and Murphy and three tours in 'Nam, the Hawaiian leprechaun, Green Beret Major Leroy Capili entertained all: to the crabbers working the deadliest catch coming down off the drugs to tattooed-up punk bands from the UK, to mysterious dudes named Hamid showing up out of nowhere after nine years gone, to well-traveled vets special forces blackamoor Cat O' Nine comrades of Leroy along with the recently freed from the joint convicts (old friends) as the parrots flew about … amongst all the cacophony of artistic debris, drugs and guns. From these memories Andre is reminded of the time, when he was a young man, and he goes to the hall of the Iron Workers Union to become an apprentice—everything is going pretty good in the interviews, general knowledge exam and the hands-on practical tests. The main dude sits down with Andre and praises him for his poise and acumen and how there's only one last question to ask—and he peers seriously into Andre's eyes and solemnly says, or inquires: "Were your parents married when they had you?" And Andre is perplexed and thinks that's a mighty curious question to ask for getting a construction job as the final question, but Andre is young and wants to get hired on with the Iron Workers and so he answers: "Well—ye-ah, my parents were married when they had me." Like … that's not real unusual. And the main representative dude exhales and responds—"Damn man, that's too bad cuz we only take bastards." And that was the end of Andre's future as an Iron Worker. Tom Rudloff was kind of relieved about that one. Hey—he did some time with the Carpenters Northwest Local 70.

This was all just wild shit that his grandfather and father had been dealing with for decades. Andre had just gotten a taste of it. The power and the glory. And the money—driving around with the top down in a sleek British racing green E-Type sports car with a pretty Puerto Rican gal like some kind of fancy frat boy—boy that shit didn't last long in his life. He remembers going to meeting with the contractors working on union issues for the spring building season, attempting to try and avoid strikes which were bad for business. Andre had been involved in coming up with alternatives insurance wise, etc. to compete with the Teamster's Central States Fund which financed a lot of Vegas casinos for the mob through Hoffa's business relationship with Sylvia Pagano. She polished the willful hillbilly in the formalities of the Italian ways of doing business—he never got the kissy stuff. Andre recalls going over all that bullshit and thinking how do we compete and why bother. Soon thereafter, it was all to be a moot point anyway. But he did like the part in his research for this Mother Jones article that Bufalino was the don who gave the okay for the movie The Godfather and took the part away from Vic Damone because it had already been awarded to Al Martino to play Johhny Fontane. Just breaking business down, with these boots made for walking…just like smoking Nancy Sinatra says. Andre fellt like jumping into a Mack truck with a thirteen speed Roadranger and hauling thirteen tons of asphalt. Set them truckers free. Let them truckers drive. We needin' a damn convoy. Badly. For FREEDOM—the heart and soul of this country. As Sergeant Warsocki was saying today like ex-Marine and trucker Duane Honz was always sayin' from not that long ago—"got all these wimps we send to government as elected representatives makin' up all these fool rules, thinkin' they're leaders or somethin'… Bunch a goddamn sissies! U-nucks! Ever heard of E-u-nucks? That's what we got. They ran the Byzantine Empire right into the ground at Constantinople. Half of them there goddamn balls haven't even dropped! Listen to that attorney general we got now. With his DOJ and FBI committing law-fare: treason, simple pure treason with that pipsqueak Fauci in Pharma's pocket—we've lost a lot of our best non-coms, cops, nurses and firemen cuz they didn't want that liar's shot. Just ask Ice Cube: he wasn't just gonna take the jab cuz the Man told him! Good on him—and he lost a lot of goddamn mo-nay for taking a stand." The trades and the truckers/Teamsters had plenty of that too—essential workers got to work…to deliver gear, make stuff and haul the garbage and trash away. It's not an abstract postmodern world of Derrida and Foucault (French guys) America needs its Freedom Fries…

How it works: in the trades—construction/contracting. The key to non-union labor was the Mafia. They controlled the unions. The stewards were made members or family. If a contractor was paying union they might have a profit of 15 percent. If they were working non-union they'd make more like 30 percent with the kickbacks to the Mob. From New York, Milwaukee, Kansas City, Cleveland and Chicago back in the 1970s into the 1980s the Cosa Nostra had the control Teamsters. That's why they needed to get rid of Hoffa. With control of the Teamster's pension fund, Central States, (Andre recalls talk of Central States though he didn't fully grasp the meaning) the Mafia had their own private bank to finance the Vegas casinos and to skim millions of dollars into their own coffers. The Gambino family in New York had the local's Irish president John Cody in their pocket. To get a Teamster foreman off the gate at a construction site would cost $40,000. This arrangement usually worked with everybody happy. But sometimes developers would not want to play. According to Sammy the Bull Gravano who was big in the construction business, back in the day—they take a developer, somebody like Orange Man Bad, just as an example—he says he wants to go with his team: a hundred percent union. Somebody goes and whispers in the superintendent's ear—don't go with this drywall outfit or this plumbing crew; they don't listen. The Mafia calls John Cody or his successor, Bobby Sasso—he arranges that a deadbeat nephew with his card goes down and works the gate checking everybody. Trucks pile up— delay, delay, delay. A hundred million project that is suppose to take two years is going to take five. Orange Man Bad flips out. Is forced to go with program. Feds can't do anything—the Teamster is doing his job. Orange Man Bad or whoever pays. Nobody gets hurt, no threats made, Gravano never even meets Orange Man Bad—said they couldn't get to him because he had too many ex-FBI agents hanging with him. How it worked…according to Sammy the Bull. From back in the day. You had to be tough-tough-tough—bite the big apple. Just ask Shaq, Herschel Walker or Mike Tyson about Orange Man Bad… telling them to tuck in their fuckin' shirts. What an asshole. And don't forget Kanye—get down girl, go head get down… Oh Kanye be crazy. And Jim Brown. Everybody presumed he was just promoting that stupid celebrity apprentice show… At least Andre did—he was for Tulsi, he recalls being out on the Left Coast at the time staying on a friend's sailboat and at that dive bar and how grandpa stumbled around the podium at the Dem debates…looking for an ice cream cone. What were they thinking? And now—he was a Kennedy man: RFK Jr. who was calling all the bullshit on the Ukraine and Fauci.

What a world. But RFK Jr. is a crackpot like Joe Rogan, Tulsi, Cha-pelle and Dana White. At least, according to our trusted free media. Andre didn't believe anybody. He'd just light a couple of candles and say a few of Hail Marys after a shot of whiskey. He was going to have to check that out about RFK Jr. and the dead black bear in Central Park. Maybe he was still on smack back then and eating too much roadkill. Maybe it's all bullshit rumors… how the fuck was Andre to know? He doesn't know Martha Raddatz. Or O'Reilly. But he does know know he went hunting for bear with a .44 mag lever action Marlin. Out near a logging town called Fall City. If they can prove you're crazy.

CHAPTER EIGHT

THE FRANKLIN COVER-UP

Something is rotten in the state of Denmark.

—*Hamlet*, William Shakespeare

Somewhere near Heaven, Tom Rudloff, a graduate of Holy Name High School where the famous boxers the Doyles were out of and Jim Braddock would crash on the couch occasionally after a long night of poker... continues as guide and narrates the saga, telling the history and story, going through all the cantos: it's 1978, Dean Beauregard is a teenager, sauntering home on Dodge Street. He's skipping school from Rummel High heading home. It's a little hot. He decides to stick his thumb out and hitchhike—see if he can catch a ride. An older dude pulls up in a flashy sports car. Beauregard gives him the address where he's headed. The older guy, kind of studious-looking, knows exactly where to go. He tells Beauregard he lives nearby. He zips right down Dodge coasting past Elmwood Park, entering the Dundee neighborhood. Pulls into Beauregard's driveway and drops him off. Beauregard's father happens to be home from the construction equipment office. The older guy from the neighborhood sped off in his fancy sports car. Beauregard thinks he's busted by his old man about skipping school, but instead his old man asks him angrily, "Do you know who that was that gave you a ride"

Deano shrugs, "No."

"That's Alan Baer—the heir to the Brandeis Department Store fortune—old money, he's untouchable. He just lives down the street from here. He's a known homosexual. You're lucky you're not tied up in his basement with a cock stuffed in your mouth and another one shoved up your ass! I ought to just beat the hell out of you right now for being so goddamn stupid! Get in the goddamn house! You'd a disappeared, nuthin' woulda happened to him."

Dizzy Dean Beauregard was a little high and knew his old man might really beat the shit out of him so he went inside without giving much static to dad. It was out of respect. And fear... Sometimes his old man drank too much: Korea and defending their construction equipment company from armed robbers and bullshit indictments from the FBI. Andre could relate some having been involved in his own family's indictments with the FBI and showing up to trial.

Before Epstein was killed by Hilary, there was the Franklin Cover-up. Nothing new under the sun: pedos and child sex-trafficking. The guy who gave Beauregard the lift was alleged to have been one of the primaries in the case. This is a story Dean shared with Andre one drunken evening while Andre was residing in the Howard Johnson Wu-tel Hotel. At the Bacchanal. The place was on fire and Hochek was in his element as ringmaster laughing the whole way—with this circus. Beauregard said these words in a low voice so as nobody within five feet could hear them—before the band started up again. Andre could barely hear him in his raspy whisper.

"You know they killed Caradori. Him and his son."

"It was a plane crash. Right?"

"That's the official story."

Andre had heard some about it from his father who followed it deeply. His father had sent him a copy of a book written by Johnny DeCamp in 1992 when Andre was working as a deckhand on a freighter up in the Aleutians for a little casual reading. The title was: THE FRANKLIN COVER-UP—Child Abuse, Satanism, and Murder in Nebraska. The book scared the hell out of the whole crew on the boat. So Andre was fairly versed in discussion with what Beauregard was to speak as well as hanging with Warsocki back in the '80s who ran DeCamp's bar called Johnny D's. Warsocki had shared some inside information over the years with Andre in regards to the matter.

"Planes crash."

"Yes they do and it's the preferred method of assassination these days. Shooting is too gangster, but a mechanical problem/mishap on an airplane… Always open. De Camp was the attorney for several of the victims. He got his pal, William Colby, who he knew from the Phoenix Program, to investigate the death of Caradori."

"Yeah, yeah I'm acquainted with that. Colby running the CIA in 'Nam—they killed a lot of VC. I know DeCamp was one of the dudes. I had friends back in Seattle who were Green Berets and a part of that as well."

"Well—you know if they can prove you're crazy…"

"All the time. Especially for assassinations."

"Colby reluctantly got involved… Back in the '70s, he was in the middle of the Church Committee hearings about intelligence activities. He maybe spoke a little too openly because shortly thereafter President Ford fired him and replaced George H. Bush as his successor heading the CIA."

"Colby was a devout Catholic. And he hated communism. Believed that the CIA should be held accountable to Congress."

"Well the Franklin Committee run by Senator Schmit wanted some answers. This is a Nebraska committee, of course."

"Yeah—I know… it didn't go national. Kept the clampdown on it pretty good. Did the Governor/Senator Bob Kerry run interference on that? What'd they name that bridge after him anyway for—shit the dude went to Vietnam for six weeks that sucks his lower leg got shot off but he's still alive and well—and pretty fucking mute… he might as well be the Catholic Church. Hey! Why didn't they name the bridge after an old Indian or something—wouldn't that have made a lot more sense?"

"Sense is a rare commodity. And the Pope's a dope and... Kerry's in New York City—teaching college at some New Age Malthusian cult school. Him and Debra Winger broke up. I don't know if he's been back to Nebraska in twenty years. I don't know why they didn't name the bridge after an Indian. Cultural appropriation I guess. He stayed very far away from the sexual plundering going on at Boys Town and throughout Omaha. "

"Well this whole deal reeks like an early version of Epstein."

"Exactly! Like Epstein—who's on the flight manifest of the Lolita Express to the island? What a fuckin' world, huh? Let's see the flight logs—what's Durbin hiding?"

"Got to be some kind of intelligence program... The list is crazy: Bill Gates, Bill Clinton, Prince Andrew. They could go to whatever island they want. Why go hang out with that putz? Gates' wife divorces his sorry ass soon thereafter meeting Epstein and publicly describing Epstein as evil. Kind of harsh right off the bat from her, pretty public and more about Bill than Epstein really....and there's plenty of guys not ever brought up—Al Gore, Prince Charles, etc. Cuz they weren't there."

"Well that's fucked up and weird. Got to be some fire. But it ain't any weirder and badder as this Franklin deal. A nationwide network. Sinister. With Larry King singing the national anthem at the Republican convention for Reagan!"

"It would appear so. And that's saying a lot. Especially after Epstein's suicide. Ja-ha! These suicides are an epidemic!"

"Yeah, right! Hilary got him. Ha! In Fort Knox jail New York. Ja-ha! Well, the fuckers got Colby too." Beauregard quiets down when a group of drunk women stagger by.

"Such strange circumstances. A whole lot of smoke. Must be some fire. The Mob dudes who spent time there say—no way. Highly unusual. Maybe it was Liz Cheney—she's a Republican; got to save the NeoCons. It's all the same party. War is a racket—got to keep'em going: follow the money… It's about the MONEY. Smedley Butler knew, one badass Marine general. What a farce, you think they're even checking the Venezuelans for COVID let alone TB? What with the fukkin' border wide open and millions of people wanting to illegally invade our country, the stupid lockdowns due to jive—if that shit was so lethal there should have been bodies pilin' up in mounds at all those drug-addled homeless zombie encampments out on the Left Coast. Old rock stars telling us now to wear a mask—that have been provin' to be useless. The whole thing is a fukkin' bozo nightmare." Andre adds in a low murmur with a grin full of contempt.

"Lame-o Howard Stern pontificating…like people think he's cool or something. What a fuckin' clown—sitting in his mansion, probably wearing a mask. And the Rage—Against the Machine… I thought they were suppose to be ANGRY singing all their protest songs rapping: 'and now you do what they told ya….and now you do what they told ya…' What a bunch of little bullshitters. And now they're telling us all to get in line, take a mandated fucked-up shot that hasn't been totally tested. Or else. What the fuck. Was at this hip barber shop off Leavenworth, all these young dude all tatted up, got the Jamal dude like it's the Mod Squad and it's cool, I'm just new in town…they start talking all this gang bullshit: Crips and Bloods… like I was well acquainted with that thirty years ago back in South Seattle. Couple years later, the Wu hits am back in Omaha: need a haircut, go up there. Oh—you need an appointment, a mask, six feet, follow protocols. Fucking bullshit sissies with their tattoos. I go down the street only a few blocks, an old girl having a cigarette out front of her shop—gives me a cut: no drama, no masks. I go to Theresa now. And we go have a drink sometimes. At Scarpello's. Theresa Swoboda—North O girl from the hood got kicked out of Holy Name High School, even knows Herky and Hurley and a few other pals of mine, ends up graduating from Tech while her sisters and brothers were North High grads and she goes to beauty school downtown Omaha eventually marries into the Swoboda clan of deep South O, she goes. My old man and family were tight with some of the Swobodas. She knows ten times what these little hip millennials know. Ah, it's a small world… Take the jab even if you don't have a compromised system. Ah yeah, it's amazing, even the cackling Veep Twinkle Toes Kamala said she wouldn't take it if it came from Orange Man Bad as she secured bonds for rioters in Minneapolis as a senator. No wonder everybody's so fucking confused. Ice Cube knows the score—NWA baby! Hey! They might be Hilary lovers…those chicks that just walked by," Beauregard licks his lips judiciously, lasciviously while Andre looks at the buoyant women of various complexions with their ball caps sideways wearing their hip-hop hoodies, neck tats, nose rings and recent Morgan Wallen tees—probably heading to the Tequila Garage.

And says, "Nah—if they vote, they ain't votin' for Hilary. Love Julia Dreyfus and that show Veep—we're living it…with Princess Giggles. But easy Pentheus, them are women of Thebes and in a Bacchic frenzy—they'll tear you to pieces. Ja-ha! Let's go over the death of Colby, then we'll go over the larger looming circumstances of Omaha's own Franklin Community Federal Credit Union. First off, according to several, though Colby never publicly say that investigator Caradori's death was murder—he apprised several people affiliated with the Franklin Committee that Caradori's death was an assassination. Colby then does an interview with some British show called The Conspiracy of Silence in 1993 about the scandal. A couple years after that he decided to go for a canoe ride at his summer home in Rock Point, Maryland along the banks of the Wicomico River, a tributary to the Potomac River. It's a cold, blustery night in April. Winds are gusting twenty five miles an hour—definitely a good time to go canoeing…"

"Go fish, baby. Ha! Orange Man Bad! Orange Man bad! There ain't no deep state…"

"Yah-yah. Calls his wife that night who is in Texas. Says he's not feeling that good, but then decides go out on the water that shitty night, right? The Coast Guard found his canoe on a sandbar the next day but no Bill. They scour the river for a week or so then lo and behold Colby's body shows up where they found the canoe, but he's not wearing any shoes on what had been a damn cold night. The Maryland medical examiner in Baltimore concluded that Colby had fallen out of his canoe that night due to a stroke or a heart attack, suffered hypothermia and drowned."

"Seems reasonable to me."

"Most people don't want to talk about this shit around here."

"As an old Chinese proverb goes—Kill one man and silence one hundred…" Andre thinks to his self—how does he get in so many of these type of discourses? Probably just luck he assumes.

"It's going to get loud here soon and those buxom Bacchanal waitresses are leering at me along with those lovers of Hilary. They're starting to scare me—with their short butchy haircuts and gnarly tattoos, but they kinda turn me on too: man rapers. Get some ecstasy. Like at a Grateful Dead show. Back at Redondo Beach. Whew! Memories. RVs full of drugs. Shiny happy people sharing EVERYTHING. And good booze. Omaha man! This is a wide open city! Half the states are still soviet right now—with goon squads. People from out of town got to let off some steam and hit some kids' hockey tournaments. From those pics of us all getting fall down drunk here—they've gone viral. Have been getting vicious attacks on Facebook from people stuck in the authoritarian lockdown states and maple fucking syrup Canada. Cuz we voted for these clowns they think they can just lock us up in some of these dipshit cities. I thought this was America. Let's hit the Holiday Lounge. Got some more crazy shit to tell you."

"Yeah—I'm here all the fuckin' time these days. Hochek laughing hard and enjoying it all like a kid at the carnival, sharing a smoke with his trusty drunk blonde assistant Mavis who greets her beau Coach Chuck with a precious kiss, who has just gotten dropped off by head of hotel security Jackson in his old Trans-Am listening to very loud white supremacist rap as the pit bull Hazard from the back seat about licks off poor Coach Chuck's ears and Jackson, the ex-con with warrants outstanding, informs Chuck that if the cops try to pull him over—he ain't stopping. Just another day in the life at the Howard Johnson Hotel. And I want to make it clear Beauregard that the Italian friends are all doing good: Mancuso, Vescio, Sacco, Billy K, Mangan and Costello. Hopefully Costello's brothers don't show up and start tearing it up—still fuckin' crazy. Go to UNO hockey games or Starksky's Bar every Wednesday—it's a family reunion Costelllo—shouting at you how they didn't see you at mass while in the same breath— howling at some godson how's that Nebraska U pussy doin' for you? They must represent close to seven high schools in Omaha. You can get your bets made good with Butch Costello. As the Italians tell old stories and maybe somewhere in the story an uncle of theirs married a "white woman" and that would get Andre cracking up, grinning. They were serious. The Costellos who have retard strength. That one knocked out the Husker All-American defensive tackle…a star who got some comeuppance delivered par avion Costello—they could get into it with the Omaha Beef, the semi-pro football team that lives here. Those games are a riot. The Beef! Andre got himself a tee! The team is in a bit of disarray because that one older waitress there has fucked over half the team. Coach isn't happy. But it's all entertaining and partying with the ex-Jet linebacker, Dante, the coach, is a blast— figuratively and literally. The band's gonna get loud—R Style. Let's split Freak Central here before the prostitutes and Aryan Cowboy bikers start arriving. But I luv gangstagrrll MC Sherri—killing me softly…man! With her song. Fuck! I live here! Andre thinks. What a scene. This place. Where America comes together as Rome's bagman Vescio describes it. Am up shit creek. Speaking of shit creek—they use to just dump the wrecked cars and trucks in the South Creek back in Ponca—this is what people saw first as they entered Ponca; Andre's mind digresses. Good thing the hotel has topnotch security with that baked badass decade plus time in pokey Jackson and his esteemed swinging around the maypole pit bull Hazard to entertain all the newly arriving hotel guests and their families. He is a good damn dog…and always carrying the goods. They just got done celebrating a birthday party for Jackson—Mavis, the blondie bar manager, had six of his aliases on the birthday cake that she looked up on him. It was a nice party, Hochek delivered a fine speech."

His life, like it just hit him. He'd been living in way worse dive hotels getting his kicks, on Route 99, back in Seattle. All you'd have to say to some people is: I'm staying/living up on Aurora Avenue…and they would grimace and shudder. Andre would wave to his neighbor the black transvestite at one joint. Every evening about the same time before heading out. He resided at about a half dozen of the dives over the years. It was cheap. There was even some community at a few of them: a communion of the down and out. Sometimes he'd reside for up to a month. Sometimes he'd just meet girlfriends at them. Andre was on the move a lot in those days—down and out in Seattle. Koreans and Indian/Pakistanis ran most of these cozy inns. Cops were pretty busy on Highway 99. Tom, the antiquarian, shakes his head recalling all the young dudes and this cocky cowboy boot wearing entitled son of privilege wreaking havoc like a demolition wrecking ball as a youth careening up the old wide sidewalks in his Camaro SS upon Tom's inner sanctuary social parlor, art gallery, halfway house bookstore and now he has sold his precious plasma and shops at St. Vincent DePaul on Leavenworth to score some fancy dead man's clothes so he can occasionally dress up and go to his rich local friends' fine parties to make connections and meet some fashionably fine old divorced debutantes. He turns the page to the next luminary literary addendum and sighs—aware that Andre has been getting his ass handed to him ever since he returned to Omaha. And so like the myth if Sisyphus, Andre keeps pushing that boulder.

The ambiance of the Holiday Lounge is ageless with the sleek colorful timeless neon sign. It's got the horse shoe bar, TVs and is kind of dark like many great historic places. They'd caught an Uber like good designated drunks and take a table in the far corner. Amazingly nobody was there that they knew. 'Lot of Rummel alumni hold their offices there. A pretty young waitress takes their order.

"Better hit whiskey now… Two Jamesons—neat."

"With a Schlitz for a chaser."

"Make mine a Hamm's. Do you know that Cesar Chavez and his United Farm Workers use to guard the border? They didn't want those on the other side of the border to undercut them—Chavez is refers to them as wetbacks."

"Fucking irony, huh? It's hard to negotiate when you got people willing to work for half the money. I've been down in New Mexico and have heard the Spanish—refer to wetbacks… Have seen big plywood signs out in the Northwest on big commercial framing project that say—GET OUT RUSSIANS. Anyway, we digress once again, but all interesting stuff. So! They kill Colby who has told Johnny DeCamp a few weeks earlier how he was going public with how the CIA has used children as pawns to blackmail certain elected representatives, celebrities and miscellaneous strivers. At least, that's one theory that has been bandied about quite a bit."

The drinks come. Andre interjects. "Do you think Liz Cheney could've killed Epstein—she's a Republican?" He's already a little drunk.

Beauregard with his sincere piercing Walloon eyes breaks out laughing, "Ja-ha! Who knows? It's wide open… One fuckin' crazy jigsaw puzzle. This Franklin deal has got a cast of characters as big as this Epstein mess. This thing is layered. Salud! To solving the sorrowful mysteries! You're a fuckin' writer, a journalist, right?" Clink go the glasses.

"Got one story published in Reader's Digest. Two in Penthouse Letters and an article in Covert Action Bulletin, Mother Jones and

Hustler and a couple letters to The Nation that were denied—they're my children, all my bastard children."

"So! Here's the quick skinny of what I got. Just to remind you or acquaint you since your banishment and extended exile has been so long… Get the whiskey flowing. Put your seat belt on. It's going to be a bumpy ride… God does not save the stupid nor does he care about a celebrity's endorsement. King had humble beginnings in North Omaha. His father had worked at the slaughterhouses for the Swift Company. He was employed there forty years starting out as a hog skinner."

"Be a rough job—black and blue. The Jungle. We all got uncles and cousins who worked at it, different friends, etc. One uncle worked with a big black dude called Hambone who just whipped them frozen carcasses around in singular motions with one arm. I only worked around there so close… all part of the same scene with Stoysich Butcher Shop just up the street. And after the football games at Al Caniglis Field, we'd pick up the seventeen dollar kegs from Falstaff Brewery that was nearby. Warsocki throwing kegger parties at sixteen years old in halls around South O. Three bucks a head. Ja-ha!"

"Well Gustavus Swift got it going with the refrigerated rail cars. Back in the 1880s. He revolutionized it. With Union Pacific Railroad headquartered here, the meatpacking industry exploded. South O—the Magic City. Anyway, comes their oldest son Larry. Goes to Central High, works as a waiter at the ritzy Blackstone Hotel—he gets a glimpse to how the rich lives. Joins the Air Force, supposedly stationed in Thailand, gets honorably discharged, has a wife, is at Omaha University and gets a business administration degree—who knows. Vietnam is happening. King works at First National Bank. He quits but gets hired to be the manager of the Franklin Credit Union in North Omaha which is operationally not doing too hot. Back around 1973, the Omaha Sun writes a glowing article lauding him for saving the credit union by his great acumen and working eighteen-hour days, etc…"

"I remember the Sun. I delivered their newspapers, running from the hoods...down at the apartments we lived near. I vaguely remember some of those wonderful pieces on King and the happy faces. We'd better order another round. I'll get the tab tonight Deano. I'll bill Mother Jones later. Or Rolling Stone...am trying to get a hold of Matt Taibbi and/or Jeremy Scahill. Them dudes should talk to Warsocki—dude's who operate a .50 cal for three years have a unique perspective. God bless the USA."

"Thanks. Good luck with that pal—think they cancelled his ass. Along with Glenn Greenwald. Probably Rogan too. With Chapelle. The Left always eats their young. They don't seem to fuck with Burr," as Dean Beauregard begins scribbling on a napkin.

"Yeah—he's too off the reservation and he don't give a fuck. But otherwise, any good liberal...don't step out of line. A fatwa against the beautiful Somali Ayaan Hirsi Ali—no problem, hear'em roar. And Julian Assange, what the fuck—where was the great Nobel Peace Prize winner Barry on that one? "He who brings the truth, keep one foot in the stirrup" old Turkish saying. Reality has been cancelled. It use to be—don't talk about politics and religion... Now, don't talk about reality. No speaky reality...like the fukkin' monkeys: monkey see, monkey do. Nobody knows why, just wear a fukkin' mask. Or else—you'll get SHAMED. It's like the fucking Salem witch trials. A lot of hysteria. And Indecision. Mock the hysterics."

"Mock the hysterics. The world now is one big political diatribe. One World Mind-Fuck. Our Bodies, Ourselves...as long as the complaint is about abortion and not a COVID jab. Ja-ha! You know Warren Buffet owned the Omaha Sun."

"Ja-ha! No, I did not know that, but I've been wandering around here the last couple of years like Rip Van Winkle; just kind of catching up after thirty-five years, pretty vacant...kind of like The Sex Pistols. Now the wizard owns the Omaha World-Herald. My Lebanese bookkeeper has got the same barber as Warren—a joint right off Dodge Street not far from the Mutual of Omaha building."

"Well that's kinda cool, kinda more down home casual Omaha—nobody get too excited. Like world champion boxer Terrence Crawford just ambles around town and goes to his kids' sporting events: track meets and wrestling matches. Plays pool at the Garage—ain't no drama. Omaha City gives him a helluva parade he most well deserves—cool as hell with all the North O marching bands and Caprices gathering in style to go party at the Steelhouse. Darling, could we get another round please—here's a twenty as a tip to keep our thirst down. Thank you so much." She walks away. Her name is Kelly: dark brown hair with a slim waistline. "Now this is going to start to get really weird and really fucked up quick."

"It was damn long time ago when I read it. And nothing came about of it. Like it nothing strange about this story ever happened—till Epstein hits the hot button and people start wondering again… Ah, y'know, maybe a little bit of that whole MeToo movement helped. Or hurt it. Fuck."

"Yeah—the little pink pussy hats. That was part of it, right?"

"Fucking triggering Shiva…ja-ha! What you writing on that napkin?"

"The broads went NUTS! The TMZ tape and Orange Man Bad with the Budweiser heir with his woke corporation. Ah-ha! Am writing a short story."

"Angie Dickinson loathed that movement—she didn't buy it, she lived it. Hot, hot Police Woman chick—probably banged JFK: they say, she don't cop to it, she don't deny… She definitely kind of had an interesting take. What'd you write?"

"Loved that woman as a kid… Let me finish it. Have got to get the words right."

"Jesus! Anyway, they went CRAZY. Orange Man Bad gets elected and Madonna rants and rages at pink hat rally to all the hysterical white women that she thought a lot about fucking blowing up the White House even though he was against the Iraq War and about the only elite publicly on the radio trashing against it and W., heard it myself. Didn't know who the hell it was, but they were making a lot of sense; about had to pull the truck over when I found out it was Orange Man Bad. No wonder the NeoCon Liz Cheney hates Orange Man Bad with her hand-washing like Lady Macbeth: guilt, guilt, guilty. Her and VP Cackler all on the same team. Ja-ha! Got to hand it to Madonna. Her too. Lady Macbeth. Blow the whole thing up. It was like a stage. But shoot—now that's a free country. No arrests: nothing. First Amendment. I think a lot of it started with that friend of Oprah and Hilary's— the fat ugly guy Harvey Weinstein the film producer… a lot of Hollywood beholden to him."

"Yeah—it was like the firing on Fort Sumter; it's some derange-ment alright: Orang Man Bad, kind of like the press's mad vitriol for Nixon—looking back on it historically. Anyway, they busted Wein-stein, Cosby, Matt Lauer, lots of celebs all running around grabbing pussies. Weinstein is still in jail, isn't he?"

"I believe so. He raised a lot of money for the Clintons and Obama. Maybe they send him organic vegan cookies from Martha's Vineyard that Obama's drowned chef baked. I dunno… He's a real charmer. As my grandfather the farmer once said: They shot the wrong goddamned man! I was like seven—was never sure who he was talking about, but I think it was the President. By the way, you ever seen any of those videos of Stormy Daniels? She likes getting schtuped up the behind a lot by a couple dudes—am just saying… Fuck I dunno—I'd do her: get some restitution! Ah-ha! Anyway— back to this Omaha mess… tell me more, back to schooly."

"Yeah, I've seen a couple of those with Stormy—not bad, not sure how many of the sisterhood of the MeToo and the View would appreciate them. I saw her down at 72nd Street at the Old Twenties Bar where I saw the Ramones play—Digital Sex opened. It's the old Club Omaha, not the new one off Center. Didn't get a go though with her. Seen a couple of her videos—the girl's not shy. The place was packed—-very patriotic night. So any hoot, King immediately buys a mansion in the Ponca Hills—where millionaires live… managing a little credit union in poor North O. Immediately alarms should have gone off, but noooo… From Pinkney Street to Ponca Hills. He is their pet, pimp and poster child, gots to prop him up as the band plays on. Some say it was tied in with money laundering for Iran-Contra. And here's the story—Baby shoes for sale—never worn. It's by EH. Says it all."

"Wow. I shudder. Hemingway! Where to start, when to begin and where to end… It is all—deep dark stuff… Yikes. Like Shaggy: Scooby Doo. 'Lot of shootings on Pinkney Street for some reason. Wasn't King getting touted as the messiah/savior of North O there for a while?"

"Yeah—kind of like the Second Coming Scott Frost was recently for the messianic starved Husker fans!"

"That's bad. The world is a mess. And Nebraska football sucks as fan plunge to their deaths from the South Omaha Bridge. So it goes. So it goes. Back in the day. Hey a dude I worked asphalt Quincy Jones, who was good on the screed and raking that asphalt smooth told me a buddy of his was back working on King's old house at Pinkney for the new owner hires a handyman to do some work cuz in the middle of the main floor was a hump. So the neighborhood handyman goes to task, gets down into through the access and comes upon a thick garbage bag buried in the crawl space full of stacks of hundreds— dead presidents. I mean we're talking a half a million dollars from all of King's drug sales and child sex trafficking. He said that dude was gone after that…had all that dough to run away."

"Yeah—urban legend. Be all renegade. That's a wild one. So much money. So few places to put it all. The laundry business is big: essential. Could be, indeed. Probably true. You want to talk about dark—look up Operation Monarch…allegedly another brainwashing op: making kids into spies. Real sinister shit—if there is anything to it…and there probably is, don't fool yourself. Like shutting down the Kellogg's plant here—state of the art facility, top producer world-wide—it's just to break the union. They had black nonunion plants in

Lincoln and all over the country under different company names, but with a Kellogg's stamp on every piece of equipment."

"Yeah, I heard about Kellogg's closing…lot of dudes we knew worked there. Our big boy Sully was a union steward there…what a shame. It's all about the greed. So, back to the Franklin cover up— King's main job was being the manager of the credit union and the goal of the Franklin Community Federal Credit Union was to give loans to the underserved black community of North O. Meanwhile, King is riding around in limos, flying about in chartered jets, wearing the finest tailored suits with all the bling as he orders bouquets of flowers to go with the best French champagne. Finally, the bust happens about 1988 as federal agents swoop down to do an audit which Larry had managed through his political machinations had staved off for years. The audit concluded that around $40 million is missing…"

"Stolen? What? Fuck—that's a screamin' lot of money! Like the invasion of Panama—what'd they do with all that money they took from our CIA asset Noriega?"

"Exactly—great question…nobody ever asks that. Buddy of mine was a Ranger and in on that one. He says they lit it up down there; bullets flying. Think about it—the military was all overhead except for the extra bullets. That had to be hundreds of millions of dollars. Where'd it go? Like King, where's all that embezzled, ripped-off stolen money? So King gets indicted on forty counts of fraud, conspiracy, etc. You know he was the fall guy—the patsy…like Oswald. LBJ had nothing to do with it and his Texas banditti. "

"Yeah, wow—where's the Senator Ernie Chambers in all of this? Spoke with him when a few years ago when I first arrived back in town—the restaurant chanteuse took me to a speech he was giving at North High. He was eloquent as usual. We had a good rap. People just don't want to hear it. We all got some brainwashing… People see and hear what they want to see and hear. Anyway, it was cool talking with him—he's a historic dude. Made it on FOX News a couple of times—with outrage. Ha-ha."

"Historic alright… He's coming, he's coming. The Senator was all over it. Ernie was relentless with this rancher from western Ne-braska—Senator Schmit. You know it would have just been another great case of shakedown like the Reverend Jesse Jackson or Sharpton, but this isn't just money and bullshit political deals. This is seedy, real dark—sinister, children. Totally fucked-up. Jesus is going to get them good. All about the blackmail," Dean peers about and around making sure nobody is listening.

"Yeah I remember it is bad like if only ten percent of DeCamp's book is true—it's real bad," adds Andre.

"Oh yeah! You remember the name Harold Andersen?"

"Nah," Andre shakes his head. "Sounds familiar, but no."

"He was the publisher for the Omaha World-Herald. Locked out the Printers Union back in the Seventies. The OWH did a lot of puff pieces for Lawrence King. More propaganda."

"Oh yeah—no thing must remain of what is passed. We did a field trip there when they were picketing. It was 1973—kind of tense. Anyway, good propaganda… always. Good for that. Like fluffers. Working for the Party. Operation Mockingbird—CIA manipulates our CNN or CIA News Network mass media circus with the likes of Anderson CIA intern Cooper and Rachel Mad-cow as FOX News sold the Iraq War as Hannity vociferously babbles on in argument with highly decorated 'Nam/Korea warrior Colonel Hackworth on the quagmire that'd become Iraq—because NeoCon Cheney needed to save Haliburton. It never ends. Just make sure they keep asking the wrong questions. Nothing new today just: Orange Man Bad, Orange Man Bad… repeat, repeat, repeat. Like the dipshit radio DJs here in Omaha—they crack me up. Don't they know there in Omaha? Me—got four decades of Left Coast utopia with hippy dippy com-munes, dystopic zombies shooting up/smoking crack on the streets, full blown riots and happy high bicycling parades with naked chicks heading to Burning Man/Rainbow Gathering/Barter Fairs—this place is so goddamn Midwest conservative and backwards they've dealt with none of the consequences around here—real immune; they just piss off all the redneck construction workers in their big pickup trucks and American flags—their audience. It is not the Woke mendicant cultural elitest Microsoft IT sissy crowd cuz mild climates make for mild people. This is Country, man—Hee-Haw Nation. It is a hillbilly state, fools! They don't coast here... Pretty funny. They jibber about doing bong hits with Cornhusker football player in the Nineties? Oh wow, whatever. Tough gig. But Orange Man Bad. Yeah he's Hitler, Hitler, Hitler—Mussolini/Stalin. Whatever. The Dems and their minions the Media are going after Orange Ma Bad hard with their hammer and sickle. Dang. Democracy for the few. The Left constantly referring to us as workers—what da' FUK... I hate working. Alright maybe I'd be a sex worker. A-ha! It is not about Orange Man Bad—it's just about the general contempt and disdain the so called "elites" have for the majority of the American people. This MAGA thing flips them out. Can't have the goddamn peasants rebelling. They don't want to lose their power and control. It's something... as Orwell writes of purges of those who don't fully conform to their ideology. Noam Chomsky reiterates and reiterates and reiterates over the decades—don't believe the lying liars of the New York Times he said in pretty much every book he wrote while not being too kind to Carter in the process—East Timor, etc. To little avail if I may say so myself. The brainwashing has worked—the manufacturing of consent has been thorough. These journalists might as well have been on Stalin's payroll back in Thirties—oh wait a minute, some of them were... paid propagandists, and they didn't bother covering the purges, liquidations, the mass starvations in the Ukraine, and then neglect what was happening to the Jews and the Holocaust as FDR sent ships full of fleeing Jews a packing..."

"Yeah, yeah... And FDR wouldn't shake Jesse Owens' hand after winning at the Olympics—he met with the whites. They don't talk much about that. And by the way, I'd like to be the fluffer on set for the gals prior to the cameras rolling. I think that'd be a great job! My dream job."

"Everybody's got to have a dream—dream big. But guy, I think that might be a myth…for dudes anyway. Ja-ha! Fuck! Get some blue chew some brothers I was pouring concrete with recommended—Shaq and Ernest. They cracked me up. Ah, we digress. Again. I don't think you heard one thing I said. It's not all about chicks all the time—just most the time. Ja-ha!"

"Okay—correct! It's three chords and the truth—'Ol Hank got it right. A-ha! Yeah, the DJs…some people aspire to be liberal here. They're just uncomfortable with laidback red-red gritty freak show Kicksville/Hicksville. Let's get to the real twisted shit. I'll give you a rough outline of some of the names of the victims, the kids and the alleged perpetrators and the institutions they were affiliated with as well as the primary defenders of the children… It's far from complete, but you'll get a grasp of the dearth of forces at work. It's mind blowing. Again, it's hard to keep track of—there's just so much shit. If a third of it is true—it's really bad. So the Republicans are pimping King, he's singing the national anthem in front of Reagan and Nancy down at the New Orleans Convention, throwing some lavish wild outrageous party. You know—who the fuck knows? Party goers included the likes of Jack Kemp and Clarence Thomas whose wife happens to be from Omaha and had ties to ex-mayor and Nebraska Congressman Hal Daub who sat on the Franklin's Advisory Board."

"You gotta be fuckin' kidding me? Gotta be careful when one gets on a lot of boards."

"Yeah—no shit. Just give'em enough rope. Well this fuckin' circus of course goes on: King, Kemp, Thomas, Anita Hill, Corn Pop, another woman named Wright—allegations, homosexuality, sexual harassment, national prostitution ring, blackmail etc. With possible links to Iran-Contra. Who fucking knows? I'm just saying. But getting back to Omaha a trail of mysterious deaths and suicides seem to hover around King. One dude had been a bouncer at The Max. You remember that joint?'

"Yeah, of course, the famous notorious gay joint—lot of drugs flowing. Back in the '80s. Was there a couple times. Check out the scene. It's gone now, right?"

"Nah—it's still around. Different location."

"Yeah, okay I walked by an anonymous looking building at about the height of the Wu and the place was packed; people waiting in line. Lots of chicks: Nebraska/Alaska. Other states, total lockdown—for a couple years! You couldn't even go out on the beach. People getting arrested for going to church! Insanity and bullshit. But here…it was hilarious. It was another fall down drunk party."

"Well King frequented the popular place a lot. Supposedly this bouncer had been making short trips to DC with King mentioning to his sister and others that he was in deep kimchi and in fear for his life. Well he commits suicide with a shotgun and leaves no note. I'm vague on a lot of the names anymore, but the Douglas County Deputy Attorney at the time had been contacted by the bouncer about if he showed up dead. A reporter had followed up on the case asking questions wanting to view the autopsy report, etcetera with the agitated prosecutor exploding on him. A couple years later Harold Anderson, after Franklin has already gone down in flames—he allows the story to run. It give me the creeps talking about it Lot of dead bodies pilin' up in mounds." Beauregard again looks suspiciously around to make sure nobody is eavesdropping. Andre shakes his head—this is crime from over thirty years ago! But even in his decades of absence, he's aware from talking with another character named Doyle who was cousin with his dear old pal Stevie Doyle and their grandfather, the famous boxer and Nebraska football player and whose father would wake up some mornings and James Braddock would be there after a hard night of drinking and cards; he was known as the Chef because he liked to cook and was the enforcer for Mickey Gaughan…that people in those years were ending up dead…like unceremoniously in a chair, tied up and naked in the middle of an empty warehouse with one of those Pulp Fiction, whatever you calls them, gag balls in their mouth: dead. Real Blue Velvet stuff. Yikes. Like LA Confidential—must be something about the water. Fucking Chinatown. Otherwise, Andre thought Omaha was pretty wholesome.

"Braddock man! Got the nickname "Cinderella Man" from Damon Runyon! Whoah! Fought and beat the killer Max Baer—who, by the way, was from Omaha for the world heavyweight championship and won. Oh my, Baer was out of order with the women and individualistic and flamboyant as Jack Johnson who shook hands with the John L. Sullivan—I've seen the picture. It's pretty cool. So hey yeah, all the Doyles are related. Somewhere back in fucking Ireland…probably to the Kennedys. Anyway, getting back…not a real pretty picture—especially for some of our most esteemed institutions: the FBI looks pretty bad on this one, Boys Town gets a pretty bad black eye in the deal, up there harvesting, grooming who they could, etcetera. Hang on—it's going to be a bumpy ride. A couple of the main kids, some of whom spent quite a bit of time in prison, like locked up to get them to shut up was a couple of sisters named Washington, an Alisha Owen, a Paul Bonacci, Danny King along with many others. Peter Citroen's in the mix too—the goofy entertainment editor for OWH and the Sun who also didn't live that far from me and my brothers at the family home in Dundee. I got an old neighborhood associate, construction dude, Joe Curry, was hanging out at bars in North O and Carter Lake getting drunk and doing blow on the tables hearing Alisha recounting the tales of blowing Wadman. This was in real time! She's a teenager! Like she's just making this shit up. How many teenage girls in Omaha could even tell you who was chief of police? Ironically, I earlier been awarded a commendation from the Omaha Police Department signed by Chief Wadman for assisting some cops who were getting the shit knocked out of them on the street downtown. I pulled over in my '74 Duster and ran over and knocked the dude out. Even went to testify at the trial."

"You made Father Laughlin proud. Good job. Yeah—in the Happy Hollow District. He did time. I know he picked up Costello and Lahood one night back in the late '70s, but figured out pretty quick he'd get his ass kicked if he tried any funny shit with those juvies. Do you know that weirdo held the Guinness World Record for eating gherkins—small pickles?"

"No way! Twisted. See no evil, hear no evil… a lot of complicity of silence. Like the Church: mute except for a few priests and nuns. Nobody at the paper saw nothing amongst Huey, Dewey, Louie and Zooey?! Not one reporter could get on his rotary phone to ask a few questions?"

"I know—it's incredulous…am not bullshitting you. Look it up. He probably still has it. I mean who would do such a stupid thing—twisted. Not ironic. I worked with some hood down at the construction yard as a kid—Tommy LaMoffa was his name. A long hair hood not much older than me but decades of light years beyond me. He was a tough kid. We got along okay. Peter Citroen approached my old man, who barely knew Citroen, to give this kid a summer job. Tommy supposedly lived with Peter Citroen. Nobody thought nuthin' of this shit in the '70s. Hell who knows what the kid went through. He wasn't there that long… When all that child rape charges first popped up on Citroen I wondered about that kid. I think Citroen was one of the fall guys…y'know like: see—we got a bust. "

"Oh, I believe it." Kelly brings them another round. "Thank you Kelly. Keep it on my tab."

"Whatever—have no idea at this stage. On anything. Normal—remember normal?"

"On anything… So this fucked up shit that's going on now with that wide open border and a hundred thousand kids who crossed over and nobody knows where they are…was going on here back in the'70s and '80s. Nationwide. These kids were getting flown around. There's even a place called the Twin Towers where a lot of the sexual/drug trysts occurred. Hell the Omaha chief of police was supposedly involved beside Alan Baer, the Brandeis heir. Dude! I mean they are moving these kids around with lots of cocaine. I will tell you another detail which points to some of the weirdness; Father Hupp ran Boys Town and knew something was up that stank real bad. He said that he'd heard rumors that staff members had been shuttling Boys Town kids off to a restaurant owned by King. Hupp wasn't allowed to investigate this because his successor Val Peters had given orders to the Boys Town police to arrest Hupp if he was ever present on the campus. I mean how weird is that? Of course—if this claim is true."

"Man—that is fucking strange like bizarre. This shit is deep. And dark. Real sinister stuff. Cynical theories."

"And supposedly Hupp brought up the matter to the archbishop of Omaha and he advised Hupp to just walk away from the whole deal. Real surprise—guess Hupp didn't really trust the archbishop or Father Val much after that."

"Shocker. How paranoid. What's the fucking endgame?"

"Always. Ja-ha! Yeah, can't imagine why. Another book has come out on it. Believe the guy's name is Bryant—it's thorough. With spooky coincidences a constant."

"Just a Hamm's for me. Thanks. Cover-up. Lots of it. To protect…but it usually makes things worse. Sanctimonious fucks. When you're so goooood… I'll have to check out that other book on it."

"So this is a rabbit's hole—a subterranean world just below the surface of all the white picket fences and bluebirds singing. Sinister. We got kids like Owens stuck in York at the women's penitentiary who says she was at parties at the Twin Towers and down at the French Café in private rooms having sex with the police chief of Omaha. Grand jury investigations determined that all allegations of abuse were baseless and a carefully crafted hoax… Amazing, the kids just made up the whole thing. Crazy how they came up with all these specific details. Wow. It's a long time ago. Shit like 1983. This Alisha has his baby and she's like fifteen! Supposedly. But she don't change her story. Ever. They just keep throwing her back in jail—for years. She's a political prisoner basically. Investigator Caradori does interviews with her. Shrinks check her out: evaluations. She gets out. She runs with some of the same boys used up in this nefarious cabal. Alisha Owens picks up a couple of felonies for like check kiting… so any time she'd hit the stand she was mercilessly attacked by the prosecutors for being a felon rather than a kid who got massively abused. The Omaha field office for the FBI it sounds like didn't treat her much better. Also, I heard recently since returning, one of the owners of the French Café had a young Italian boy maybe fifteen—everybody knew. A conspiracy of silence."

"Everybody's got to cover their ass and protect the powerful. She was one of the most damning I remember…a lot of the others particularly the boys were so damaged from all the sexual abuse and drugs… When the hell did she finally get out of the women's reformatory in York?"

"Jesus—she'd get out for a little while, John DeCamp might defend her or some other attorney. They'd throw her up on the stand and put her back in the pen for perjury. I think she was behind bars sometime up until 1997. I think the College of St. Mary eventually gives her a full scholarship. And Metro Tech did something like that."

"Whatever happened to the police chief?"

"I don't know. He went away somewhere. Maybe The View knows. That's where I get most of my pertinent info: Ode to Joy, Sunny and Whoopi—whose real name is Karen. Spelled a little different, but what the hell, irony abounds. Those broads know what the fuck is going on."

"Ha! Hell yes they do… They're my main news source also! How about the chick you were dating—the publisher's daughter, a Ghislaine Maxwell?"

"Aw she was a good gal—she didn't know nothing. It's a one newspaper town. She was no Ghislaine and she had too much sense to go out with me. I like to party a little bit too much sometimes—

you know. The publisher had to protect the rich and the powerful. That was his deal. Shit –you got Boys Town, the Church, scandalous stuff with Creighton and the Jesuits in the Dominican Republic— well-meaning coeds in harm's way going down there to do works of mercy and care getting sexually assaulted from DR boys who after getting raped by that one priest I can't remember his name, were pretty fucked up. Heard that Father Paco or whatever his name was, even had some of them boyos in a dorm up here—a real shit-show. With true believer/social worker-type chick whistleblowers getting fired—all the poor Margaret-Marys. What a mess. What can you do? Move them around? Cover it up? House den mothers running off with a young male student—FBI shows up at downtown hotel. Coach Chuck somehow ended up in the middle of one those trying to save the kid. OPD and FBI severely question him and he ends up spending the night in jail. Twenty five years coaching and thirteen shot dead players—a whole year's team gone. Can't save them all like a catcher in the rye—the gangs groom them young. And of course, they banned Father Hupp from being on the premises of Boys Town—he knew something was going on. Got some bad apples— got to protect the rich and powerful…strange are the ways of evil. Look at Charlie Hochek telling the story on Herek at Saint Joan of Arc. He was an altar boy there, saw kids getting raped—reported it to his parent. Said the priest was "gay" didn't know any other way to explain it. Father Herek as a kid in the mid-Seventies. Herek shows up, his parents don't believe him—how fucked up is that? They eventually put him in prison."

"I heard about that priest—a real baddy. Innumerable assaults. Another cousin of Doyle was raped by him at St. Joan, not as lucky as Hochek, kid told his dad—his dad didn't believe him and beat the shit out of him. According to Doyle his cousin was a wreck and eventually committed suicide. But the newspaper needs to sell that advertising. People really didn't know or something…look the other way. Kind of like today. Naïve. Yeah, yeah I get that and yes…have happened to notice that. You getting pretty fucked up. But man, this thing is a fucking mess: assassinations, sex trafficking, drugs, abuse of children, massive graft, homosexuality, more murder… No wonder nobody in Omaha or the whole United States country wants to talk about it. Hear much more of this shit I'm heading back to Church—and they got enough of their own problems. Man—missed the whole boat on some of them priests at Rummel. The one who ran around as a chaplain—Father Cannon—had no idea or suspicion on that one… The Monkey Priest was always a little strange. I mean the whole thing's a bad construct. Some kid dropped his drawers for him once…who knows. But anyway, what do you fucking think is going to happen? You can't fuck… It's against biology—not following the science which is the fashionable way of saying it now. Ja-ha! Men and women fuck. Males and females fuck. Whatever animal. Whatever species. Breeding happens. Life. Biology. It's all Ancestry.com. Three quarters of our behavior is coded in our DNA. Just ask a kindergarten teacher. The Latin rite should have gone the Orthodox rite—priests married."

"Ja-ha! No doubt. Breeding happens. A binary world. Yeah—y'know, all those novitiates coming into the Christian Brother Jesuit program when we were sophomore were so young and effete looking. Nice enough guys but definitely much on the lavender side. Some of them I thought were just other students. Hey, you know Malone the runaway, living alone pretty much, sent off for a while to an Irish boarding school, was getting groomed by that priest Cannon who had a mile long record from the East Coast. They'd been out for pizza at Godfather's and had imbibed in some beer drinking and ended up in the priest quarters and Malone had to fight him off—went screaming running out of the joint. "

"Yeah—that one was a surprise. Wouldn't have guessed on him—thought he was alright. Guess not. What a fuckin' program that was. Must be the end times… I heard a lot about this a couple of years ago when first in town. Doyle told me a lot on a job site. Two months later, it's all in the Omaha World Herald. Y'know, a couple of years before the Wu hit. Turned to one guy who was a few years behind us and sez to him, "Ur gonna have nightmares tonight. Ja-ha!

I then says to Doyle there was only one normal one out of the seven and I tell him which one: Pavelka—and Doyle who has got like a hundred cousins in Omaha replies—he dated my cousin and he never told her he was a Jesuit! Ja-ha! Now that's FUNNY."

"Got to laugh about something…"

"Or just hang down your head and cry. Fuckin' real blue velvet world we grew up in."

"You got that right. Forgive them Father for they know not what they do."

"Bullshit! They know exactly what they do! What's up with that prez they had a while ago back at Rummel? He was a novitiate when we were sophomores—little rosy cherub cheeked fellow the John Lennon glasses and the milky soft white hands like they paint of Jesus in those old paintings? Heard he was from some real "established" Catholic family here in Omaha—whatever the fuck that means… You gotta play ball. Didn't even know he'd become the president which means/translate—he's the king gold digger. 'Course I been gone thirty-five years or so."

"Father Schapps."

"Yeah when I first got here and heard about that scandal whenever I was with a crew of us at a bar—say Office West: I would raise a toast to Father Schnapps. That was often not a crowd pleaser. I thought it was funny."

"Last call." Kelly shows up and lets them know. They order shots, doubles and call for taxi rides. Uber in Bogart's case. Andre liked catching the orange Happy Cabs with the rick-shaw sign on the side with an Oriental in conical Viet Cong hat pulling it. His father had interest in it back in the '70s along with a bunch of lemon groves outside of Yuma. They were down there once as a family on vacation and went to take a look. Harvest time was happening and the bracero pickers were hard at it. What you gonna do? His father once had interest in a charter sailing yacht down in the Caribbean as well. It was hard to keep track of all the businesses Mike was involved with. He was part owner in some racquetball clubs as well.

"Yeah people are a little sensitive about that one. Y'know—the optics are bad."

"Ja-ha. Yes! Have heard that one before—the optics are bad. FUNNY. The beauty of understating… Ah, it was amongst consenting adults. It's lite stuff from all this prior subject matter—it's just the holy sanctimonious bullshit that's the problem."

"Let's head to King Fong's for Chinese. I'm hungry. Wish Mickey's Nite Club was still around. "

"Excellent. I'm hang-ry too. Love that old joint. Both of them. With a great marquee. We had a late night one in Seattle called Tai Tung's. We had a lot of them in Seattle. Ruby Chau's where Bruce Lee had worked. Etcetera. Call up a cab. It's a nostalgia thing. Too bad about Mickey's: cocktails and dancing—girls, lunch, girls. Warsocki hung out there with his cop buddies. The South High wrestling coach owned it. And, alas, the Cheetah Lounge: no mas either. Like the destruction of Jobber's Canyon all for glory and profit of corporate ConAgra who splits in 2015 anyway to move their headquarters to Chicago—it was the largest razing of buildings from the National Register of Historic ever committed in America."

Beauregard shakes his head in sympathy and calls them up. "Yeah—the wifey of the CEO didn't like it here; Nebraska—it's not for everybody. By the way, stay out of the Carter Lake strip clubs; Warsocki and crew decades ago got in that huge brawl with knives and clubs pulled…was a bloody mess. Fighting with outlaw bikers is rough business." Andre just nods as he recalls…it was wham-bam thank you mam the first round. One of them jacked asphalt man/ done some time Mikey. So Andre cracked him. The biker must have had a head of cement. Andre didn't believe he'd get back up, but he saw some of them running back into the club and knew they'd better move fast to his car and get the fuck out of there before the guns came out, but they didn't, fortunately they wielded only knives and axe handles. But Mikey and Warsocki fought back with fury. Andre later on clings to paramedic's hand—he don't want to let go… One week later in Saint Joe's Hospital with a variety of women and nuns visiting with holy water, petitions and centerfold posters while raucously drinking, laughing and playing bumper cars in their wheel chairs— they were released somewhat on their own cognizance from medical jeopardy Andre vaguely reminisces: nobody learned a fuckin' thing. "So, back to the issue, Father Schnapps according to a wedding Tim Doyle was at in Chicago for some Rummel dude a few years behind us says Father Schnapps kept going on about how good the groom looked who he had mentored when he was a young novitiate. The kid had a mother around but no daddy—you know how they find these guys. So anyway, Schnapps is just lit and everybody is like we gotta take care of Father Schnapps. Meanwhile, Father Schnapps doesn't once mention how fine the bride looks—it's all about the young groom. Doyle is pretty drunk, but nothing like Father Schnapps. They're outside the hosting hotel, he's kind of keeping an eye on Father Schnapps. Y'know, he's a pretty open minded guy."

"Was a helluva nose-guard and fullback in the football sport. Pretty chilled dude. Really took care of his chemically imbalanced schizophrenic wild man cousin Big Ten offensive tackle Stevie: motorcycle jacket on saying—Hate & War on it, punk rocker wild man! We should've listened to Stevie and started that band. My regret. Our regret. The crew."

"Well out of nowhere…downtown Chicago, a big limo comes flying up out of nowhere. The door pops open and Father Schnapps jumps in and it jets off. Doyle is standing outside there with others as they're all wondering what the fuck—right?"

"Doyle told me this story when I first come to town—it's pretty funny. It was on a construction site. Doyle Painting: there's like seventeen contractors in Omaha with the name Doyle. The rest are attorneys—some canon lawyers. Bagmen for Rome, handling the Church's business. Like Vescio. The dude's got the juice and skinny on this town."

"He's definitely a Blues Brother. Finish your drink. Taxi's here. Let's hit Milt's for golf sometime following an afternoon at Horsemen's Park betting on the ponies. A little relaxing nine holes. The joint has a Madonna in front—prayer before golf. My kind of place! Then end up at Tequila Garage for some sampling. See if Costello and Hochek want to join. Hey! I already got the tab."

"I'll leave the tip for Kelly. I use to date her sister."

"Oh I know. Bragging all the time. Get over it. You got arrested development. You're old."

"Kelly's fine. Maybe I should ask her out. I know she's a good dancer."

"Jesus! Such audacity of hope you are."

They catch their ride. With a little chit-chat they come to know that the driver is an Eritrean. He's been in Omaha about five years. Before that he'd been in Israel as an asylum seeker. Andre tells him he knew some Eritreans in Seattle. He had worked with them in the tradeshow industry. Beauregard and Andre, quite drunk, look out at the neon lights as Danteque clouds of steam roiled up from the manhole covers going down the wet six lane pipeline of Dodge Street.

"Remember sneaking into the drive-in there off 72nd? Christ! They were X-rated movies. That's hilarious! Can you imagine that now? You could see giant boobs from the streets everywhere. All the hot rods and muscle cars racing up and down the way—hundreds of them lined up on the old main drag of Dodge Street!"

"You had to see it to believe it. Like American Graffiti except it's the '70s."

"Warriors come out to play... It was like that, with Burke and Westside High going at it every weekend with fucking armies. My pal Larry, punk rocker/union brother from Hell's Kitchen NYC gave me the whole skinny on it—he was there. With the skinheads brawling on the streets, in the projects, how his Filipino wife first met him, literally. He lived it "The Warriors" the movie. It was great! It inspired a whole generation with Joe Walsh singing Funk #49-like shit—'somewhere out on that horizon faraway from the neon sky'… Omaha was like that with beaucoup Urban Cowboy in the mix. Roll out the pony keg."

"Exactly… Ja-ha! Didn't Hochek mostly organize those hit the drive-in parties. Miss Nude America was one of the shows. Some French ones. Alice in Wonderland. He was always leading us to salvation as we clamored over the fences sometimes."

"Yeah—he had the keys to that no-tell hotel off Center Street somehow. We'd be wandering around up there—put a quarter in. Laughing our asses off. That reminds me, had a big party for my birthday at the Wine Shop. Hochek ends up taking me to the strip joint Club Omaha. He paid for everything! Crazy night! Place was packed! Some young black kids got their fat stacks—a thousand dollars just showering the dancers with them like Saudi princes. And next thing I know Hochek is interviewing a few and I casually tell one he's a priest and next thing I know all these girls start lining up like at a confessional to talk with Father Hochek. With a packed house and between the young bloods raining down money on the dancer and Father Hochek's blessed counsel to the lasses—because Jesus loves strippers… as do I and Hochek: for they do much saintly work if you really think about it; over the years at least what I've seen—goddamn blessed saints some of them with their works of mercy, almost like nurses. Now them women are saints! Good heavens what they do, ain't just a little rag-tag for the handicapped. Anyway, it was a sight to be seen. He got me a helluva young acrobat that evening for the VIP. She had some interesting tattoos and knew how to make ya feel alright… I just can't afford with all this debt and rebellion I've incurred over my life of dissolution. Needless to say my date abandoned me that night. We returned to the Vino Paradiso, but everybody was gone. Father Hochek dropped me off at her place. Must have been sometime well after midnight. Oh—what a night as the sun came upon my eyes in the morning."

The Eritrean is smiling but understanding enough. Who could understand this madness of free range feral children drunk and running amok with no direction and no guide in life from anguished moms helicoptering them, droning above their heads, monitoring, filming and phoning them constantly as to their screaming whereabouts. Parents had their own lives back then.

"Hochek is great for that—dude missed his calling. Sounds like an evening to remember. Like the Vegas road trip infamy with Joe Steele and Walker. 'Oh what a lucky man he was...' Jesus loves strippers. I think it's true. You remember? Hochek had the keys to the rooms of that one hotel, the Deluxe, off 72nd and Center; put in a quarter for the dirty movies. Then we all migrated north to the other hotel. They all got arrested at the Aksarben Suites: Hochek, Fitzpatrick, Paladino; shooting off the hotel fire extinguishers. Some of us were with them earlier—we're like fourteen, fifteen years old. I dunno how we escaped. The Bolampertis, their cousin Johnny Wills and I took off. Was there for homecoming listening to a lot of Led and just a few years ago again for a couple of nights with Faye Louise who'd come in for a visit from Canada. The place was a zoo. A stay-cation like the Howard Johnson, with little black kids running everywhere, at all hours, hitting the swimming pool. You got to see it to believe it: several times. First of the month when that Wu relief check come in. Party! Steak and lobster. With another generation of free range kids just out having fun... She got the place—sweet beautiful Faye Louise de Quebec: Montreal. We had a great time, a great time! We drank wine and laughed. We got simpatico, her and I. But—what a scene. Hilarious. Can't make this shit up."

"Sounds like Hochek—he got pretty busted as a bookie with Spike and Kuhn back in the mid-80s."

"He's the quintessential Omaha dude: part Itai, part Irish, part Pollack—a big boy playing football laughing his ass off the whole time. Hochek and Costello were the first two dudes grabbed by Father Laughlin after the Volkswagen stunt/prank/political statement—whatever you want to call it."

"Nothing has touched that ever since. It still comes up on the rock 'n 'roll radio stations as the greatest ever. Kind of political may-be—'he who fucks nuns will later join the Church' it's a lyric from a Clash jeezus—what were you nuts thinking. Am surprised your desiccated bodies are not still dangling/hanging from the yardarm goal posts with a murder of crows perching all about thee—as a warning to all savages and fine young cannibals. A house of pain, what a motley crew of dead rabbits it was: Kirby, Keiny, Mangan, Kennedy, McCoy, Hogan and Doyle..."

"One step beyond... Yeah, I heard that not too long ago. Was pretty surprised. We were so much younger then. Costello told me on a visit from back when I was living in France."

"Father Laughlin was a great guy, ex-Marine with his crew cut, could send a dude sailing with his finger thumping you in the chest. I spent a lot of time in JUG and I wasn't very good at math. Or re-membering poetry. You could negotiate with him. A hard man, but a reasonable man."

"That dude was the Dean of Discipline—righteous. Old school Jesuit. Was at Iwo Jima. Like Warsocki's uncle who was the chaplain for decades at the VA off 42nd."

"Yeah well we're at King Fong's. Pay the man. This is getting like that movie—My Dinner with Andre."

"Covering a lot of territory. Do not confuse the map with the territory."

"Indeed. We're all just trying to figure out the ninth configura-tion...like a parallax view."

"Good group, good movies. Like Repo Man."

"The life of a repo man...is always intense. Says Harry Dean Stanton."

They stagger in loudly knocking down some ferns and a couple ceramic jars. A gracious older Chinese woman in silk is there. They order drinks and food. She bows. They bow stupidly as they follow her to a booth.

"Place looks about the same. Like an old opium den. Takeuchi Jewelry still around? Mancuso's office was right next door. You know the Japanese showed up to work in the slaughterhouses around 1900. The Chinese were already here from working on the railroad and following the silver and gold mines supplying the offices of inequity."

"Yeah—in South O, they had that place called Japan House. Brought in so many Japs to work in the slaughter houses like our old friends the Takeuchis…the hundred year old mother Kimi still working there at the jewelry store."

"That ties in nicely to Father Schnapps…and the Confucius Trading Company story. You know—the Orientals…"

"The cat made it on 60 Minutes—blew through that much dough with the cocaine and gambling. Talk about leaving Las Vegas. Incredible—why couldn't I have been there to enjoy the spoils? I'd a' been a great wingman for him, even though he's gay—I'm a local Omaha guy! Think global, act local. I'd a looked after him. All that blow…the mo-nay just falling about, gambling at the roulette wheel, at the craps table… I love shooting dice, pai gow, the dance girls, strippers. Dude blew millions. Dang. My dream."

"Everybody's got to have a dream. Yeah—didn't hear about that till I moved back here. Actually was just visiting the sweetie back then—was still out on the Coast. Met his brother; didn't have a clue who he was: RICH. Was up at Bergan Mercy Hospital most the time. The poor woman and her family who I'd known my whole life. Her nephew had OD'd. Talk about despair. I'm catching the bus up to the hospital—they're all holding vigil up there. The whole family with lots of friends; staying overnight. It was the saddest thing. The fentanyl was just starting to creep into the picture. Now, of course, it's everywhere. Only getting worse…with the border wide open. Nearly a hundred thousand dead a year. Young people mostly. Take the wrong pill—could be an aspirin. Vietnam and Korea both wars—

we lost roughly 60,000 men. What's drill instructor Warsocki tell his soldiers? 'You're worth seven cents—seven cents is what the cost of a bullet is.' The fentanyl is even cheaper than Russian bullets from Moldavia."

"Both wars we were fighting the Chi-Coms—sometimes with bayonets. Dropping this fentanyl off in Mexico is a whole lot cheaper than military battles. They gots to get back after all that opium we dumped off on them—with the British and French."

"The Boxer Rebellion. The politics of heroin—drugs. Making cities, making empires. The Chinese brought the poppy seeds to Mexico back in 1820. They hadn't had their independence very long—they needed people. Eventually morphine happens about the time of the American Civil War—and a very large demand is created."

"Yep—and the Chinese in Sinaloa get rich, the original cartels and later the Mexican cartels get to fuck us up. It's a win-win for them. Kill the gringos. Ja-ha! The Triads make money moving the dollars back to China… And they exact some revenge with Mexico for slaughtering, purging and deportation of the Chinese during the Mexican Revolution back in the 1920s."

"So yeah—sad story. The Mexicans expropriated the Chinese wealth and property—a few hung in there back in Guadalajara to become the bank for the cartels. It's a revolving door. China don't forget. And now the youth of America pay."

"I know the crew—great family, the Twohigs. A fun bunch, a little wild; tight with the Prochellos… But from my clan—who am I to judge? From Blessed Sacrament. It was like Angela's Ashes in Omaha in the Seventies. One of the brothers and one of the sisters got kicked out of Ryan High. It took a lot to get kicked out of Ryan High…bean bag chairs, everybody high like the corny show Room 222. The expelled sister eventually graduates from Tech and cut hair, mine—funny broad. Hated to hear about it. But it's a goddamn all too common story these days with millions of illegal aliens having crossed the border the last two years since the corrupt retard took charge. But let's defend Ukraine's border. Fuck! I voted for the clown—thinking lesser of two evils."

"Well we all make mistakes sometimes… It's always a 50/50 vote in this country except when Nixon beat McGovern by 17 million votes with the help of Hoffa and the Teamsters going with Nixon. Then they got rid of him—can't let the peasants decide who is going to be president plus he'd gone after the communists so hard and he was poor and not an Ivy Leaguer. That was coup d'etat. The first big one. Ja-ha! What about Father Schnapps and Wayne? That's his name, right?"

The Chinese lady brings their drinks in paper cups—it's after hours along with the chow mein, chop suey and pot stickers. Sticking with the basics.

"Thank you. Send in Jimmy Carter."

"Thank you. Yeah—we need to get Burkina Faso over here to monitor our elections."

"Am pretty sure about that. So Wayne blows millions on blow and roulette. Becomes famous for it. Lots of mo-nay. And—the kicker…Father Schnapps and him are an item. Like the little office ladies of administration at Rummel receive a splendorous bouquet with a dozen roses—for Father Schnapps! This was regularly happening. But that's just the beginning. We already went over the wedding story like he's homecoming queen. Well—BASH is coming up: the big shakedown auction amongst all the grand poobahs with all the moolah for Rummel." Andre is grinning. "It was amongst consenting adults… Nobody cares—just leave the kids alone for fuck's sake— evil fucks!"

"Amen to that," replies Beauregard.

"Speaking of war…was subbing at Central High the other day, they've got their plaques and Hall of Fame with the likes of the great Gale Sayers, etc. And they had the names engrave upon the entry of those Central grads that had died in the wars. I thought this was wild—World War I had twenty three dead dudes, casualties, KIA. Twenty three! In World War II they're were fifty. Korea had there were thirteen killed and surprisingly there were only six deaths from the Vietnam War."

What? We were only fighting in World War I for barely a year! I get World War II with fifty deaths but World War I... That many?"

"I know, I know... That's why I brought it up. They got slaughtered in World War I.""

"Dang. Surprised Vietnam didn't kill more. Central ain't hardly no rich kids' school."

"Yeah, alumni Gale Sayers, etc...'lot of kids from the hood. We'd be getting ready to play them and their running back was out cuz he got knifed... I was real surprised as well, that's why I bring it up. There was a whole lot of shooting going on in all four wars. And even by 1975 at the Fall of Saigon which looked organized compared to the Fall of Afghanistan, but anyway, according to a buddy of mine who was a Pathfinder Airborne there in '69...they still hadn't used up all the ammunition from the World War II depots—.45s and .50, howitzer 155s, etc."

"Ain't that something—if that's true... Heavy. Crazy. Hard to imagine. They had that much shit still stockpiled from World War II."

"I don't think it's like that now. Probably got enough for ten days—been sending so much ammo to the Ukraine so they can defend their border from the Russian communist horde. By the way—the original code-talkers were the Choctaws, Cherokees and Lakota in World War I. Confused the shit out of the Germans. Just reading a book about the Dull Knifes of Pine Ridge: Lakota. One was a chief who fought with Crazy Horse: Fetterman Fight/Massacre, Battle of Rosebud and of course, Custer's Last Stand. Later on he led his people out of Indian Territory/Oklahoma on a six hundred mile trek. His son Dull Knife fought in World War I and was at the Siege at Wounded Knee in 1973 along with his son who fought the Viet Cong in Vietnam. What can you say? They're warriors. They like to fight. Second lieutenants would tell them to knock off on the war whoops—you're giving our positions away."

"Got to call it a night. I'll go over my old notes on the Franklin Cover-up and get back with you."

"Sounds good. Let's meet at Josephine's next time. Give Frank some business. Nice quiet place—cozy. There off 19th and Pierce and always interesting converse with Frank."

"I dig Scarpello's. Interesting joint amongst the nightclub denizens. Ja-ha! Love the décor. With the mannequins like your Volkswagen prank putting it in front of the library on the second floor. Wasn't he a fullback for the Huskers?"

"Yes—nice wigs. The décor is impeccable with the pinball machine, pool table, jukebox and mannequins—they're not done up as a priest and a hooker. Doyle carried that baby up that flight of stairs: incredible. Yes, Frank played for the Cornhuskers with great pic of him in uniform as you enter: a tough guy. And—his uncle was the famous wrestler—that really got the wrestling program going at Iowa before the Gable brothers. You can see photos of his famous uncle down there at Orsi's Bakery along with all the other Itai star athletes like who we use to play with like there's a Marfisi, there's a Caniglia. It's like another Sons of Italy."

"Best pizza in town…next to Big Fred's. Fred Bruno! What a place! The original was down at here Dinker's Bar is. Big Fred's—back when Nebraska was great! The football. One of the Marfisis played linebacker with McCoy for the Huskers—they nicknamed him Crash."

"I remember—he was a crazy fucker. Hey! But don't forget Pepe and La Casa's! Anyway let's make it Josephine's. I want to hear more. I'll let Omar know. He doesn't live too far; never moved out of the old neighborhood. He can join us. His grandparents were first cousins—they hadn't been off the boat too long from Lebanon when they got married in East Omaha. He's a good drawer and my accountant. I want him to do some illustrations."

"For what?"

"I dunno man…we got such a hot volume of talk, am thinking about writing another science fiction western romance novel."

"Oh that'll be a classic—right up there with Captain Kangaroo. Hey, by the way, you, me and Malone are spearheading the class reunion."

"What the fuck you talking about? Man if I've ever heard of less likely: the usual suspects—it'd be us three. Didn't you spend more time in JUG than school? Ha! Justice under God!"

"Yah-yah whatever. We're going to have the dinner at Cascio'c Steak House. Or Fucinaro's Anthony's. If it's too expensive for some people—Malone says: Go Home. Get a refund from Rummel."

"Ja-ha! Nice. The man's a mindhunter and rebel-rebel. Always was."

"Definitely one of the leading members of the fight club."

"Fucinaro Excavating—good company."

"She sang Blue Velvet…" is playing in the background. This make Andre think of the part Russian chick Phaedra the cello player. Would she ever go out with him? She quit waitressing down at the Havana Garage; her boyfriend, the two tours in Iraq with the Marine Corps was moving gear in Cali. The brother was well over fifteen years younger than Andre; black as coal with a face etched in stone and he was in top shape and a smile that flashed brightly. Andre considered him a worthy rival for her affections. The PTSD Marine and her had a love affair—tumultuous but real. Thought she wouldn't mind some white snake occasionally Andre thinks. They had a lot of dialogue with him drinking that whiskey over a cigar—she was his captive audience. Met her as he picked up a young thing with long legs on the cobbled streets of the Old Market. She was their tatted up very sexy waitress (the long legged gal was in the Air Force and got shipped off to Japan). He figured she was cool, kind of a Nirvana chick with that good wagtail wagon, and he was right he learns later on. She saw Nirvana play at the Civic Arena when she was in high school—so she was deep. Phaedra had joined the Army after high school. Andre didn't know much about that part of her life. In fact, he barely knew her at all…he heard her play the cello down at Our Lady of Lourdes. And he heard her hitting that cello hard in his mind often at the damndest times—driving, rhythmic. She sang Blue Velvet, just like Bobby Vinton… Frappez Moi. Andre sought to see all her tattoos.

"We just passed Vinton Street."

"Man we are lost! Like the black cops said to us once down in Houston on that road trip to New Orleans seeking the House of the Rising Sun like that quest down to Mexico looking for the Hotel California—didn't even see no Mexicans for miles, thought I was in the heart of Africa. Them cops said with humor: MAN U GUYS R LOST! Ja-ha! Frappez Moi. Frappez Moi. Man, they like to party down there!"

"We'll get there. We're going to make it—like Easy Rider. Don't tread on me mutherfukker."

Andre slips into drunken reverie and nostalgia like the passenger: he rides as the city lights go by. He thinks more of Phaedra, he remembers Nirvana, back at Capitol Hill, the late eighties/early nineties—the house band was Sky Cries Mary. The band was usually on tour. The sexy raven haired with her flowing gowns Anisa Romero wailed with high-charged dynamite in her voice. Artists, junkies and degenerates. Andre was a Midwestern boy on his own… Some chick with a fat lip kept coming up to him. He was with a buddy Donnie who was in the Navy and seeing the world was stationed at Bremerton Naval Shipyard across the other side of the Puget Sound from Seattle. For it wasn't just a job for Donnie—it was an adventure. The chick with the fat lip kept coming up to Andre. She was kind of cute. Andre said something to Donnie about the chick coming up to him…"You dumb shit can't you read? It's on the inside of her lip."

Andre took a more perceptive angle. It read: FUCK ME. Damn that would hurt he thinks. Andre took her hand as she led him off— for a fast and furious tryst. Kind of crazy. In the heat of the moment.

Decades later as his buddy Donnie and Andre are back in a place called the Happy Bar, Donnie recounted tales from Tijuana brothels and running from the Mexican police to being fucked up out of his skull with some of the lads, the usual suspect and at hotels with hookers in Omaha off Cuming Street to running around with 14,000 dollars after retrieving it from the bushes as the runner was getting chased by the police around downhome Rosenblatt Stadium with the College World Series going on in South O and people renting out their front lawns for parking, with the bookie's stash like a Keystone Cops show… calling up his bookie friend who ran the trophy shop: you REALLY want to open up the door and let me in… And all the other general mayhem and youthful high jinx tales of the days of our lives.

He says to Andre, "Man—we were really fucked up. Really fucked up… But that's Life. It's just the fucked up people taking care of the more fucked up people. Andre get out. We're here."

Wherever here was—Andre got out. Like a profile in courage, like a Hollywood star who plays a doctor, cowboy or soldier on TV. He fumbled with his keys. Got in the door and decides to oil and clean his Chinese SKS. Don't tread on me. Perusing through some of the copies of the material of his: Payoff, three meetings near Hanscom Park, with Richard O'Konski, Jones Construction vice president Raymond Johnson, Land Paving convicted of bid-rigging and mail fraud, Johnson perjury, lied to the FBI and the grand jury, he was scared of Miguel Jones and Tony Dambrowski, claimed he had not participated in bid-rigging, scared of Mike and Tony, for project in 1979, Nebraska State Highway 31 from Elkhorn to the Washington County Line, make the bid $960,000 to Matt Flinn says O'Konski the vice president for Land, Land gets contract for $849,000, Jones and Flinn give complintary bids, outfit called Midwest gets checks cut to them for $35,000, Tony Dambrowski is president and principal owner of Land Paving, Richard O'Konski is his cousin, O'Konski gets fired in 1981 for having an affair with a female employee according to O'Konski, and argument ensues, Dambrowski has his cousin

O'Konski "involuntarily committed" to Richard Young Hospital for mental treatment, eventually the psychiatrist releases O'Konski—can't make this up. Then bankruptcy, bankruptcy, bankruptcy—cuz bankruptcy happens... The world is a casino. Like Mutual of Omaha's Wild Kingdom. Don't tread on me. Business: they oil more during an election year.

CHAPTER NINE

BACK WHEN MAMA CASS DIED

Life is full of surprises, some good, some not so good.

—Pablo Escobar

A young Tom Rudloff graduates from Holy Name High, prefers reading Virgil, he's not very interested in girls. He'd helped out quite a bit at the church for the Lenten fish fry. Every parish in Omaha had them going on—bars advertised them on their marquees. His folks drank at these bars in North Omaha like the Nifty Bar where Andre came upon the band Ween's particular mascot/logo in the men's head— seen them a couple times out on Left Coast, even had it on his hard hat so it made him feel right at home. Next to the College World Series down in South Omaha at Rosenblatt Stadium, the Lenten fish fries from Holy Name to Holy Ghost, to St. Benedict's, to Our Lady of Lourdes, were the biggest social event in Omaha. People from out of town even from New Orleans were impressed at the amount of people and beer drinking. Tom's father participated with gusto. Tom was of a gentle and scholarly nature so it was of no great surprise that after graduating he heads to a seminary bringing joy to his mother and much relief to his father and that is where he crosses paths and meets the itinerant and outspoken monk, Senor Agape. They become fast friends, its pre-Vatican II, the early sixties, things are just starting to burble…with the mamas and the papas, Vietnam and protest for these two young highway apostles of Rabelais and Christ.

Andre, a man of peace, except occasionally with the misunderstanding of others—that would lead to violence, come across a letter in one of the notebooks from Mac that is addressed to Walter and Warsocki. He obviously didn't get the news about the death of Walter. Mac claims he is back in the Live Free or Die state of New Hampshire, working as a veterans counselor and assisting as a nonpartisan poll worker while stuffing bags full of ballots and tossing them in the river to float down to Massachusetts where they can use them accordingly, after abdicating his undercover duties with the Detroit police, Mac, in the letter, says he knows Warsocki is somewhere in Chad training some other praetorian guard with his Shin Bet cohort—Kinski: remember when Mama Cass died. All the kids in the neighborhood were running around saying, "Mama Cass died! Mama Cass died!" It was a big deal. The year was 1974—everybody was being like hippies. Mac describes running with the Marine Recon in Cambodia carrying a .357 Dad who'd been with MACV earlier in the "conflict" sent him as he's tossed in a tunnel of the Khmer Rouge—to check it out. He briefly discusses losing his brother who was there with the Airborne in '68. The American riots had slowed down, the Vietnam War was winding down, still a lot of bombs going off and cops getting assassinated, President Nixon who had won by a landslide was kicked out of office after taking more than 60% of the popular vote and carrying 49 of the 50 states—it was all about the call girl ring, and it was all still very tumultuous. Though he garnered 17 million more votes than McGovern (who Andre's mother voted for with about twenty three more people in Nebraska—one being an aunt, an uncle and his maternal grandmother). Also, Colonel Corn Pop/ Lunch Bucket best grandpa ever Sleepy Joe and the smartest guy he knows—his son kicked out of the Navy for smoking crack Hunter— hey his brother's widow wasn't bad looking either, was already a year in the Senate representing the Dupont duchy of Delaware with all those HQ corporations centered there…what's up? All some hilarious overt shit, as Bill the Biographer Ayers and Bernadine Dohrn with their Weather Underground comrades continue their bombing campaign to achieve "the destruction of US imperialism and form a classless communist world" to save us. From our stupid selves. By believing in a fantasy. Some people may have an overly optimistic idea of progress. A temple of chance. Seeking our American Dream which is already behind us. This different brand of nihilism: play it as it lays…play it as it lays… Contempt for the hoi polloi. And dirty stinky hippies—which is understandable. In most regards. But. It's all about the advertising. And sports. Rants Mac. In this manifesto. Ain't no country for old men! He writes. And all the media wants to cover is January 6, which was a glorious day for America as the throngs raided Versailles. It was like the masses storming of the Bastille—Peasants you know, French Revolution, let them eat cake stuff like the French Laundry. Mac thought all that stuff was suppose to be cool with him and his liberal brethren—y'know: Sandinista, man! The glory of it when they stormed Somoza's palace in Managua for I was there Walter—way before your liberal buddy Andre was there picking commie coffee beans. Had been working as a kicker—bale after bale; sometimes palletized. Not sure who was paying us—the Cubans, the Russians or the CIA. Nambu was the pilot. Mac ponders aloud in this essay…should Walter write another letter to Woody and see what him and his Jesuit minions think? Can he arrange a visit with the pope—y'know…two communists having a little meet and greet. That would be grand. And there's always Che Guevara…right? A committed psychopath killed while trying to foment revolution in Bolivia. As the trucks from Ben & Jerry's pull up to give ice cream to all the screaming sweaty college white kids hollering for Black Lives Matter down on a hot sunny day in the Centennial Park in Atlanta: singing protest songs: misguided and confused—wouldn't it be great…like a Beach Boys song. The criminal overdosed on drugs! Mac hollers in his treatise. Do you think that bullshit about Helen Keller is true? She wasn't able to see or hear since she was an infant? Santa

Claus or the Easter Bunny? Her mother wrote the story! Ask yourself and think…WHO DO YOU KNOW KNEW HELEN KELLER?! That was an amazing riff Andre thinks. He wishes Chris Hedges was still around—he just finished reading his Empire of Illusion. How we are ruled, informed and entertained by the courtiers. As Kurt Cobain screams: HERE WE ARE NOW—ENTERTAIN US! It's all kind of like: Reimagining CRIME (or the police)…just send out a couple unarmed social workers—these are very naïve people who've never hung out with criminals. And according to the great liberal Hedges, that's all the media is now… courtiers seeking the spectacle… For we desperately need more awards shows for all the celebrities—for there are not enough of them happy people, bullshit happy people… (Mac rambles on, Andre tries to discern, tries to translate). And most of the Republicans (especially the ones that got hijacked by the evangelicals: they like there role as the minority party—I'm falling and I can't get up) and Democrats are the same—courtiers for K Street and Silicon Valley: the lobbyists. So go ahead and get your panties in a knot…you want an abortion vote Democrat, you want to keep your guns vote Republican. It's hollow. Kabuki theatre, stagecraft erected to strip us of power—not really brainwashing, but through good casual indoctrination to a totalitarianism RFK Jr. is desperately warning us of. Smoke and mirrors. Won't even give the poor bastard presidential candidate Secret Service protection—not enough dead Kennedys I gather; was a great band! The television is the worse Hedges goes on… How can you pay political apparatchiks posing as journalists millions of dollars as they get all cozy with the likes of Joe Biden, Hilary Clinton, or Lawrence Summers is who Hedges brings up—as they squat in a studio getting their makeup pasted on them? Mac writes that he has heard they are paying Rachel Mad-cow upwards of 15 million dollars… or was it 30? For that kind of money Andre thinks he'd probably read whatever they tell him to…seems reasonable if the oligarchic rot pays that well, Mac says, shouting expletives into the night like a journey to the end—people just can't get their heads around the notion that old Uncle Walter Cronkite lied to us every evening—"And, that's the way it is …" Just like they are now. On pretty much EVERYTHING. Chomsky, Chomsky, Chomsky. It is Pravda. So what do you bastards think? "If we don't believe in freedom of expression for people we despise, we don't believe in it at all." Noam, Noam, Noam. Right on, right on. Also: as George Orwell so eloquently put it, "All tyrannies rule through fraud and force, but once the fraud is exposed they must rely exclusively on force." Get ready—too many people choosing to be blind in this world: "If you will not use your eyes to see, you will use your eyes to cry—Jean Paul Sartre… Mac writes to Walter on and on of cynical theories of Marcuse and the Frankfurt School of Critical Race blah-blah and the Institute of Social Research in their quest to make the populace a gaggle of individuals devoid of self-respect that hate what they love and love what they hate as Mac declares what Boris Pasternak and Bulgakov were driving at—destroy human dignity and independence: what the communists want, with all the other reasonable liars.

It's a good letter. A raging manifesto. Like notebooks full of rambling material excoriating the despotism and doctrine. A rejection of reality! He shouts: Humanity! From the simian fellow who knows that truth doesn't care about your feelings. And most important point he makes is that he thinks it's possible that he could get his job back as a roadie for Molly Hatchet that are scheduled to be going back on a revival tour this next year. Everybody has got to have a dream…dream big Mac, Andre thinks. And he thinks hard and it hits him, Andre realizes Mac must have been out crabbing, working on the ships in the Eighties out in Bering Sea back when Andre was there. He recalls meeting Mac, the provateur, down at the zeitgeist art gallery in Seattle back when Walter briefly resided there in '97 when the WTO came to town. Dude seemed familiar, probably running under another alias back then. You met all kinds up there, out there— Naylon, John Courage, Harris, Greg Lee, Doug; Andre had met them all. Yeah, the WTO protest—like it was just a bunch of French farmers and dirty stinky hippies protesting with the unions against globalism and giving membership to China. Like the oligarchic elites figured they'd just give the Chi-Coms enough Happy Meals and Disney that they'd abandon their totalitarian traits and free Tibet. Guess not. Just ask the Uyghurs. While they buy up ranches and farm land across Canada and the United States. Hey! Nobody is forcing these sales. The Americans like to play victims. The question is: what's the end game? Or is it just incompetence and greed? Probably need to put the Indians in charge again. A few years or decades ago everybody was whining about how some Arabs were going to buy some East Coast port like in Baltimore or something—and it was like if it bothers us so bad...then don't sell it to them fer Chrissakes!

Mac ends the note with a prayer and a song. The prayer is on a laminated card and has the Madonna with child in the clouds above a wooden row boat with three men aboard—two whites and a black as they attempt to survive the ocean's fury. Two cherub angels are too slightly upper to each side of her. The other side of the prayer card is titled: Prayer to "Our Lady of Charity" it reads—

Oh, Holy Virgin and Lady of Charity, with happiness and humility I come to your feet!

Virgin of Miracles! You cure the sick, you give hope where there is despair, you give strength to the afflicted, preserve from disgrace our families, protect the youth, guard our children.

No one can explain all the miracles and fortitude you give to the souls that come to you

We, your children, thank you for all your grace. Amen.

For the song he has the lyrics written to Brandy (You're a Fine Girl) by Looking Glass. Andre finds this all very interesting while seeking meaning: good luck.

Doo-doo-doo-doo

Doo-doo-doo-doo

There's a port on the western bay

And it serves a hundred ships a day

Lonely sailors pass the time of way

And talk about their homes

There's a girl in this harbor town

And she works laying whiskey down

They say Brandy fetch another round

She serves them whiskey and wine

Yeah your eyes could steal a sailor from the sea

Brandy wears a braided chain

Made of finest silver from the north of Spain

A locket that bears the name of the man that Brandy loved

He came on a summer's day bringing gifts from far away

But he made it clear he couldn't stay

The harbor was his home

The sailor said Brandy you're a fine girl

(You're a fine girl)

What a good wife you would be

(Such a fine girl)

But my life and my lady is the sea

(Doo-doo-doo-doo)

(Doo-doo-doo-doo)

Brandy used to watch his eyes when he told his his sailor stories

She could feel the ocean fall and rise

She saw its raging glory

But he had always told her the truth lord he was an honest man

And Brandy (a-a-a-h...) does her best to understand

(Doo-doo-doo-doo)

(Doo-doo-doo-doo)

At night when the bars close down

Brandy walks through a silent town

And loves a man who's not around

She can still hear him say

She hears him say Brandy you're a fine girl

(chorus)

You get what I'm getting at Walter? Play it as it lays Walter... play it as it lays. Ever noticed Walter how boring it is to hear about successful people? I want you to know that I've been acquiring all the trinkets and groovy garb—you know, the accoutrements of the hipster. Life on life's terms—can you dig it? What I've read, I think you need to get more graphic in your porn for Fifty Shade of Jones— we have a lot of mentally unwell people in this country. Just a suggestion. One man's opinion. I've added some literary smut of mine own here from my western romance novels to entertain you, and the women folk—we'll all be speaking Chinese here pretty soon anyway, wearing our little gray caps with a red star on them, but at least we'll all be able to have an abortion. Thank God!

Siding with the perceived or produced oppressed creating a hijacked morality based in a fraud morality as a weaponized construct. Marxism as a Cain and Abel construct: the have & the have-nots. Divide and Conquer—basing bullshit on religion, race, ethnicity, party affiliation. CREATE ANARCHY TO IMPOSE TYRANNY: BLM/ANTIFA. What you see or hear with your own eyes…day of visibility etcetera, man is a woman, gender is constructed, everyone has their own truth…misguided simple feeble attempt at authenticity. It's all an embarrassment to Western Civilization. And that's the point Walter, don't you see? No borders… Coincidently the Indians had territories—borders, that they, Pontiac, Black Hawk, Geronimo, Quanah Parker, Crazy Horse fiercely defended from encroachment from the Europeans and other tribes. To quote George Orwell—"some ideas are so stupid that only intellectuals believe them" another good one by him is…"in times of universal deceit, telling the truth will be a revolutionary act." They're all shameless liars Walter—highly paid shameless liars. For instance think Walter—Rachel Maddow gets paid $30 million a year by NBC Universal. Just give her the script for those hormonal theories into Byzantium that she so deliriously inflicts upon her audience of cultured intellectuals. Know this Walter—they're not on our side as the Irish/Basque patriot Chris Plante says so aptly… as they censor liberals like Shellenberger for posing questions: don't be articulate. Like it's 1917 and the Hun music is being banned while Congress passes wartime laws against sedition and espionage against speaking or printing anything that expressed contempt for the government… The First Amendment? 'Congress shall make no law respecting an establishment of religion, or prohibiting the free exercise thereof, or abridging the freedom of speech, or of the press; or the right of the people peaceably to assemble, and to petition the

Government for a redress of grievances.' Free speech was the greatest casualty, like in the First World War...when the Wu hit. But it was nothing like the Spanish Flu which, by the way, came from Kansas and killed 50 million people—went through America like a prairie fire with folks dropping right there at their work as the anti-German propaganda flew so that we could save the British Empire. Always the same story, wartime laws kick in against sedition and espionage as Hun music is banned. The song remains the same. It's the elites vs. the deplorables. We are the deplorables. The establishment versus populism. Progressive versus the backwards people. The managerial class versus the rabble. The U.S. Army versus the Indians. What it is. Don't jive yourself with their saccharine platitudes. Kumbaya my ass. The Pope's a dope. Joker's wild. Crime always finds lawyers and innocence only rarely. Don't worry, the health alteration committee may be knocking on your door late some night if the preemptive neutralization crew hasn't already gotten to you. Remember we took an oath: I, Mac (and you Walter), do solemnly swear that I will support and defend the Constitution of the United States against all enemies, foreign and domestic; that I will bear true faith and allegiance to the same... That's the number one part of it Walter—what to do when we've got a corrupt retard for President? The cover up. The lies. The coup. He's the Trojan horse for the Left. Mock the hysterics. Mock them. Dear Walter. Mock them: cuz we're—Ridin' with Biden! We know they are lying, they know they are lying, they know we know they are lying, we know they know we know they are lying, but they keep lying...something like that: from Gulag Archipelago dude. We are just waiting for the political commissars to arrive like Nambu and I were back in Africa—waiting for air cover.

Andre, dressed up so natty, wraps up reading the entries of this vast dissertation of Mac's that is chronicled almost like a diary—the western romance novels of his have a whole lot of pussy... Maybe Andre, who only seeks copulation, could have Mac finish up Fifty Shades of Jones. Mac describes how he and his Shin Bet associate, Kinski, had to bury Nambu, who got clipped by seven cents just behind the ear, on a shallow beach in the Spanish speaking country of Equatorial Guinea after running guard duty for the President-for-Life of that great nation of West Africa. They got sent out on a mission with a platoon to some islands off the coast to round up some pirates. Seventeen wars and campaigns later and Baby Nambu finally reverently arrived at the Gates of Saint Peter, well-armed, Mac adds. His number came up, he looked so peaceful, 'twas finally his time to meet the Maker. Lord have mercy... And by the way—now the Wagner Group is running things there for Putin—with the Chinese building the ports. Ah—that was Mac's impetus to retire to the Legionnaire home in Orange, France with Maurice's papers. It was a good run till Didier happened to show up and fuck that up—getting his revenge, but I got mine—split his head open like a cow's vagina. Aw—it is good to be back home to the White Mountains of New Hampshire with Ma where his mother would proudly tell her friends that her son was a writer—"he writes PORN!" and he even got a parrot named Mickey and it was bestowed upon him because he had been a Marine and the parrot Mickey could only go to a Marine. Mac was the third Marine Mickey had hung with—the other two died already (there'll be five before Mickey goes). And then he adds—Ah shit! Another broken toy has OD'd on me and collapsed through my doorway. Thought I heard a loud banging. Got to Narcan him, get him to ER. Goddamn jarhead. Too many deployments to Kandahar. Seeking a separate peace. Over and out.

The last passage of the letter from the nonpartisan poll worker is:

There will be no more Hope. No more Glory. Not for the nation. There will be no more parades

—Ford Maddox Ford

And Andre concludes, it must be—all because Mama Cass died... she was the glue that held the insanity together.

After taking that all in, he goes to pick up Terri Baby as they are headed to the Thirty Club Bar off West Broadway not far from Sunset Speedway, to get back with her roots of Counciltucky/Missouri Valley. Her grandmother would send her in there have to retrieve her drunk ornery grandpa the heavy equipment operator contractor. Sweet home Counciltucky where you'd drive around and casually see the occasional Confederate flag present in the squalid fronts of the residences of the greatest country. Andre had ended up working quite a bit putting up steel buildings and getting to know the locals going to get a beer at two in the afternoon sharing the death and prison toll in the neighborhood and asking him if he was from here, or there and Andre informed them that—No: he was not from here, or there… They'd steal a box of bolts there. Most of the homicides were in North O but the real crazy crimes in the metro area happened in Counciltucky—Bonnie and Clyde car chases and shootouts with the police as they made their escape from the law takin' the money. With weird kidnappings and big meth busts to boot. His foreman by the name of Jack, on that project was cool—with the whole crew but Andre smoking cigarettes. A buddy of Jack's was on the crew and after a week out of nowhere asks Andre if he knows how Jack got into putting up steel buildings? Andre said he didn't know the story… So the story goes—Jack meets a young thing in a bar. Things go well. He winds up in the sack with her. But the next morning he is abruptly woken up to a burly man kicking his feet telling him it's time to get to work. It was the sweet young lass's father. So Jack put on his boots and got in the truck and went to work. The father didn't bother telling Jack he'd be on the road for the next two weeks. And that's how Jack got doing steel buildings a dozen years ago or so.

With that pertinent information Andre surmised that pappy told daughter to go out there and get him a strong, strapping lad—he needed some help on this construction project coming up. So Andre's main question was did she call that night or early that morning, "Daddy! Daddy! I got one!'

Terri Baby's familia was rife with this for it was a big clan to begin with and then became ever expanding as a cousins would have children and then get divorced and marry Mexicans who had children to have more children with. Less the uncles that were equipment operators and hard men livin' hard lives some of whom hadn't been right since Viet-Nam and some of whom didn't go to Viet-Nam but just weren't a right anyhow, but all of who had had premature deaths and some of whom weren't that much older than Terri Baby along with a couple of her aunts that were Andre's age. It was all very confusing for Terri's sons to keep track of at the family reunions. And to think it had all started with a couple of orphans on a potato farm that got married at fifteen years old—her grandparents. An American story. Another one. Not so much privilege there.

They drive past a King Kong restaurant with all the various sized ape/monkey statuary prominently displayed in the front of their cafes. With the odd deer and Madonna. The two of them decide they should get a bite to eat before hitting the Thirty Club. The place is full of palm trees, Christmas lights, King Kong movie posters, funky monkey accoutrements and paraphernalia. And the food is good. Better than Hooter's.

CHAPTER TEN

THE RIVER RUNS DEEP

Lies! You're all lying about my boys!

— Ma Barker

Seeking La Llorona again, she came to Andre in a dream. At least he thinks it was a dream... He was all scratched up—he was ALL scratched up: what the fuck? Couldn't remember much. Probably too much Irish yoga. He fuzzily recalls glimpses of screaming around town in a gold convertible Mercedes coupe with Dardan. Dardan half artist/ half gangster Albanian stone mason/tile setter was very high, getting his powdered combination shit from back East somewhere in Jersey (probably not far from where Matty got shot in that drug deal gone bad in Newark—he survived, shot in the leg, Matty—who claimed he wasn't like that anymore, at least that's what Walter—before he died) told Andre: Andre digresses, again about true crime stories). Dardan had joined the Navy to escape judicial prudence as had become a Christmas ornament on the FBI's investigation holiday tree. And that's the short version of a long story of how the Albanian stone mason ended up leaving the pawn store in Hoboken, New Jersey and winds living in the tony neighborhood in a prosperous fine brick house of Regency—in West Omaha...he'd become part of the Nebraska Navy. He was some kind of loader of ordnance and picking up buoys and drowned bodies along the Missouri River—a strange assignment, hurt locker kind of shit, but it worked for him, kept him from getting busted like band on the run. The ordnance part, now that sounded safe—so the story goes and he got some kind of medical: a ticket to ride for Dardan the Dodger. Got to admire the hustler in this dope fiend. When Andre first met Dardan they're working on a small trim job (ironically a cop's place) Andre's got from a cop friend of his and Andre started doing a little math and finally asks Dardan how old he was when he enlisted in the Navy? Dardan tells him he was about twenty five and Andre not knowing this guy from Adam retorts—"most the time when a guy signs up for the military at an older age like that...they're in trouble." That was kind of a BINGO—let's just say Dardan did not join under any auspices of patriotism, but more from a necessity to evade the law. Andre remembers talk of giant five foot butterflies from the Amazon. He thinks he should still be able to make the funeral of old man Malay at Saint Mag's with seven priests presiding, twelve grandsons as pallbearers and Andre had heard the bishop may be attending. He also thought there was still time to turn his life around. Too much fun the night before starting out at hip howling coffee shop that use to be the gay blade Diamond Bar to meet with the great artist Patrick Williams, who Andre considered the technically and conceptually the best artist in Nebraska, was doing paintings of all the statues torn down from the mostly peaceful protests with artist/sculptor's name, date of birth of sculpture and date torn down, interesting—history erased...then down! Patrick and Andre had ties back to the Nineties in the art scene in Seattle and Portland. He had just gotten rejected by Lauritzen Gardens for his flower murals which Andre considered a pure unvarnished deal of politics, Andre had seen the paintings and believed they were perfect for the botanical garden setting. Patrick had said something about giving the powers that be five hundred dollars and Andre quickly retorted that Williams probably needed an uncle who could donate at least five thousand to the Amplify Arts Team nonprofit. Williams had also just gotten his submission to the brand new Omaha Central Library call for public art which was getting constructed by Peter Kiewit Corporation denied. They were casually waiting for Dardan drinking their coffee chatting on and on sometimes with the gregarious coffee publican owner. Patrick shows Andre some of the emails exchanged. The artist tells Andre how he'd done paintings of Nebraska writers such as Mari Sandoz and Willa Cather—cuz like y'know, the building is going to be a large library… Here was one of the responses from one of the selection facilitator design team process external panelist's feedback: I appreciate the idea of representing significant Nebraska authors. However this is a general approach and this project does not address the inclusion of historically marginalized groups or the process of colonization that led to the displacement and genocide of Native people. Integrating complicated, troubled, and unsettled histories would encourage blah-blah, say no more. Thank God! Dardan finally shows up arriving as high as a Chinese weather balloon. WTF Andre couldn't read any further; backwards, redneck, hard working, alcoholic, hillbilly sweet home 'we don't coast' Omaha has gone FUCKING woke. Introductions made, pleasantries exchanged with the artist soon having to return to his studio leaving Dardan and Andre to their own devices that eventually led to the enchanting Old Market to La Buvette to drink glasses of French red wine barely delivered by surly skinny tee-shirt wearing waitresse upon brick paver sidewalk patio to peer out over the chalky red bricked streets, eventually screaming around the afternoon in gold coupe convertible (reminding Andre of screaming, careening around in black Porsche around Fall City, WA with armed and dangerous hillbilly pal on various deliveries) onto the Interlude, the VIP Lounge, the Green Onion, the Holiday Lounge, the Happy Bar, enjoy some at the Tequila Garage, drag into Cohen & Kelly's and concluding the evening at the Bacchanal as Hochek barks orders at his wacky staff where the artist as not so young a man Andre resigns to leave the other artiste'/artisan Dardan to his own stone broad vices as he's chatting it up with an ex-Mrs. Nebraska and her rapper hip hop well pierced chick friend, to go MIA and stagger to his Howard Johnson hotel room—collapsing to find blood all over his sheets like a baby seal had been slaughtered to find a cute fat naked waitress smiling in his bed. Another one. Those poor baby seals. What was that about here all the time? Just Andre's luck. Andre had had a lot of chaos in his life. This one was a little dusky one—and the hurdy gurdy, hurdy gurdy gurdy man comes singing songs of love. It's all about the Re-Search. And finding La Llorona. His quest. He knows he was with that bitch last night. He's getting too old for this shit— but he can't help it…the drama, for he is a man of the opera, just trying to deal with his summertime sadness. A couple of months later he would get a call to pick Dardan up at the airport after he escaped from a rehab center in Michigan. It's all part of the process. After a few rounds of whiskey, trying to find a bigger bag of some stronger stuff for Dardan, Andre returns him to his wife of French descent, a classical concert pianist and debutante alumnus from the prestigious Duchesne Academy for girls. Like a Neanderthal, her playing would soothe his naked savage soul. He'd rest by the side of the baby grand as she played.

Later on, he laughs after enjoying the sumptuous breakfast buffet at the Bacchanal with the varied guests of the Howard Johnson Hotel. Andre says hello to all the regulars and employees that lived there. Hochek was somehow up doing inventory. Andre had no idea how he got up after all these festive gatherings and alcoholic powwows and did it. But he did it like clockwork when Andre barely staggered and could only see with one eye… Thankfully the security detail, Action Jackson, was around with his trusty pit bull Hazard that swung from the pole clenching the rope pull with mighty jaws—that spectacle always made Andre feel safer. It was kind of the greeting party for the potential patrons to the hotel just off I-80 in the heart of Omaha. Andre gives him the peace sign as he gets his Eggos and sausage. His girlfriend, Annie Scavio, the bookkeeper for the hotel is sipping her coffee. She was from St. Ann's right off Poppleton just down from the yard she had casually told him one evening at the Bacchanal. Andre casually mentioned his familia had built that church; slaughterhous- es and churches all throughout the mecca of South Omaha— along with paving the streets, brick after brick. She nods with a grin. He is sure it's something funny. Half the people that worked at the Howard

Johnson lived there. That's how Hochek's buddy the manager, ran it—they were like indentured servants. It was a cast of characters. Windows on the seventh floor getting blown out as the cops busted a meth lab with a little too much exuberance: exciting times. Andre recalls or has fate simply reminded him once again? Been getting his ass handed to him ever since his return—back to Omaha.

Many truckers stayed at the hotel where they could park their semis along with the various traveling construction crews from states like North Dakota and Indiana, et cetera along with the families in town for a kids' hockey tournament or a Pope Paul the VI convention after or during the swingers' happening on Floor Nine. And then there's the hookers…pulling up and hustling that wagtail at the bar. Some of them lived there. Andre gets a call out of the blue from Doug who is pulling into Omaha in his eighteen wheeler heading to join his Canadian brothers protesting the French guy's dictates of mandatory vaccinations, then he's on his way to DC. It's a long voicemail. He's part of the "Freedom Convoy" and the "People's Convoy" and one of the organizers of it cuz everybody's had enough of all the bullshit! It made sense to Andre as he hit them truck stops along I-80 with all them truck drivers black, hillbilly, Mexican and Sikh—all driving and everybody moving about with no masks on, just hauling goods: essential workers. Like magic, they couldn't get infected like the tough old clerk-chicks with their tattoos smoking their cigarettes taking a break outside amongst all the diesel fumes. Then Andre, just to remind those not paying attention—he'd go a few miles east and get a coffee at Whole Foods where masks and lotion were being dispensed everywhere and six foot Big Pharma Fauci protocols being readily consumed by all party members. Andre felt safe there…like being back in Seattle amongst progressive people. He returns Doug's call. Why not? They've had a few adventures together.

"What the fuck?"

"Am just pulling out of O'Neill, Nebraska. Got me a load of pork bellies to drop off in your neighborhood. Would say hello if you happen to be around and not in Kenya or Guatemala or somewhere.

Lots of crazy people here in O'Neill. A bunch of Fenians. We gots lots to discuss. Need to bring back Civil War veteran John O'Neill and the Fenians and invade goddamn Canada!"

"Yeah—am here, staying at the Howard Johnson Hotel."

"I know that goddamned place. Ha! I see ur still livin' large Andre, livin' large. Livin' the dream. Glad to hear it—not much has changed. A couple decades later. I'll see you in a bit."

"Oh boy. Can't wait. Interesting story—John O'Neill did a lot of fighting in the Civil War, was captain for the 17th United States Colored Infantry. Started out as a sergeant in the cavalry. Kind of like my ancestor General Jones who fought at Kennesaw with Sherman. Wounded three times. Cavalry. One of the few Irish born generals. Yeah that O'Neill dude invaded Canada three times to get back at Britain for what they did to Ireland. Ulysses S. Grant pardoned him. Then he invaded again. In the Dakota Territory. He was setting up O'Neill as an Irish homeland. I'm sure you fit right in—rebel rebel."

"10-4 copy on that pal. Breaker one-nine bringin' in the bread, some Old Homey Bread. For the pork bellies. Tell Mavis: hi, and her mother CW."

"Getting a lot of radio chatter. On citizen band. Put the hammer down, I'll have the Old Crow ready."

"We got ourselves a mighty convoy. A might convoy. After Omaha—we be crashing Chi-town to make the dance before blowing our horns onto DC and Canada. We getting' tired of all this negatory."

Jesus—what was Andre thinking? This will be a night to remember. Like back with Hochek, the coke dealer chick and the ex-NFL dude who coached the semi-pro Omaha Beef football team. And it was. Got really queued up on Q-Anon that evening. A lot of it made sense to Andre by the end of the evening and so much Old Crow down. Doug was all about the present… and his family and the future of America—there wasn't that much on the fishing yore of Alaska and the past-past of Iraq. He met a lot of the crew and got on well

with the pit bull Hazard and his owner who was head of hotel security—sharing prison stories. Then they hit the American Dream. It was
a busy night there with a band outside. Xtasy was looking exquisite
as usual with that Bantu backside of hers, this time as a 'blonde' black
chick and always very leggy leg. "Blondes have more fun," she says
to Andre—they kind of have a thing... money helps. And then there
was Baby—a little cutie brunette. A couple of rounds of drinks with
some generous tips for the women folk and discussion of matters of
political import. The next morning Doug was on his way: hauling,
trucking. An essential worker. And hard-working patriot. Doing the
best that he could for his wife and family. That was a blast from the
past, Andre shudders.

The next day Andre takes off to hit the cabin along the Platte
and visit his father. He's driving the old Chevy K-10 square body
pickup with a cracked windshield and busted fuel gauge. He's about
to Sapp Brothers Truck Stop and he knows he's got to get some fuel.
He's about a half mile or so from the exit. He pulls over to the right
quickly to get on the shoulder for he knows he is running out of gas as
the vehicles careen onward. He gets out and is just beginning to walk
when a car pulls up. It's kind of a shitty little car. And a little brown
man gets out. Andre looks at him. He's not Mexican. They talk, he's
wearing rumpled khaki Dickies and a gray t-shirt with tennis shoes.
He seems together enough and friendly: not a psycho killer. The
dude says he'll give him a lift. Rock on! They get chatting, the cat's
name is Mego and he's heading that way to the auto auction—to buy
some; he's got a car dealership in South Omaha called Jeddah Motors
off N Street. Mego drops off Andre. Andre buys a gas can.

Mego says with a smile. "Hang tight... I'll be back."

Andre can't believe his luck. Mego shows up grinning. Andre
fills his car up with fuel even though Mego says just put five bucks
in. He's getting a ride back! They get talking more. Got it –he's from
Saudi Arabia. Back in the early Eighties he was on a full ride scholarship at Creighton University to become a doctor. Then with his older
brother and other Saudis got mixed up in a scene... he said it was

gambling and things … and lost his scholarship. He couldn't blame his older brother for leading him astray. It was his decisions, his choice, his call and responsibility… nobody else, in not making it through medical school. But Andre knew that was all bullshit. He knew of these guys. His girlfriend sold to them. They bought lots of cocaine. Those Bedouins.

They got to Andre's Chevy truck not far from the levy. Andre puts the gas in, Mego gives him a few tips and the breaking bad baby fires up. Andre don't say shit to Mego about how he knows him and his story pretty intimately. They shake hands. Barely a half hour has been wasted. Kind of bizarre. Andre will righteously buy a rig from this dude someday. Maybe two or three. And Andre has people that can verify what he speaks of… oh glory days, glory days. Ode to Gloria!

CHAPTER ELEVEN

BROKEN APPLES

All unhappy families have unique stories,
all happy families have the same story.

—Leo Tolstoy

Andre had hit some of the mostly peaceful protests in Seattle, Portland, Omaha and Atlanta. Nothing like a little political mob violence to keep the community spirit up: it takes a village as Hobbes and Rudloff look on from a nether world. He'd been chilling out in Costa Rica with his actor/comedian buddy Barger down at his condo on the beach because they both knew lockdown was coming to California—and that you wouldn't even be able to walk along the beach because the authoritarian fun-hating hysterical control freaks had inculcated themselves amongst all the mamas and the papas so thoroughly into the Beach Boys' golden state of surfing U.S.A. Couldn't have it… no more California dreaming there while the slick ex-mayor of San Francisco and the present Cali governor hits the fancy Napa wine country restaurant The French Laundry for a birthday party with his Silicon Valley pals and donors while shutting down the state to all common sense—let them eat cake…(the peasants) kind of clown guy he is. So after a couple months of enjoying the Guatemalan Zacapa sexual rum and sandy sunny parties of Costa Rica Andre makes the fateful decision to return to the States to see how it's going. And he thinks, let's make it Seattle. Wrong move. And Andre the flowering shoot of the Merovingian vine…gets off a crowded bus downtown and ends up in the middle of a riot amongst masked fascist malcontents. He's having flashbacks of the flash grenades from the righteous 1997 WTO protest/riots of trying to keep complete supplication to the CCP Chi-Coms from happening across the globe. But this is bigger. Much bigger. Winds up in King County jail and had been only listening to Pearl Jam four months earlier in Seattle and everything had been laid back/uptight normal cool kind of hip groovo, boring Seattle. Now his old happy gay neighborhood in Capitol Hill from the 1980s was called the Chop Zone (and then they called it CHAZ) and had declared its "autonomy" from the rest of the country. Antifa goofballs were traipsing around playing Che Guevara checking peoples' papers and doing other fascist Brownshirt harassing bullshit like that. The black bandanna face covered fools he found himself surrounded by that night kept attacking the federal courthouse building. It was a bad clown show and of course none of those idiots got arrested. The debutante mayor had poignantly declared it was going to be a "summer of love" after doing a bunch of blow one night of partying hard at the Wild Rose with her sisters and Andre proscribed like most things involving the word 'love' was an elusive matter of definition and interpretation. The good Catholic mayor from the best all-girls plaid skirt-wearing high school, with her degrees from Notre Dame might have miscalculated on that prophecy. Fuckin' stupid, like what—Homage to Catalonia? Haight-Ashbury which was pretty fucked up and gave us Charlie Manson? An MK Ultra project gone wrong, way wrong. The nuns obviously got to her…in some delirious way. 'They're not liberals. It's the Left'—dummy, ja-ha! What a world. What a savage nation—all foggy and drunk. Some of this coined by an old school liberal journalist, what's his name?—catching him on the AM transistor radio occasionally: got Andre laughing, FUNNY, if you're a little twisted, in an un-funny world. And— 'they're not on our side': America. Such a savage nation. What the fuck were those nuns teaching her back then, obviously not enough compulsory prayer to inoculate her childish soul from this virulent infection… and what's Woody going to think when he hears of Andre's arrest—

fuck he might be proud of him. He's better call Ed Sledge. Though it was just an accident and Andre was an innocent bystander. Better call Gibson his criminal defense attorney if he's not out on the coast in La Push serving as a judge for the Quileute tribe, or up in his treehouse tripping. Fucking Eric could be attending an Indian women's legal conference/convention in Vegas right now. Andre barely managed to get him to SeaTac airport in time to catch his flight to the last one—surprised they let him on the plane given the condition he was in. Charmed life old Gibson—oh what a lucky man he was. Crazy as it seems Andre finds on the steel bunk a copy of Eric Hoffer's The True Believer. He'd read it thirty to forty years ago or so...

The fanatic cannot be weaned away from his cause by an appeal to his reason or moral sense. He fears compromise and cannot be persuaded to qualify the certitude and righteousness of his holy cause... His passionate attachment is more vital than the quality of the cause to which he is attached. To live without an ardent dedication is to be adrift and abandoned. He sees in tolerance a sign of weakness, frivolity and ignorance. He hungers for the deep assurances which comes with total surrender—with the wholehearted clinging to a creed and a cause. What matters is not the contents of the cause but the total dedication and the communion with the congregation.

What a world.

And Gibson takes his call and bails the dear boy and heroic dandy, out of jail picking him up in his red Jaguar convertible E-type: a beautiful automobile. It feels good to drive away in a Jag. Gibson gives him a little bump. It clears Andre's sinuses. Makes him think more clearly. He post Andre up on Connolly their globe-trotting mountain climbing guide buddy on his latest walkabouts and whereabouts. It's all good clean stuff. Andre might be getting off the airplane after being gone months and it'd be Connolly who'd been pretty vacant for years and would tell Andre he's in town from the Andes and they' make the rounds, hitting the old haunts and dives about Seattle, recounting the raging parties and back country mountain slopes skied and blazing white water rivers ridden with some electric golf thrown in occasion-

Parks • Sempek • MacNeil

ally as jets careened above, neglecting to go out on the Ferris wheel in downtown Seattle out overlooking Elliot Bay or participating in any walk-a-thons while the Space Needle burns on fire.

CHAPTER TWELVE

WEIMAR REPUBLIC

Protest is when I say I don't agree with something.
Resistance is when I ensure that things I disagree with no longer
take place.

— Baader-Meinhof Gang

It's not that complicated... The mob put together a lot of shell corporations.
What do you think they got paid direct with a little check and their
name on it? Mock the hysterics. How did we get so many hopelessly
naïve and dangerously gullible people in this country? Giving money
to all these shakedown operations run by reverends. Andre does
some Re-Search trying to figure out more about who some of these
goofy black bloc lunatic militants were. He remembers a number of
them running around at the WTO protest in Seattle, but this is different—they have greatly grown in number and aggression. He goes to
the public library downtown—zombies abound everywhere staggering, shooting up with rigs hanging off their scraggly arms, defecating
on the sidewalks in front of fine boutique cafes. Omaha doesn't have
these problems—they don't coast as the slogan goes... along with
the official tourist motto—Nebraska, honestly, it's not for everyone.
Not sure what all the blue dot hee-haws in Omaha are thinking with
their irrelevant virtue signaling. Well no doubt, one could keep
wondering, as Andre scans the dystopic horizon surrounding him.
No need to put Mad Max movie sets together—just go under the
West Seattle Bridge. He continues his studies, his Re-Search... all

part of the down and out in Seattle gig in the cheap fleabag motels along Route 99 where the pimps shoot it out semi regularly as the hookers scatter in their high heels, not far from the Fifth Precinct. Andre recalls waving to his neighbor the black transvestite every evening: "HI," as Andre pays little attention to the hapless mental patient sitting and gibbering next to him. There were always crews around one foot away from living under a blue tarp: the Seattle City Council might try calling it: affordable housing. Again Andre thinks careful what you get good at. And maybe he should change genres... literary-wise. There's method acting and there's—method writing. It can be an occupational hazard.

The Treaty of Versailles was economically crushing the Germans after World War I. This led to much political instability. The German government faced many upheavals right after the war. Many of the Germans could not believe they had been defeated. In January 1919, around 50,000 communists led an uprising in Berlin. It was known as the Spartacist Rebellion. Rosa Luxemburg was one of the leaders. It was backed by Lenin and the Bolsheviks. It was crushed. Rosa was executed along with many of the leaders who weren't killed in the battle. Later on the communists regroup and align themselves with the Sturmabteiling, the original paramilitary of the National Socialist German Workers Party better known as the Nazis who wore Brownshirts and were Hitler's violent thugs.

In 1924, the German Communist Party formed their own paramilitary group. They had their own uniforms and the group adopted the clenched fist as its symbol which the leftist groups of today from antifa to Black Lives Matter have adopted. The Red Front Fighters' League as it was known, clashed violently with liberal groups and social democrats who they considered cultural fascists. It is believed that by 1929 there were upward of 130,000 members in the communist Red Front Fighters' League before it was banned. In 1932, the German Communist Party change their name to antifa for Antifaschistische Aktion (Antifascist Action). And Andre thinks, man—it's a lot fighting stupid. Everywhere you look. God doesn't save the stupid. This country is doomed. It's all an emotional tantrum. And we barely had clean running water here one hundred and fifty years ago. Plumbers: protecting the nation. And another reason we don't die like flies? The garbage men haul our garbage away... Whaaah? Talk about essential. Mock this squad of hysterics who just want to drag this beautiful backwards very imperfect country to its knees. Andre ponders nostalgically to the Seventies and Eighties—not a cellphone in sight...just people living in the moment fighting and fucking and going to church on Sunday. We were the last of the feral children. The parents all hanging around the card table drinking a six pack of Falstaff, Schlitz or Hamm's, smoking cigarettes having no idea or worry where their offspring was wandering for the last eight hours... much in black and white photography. And now Andre realizes we're all dealing with the goddamn Nazi communists again. What a shame. Thanks CIA News Network: Operation Mockingbird. He reads some da Vinci, thought it might help...ward off some against the totality of lying and cover up by the media/industrial/political complex.

Creature shall be seen on the earth who will always be fighting one another, with the greatest losses and frequent deaths on either side. There will be no bounds to their malice; by their strong limbs the vast forests of the world shall be laid low; and when they are filled with food they shall gratify their desires by dealing out death, afflic-tion, labour, terror, and banishment to every living thing; and from their boundless pride they will desire to rise towards heaven, but the excessive weight of their limbs will hold them down. Nothing shall remain on the earth or under the earth or in the waters that shall not be pursued, disturbed, or spoiled, and that which is in one country removed into another. And their bodies shall be made the tomb and the means of transit of all the living bodies they have slain.

O earth, why do you not open and hurl them into the deep fissures of thy vast abysses and caverns, and no longer display in the sight of heaven so cruel and horrible a monster?

Nah—it didn't help at all. In fact, it made it worse. No rest for the wicked—a closing door. He'd like to think Tom Rudloff can lead him out of this hell someday.

CHAPTER THIRTEEN

JUSTICE UNDER GOD

And I saw the beast, and the kings of the earth, and the armies, gathered together to make war against him that sat on the horse, and against his army. And the beast was taken, and with him the false prophets that wrought miracles before him, with which he deceived them that had received the mark of the beast, and them that worshiped his image. These both were cast alive into the lake of fire burning with brimstone.

—Revelation 19:19, 20

Reflections of...the family business—asphalt and inheritance. The politics. Son of a Bitch! What'd his grandfather Fast Eddy use to say—"They oil more during an election year." Piercing the fog of reality. A wigged wonder of a working girl calls out, "Hey baby! Are you down...? Andre says, "Maybe I'm down for what's up... What's a donation for the cause these days?"

"Oh I think Benny and his General Grant should fix what's ailing you," she smoothly strokes the reply.

"Damn!" Andre thought, "I have been judged by some experienced eyes and have been reduced to $150!"

From the looks of her, and her take on him, he'd hit low... real low, all-time low. He was starting to get use to it.

"Nah! Sister Souljah got no play, not enough dimes," says Andre, "Be a waste of your time and mine!" as he headed out into the great known unknown, forgotten and remembered ... feeling like how Rumsfeld must have felt sometimes. Been down so long... nowhere to go but up. Life on life's term amongst this tapestry of contrasts. The Neolithic dude springs her a tip just to help pay for the house.

He was beginning to get all these episodes confused in his pantheon of time... How life use to be.

He goes over some of his notes from the microfiche on the brothers Jones—which was extensive. Headlines like: Did The County Get All It Paid For? City Inspector's Arm Broken by foreman George Jones (they weren't suppose to throw dirt clods in the concrete mix), Mysterious Oil Deliveries, Phantom Oil Deliveries, etc. With the spokesman for Jones Construction being Andre's grandfather retorting with phrases like; "never paid a dime" "once or twice" "we routinely rented a dragline or a tractor and lowboy trailer to the county". The councilmen were NP Dodge, Dworak, and Al Veys with Rosenblatt as mayor. These Omaha World-Herald articles were in the fifties. Morgan was often given a summons and hauled into testify along with city inspector Jim Brick. Like a ritual every couple of years, part of the process. Of doing business. Before the overzealous FBI agents in their American hustle mode got draconian with RICO and decided it was time to put Flinn from Flinn Paving and Dambrowski from Land Paving in jail along with Andre's father and grandfather. The retired superintendent Morgan showed up every day down at the yard when Andre and his brother were working down there in the summers back in the Seventies. Again, to reiterate, Morgan had fought with fury at the Battle of the Bulge with a tank division. He would just say—it was cold. Yeah—cold alright as Andre recounts his grandfather telling how James J. took the back of a shovel cracking it across the backs of men he deemed who required some motivation.

Andre recalls, on that matter along with many others, so did the retired city inspector Jim Brick... He showed up every day at the construction yard or on the highways and streets getting paved. It was in these men's blood. They had passion for what they did. And everything they had gone through, fought and endured in their lives. Another line Andre comes across in the newspaper articles from the Fifties and Sixties with contract awards of up to 53,000 tons of asphalt paved a year—from Eddy with a casual succinct quip that kind of summarizes EVERYTHING. "They oil more during an election year."

As the heat of the day lingers, witness to a wedding, knowing full well it is an abortion ready to happen. Should Andre, a man for others, stand up and call the bride out for the nasty package of bipolar fun that she is? Save his bro from the eternal vixen ho? Andre ponders as the clock ticks…and the celebrant asks, "Is there anyone here today that…" Seeking jihad with a little bushido, Andre nearly feints. He loves weddings and the maidens in waiting. Got to follow the science. Fresh baby.

It's down at Sokol Hall. The ceremony had been done at Saint Cabrini with all the old statues. Andre hit every shrine lighting a candle praying for his soul and praying for his buddy—poor doomed son of a bitch. But he was definitely going to have some fun.

The band was good with some rockabilly to keep with the theme. The Mezcal Brothers with Gerardo in his best suit of lights. Andre had seen them back in Seattle years earlier playing with a couple of his loose musician associates, Knut Bell and Gerard, the bass player. That was a party. They got bullshitting and Andre had to ask them if Charlie Burton was still alive—(Nebraska Rock' n' Roll Hall of Fame: opening up for the Ramones). They laughed and said he was. Andre went up and reintroduced himself to Gerardo. He was the bridesmaid's cousin—all kind of a Sicilian/Irish/Mexican thing. It was all abrazos like a Costello wedding.

They smoked a couple of cigarettes as they pounded some shots of whiskey—one of the main fuel ingredients for rockabilly while throwing in a few signs of the crosses… He decides to forget about his buddy and the bride figuring they'll figure it out or they won't in this celebration of breeding. It was too good a damn party at Sokol to get weighted down by a few details from history. Besides there were some nice bridesmaids about—all in heat. For the body count—Andre's. And there's just something about weddings that makes people want to shed their garments and get back to apples and Eden.

Later on, like a romance novel… animalistic the way she kissed him. It was passionate. Tongues dancing fluidly, sensually. He bit her lower lip and ran his tongue across it. Then he threw her up against the wall. His hands all over her pushing up her dress. His hands big and strong grabbing her all over, squeezing her beautiful breasts hard and roaming all over her ass. She moaned with aggression biting his lip and holding back screams of delight and pleasure. His hand tightened on her chest as he kissed and sucked on a nipple then making his way up to her throat as he bit down on her neck. She let out a grunt of ecstasy and pain. She kissed his neck violently, she couldn't take it anymore, like a cat in heat, as she ripped his shirt off and they fumbled with the rest of the formal attire they donned for this official festive event and affair. He didn't even know her name nor, he was convinced, did she know his as they grappled in some backroom of the ancient great hall. Nothing but straight up lust emanating as they glared into one another's eyes longingly. She grabbed his cock with abandon and he shredded off her thong. Kissing slowly then fast from her neck to a lingering suck upon each nipple to softly biting her lips then sensually finding the sweet spot back on her neck. He dove down to her belly button and further. A small moan escaped her. His tongue flickered past her cute little perfect muff inside it just above her clit. Aw—she smelled and tasted good… this woman. He wanted to fuck her now, but he held off.

He slowly kissed around her shaven mound. Nibbling, then placing his whole mouth around her the folds of her lips. She getting wetter and wetter with each passing moment and movement of his. Almost like he wanted her to beg—teasing her. He was holding back with all his strength. His tongue slithered into the longing slit. Her hands were on the back of his head as she pushed his tongue deeper inside her. Her moans were getting louder as her juices flowed. He had her on the verge of a powerful orgasm as he flicked her clit with his tongue. She began shuddering, trembling. Her whole being down there. He knew it was time to enter her for real now. She gasped as he pounded her as they grooved in synchronicity. It was too much. She shook and struggled, seeking oxygen. He decided to waste no more time as she kept coming involuntarily. It blew his mind, it was that good, that high. They collapsed upon one another like a sacred eternity.

Not bad Andre thinks as he reads this from a letter he picked up of Walter's. He had only described the sumptuous coming together with the bridesmaid. Walter was putting it in as an installment for the Fifty Shades of Jones book. They had planned one that one being the money maker: to recoup all their losses. From the debt and rebellion. With some expounding upon the Delilah complex. But then sadly Walter died. Andre and the Lebanese guy, his bookkeeper, were slowly going through the mass of notebooks assembled over the decades. They'd come across a crazy letter Mac had somehow managed to get to Walter. It was a long drawn out tale from the aftermath of Iraq, Matty (recovered pretty much from the bullet wound from drug deal gone bad in Newark) Dubois, Louis Willy, Senor Agape', Doug the Bug leading the truckers' convoy, Alaska, the WTO protests, Judy and the kids, the Wu, the lockdowns, Castro, Canada, Trudeau, authoritarianism, Saddam and the savage death of Maurice. It all roiled together in the slurry of his Bukowski-ed out mind amidst the pools of alcohol and erotica.

He takes Maurice's papers and winds up at rest home for old French Foreign Legionnaires not far from Orange in France. He said it beat the hell out of Guyana and Devil's Island. And was better than Jonestown. Andre thinks with the brainwashing that's gone down in this country... we've all been drinking a certain amount of purple Kool-Aid. Eventually, he gets outed by none other than Didier. Winds up in the Live Free or Die State New Hampshire and becomes the house director at a veteran home that he describes to Walter as the house of broken toys; Mac the counselor—that all sounded very reassuring to Andre. This was all after Mac had made his first detour to Detroit to check on his cop buddy Derek who he said looks and acts a lot like Shaft. And that reminds Andre who once awhile back was golfing in Portland with his Harlem Globetrotter friend, one of the many brothers Harrison when a dude happens to call up the basketball player. For one reason or another, Andre overheard enough and not usually his habit, asks him who he was talking to…and Les replies: "Richard Roundtree." And Andre said: "Shaft?" And he said he doesn't really dig being called Shaft. Oh well, as Meadowlark and Curly Neal stayed in his place on Miami Street back in North O just a couple blocks from where the cop killing bomb went off and they pinned David Rice to the murder—the Globetrotter's older brother Richard remembers hearing the explosion; burn out the night man. Funny world. Anyway, now the inmates are running the asylum if Mac is in charge—kinda like the whole country. Andre decides he'll read more: later, takes a lot of energy—dealing with that rummy character.

It had been gnawing at him for some time…so Andre finally begins to compose a love letter to his girl AOC. He loves her and hopes she will go on a date with him if he can write a good enough letter. Andre believes in courtship. And believes AOC and him have a future. With her beauty and brains. And his moral compass. It begins.

Dear Sandy,

I love you. And always wanted to attend Boston University. And study economics. And get a degree in it and international relations. Just like you. How was it being an intern for Senator Ted Kennedy? He was a good swimmer and almost President. I like French bulldogs too. I think we have a bright future. Give all my love to the Ilhan Omar and the crew. Or squad: always TEAM AMERICA. Pocahontas is my favorite movie. I am part Cheyenne. But am not part Latinx, but am part Latin. Mucho French. And Basque. Habla espanol? Baby girl I really think we have a thing and should go out on a date.

Con amore,

Andre Jones

What a feelings arranger—he is… Ode to joy. And love. Andre the Eagle Scout and romantic diplomat. Trying to make America great again. Ah Baby Girl! Nebraska's already great. As Andre directly faces the sun, staring into the eternity of it all while his bittersweet women wear long black veils. They shed not a tear. But they walk the hills.

And in a preview to our next episode: stand by for news—a beautiful Czech psychiatrist continues to off her clients. For their own good.

Staring at dirt. The cold lumpy mound, recently disinterred, waited anxiously to take another victim, over time to claim and absorb it—reducing… to its soulless disintegrating fate, feebly protected by a metal box and a concrete vault. Another funeral to attend. It was like getting to be a hobby for Andre sometimes with Lahood and him in the front pew faking it like they knew how to do the Rosary with all the Luminous, Joyful, Sorrowful, Glorious Mysteries. Well, it's all about the weddings and funerals—for how people get together in Omaha. This one was Warsocki's father. He had returned a few weeks earlier from Mexico for his father, the kind of a Cro-Magnon dude. Nebraska strong, South Omaha Polack strong, but a philosopher and builder as Warsocki tells a story of him and his brother down along the lowlands of the Elkhorn River where they had a little land and kept a trailer and plywood shack in Dodge County with dad in a fedora on a cool crisp autumn day—as they pull up in the 1960s station wagon with the fake wood paneling. The boys are under ten years old. It's a cornfield with a giant cottonwood tree in the middle. It's all stranger than paradise. Everything is black and white—maybe it's 1970. The old man is going to cut down the tree, but it don't come down. So he hooks up some rope and chains to the station wagon. The boys look on in bewilderment. Something don't look good or right about this picture as dad starts revving up the station wagon as the boys look on from the sidelines. And with Polish will, like Atlas shrugged—the big tree starts to lean. And then comes crashing down and between two giant forks of the tree—sits that little station wagon and their dad in his fedora. The boys open mouths stayed frozen. He got out of the station wagon unperturbed like everything was normal and unhooked the rigging—because that was always his plan...as he coolly adjusts his fedora hat. That's where Warsocki's old man would get drunk with his South O buddies and shoot the Thompson machine gun—shredding the corn stalks. That story reminded Andre of when him and Warsocki after having spent near a week in the Saint Joe's knife and gun club hospital after a Carter Lake Chez Paree bar fight—got picked up by him wearing a porkpie hat and he acted about as cool as if he was just picking them up from District 66 wrestling or football practice. Very stoic and nonplussed—stranger than paradise, no fucking lecture: what the fuck to say? Put a spell on them...some Polish shit, he knew—Nothing.

The cemetery was south of St. Peter and Paul Church on 36th Street and full of Polacks, Croatians, Bohunks and proud Nebraxicans with names like Valdez and Martinez. It was near the Indian Hills Elementary where Terri Baby taught and the parents had the kids deliver her bottles of booze at the end of the year for a present (no shit) and Andre occasionally worked as a substitute teacher (trying to get along with her) as he filled in at a multitude of schools throughout North and South Omaha (him and Terri Baby were working together—to make Nebraska great again). It was kind of fun (that is being a substitute teacher, not a full-time teacher which looked goddamn demanding and awful to Andre).To him it was kind of volunteer work helping putting out fires—it just paid a helluva lot better than being a volunteer firefighter. Fortunately Andre spoke pretty good Spanish which was very useful given sometimes in a school like Castelar Elementary School not too far from the old Stoysich Butcher Shop and the Jones Construction Yard, Andre would have a class of twenty one kids and three of the kids' backs would still be wet. Andre would have to teach them in Spanish. He'd have beautiful upset Honduran junior high girls nearly crying, not knowing what was going on with not speaking the language and the general chaos of the classrooms. Andre did his best, but couldn't help but feel a little bad for them. Many attended—the wake and the funeral. Throwing some dirt six feet down the cold sad hole. Dworak was the mortician. Andre knew him from St. Joan of Arc and Dworak had been on the Kennedy's Mets team. Dennis Kennedy was a well-known artist and mad drinker in Omaha—with about nine kids; and also, a friend of Andre's father, but of course. As they would be hanging down there carousing at the Paradise Lounge in Westgate Plaza. Everybody knows everybody in Omaha.

They hit the streets afterwards, after the tears and reception and blessings from the priest. Andre drives, they recollect. Warsocki has only been back a few weeks. They decide to hit Shaheen's for some chai, goat and jirga with his Afghanis bros of the Shin Wari. As they amble their way to the café, Warsocki tells him of this recent happening from his home in Ciudad de Dios, Durango: Walking out of the store, something stood out—a big dreadlock wearing black dude, his family stationed across the street in the shade of a tienda/ store. He was asking for money. Asking for money didn't make him stand out here in the Sierra Madre, it was obvious that he wasn't from here. I walked up, gave him thirty pesos, he thanked me. I asked him where are you from? San Pedro Sula! I knew it before asking him. The majority of the immigrants going North are from this part of Honduras. Drug wars there and extreme poverty are the catalytic converter pushing them North. The Soros funded NGOs are part of the converter too. I advised him not to detour towards the mountains or he might be planting poppy for the rest of his life, and his wife and daughters sold off. He nodded grimly. I added that the Padre at the Catholic Church would help.

In silence they drove the end of the trip. That's a wrap dude… Nothing else to say.

The dust shrouded the scene, men hollered amongst the shadows, the noise of the machines and equipment, the whine of the cables and lifts…he thought he was playing the part in the Zola novel Germinal about the miners. Andre is working on a seven story hotel. There is a large crane and several aerial lifts. There's a hundred dudes demolishing the interior of this large building. The roof collapsed. It needs to be replaced. The work is dangerous. These are desperate men. Its seven days a week with ten hour days: grueling. Scaffolding is getting erected, up and up. Andre is often a minority in these improv crews as they push the carts of steel, wood and gypsum debris out the chutes, out the windows, out the container boxes. Some of the hillbillies worked at chicken slaughterhouses. Some of the Mexicans or Salvadorans went by the name Robert or Doug. Some of the blacks called their women who were in jail for cutting someone up. The cool black foremen named Steve who was built like a lean jaguar empathizes with Theo having to call his old lady up—hands him a smoke. Everybody on this gonzo construction project works their ass off. Taking the collapsed roof off was a wild process; a dodgy bit of business. Living a life of danger. The sun beat down. Sapp Brothers arrived every day to fuel all the generators and machines required to make it happen. Andre loved seeing the Sapp Brothers' tankers arrive—they'd been associates of Eddy's and Eddy's alcoholic brothers—who were more ruthless than smart. Eddy financed them through loans when they started and the company became a big customer of theirs. Now here he was. He came. He saw. What the fuck. Of what life use to be. Talk about hangover—Andre didn't need any. Every day in Omaha was a financial hangover to him. Putting the roof back on the beast was another harrowing prospect—what we do for money… He worked/ partnered a lot with a dude with dreadlocks named Ray, Lopez, a chilled smooth guy from Belize, a thick as a tank gregarious high yellow from New Orleans named Turk, a funkadelic refugee called Eclipse who must a been a roadie for George Clinton and crew back in the day and had crazy voodoo Halloween stuff as the decor on his red car while calling Andre "Brother-Man" along with hard-working, chain smoking tough and unflappable hillbilly who lived in a trailer out of Wahoo called Chad—they'd framed a church the winter before together, shoveling snow off the site at times working with a mad black bearded big Croatian hillbilly like grinning Ustasha who was the foreman named Willy who really knew his shit, knocking the piss out of that frame. Anyway, the job/project was about as weird as building that fancy brand new golf course was. What crews—with tattoos all over their heads, some on their faces, and of course plenty of neck tats! Yikes man. Too live crew—these weren't these airy-fairy, hippy-dippy freaks of the Left Coast, nah man these are some gritty freaks…making Nebraska great again, making America great again. Amen. Since coming to Omaha, Andre had poured a lot of yards of concrete on commercial sites, framed a lot and had hauled miles driving dump truck—for half the pay he was acquainted with. It was like starting over. He was learning a lot. Like an apprentice. For some reason, inspired by Larry from back in Iraq, he wrote way big on the wall down in the cement parking garage:

Kill a language, kill a people.

Chaldeans

Virtual court of estrogen

I feel, I think, but I do not know, but it doesn't matter, because I feel.

Marxism is just a twisted inverted form of Catholicism/ Judaism eating its own tail, racked by guilt and feeling bad…

Andre enjoyed writing obscure stuff in public places. Call it poetry, call it graffiti. Get people to think…that might be a stretch. Getting back to last week's episode…as a reminder for our short attention span deficits.

CHAPTER FOURTEEN

GOD'S KIMONO

"Death is our Business and Business is Good!"

—painted on the side of a U.S. helicopter team in Vietnam.
(Warsocki had same painted on side of track with .50 in Iraq)

Andre reminisces that much of his life he has spent with a floating population. If you just counted the laundromats he had frequented—it was enough to make one's head spin. Mucho chaotic scenes going down at laundromats across the fruited plain of this great hillbilly nation-country. It wasn't too bad of one here off Leavenworth, not too far from Alderman's Bar where his sumbitch redneck looking like a hard James Caan, his buddy Billy's mother would go with her father after mass at St. Peter's—back in the 1940s. The joint had a very celebrated karaoke where the girls would get fall-down drunk as a third of the country was in full-on China/Bolshevik lockdown nanny state syndrome. Nebraska/Alaska is what Andre determined—his most liberal hippy bohemian beatnik pals in San Fran, Portland and Seattle would be aghast in horror if they could have witnessed the sacrilege of it all; not following the science. These backwards people needed to be supervised. No masks, no vaccinations, no worries—Andre loved it like a Sex Pistols song: Anarchy in the UK—always. The Dinka women wore their colorful garb, the Mexicans seemed to be having a piñata party, the poor whites and blacks went stoically about their business of getting their clothes washed. The TV is blaring Jerry Springer who

Andre didn't realize was still around: something about trannies and nancy boys playing sports against girls—so much for Title 9 and I Am Woman Hear Me Roar; Andre recounts again and thinks after enjoying so many mornings for years chomping on Grape-Nuts hearing feminist theory expounded upon by psycho-muppet chicks...where's all the feministas now—Helen Reddy, Gloria Steinem, Hilary and Madonna? Madonna was still probably too busy threatening to blow up the White House with all the ladies wearing the pink hats. Hilary was probably at home going over classified documents on her personal Apple server before she starts smashing them with a hammer to destroy the evidence: oh well. Andre was getting tranny-ed out. It all had a different meaning back in the '70s and '80s when you blew a tranny than it does today. Could all be bullshit anyway... a Russian hoax, etc. But probably not. So much confusion. What all happened to black lives matter? Guess just send a check to some PO Box at some obscure USPS office—somewhere. Good fuckin' racket and shake-down that one—with all the idiot woke corporations dumping millions in that bullshit scam while a slaughter every weekend goes down in South Chicago, Philadelphia, Tacoma around Hilltop and North Omaha with nearly 10,000 black homicides a year, that's black on black crime. The numbers are way higher than any other ethnic group... Vietnam War with a whole lot of shooting happening and about 60,000 dead American military killed with around 7,500 of them soldiers being black: that's a lot of blood shed by black Americans—got that every year in American cities! But what to say, don't say their names. A whole lot of those woke well-meaning corporate suck-up sissies must have a lot of guilt—they don't want to be all Marxist about it and say perhaps the system is rigged and that the individual cannot overcome (their philosophy)? Nah—we'll just blame it all on race. And white privilege as he observes two young Mormon men in short sleeve shirts and ties around their necks bumbling across their bridge—the Mormon Bridge off Florence in North Omaha. Clueless! Salve for the soul. For Andre it was good to be living amongst sane people with real problems. The Wu numbers were picking up and the bats were flying, Andre didn't want to infect his father. He was working for a contractor and had fixed up a couple of ex-military houses for Fort Omaha. The contractor was eventually going to rent them out. That's how he ended up residing in North Omaha. Living in North Omaha wasn't too bad—people mostly just doing the best they could amongst the Crips, Bloods and Clicker-Clackers, the Sudanese Dinka and Somali gang that mixed amongst the Hmong in the nearby projects tilling their small garden plots, barefoot in their conical straw hats carrying buckets of water with wooden yoke upon their shoulders—Andre be tripping at this Third World spectacle here in Omaha. Living next to Sanford and Son, always working on a couple of beat up cars or trucks in the back: Theo was cool as they shared a chaser of Olde English 800 occasionally with Theo's favorite bottle of bourbon—we're speakin' George Dickel by gum! Out on the white plastic lawn chairs around a rickety card table on an occasional balmy fall Sunday playing some cards. Theo wasn't much about or for these mass movements—thought they were mostly filled with a lot of frustrated misguided spoiled people. That was his take—a bunch of fun haters he calls them. Andre had several interesting discussions along those lines—some of the old black metal salvagers brought illumination to matters—here and on the West Coast. And the bars were friendly along with the local food mart/café and its Afro/Carribe village mural on the old brick wall with good biscuits and gravy though there was a shooting there the other after midnight—always after midnight to five in the morning, ninety percent of the shootings. Andre did find it disconcerting that about whatever bar he went to the bartenders would have a sacrament of Jameson whiskey neat waiting for him and maybe he didn't even recognize the bartender or hadn't been in that particular hole in the wall in weeks or a couple of months. And also when the young brothers dealing the powders referred to him as OG in the various dives as they shared a little with him in their vices for sale as he tipped them generously. It gave him pause to reflect…besides being out of money, not working a great deal, writing furiously for seven hour stretches at the Wahoo library to desperately finish Fifty Shade of Jones for the Omaha libraries were still closed due to the Wu. On those cold winter nights he would make the rounds, play a little pool up at the Musette and then hobble back to his cot in the empty little well armed house about the size of a cottage just off Omaha's famous Lake Street and Thirty Third.

He went to reading while he waited for the washer to finish its rinse cycle with his fancy duds. Given the strangeness of the times and all the cancelling and double-speak a happening out there in social media Twitter land, Andre felt the necessity to revisit Orwell and Chomsky. Also, given the irony of his socio/economic station/ situation, a stark example of reversal of fortune, back in the old town again, he felt an obligation to read Orwell's down and out travels and travails in Paris and London. For he still thought, no! he believed in the words: Liberte', Egalite' Fraternite' for Andre Jones was part French. His great-grandfather had come from Aquitane and the great-grandmother from the watery La Camargue region with the white horses.

"There were eccentric characters in the hotel. The Paris slums are a gathering-place for eccentric people—people who have fallen into solitary, half-mad grooves of life and given up trying to be normal or decent. Poverty frees them from ordinary standards of behavior, just as money frees people from work. Some of the lodgers in our hotel lived lives that were curious beyond words.

I am trying to describe the people in our quarter, not for the mere curiosity, but because they are all part of the story. Poverty is what I am writing about, and I had my first contact with poverty in this slum. The slum, with its dirt and its queer lives was first an object-lesson in poverty, and then the background of my own experiences. It is for this reason that I try to give some idea of what life was like there.

Life in the quarter. Our bistro, for instance, at the foot of the Hotel des Trois Moineaux. A tiny brick-floored , half underground, with wine-sodden tables, and a photograph of a funeral inscribed "Credit est mort": and red-sashed workmen carving sausage with big jack-knives; a splendid Auvergnat peasant woman with the face of a strong-minded cow, drinking Malaga all day 'for her stomach"; and games of dice for apertifs; and songs about "Les Fraises et Les Framboises," and about Madelon, who said, "Comment epouser un soldat, moi qui aime tout le regiment?"; and extraordinary public love-making. Half the hotel used to meet in the bistro in the evenings. I wish one could find a pub in London a quarter as cheery.

It is altogether curious, your first contact with poverty. You have thought so much about poverty—it is the thing you have feared all your life, the thing you knew would happen to you sooner or later; and it is all so utterly and prosaically different. You thought it would be quite simple; it is extraordinarily complicated. You thought it would be terrible; it is merely squalid and boring. It is the peculiar lowness of poverty that you discover first; the shifts that it puts you to, the complicated meanness, the crust-wiping.

You discover, for instance, the secrecy attaching to poverty. At a sudden stroke you have been reduced to an income of six francs a day. But of course you dare not admit it—you have got to pretend that you are living quite as usual. From the start it tangles you in a net of lies, and even with the lies you can barely manage it. You stop sending clothes to the laundry, and the laundress catches you in the street and asks you why; you mumble something, and she, thinking you are sending the clothes elsewhere, is your enemy for life. The tobacconist keeps asking why you have cut down on your smoking. There are letters you want to answer, and cannot, because the stamps are too expensive. And then there are your meals—meals are the worst difficulty of all. Every day at meal-times you go out, ostensibly to a restaurant, and loaf an hour in the Luxembourg Gardens, watching the pigeons. Afterwards you smuggle your food home in your pockets. Your food is bread and margarine, or bread and wine, and even the nature of food is governed by lies. You have to buy rye instead of household bread, because the rye loaves, though dearer, are rounded and can be smuggled in your pockets. This wastes you a franc a day. Sometimes, to keep up appearances, you have to spend sixty centimes on a drink, and go correspondingly short of food. Your linen gets filthy, and you run out of soap and razor- blades. Your hair wants cutting, and you try to cut it yourself, with such fearful results that you have to go to the barber after all, and spend the equivalent of a day's food. All day you are telling lies, and expensive ones.

You discover the extreme precariousness of your six francs a day. Mean disasters happen and rob you of food...

You go to the baker's to buy a pound of bread...

You go to the green grocer's to spend a franc on a kilogram of potatoes...

You have strayed into the respectable quarter, and you see a prosperous friend coming. To avoid him you dodge into the nearest café. Once in the café you must buy something, so you spend your last fifty centimes on a glass of black coffee with a dead fly in it. One could multiply these disasters by the hundred. They are part of the process of being hard up.

You discover what it is like to be hungry. With bread and margarine in your belly, you go out and look into the shop windows. Everywhere there is food insulting you in huge wasteful piles; whole dead pigs, baskets of hot loaves, great yellow blocks of butter, strings of sausages, mountains of potatoes, vast Gruyere cheese like grind-stones. A sniveling self-pity comes over you at the sight of so much food. You plan to grab a loaf and run, swallowing it before they catch you; and refrain you from pure funk.

You discover the boredom which is inseparable from poverty; the times you have nothing to do and, being underfed, can interest yourself in nothing. For half a day at a time you lie in on your bed, feeling like the jeune squelette in Baudelaire's poem. Only food could rouse you. You discover that a man who has gone even a week on bread and margarine is not a man any longer, only a belly with a few accessory organs.

This—one could describe it further, but it is all in the same style—is life on six francs a day. Thousands of people in Paris live it—struggling artists and students, prostitutes when their luck is out, out-of-work people of all kinds. It is the suburbs, as it were, of poverty.

You discover boredom and mean complications and the beginnings of hunger, but you also discover the great redeeming feature of poverty is that it annihilates the future…

And there is another feeling that is great consolation in poverty. I believe everyone who has been hard up has experienced it. It is a feeling of relief, almost of pleasure, at knowing yourself at last genuinely down and out. You have talked so often of going to the dogs— and well, here are the dogs, and you have reached them, and you can stand it. It takes off a lot of anxiety."

Andre read that and thought: Man! He really needs to get the fuck out of Omaha—all these happy successful people…they really got on his nerves. He sent a text with a plea to Celine Reval, his beautiful ex-junky Alsatian editor and bon amie muse from Paris. Smoking just like Jackie O or Bacall, taking meds in the middle of the night and laughing, she is beautiful and a professor in literature and philosophy and had turned him on to Baudelaire decades earlier back in Capitol Hill/Seattle when pride meant something—the bad old Eighties. She was versed in Nietzsche, wine and the streets like le moulin rouge. She with two ambitious sons, Romulus and Remus (Andre could never remember their names) from a father of unknown origin, some rumors say he was a Russian oligarch living upon the isle of Crete, others, that he is of Dalmatian heritage and a captain of ships, anyway, she is a painter of bold abstract—with her tour de force of personality and love of the humanities she, like a Simone de Beauvoir, gave Andre, in aggressive and stoic argument, a push for renewed strength in his trials and quest. He needed that, like a baptism of fire and confirmation, for this entitled dandy, believed he was some kind of goddamn Don Juan prince wanting it all, and was relating all too pitifully well to Orwell's tales of woe. Poor, poor pitiful Andre. Like a prodigal son who'd been with many beautiful harlots. They wouldn't let him be. Grateful to Mercury and back. But dang there was no fatted calf left... Andre seeks his empire: Lectio Divina from his Latin classes at Rummel. Ah—those diamonds in the sun: silver and gold. It's so cold. The river—against the current, he doth goes. And visits he—fine partner in crime, a Polish countess of Krakow... who wound up in Berkeley via Chicago, Florida and NYC, in the early Eighties, waitressing in San Fran because of the Solidarity movement and due to a loss of her papers (passport being invalidated), with Lech Walesa and Pope John Paul II with the Vatican banks and money from the Mafia all over it, to break it all up with Reagan: the communism, the wall and the dictatorship of the proletariat... she ended up being a no papers dp refugee in America, shakin' that thing—they coming to America... Maybe this wop (without papers) had been a spy. Probably—Andre thinks, definitely some espionage going down with this one. She claims nobody ever approached her on the subject matter... She quoted Hamlet and sometimes Macbeth with full recitals of poems by Faulkner, Yeats and Stevens to Andre. As she did this, she'd get this possessed look in her eyes and Andre concluded that if she wasn't a spy, she was at least a goddamn Polish witch. Anka was really a peasant of hearty stock with exquisite looks and bendy body with rough blunt hands from so much gardening, sculpture and equanimity. Poor Andre thinks: have to get back to Krakow and visit Anka at her studio apartment in the heart of the old city and have her cook him some borscht from scratch with some pirozhki. It was all good—this borscht and bam-bam with a couple cigarettes. And then Andre thinks—where have all the babooshkas gone—long time ago? She got back occasionally to Portland and San Francisco to run with the Reval woman—Celine. Celine and Anka together had formidable elements of Thelma and Louise—no denying this. They soothed his restless, tumultuous soul and fumbling attempts seeking love. Sometimes with gratuitous torment. But he knows, for the sun also rises. From his world of bitterness, fighting the weight of time—getting older. But they won't let him be. Either. Like Patty Hearst. For the SLA. With a machine gun. Robbing a bank. Poor, poor pitiful Andre as he tries not to go off the cliff like a lone hitchhiker with these two Euro beauties—too many times, anyway. For as smoking hot Anka aptly stated to Andre driving by the nuke subs of Bremerton: if peace ever breaks out...the whole thing will collapse. The world, like his mind—against the current, in this age of reason.

And with that, it would appear, once again; only seeking diamonds and silver for politics was not Andre's religion, there is... Nothing else to say.

CHAPTER FIFTEEN

IN CRAZY FAITH

Ah you too Vanity!
I knew you would overcome in the end.

—Cyrano de Bergerac

As Andre so vividly recalls, it was such a perfect day and with night splendid before. They'd made up from the night before when Andre had called Terri Baby a bitch at Anthony's Steakhouse. Mavis, Coach Chuck to his players Boys Town Globetrotter (YOU SHUT THE FUCK UP! YOU SIT THE FUCK DOWN! Then he'd take them all to Goodrich Dairy for malts and root beer floats—Coach Chuck had taken cue from Brother Mott back in the day at Rummel) with the very nice stable hard working from the farm Bohunk couple originally from Wahoo that massively counterbalanced the rest of the dysfunctional alcoholic lunatic peeps, and them had all decided to go to their bar the Vino Paradiso, the bar owned by Mavis and Coach Chuck, to celebrate the rest of the evening. Everything was going pretty well till Terri Baby took offense again with Andre for calling her a bitch. He refused to apologize and thought she should be grateful he didn't take the whole platter of Fucinaro's spaghetti and smash it on the floor at the restaurant—sometimes Andre got angry. Others arrived at this place to join in the festivities. But Terri Baby wasn't letting it go, and kept telling everybody of this faux pas. Andre and Terri Baby danced to Lynyrd Skynyrd's Tuesday's Gone and he figured this

probably the end of the road for him with her. Then one of Coach
Chuck's five daughters shows up at the bar—the nineteen-year old
raven haired always tanned and barely graduated from Mercy High,
Abbie who was kind of Abbie-normal and often in trouble with the
nuns for how she wore her plaid uniform at the all-girls Catholic
high school in South O across from Holy Cross...and Terri Baby
tells her of this tragedy and Abbie not so normal simply says to Terri
Baby, "Well what'd you expect when you pick up a street guy from
33rd and Leavenworth?" Abbie always had Andre's back—laughed
her silly head off when she found out Andre wrote books: she had
never read one. And later that evening Andre told Georgia cracker
Mavis that he'd make a point to make it up for Terri Baby good that
night. And he did. So she, Terri Baby gone, like she does...with the
wind, had gone to work out early that morning at Orange Theory
with her sprinter's iron constitution. Somewhat grateful, riding his
blues, Andre decides he should celebrate with a little more drink of
tequila for it was Palm Sunday and what a year it had been with the
death of his father, assisting the coroner that night gently desiring
Miguel to get at least that respect, the funeral (and others)—Easter
being his father's favorite holiday resurrection. Maybe it was a very
good year for—gonna see where this train ends Andre. The pit bulls
wag their tails like conscious of his crusade. Terri Baby returns all
sweaty from her organized exercise, Andre takes her down. He's
going to be leaving Omaha. She says the son who works in Miami
wants them to meet with his crew of pretty chinchillas for brunch at
a hip downtown Benson spot. And they've got endless mimosas...
yay, says Terri Baby. At this point Andre is going with the flow...he
is in flow-motion and his loins are weary from the night before. She
really worked him over good. She is feisty; he is at her command.
They get in her old Cadillac and head north to Benson. To his destiny
and fate. At least this morning, after she pinned him down and then
let him be free, he shared some philosophy, stories and feelings with
her—and she didn't throw a blanket over her head: this time. He
had poured quite a bit of tequila down her belly that night having
lapped up much of it with a great afternoon of bowling at Western

Bowl (or was it Chop's Bowl?) with a merry crew was a steady stable Bohunk couple straight out of hardworking family farms circa 1930s, who served as the ballast with a sense of humor for this erratic gang of dysfunctional alcoholic lunatic clowns, they were originally from Weeping Water and Wahoo over near Waterloo (Czech Land, Nebraska—farm kids done good, with husband going from pipefitter/welder to VP of national corporation) as well as hitting an Irish bar with a Jewish manager for an Irish wake for a friend's dead father who was originally from New Jersey and had married a Quebecois Metis with some Jameson on top of all of that—Andre was well on his way that morning with a little top of the morning Patron tequila by the time they got to the celebrated hip brunch joint where all the young groovo-es hung in hip downtown Benson. They had to stand in line a bit. It was a dang good breakfast and his glass of endless mimosas was never empty—so you see, he was getting all that vitamin C he needed for the busy day ahead.

Terri Baby and Andre leave the young and the restless troupe of half a dozen and start meandering their way through the heart of the borough of Benson eventually finding themselves initially at Jerry's Bar with the cool old marquee to cool down with a cold can of Schlitz. Andre had not seen a can of Schlitz in decades. He had believed it had gone extinct, but here it was in this place that hadn't changed since maybe the early '60s. He had to go for the gusto! It was a nice speakeasy joint with regular friendly neighborhood patrons for a gentle nice spring early afternoon. Chitchatting away probably not about much the dynamic duet made their path to the next casual dive for another cool one. Andre might have had a shot of whiskey at that one called The Musette for a round of pool. It's an old pool hall that's been around for over a hundred years. Everybody is there, sometime...especially late at night. Andre casually says to Terri Baby: See—I take you places. She nods agreeably, almost stoically recounting the visits to soup kitchens and street missions. And Andre with that drunken lucidity realizes that Terri Baby and him still don't really talk much. But that was okay. It was a perfect day. Might as well hit the Cornhusker Bar to drink Hamm's—the land of sky blue waters and talk further about his life and put a little more of a wrap on it for the afternoon. They hit the Saddle Creek for some champagne from the tap tinking the glasses in salutation. Maybe gonna have to take her to church again someday. Still kind of a heathen—savage at times…hurt him good. She was so rough. Kind of Daisy Mae… Missouri Valley style/version nature gal.

They, the train wreck couple eventually make it back to her place where they are graciously greeted by her pit bulls. Her blonde friend Mavis calls and invites them to join her and Coach Chuck with five daughters and always going to save the Boys Town Cowboy basketball team…up at Happy Hollow Country Club (where Andre and his brother were barred from as kids because his father wasn't going to allow his sons to become country club boys) for cocktails and dinner. Andre responds on the phone to Mavis that he is: incoherent. Terri Baby leaves him to his own devices with the lascivious mongrel pit bulls and a half bottle of tequila to continue on her quest to fulfill-ment. Andre thought he was the fulfillment center. It's all a staggering prospect for Andre has to go to work the next day and it is creeping into late afternoon. Should he stay or should he go? He should obviously stay. But now he has to deal with his abandonment. By yet another woman. She uses him, and then she just keeps on a using him up some more. It's not really fair. He drinks some more and fatefully decide he can just slowly amble his way back to his trailer along Platte River where the upturned dead cows float by, to assemble himself for the coming week of commercial construction. In celebration of the concert he had attended to the week before of Kid Rock with Grand Funk Railroad opening before he primed up at the Tequila Garage to hit the MMA bouts to watch Crawford's man, the mighty Sullivan in his professional debut, he listens to: We're an American Band… way up loud. Him recalling at the concert how people were chanting so loud: Let's Go Brandon! Fuck Joe Biden! Tens of thousands. He remembers how a year earlier at the Eric Church concert how much audience participation was going on with the same little ditty. Not really the Pelosi/Hilary fan club around here. Terri Baby had gotten the tickets and they had all met friends of hers at Barrett's Bar off Leavenworth. It was a crew of young teachers gone wild with a couple of coaches—good group. Terri was senior by twenty years to some the teachers gone wild from podunk Nebraska towns with names like Beaver Crossing, Long Pine, Keya Paha, Bucktail, Broken Bow, Loup City and Hay Springs. Ah yeah and Custer County along with Sioux County. They were all still recovering from the night before from the Thunder Down Under male strip tease show where Terri Baby had been put on the stage to sexually assault and get sexually assaulted amongst the naked men from Oz with their cowboy hats on... Which later on entailed body shots backstage with the country band as the nature gals clamored and jumped in—"Shot! Shot! Shot! Don't be a pussy!" Terri Baby shouted at her younger peers. Or that was what was the casual out-take to Andre by a few of the younger novitiates. So Andre makes the acquaintance with these young Americans and notices one of the dudes had a tee that read on the back in red letters: GUNS CORN FOOTBALL and in the middle of the shirt was the word NEBRASKA. What a fuckin' backwards country, definitely where the N stands for nawledge—ain't gonna change these people with bullshit dumb motherfuckin' progressive notions of equity and Marxist guilt: FUNNY! Try to make people feel bad—shit's as bad as Catholicism. Kumbaya communist fucks like evangelicals messin' with young hearts and minds. TIME! Andre finds himself in seeming to always look for where the wild peaches grow—wasn't even drinking when he first got to Omaha. Third fuckin' drunkest state in the union—Nebraska/Alaska. Most of Wyoming use to be part of the Nebraska Territory. Seven years sober down the goddamn drain all in crazy faith he came—kind of like his erratic collegiate career and his misbegotten senatorial aspirations. What a hell of his own making! In drunken reverie he takes another jolt of tequila and makes that fateful decision to slowly assuage his way back to the humble cabin abode out upon the glorious and historic Platte River where the dead cows slowly floated by during the flood and turned the Great Plains into an inland sea and Andre couch surfs through Omaha, homeless once again as he had walks out of the flood between the Platte and the Salt Creek like it was the Sea of Galilee up to his waist in the churning frigid waters amongst large logs—and he thinks...no one saves Crow Dog. He reports to the firemen on Highway 6 as they airboat out the straggling residents. Andre's mind keeps floating; the past, the present not so much. In his old pickup truck it's not going well. The music is good and loud and based upon a true story, Andre is drunk and reliving the concert playing Grand Funk's: We're an American Band—

Out on the road for forty days

Last night in Little Rock put me in a haze

Booze and ladies, keep me right

As long as we can make it to the show tonight

Four young chiquitas in Omaha

Waitin' for the band to return from the show

Feelin' good, feelin' right...

Now these fine ladies, they had a plan

They was out to meet the boys in the band

They said, "Come on dudes, let's get it on"

And we proceeded to tear that hotel down

We're an American band

We're an American band

Minding his own reckless business, tooling up Highway 370, everything is going swell till Andre notices a group of many several motor vehicles with red lights flashing behind him. It is Palm Sunday. Like pulling into Nazareth (again). There is a drizzled awakening happening to Andre as he pulls the rig off on the shoulder with his hands high upon the steering wheel, but upon closer blurry examination Andre becomes aware that the police have guns drawn and are behind their car doors pointing them at him and over a speaker instructing him to get out of the vehicle. The dude abides to their wishes as they proceed to tell him to raise his hands in the air and behind his head and to get down upon his knees ... which he dutifully does while looking out upon the late afternoon rays of spring as the cars careen by him with arms out stretched—the roadside attraction. People would have hypothesized that he was a bank robber or something. Or that his daddy was a bank robber. But he never wanted to hurt nobody—Andre's daddy. As he goes down in a blaze of glory, as per usual, this is the apocalypse and his sabotage, Andre stares into the sun seeking an epiphany of a world everlasting, a world without end ... Knowing eternity is always near us. We're all on borrowed time.

Down on his belly, the police handcuff him, ask him a few questions as he cooperates fully because they are his brothers for he has worked with them much before and they are doing their job keeping the streets safe from derelicts like Andre. They are polite and professional with him as they haul him to jail but with one caveat—Andre, the tourist attraction, had forgotten about stowing one of daddy's German Lugers underneath the seat of the truck and had thus neglected to inform the police officers of his concealed weapon that he'd packed in these lawless days we, the people, were enduring through and tolerating. He'd let his CCW with Washington expire and had not taken the class required in the state of Nebraska. To Andre's surprise and dismay, it was much more difficult to obtain a CCW in conservative Nebraska than it was in liberal Washington. 'Lot of things were more liberal in the NW—strip clubs, drugs and property crime to start with ... plus not to forget the girls riding upon their bicycles naked in parades (it's not all bad on the Left Coast—lighten up). He did not expound upon this with the police officer much as he hauled him to jail and they discussed other general matters on life and the state of national affairs given the strangeness of the last two years. They get to the station and then the damnedest thing happens—they allow him to make a call so he tries to get a hold of Terri Baby, but to no avail...she's not answering, probably passed out. And Andre tells the cop that no dice with getting a hold of her and this is where it gets wild—he offers to give Andre a lift to her place. Andre was incoherent but coherent enough to be surprised as hell to hear that—thought it might have something to do with his seven year volunteer hitch/ deployment as a fireman/medic. Hadn't quite worked out that way for him in his past career in low intensity crime. A couple hours have transpired at this point. So he gets in the cruiser attempting to point in the right direction for he is not exactly sure of her address while the two of them carry on an interesting conversation about the curiousness of the national political scene—it was all very reasonable and common sense based. The police had been getting a hard time from some sectors of the community and society at large while other less productive sectors received no such criticism—nothing at all about defunding them from emotionally disturbed political activists with hysterical rants of protest and catharsis. It all seemed to lack equity: a world out of balance, a very upside down time for the nation as a whole in these most emotional times where all the criminals are victims and the victims—oppressors. Orwell couldn't have written a better script. Then Andre came to the realization that this arrest would probably dash his senatorial aspirations.

So they arrive near where Terri Baby's home and they happen to drive by it and Andre shouts, "There it is!" And the policeman slows the vehicle down and is about to turn around and Andre tells him, "It's okay—close enough." And he thanks the officer and thanks him again still in a bit of a state of shock at his good luck and bad luck at the same time as he jumps out of the cruiser. He heads to her place. It is near the midnight hour. He enters through her front door that she leaves open for Terri Baby doesn't worry too much about things. Andre is also keenly wary of getting greeted ferociously by her two pit bulls. He makes a loud racket as he enters so as not to startle and scare her and to let the pit bulls know it is him so he doesn't get his leg bitten off or have his neck ripped open. There is no response, no barking, nothing...so he continues walking to her room proceeding with a loud racket, flipping the light switch on to find the two pit bulls and Terri Baby all sound asleep sprawled across her generous bed. He shouts as Terri Baby rubs her eyes saying—what? where? when? why? As the pit bulls slowly peek their eyes open.

"I just got out of jail!"

"What? Where? When? Why?"

"I tried calling you!"

Slit-eyed Terri Baby is slowly coming into a vague consciousness.

"The cops gave me a ride—told'em to drop me off at my girl-friend's."

And without missing a beat Terri Baby says to Andre, "Well then—why would they drop you off here?" She might as well have just punched him hard in the head right between the eyes. It's a technical knockout: crushing. Andre knows the agony of defeat... and responds, "You fukkin' smartass!" Both of them pretty much still drunk as skunks. Finally, the pit bulls wake up, start growling at Andre as per usual and baring their teeth—grrrrr, grrrrr.

Early the next morning, she gives him a lift out to the hinterlands amongst the gray brown fields to get his truck out of impound as she heads to work. Andre has to wait around a bit. He observes a big feral black dog appear out of nowhere scavenging for a meal amongst the junk cars strewn across the lot. Andre feels for this dog... he relates to this dog in a weird way—this poor, poor abandoned beast. That he has become. Saddest sigh Andre had ever seen. Fucking brave dog/dead dog... son of a bitch.

He gets to the construction site that morning late. He had given the lead a text that he'd be late. It was of course, a very hectic dangerous day of setting steel with heavy equipment and the cool brother from Baton Rouge at this commercial project with the cowboy superintendent showing up that morning. He barely survives.

At end of day he makes a call to McKay's second cousin (poor old 9/11 McKay), Danny O'Dea, a fixer and consultant and nephew to Peppermint Patti, the old West O madam at large, riding around in her little red Corvette with the vanity license plates that read: CATCH ME. Danny happened to have just smoke a spleef leftover from Bono, or Sting, at a very rich client of his—who had a little birthday party with a fleet of Lear jets swooping into Omaha as he picks up his rotary dial phone. Demure Andre asks him if he knew of a good attorney. Dan O'Dea is also a bookie who works a bit at an all cash bar in South O and has his sources and finds him a great criminal defense attorney named Nick Radek who deals in homicide, border issues, assailants, miscellaneous mafia-type rough stuff, labor arbitration, cartels and drunks. They meet at a bar. In fact all Andre's meeting with Nick are at a bar. Kind of poetic. Justice. Almost. Nick asks him a few questions and Andre asks him a few questions about defending cartel members and Radek retorts casually. Radek says about the lawyering for criminals and writing such jurisprudence with the line from the old-time bank robber Willie Sutton: "Because that's where the money is." No rhyme or reason really, but money is in the stories...like a good Rock song where the song remains the same: of isolation, elation, vulnerability, reckless jubilation, suffering, misery, unvoiced/unspoken shadows. It's a sound start. To their working business relationship. And Nicky's got the scoop on a lot of the skinny on Omaha with a certain panache and casual outtake that Andre can appreciate measure for measure.

CHAPTER SIXTEEN

NOTHING ELSE TO SAY

To you only do I tell the enigma that I saw —
the vision of the lonesomest one.

—Friedrich Nietzsche

Nick gets him on a program that eventually will allow Andre to possibly get acquitted, but Andre has to attend AA/NA meetings where he works hard on the thirteenth step with modest success. He also has to do some community service where he ends up working along the highway on weekends. It all seemed pretty fair to Andre realizing how fucked up he was in the mourning process since the death of his father. Andre needed to straighten up. There was still time to turn his life around. I mean he was still in his fifties like not sixty years old yet … with the normal amount of girlfriends. It should have been a sign months earlier, after hitting the music scene at the Omaha Lounge dancing with Chanel and some of the sisters amongst glasses of champagne while MC Sherry making Roberta Flack proud, tore it up hip-hop with the R-Style Band 'killing me softly with his song…' and then rounding out the evening at the Green Onion amongst the ghosts of his grandfather and associates, to wake up that Sunday morning in his pickup truck to the friendly sign of the Green Onion. Could've been a clue. That blackout. Having been dancing with the beautiful African girls, drinking and carousing earlier that evening at the Omaha Lounge—seeking to forget all that ailed him … then hitting the Green Onion, not remembering much after that last shot of Patron amongst those most beautiful brunette bartenders in the world. Whenever that was in the evening late. But the bleary-eyed Andre seeking his medicine hat would not be defeated. He rousts himself looking around wondering what the fuck time it was? The sun was already pretty damn high. Somebody drives by with The Beach Boys playing loudly: I Want to Go Home. 'So hoist up the John B sail. The first mate he got drunk. Well I feel so homesick I wanna go home...'

In his orange jumpsuit, Sunday morning, Pentecost, working along the highway, fulfilling his civic duty judiciously bestowed upon him by the designated civil servants busy herding cats—all part of the diversion program. Andre picks up the trash littered upon the roads byways. He is at an intersection amongst his fellow inmates waiting for the van to come pick them up when Andre happens to see Terri Baby with the pit bulls come pulling up the cross street in a brand new Cadillac and Andre thinks and then says quite aloud, "Son of a bitch! Where'd you get that Cadillac!?"

He looks at her a bit sheepishly as he lightly waves. His new friends, his cellies, appear to be surprised at the scene—smoking hot blonde pulling up in a Cadillac, with pit bulls that might eat the fresh baby. Her window is open. She is smoking a cigarette which the state medalist track star hardly ever did. She drops her shades a little upon her pert arrow nose and looks at him with her slit green eyes. She's got playing Elle King's song "Ex's & Oh's. The pit bulls recognize Andre and begin to bark and snarl at him vociferously. She taps a few ashes off the smoke and sped off as the light changes kicking up some gravel. Brand new Cadillac. Terri...Tora! Tora! Tora! Like Japanese Zeros coming down on him at Pearl Harbor with the clash of explosions. Cuz he luvs her! Baby, baby... No more Roman holidays. Dang, man—she ain't a never coming back! Stunned, but defiant, his hallelujah had come and gone. Andre raises his fist in the air with a black glove on John Carlos style, staring at the sun like Crazy Horse like Quanah Parker, like Geronimo, hearing the pounding hoofs of millions of buffalo…as the Indian ponies run wild with them—hear the sound…the dance, feeling: the agony of defeat, looking out across the Plains, thinking: Delilah, they know not what they do. To us. This love for a woman. Kill you about every time—desperate. Proclamation. Ascension. Holy Ghost. Like a disciple he goes. Every time. The other inmates slowly begin clapping.

Eventually, Andre got his truck. In his pursuit of happiness— (kind of a First Amendment thing). With the 13-speed Road Ranger tranny he strums through the gears and drives around and around. Hauling whatever: rock, asphalt, dirt. Andre has got the old Mac dump truck painted up just how his father had them all done up with that black and lime green… On the tailgate he's got the ten pallets sign painted on the back of the truck's tailgate. It's the communication they'd share at the docks on the waterfront in Seattle back in the Western Pioneer days for another load of ten pallets. It's the middle finger set sideways. Some Fallen Angel bouncer/Montana dude door gunner longshoreman mutherfukker probably came up with it as Andre recalls—what a crew; the art gallery was nothing but a rogues' gallery—couldn't make this shit up with Walker, Murphy, Capili, Rolle and the boys. It all seemed appropriate to Andre. As a signal. For Andre chose his path. Let people know, as he waves his fist—he's still the Boss! Been getting his ass handed to him since he got to Omaha from his ever fateful return of exodus and banishment—in so many ways…seeking redemption song. For all the pain, indignations, humiliation and public embarrassment him and his familia had endured and suffered through. Be it from the fucking corporate bureaucratic fascist deep state lying Indian killing FBI indictments trying to put them all in jail for RICO bid-rigging conspiracy charges with the union shakedowns, et cetera or from the injurious, nearly libelous bankruptcy courts or the whispers and laughter of the measly fuckin' weak who always tear down the strong, bold, combative and unafraid like his father, rebel-rebel. Fuck this noise. Such dramatic work. It wasn't worth it—Andre's rebellion, his insurrection: the travel, the women, the parties, the writing and the curse of it with the books, oh the lust and the glory—in vain, in perdition…his delusion, the anguish to a mother and a family, the destruction of a company—he was warned by the Cassandra—Victor, the thick accented speech impedimented Walloon displaced person/dp refugee, who deserted the Belgian army to evade going to fight in the Congo, and had worked as a laborer for years for the company mostly with Chief, the Omaha Indian and Louie Harris, the old black foreman WWII veteran who was like another grandfather to Andre, Victor had warned drunk Bacchic Andre that he needed to take it over, they were stealing, stealing, stealing from the company, but now Andre knowing—now, his deaf ears opened, his eyes can see…he could have been a contender! The end of the dream. Grasping this empty bottle of smoke of his. Chasing the dragon, so to speak, of fame and fortune with nothing but debt and rebellion to show. He knows dissidence—like smack, he blew it man… Can't kill the rooster, but don't kill the golden goose for fuck's sake! The grandfather Eddy had warned them as boys—the workers will steal as they smile at you: the accountants too, especially the accountants; trust no one. The hope, the hope, the goddamn hope, how Andre detested that word…and. The fucking tragedy. Where have all the lemon groves gone? And the pretty paint horses, the oil and the asphalt? So now, with ball and chain, and all the breakage…he sees, he seeks…rebellion, revolution, bemoaning a dirge. Sad song: everything's his fault. Disintegration. Entropy—decay, space. Like last tango, the last picture show, a last hurrah. With motorcycle jacket on. In Omaha: downtown. Staggering. Lurching sideways, weaving forward like a boxer on the ropes, down and out, but not defeated. No Cinderella aqui. Reeling through his ancestors' built chalky red brick paver cobbled streets. The rain drizzling down, the street lights glow with no direction. He's unknown, him, seeking love. The love of… The beautiful heroine woman, with her tattoos and dark brown hair, Phaedra—wearing a satin blue dress, plays the cello hard, with purpose, rhythmically, driving: frappe-moi, frappe-moi, Andre hears her having given away so much he loved. Andre imagines kissing her hard on the mouth as he whispers—we were born to die, like an echo. It was his to take. His to perish for...this waking dream. The end of—what he needs. He got nothing else to say. And nothing to lose. A broken man, Andre seeks love, and revenge...

EPILOGUE

Once upon a time, Andre is having a sitdown at a bar with a sexy literary agent/provocateur he just met a few weeks earlier at a fancy West Coast authors' conference. He's got two manuscripts of western romance and adventure he thinks he can sell. He starts out the meeting looking straight at her from across the table banging his straight fingers down hard on the wood saying to her, "I want to make a lot of MONEY!"

Many years later, Andre realizes—no amount of money could recoup much of his losses.

Acknowledgements:

to our poor mothers

About the authors

CONON PARKS is a card-carrying liberal and member of AIM, the American Indian Movement. He sometimes works as a substitute teacher.

CHRIS SEMPEK was a drill instructor with twenty plus years in the military which involved three years of deployment in Iraq and Afghanistan. He speaks five languages and lives in Durango, Mexico with his wife Lupe and works in the film industry with a multitude of credits to his name.

MIKE MACNEIL has a parrot and works in Detroit—sometimes with the police… He was running in the jungle: of Cambodia and the Philippines with the USMC back in the mid-Seventies. Later, he worked as a commercial fisherman, crabbing and long lining in Alaska. Out in the Bering Sea. His parrot's name is Mickey.

NOTE

*the writers have no idea if Chuck Hegel and John DeCamp ever so much as had a beer together…

www.ingramcontent.com/pod-product-compliance
Lightning Source LLC
Chambersburg PA
CBHW020003140726
47904CB00018B/1755